BLADE OF REBELS

The Lost Sect, Book Two

JULIAN GYLL

PORTAL BOOKS

For Rosa

Contents

Chapter One

I had never seen the world.

Not really.

That was what hit me as I clambered up from the canyon walls, emerging out of the valley of the Hollow for the first time in my life.

I had seen pieces of the world, of course. Down there, in the valley where I'd grown up. I had spent my life in caverns and gorges, chasms, and jungles. I had gazed up at the same line of sky, framed by the cliffs that had always towered around me.

Nothing could have prepared me for the sight in front of me now. The true shape of the world entire seemed to stretch out before me, laying itself bare for the first time.

It was all I could do not to collapse to my knees at the sight of it.

The main thought ringing in my mind, the one which my brain could not let go, was the sense of hugeness. Everything I'd ever known was dwarfed into *nothing*.

A plain of dust and rock stretched out in every direction, losing itself in faraway horizons where land and heaven met in a haze. All around me was an expanse greater than all the expanses I'd ever dreamed of: an infinity of space and air.

It wasn't just that the world was huge: it was that it was

flat, too. Nothing was flat in the Hollow. Nothing apart from the surface of pools; the length of a sword. Here, though, the universe was one long unbroken stretch, like a deity had cut existence in half with a blade. There were more valleys, more canyons, all gouged into the floor of the plain. They were just fissures in one long plain of rock which went on, unblemished, until the world passed out of sight into a sinking sun. A copse of trees, and some peaks of rocks in the North were small deformities in a world as smooth as parchment. There were clumps of trees, and a stone hut to my left, a fact my mind registered as important but could not fathom yet, but they dwindled into insignificance against the enormity of the universe.

Dizziness overtook my body as I struggled to take the sights in as the newly enlarged world whirled around me. The shrinking red sun, and the canopy of stars blurred together.

Shielding my gaze so I would not have to deal with the vastness of the sky, I mentally followed the cracks of the rock, tracing one line with my eyes like a fish follows a river. I rose and took one step, then another.

I closed my eyes. My breathing slowed and the dizziness ebbed. Sounds came to me then. The wind, free of trees and cliffs, whistled by and disappeared like it had never been.

A trickle of water gurgled nearby.

One of the last things I had done before leaving the valley was create a new waterfall, tearing a hole into the cliff walls and releasing a jet of water. That water had to come from somewhere.

That somewhere was here.

I managed to walk a few steps. Still, I kept my head low, looking up to the expanse of sky was still enough to make my stomach lurch with discomfort. Following my ears more than my sight, I strode forward — focused on the slits in the rock, like a child playing a game where they avoid stepping upon cracks on the ground.

I picked my way until, a few heartbeats later, the rock sloped downward into a body of lowering water. It was a large pool fed by a network of streams coming from the plains, but the waters were not still. They were circling, restless. Sucking down into a sinkhole, feeding the new river-fall I had created earlier that day.

I waded into the waters and cupped my hands in order to drink from them, and then to throw water onto my face. Just like the rock and grass, I'd wondered whether it would feel different, here in the world above. It was cool and delicious, and everything water had been back home.

Relieved, I plunged my entire head inside, and then reemerged, gasping. The long trails of my hair hung heavy, and the cool liquid dripped off my face.

The world remained, proving to me one last time that I wasn't dreaming.

My whole life, I'd been told the Gods above would punish me for climbing out of the valley. Even now, though I knew that such scripture was a lie conceived to keep me and my people contained in the Hollow, I still half-expected a deity to reach down from the twilight and throttle me as punishment for my trespass.

But nothing happened. I was alive and awake.

This was the world. It was foreign and startling… yet the one I needed to traverse if I was going to find a cure for my father's illness.

Sitting there in the pool, with my gaze still firmly fixed on the water a wave of anxiety washed over me, and I thought about everything I had left behind in the valley.

I thought about Rana, my little sister. Just days ago, she'd been a carefree little girl, scampering about the jungle.

But now I'd left her to look after my father—a surefire way to ensure that she would never be carefree again. I felt a yearning to be close to him, not because he could help me feel better, but because he was so ill that I worried I would not see him the way I knew he should be. Instead, his mind was consumed by shadows, swamped by a sickness which plunged his mind into the past instead of the present, all because he had tried to help me. No one in the Hollow had ever seen anything like it, and it was the main reason I had decided to leave: to go and find someone who could help him.

I'd been told that our enemy, the Lightguard, had the answers. So I was headed to them—into their city, to learn their ways and see how they could help me, and if they were willing.

But I knew it wouldn't be easy. The only Lightguard I'd met had pretended to be a prophet, keeping us fearful of her false gods. When I had stood up to her, she had been powerful, weaving beams of light into a staggering variety of forms.

To think that I would infiltrate a place full of such foes by myself, under this heavy sky, was a terrifying one.

And then, finally, I thought of my childhood friend Yennenga. She was the person who I wanted more than anything to have with me now. Mostly, because she was so capable; that was the reason why she'd stayed behind in the first place—to be a leader along with Commander Corinthia and keep the Hollow safe.

There was another reason, too. I had a strange sense that we hadn't said goodbye properly, and that this was important for some reason. I wanted her to be right here, so I could rectify that mistake, as mad as that sounded.

I thought of all the people I was leaving behind.

The temptation to turn around and shy away from this gargantuan sky was strong, strong enough for me to turn back and look at the edge I had just crawled from. For a moment, I wondered what I would see if I walked back to the edge and saw my family and friends. I shook my head and turned away from everyone and everything I'd known until now.

If I walked back to the edge and looked down… the temptation to climb right back down and return to my canyon would be too strong to overcome.

I turned back to the water and cupped my hands, trapping the liquid as it swirled about me. I took a drink, and then another… and then just let my fingers play in the current for a minute, letting the continuous movement calm my mind. I let the circulation around me remind me of the power of Anima, which ran through the energy channels in my body.

Then I settled my thoughts, enough to focus on my next step.

They would be small steps to begin with, one rock at a time.

But, I didn't really know where to start.

I raised my head and looked around at my surroundings. I could still see the stone hut not far off, overlooking my home in the Hollow.

That's when the thought fully came to me. Why was there a hut? Who would live in the middle of nowhere, with no other human in sight, overlooking the valley?

The answer arrived, painfully slow.

My people had been prisoners in that valley. Forced never to leave by the threat of false gods, our cage was meticulously constructed in the architecture of our own minds. But when someone broke out of that cage, like I had…

A sound, sharp and cruel, pierced through the air. A shout.

In my blurred vision, two people emerged from the hut and ran toward me.

The guards of the valley.

The gods were false. I had come out of the valley, and into the plains above, without a deity striking me down. A dark, ironic thought filled my head as I witnessed the blur of two warriors rushing towards me.

Perhaps I would be punished after all.

Chapter Two

Still in a daze, it took me a moment to make out who was coming toward me. I couldn't move, paralyzed by indecision.

There were two warriors, a man and woman. They ran across the side of the pool, holding up their hands and summoning strips of light from the air to their fingertips.

For a long moment, I was too overwhelmed to process the sight. The last time I had seen someone summon light into their hands, it had been to Weave the light into weapons designed to torture and kill me.

I'd barely escaped alive.

The enemy ran along the edge of the pool, and finally stopped at the edge of the water. They glared at me with a dark intent in their eyes.

My attackers were superficially like the kind of warrior I knew from the Hollow: long tunics layered with shoulder plates and body armor. But they were still worlds away from the kind of rusted, scratched, and patchy clothes I was used to seeing. Their armor gleamed as if new, and the tunics had lost none of their color.

The woman wore a white garment, and it shone as if it had never met blood nor earth. Her hair, black as subterranean caverns, was bunched up in perfect patterns, with nary a curl out of place. The man, who wore a black tunic, was equally without blemish. Even their skin had perfections which I had never thought of, the man had a glint of gold jewelry studded into his brow in the shape of the sun. The woman wore a silver necklace shaped like the moon and stars.

It was like all of the hardships of living in the Canyonlands, the hardships which my people had dealt with all their lives, had not touched them at all.

All in all, they looked formidable. The only thing which gave me any sense of confidence whatsoever was their hesitation, even confusion. They glanced at each other, almost as if trying to egg each other on.

Still, it was obvious they'd trained together. They moved as one, finally deciding after their initial reluctance to enter the pool. They looked about the same age— and they had the same movements, the same way of running. Like they belonged to the same body.

The man summoned more light in his hands, as Echo the Endless had done. It immediately Wove into a shape, the light concentrated and solidified. Beams from around him gathered, the crimson gleam of the disappearing sun turned into blood red chains in his hands.

The woman, however, did not seem to Weave daylight at all. Instead, an orb of grey and white light appeared, summoned from the air around us and spinning around her hands.

I realized that she was not using the light of the sun. She seemed to be using a different light, perhaps from the stars or moon, snatching it from the surroundings and Weaving it into a weapon. Wisps of grey whirled about her like tendrils of fog before hardening into an implement of war. She wove a net of light in her hands, ready to throw it and ensnare me.

The warriors before me complemented each other. One was trained in using the Essence of Sunlight, the other for using the Essence of the moon and stars. Perhaps this way, whenever they needed to fight, in night or day there was always someone who had the source of power needed to strike.

Only now at sunset, the cusp between light and day, I had the bad luck of facing them both.

Finally shaking out of my paralysis, my instincts kicked in and I put my own hand out, drawing out the shadows stored inside my body. The darkness, flecked with lightning blue, flowed out of me and into my hands. I used up energy in my body, the Anima coursed through my channels to form the black into a shadow-staff, a long spear with blades at both ends.

I was ready.

But they did not attack immediately.

Just as I expected them to pounce on me and begin their attack, they diverted, no longer racing toward me but circling me instead. They bumped into each other at first, both wanting to go in the same direction, but then the woman barked "That way, you fool!" The man did as he was told.

They revolved around me, while I had to constantly shift my gaze from one to the other. The woman continued to give orders to her counterpart. "Keep your eyes on him!" she said, although I had the impression that he was already doing so.

They circled around me like water swirling around the sinkhole. I noticed lines of sweat dripping down their brows.

The two were nervous.

I turned from one side to the other as they circled me, taking their time. I jabbed my shadow-staff in one direction, then another, as if that would be enough to warn them off.

"I don't know who you are, but I don't want to fight anyone, and it looks like you don't want to fight me either," I said to them. "I have no quarrel with you. I am just a stranger here."

"You're to come with us," the man replied, his voice a little unsteady.

"And if I refuse?" I asked.

"Then you're to come with us all the same," answered the woman from behind me, even though I had addressed the man. It was like I was talking to one person divided in two. Even the intonation and voice were similar too: their diction seemed too practiced, like they were trying to overenunciate. I wondered if this was how the Lightguard spoke. Perhaps they didn't slur their words together like we sometimes did in the Hollow.

"What's it going to be, then, stranger?" the man asked, his voice growing in anger to match the woman. "Will you obey, or will you need to suffer first?"

The threat sent a flare of fury through me.

"I've suffered quite a bit already," I said, gritting my teeth. "But then I've also been imprisoned a whole lot longer. My whole life, in fact. And it's thanks to you Lightguard on both counts. So no, I'm not playing. Even if it kills me."

"Suffering it is, then," whispered the woman, almost to herself. She seemed disappointed by my response.

I grasped my shadow-staff tighter, until my fingers went white. My heart thrashed in my chest in anticipation.

The man started to wrap a bunch of light-chains about his fists, ready to swing at me.

And then it happened.

The woman feinted, pulsing forward, and stamping into the water while the man threw the chains in my direction.

But I'd waited for an attack from both sides and was ready.

The light-chains surged through the air, as if ready to coil around my chest, but I ducked, holding my shadow-staff up. The chains wrapped around my weapon instead of me. With one end planted on the ground beneath the water, I levered the staff, pulling on the chains. The warrior stumbled forward, surprised by my speed.

In the meantime, the woman rushed forward, raising the light-net above her head in order to fling it down at me. The light-chains around my staff dissipated back into light, so my staff was free. I swiped away at the net, hooking it on my weapon.

Then I tossed it toward the man.

The net fell upon him. He cried out in pain as he frantically tried to tear the net away from his skin.

There seemed to be some kind of unknown type of magic in that weapon. Something torturous.

The woman ran forward, shrieking a war cry, and jabbed forward with a hand which had already formed a new Weave, creating a leaf-shaped sword out of starlight. I instinctively held up my staff to block her jab, but it cut clean through my staff, dispersing the shadows as if they had been nothing but air.

The shadows, torn from their form, faded and I backed away.

Skies, they're fast.

The way in which the woman had Woven her new weapon had been quicker than anything I had ever seen. It was like she hadn't had to create a new form at all and had just taken the essence from her light-net and repurposed it into something else.

The man, freed from the net, gathered himself up and advanced. With what seemed like just the arch of an eyebrow, light summoned to his hands. Light-chains danced into his fists, but also encircled his body. They wove together in a layer around his torso and stomach, creating a mail shirt of blood-red armor.

I held out my hands, and summoned shadows once more. They interlaced into a shape, creating shadow-khopeshes in each hand. I pulled from my core, making my weapons dense with black, a smaller but sturdier weapon, created in the hope that they would better withstand the blows of my enemies.

Two opponents, two blades, I reasoned.

As if that would be enough to save me.

The woman ran to my left, the man to my right. She leapt into the air and drove her leaf-shaped sword with both hands in the direction of my neck. I swerved to avoid her, only to see that it had been part of their plan from the start: my direction immediately brought me into the man's reach.

Chains wound around my shoulders. His chains did not seem to have the pain-inflicting charge which his partner's net possessed, but they wrapped tightly around me, biting into my skin.

I threw myself to one side, pulling on the chains so that the man would come down with me.

We both crashed into the water with a splash, and I squirmed out of the chains and rolled to one side as he flailed on his back. With the man on the ground, I got onto to my knees and tried to jab a khopesh in him— but to no avail. My blade hit his light-mail and could not pierce through it.

A look of satisfaction appeared on the man's face as he realized what had happened.

His smirk only deepened as I felt a blade touching the back of my neck.

The woman was behind me. She held the same sword which had cut through my staff as easily as an oar plunges into water.

I froze, not daring to move.

"Finally," the woman said, sighing with relief. "Now get rid of your puny little blades, before I give you a taste of what a real weapon feels like."

My mind raced.

What could I do?

I was obviously outmatched. I didn't even know where to run, even if I managed to get away.

There was one hope, and one hope alone.

They had said that I had to *come with them.* The woman had chopped through my staff, and then feinted at me with her sword in order to drive me into the man's chains. She had never gone for the kill, not once. It had all been feints to drive me into chains and nets.

"You're not supposed to kill me," I surmised. "You're supposed to take me alive."

The man got to his feet, dripping from his tumble into the waters. He looked down at me.

"Being alive has nothing to do with how hard you're screaming," he said.

"Good one, brother." I could hear a smirk in her voice.

I still hadn't moved. I was on my knees, the wash of the water still about me.

I still held my khopeshes.

"I would let them go, if I were you," warned the man. "My sister doesn't tend to joke about these kinds of things. In fact, she doesn't joke about anything at all."

I finally relented, letting my weapons unfurl.

I then held my hands up, furious at myself for being captured so quickly.

"Thank the skies for that," said the brother. "Sister—do you think he needs to be light-charged, though? With your net? Shock him until he's more obedient?"

The woman thought for a moment. A chill went down my spine.

"Maybe," she said.

In a heartbeat, the sword in her hand morphed into a light-net once more, and she cast it upon me like I was a fish.

My mind screamed *immediately*.

I'd never felt like this before. It wasn't pain, as such. The word *pain* wasn't adequate for what was happening to me. Rather, it just felt... *wrong*. My mind lurched, filled with a spinning movement. My muscles spasmed, and I lost control, slumping down into the water.

Everything swam, and it wasn't just because I was semi-submerged. It was like the whole world was underwater.

I rolled, turned, and cried out, gulping down water as a result, all while they stood there, looking down upon me.

Waiting.

All of a sudden, the sensation stopped.

The sister eyed me with satisfaction. "My light comes from other corners of the universe. From stars and moons, further away than the mind can fathom. It comes from other times, and other galaxies. It can have a way of... disturbing the mind and body, let's say. Can you feel it? A light so foreign the body wants to reject it?"

Then it started again.

It was only for a few heartbeats, but I felt like my body was going to give up on me. It seemed like my bones would crumple, and my muscles give up, and I would die, then and there, left to float in circles and be swallowed up by the sinkhole.

But then there came a voice, coming over from behind me, distracting the sister and stopping the pain pulsing into my body.

A voice I thought I'd never hear again.

"Please… You have to *stop* this!"

Chapter Three

I couldn't believe my ears. I thought that the events of the day had finally overwhelmed me, or that the magic of the chains had perhaps damaged my senses.

Tende stood at the edge of the pool, his palms out in a futile gesture of surrender.

He was drenched, water gushing off every edge of his kaftan. His clothes were so wet that they clung to his thin, lithe body and stuck to his long, dark locks of hair.

Apart from that, he was exactly how Tende always was. I felt a rush of heat in my chest as I took in the sight of him. I'd seen him just earlier that day, but so much had happened since that it felt like an age.

The last I'd seen of him, he'd been battling away at the monsters of the Deep, facing off against the creatures of the Void while the river had born me away.

I thought he had died, and I'd grieved as much as I was able during the day's mad events. I'd thought of how he'd shown me that water could be Woven and shaped like shadows, how he'd taught me the ways of the Riverkind.

Now he was in front of me, trying to save me once again.

"I'd walk away, if I were you, Riverkind," grunted the man. The sibling warriors immediately faced him.

Tende held out his bare hands again, demonstrating once more that he was not Weaving nor holding a weapon.

He flashed a look of worry at me, scanning me for injuries.

"I cannot walk away," he said. "It's against the current."

"Then *change* the current," snarled the sister. "By all the valleys, I can't *stand* how Riverkind speak."

"I cannot. That man"— he pointed at me— "is my friend. I cannot leave him. My flow is with his."

"I swear, if you speak one more water metaphor, I'll light-spear you on the spot…" sneered the sister.

"Sister, be calm," said the brother.

"I *am* calm!"

"Then be cal*mer*!" the brother shouted, losing his patience. Their words had the speed and patter of siblings who had lost patience with each other years ago.

The brother took a step forward.

"Listen, Riverkind. We both know that your tribe doesn't fight. You've all sworn never to raise a hand against your fellow man."

It was true, Tende's people had renounced war hundreds of years ago. He had even scoffed at me and mocked me for how my people were so focused on warfare. Fighting the monsters didn't count, that was just *hunting*, apparently, but he was not allowed to confront other humans.

"So…" the brother continued, "there's nothing you can do to stop us. We are carrying out the work of the Emperor himself. And the Emperor wants the valley folk captive. So unless you're going to break your pacifist traditions, there's no way of swaying us. You'd best step away, or we might have to hurt you. I imagine there's nothing worse than being hurt and not being allowed to hurt us back."

Tende's eyes shimmered. I could sense confusion in him. I knew him as calm and balanced. He accepted the duties of life and was joyful of the pleasures.

As his eyes darted from the warriors to me, I could see that he was racked with guilt. Either he would have to renounce his ways or leave me to these siblings and the pain of their light-net.

I met his gaze with my own.

Please, I implored with my eyes.

I didn't want him to break his traditions, I knew how important they were to the Riverkind.

But judging by everything I'd learned today, I knew that traditions could be a stranglehold as much as a blessing. If I was going to have any chance of getting out of my physical chains, he was going to have to break out of his mental ones.

Tende shook his head at me, his eyes full of sadness and regret.

He began to turn away.

My body suddenly felt heavy, and my heart plunged.

I was going to be left at the mercy of the siblings.

"You've made the right choice, Riverkind," the brother said.

"If your friend had been as compliant as you, we wouldn't have to teach him a lesson, would we?" the sister said, her voice tinged with relief, as she let Tende walk away and turned back to me. "Now, where were we? Oh right, more pain." Her delight in being able to manage the situation seemed to have brought out a sadistic streak in her.

The brother turned back, towering over me. "Our captive's ready for another dose," he agreed.

I shook my head, and tried to say something, but words did not come out.

Then I heard cracking, like a hundred twigs snapping in a fire.

The siblings jumped in surprise.

I looked up and saw Tende with his hand in the water. Facing us again.

A line of ice emanated from his fingers and stretched all the way to the siblings' heels.

He'd frozen the water around their feet.

I took this as the opportunity I needed. I squirmed through the water, rolling away from the siblings, as they bickered and shouted to each other. The brother tried to put his hand on me before I rolled away from his grasp, only to lose his balance in the action, his stuck feet stopping him from recovering.

The sister's lost concentration weakened the net on me, and light leaked off of it, steaming back into the air.

This was my chance.

Adrenaline coursed through me, clearing my mind. I writhed and pushed the net off.

I got to my feet in the circling waters, anger clenching my jaw, while the sister started to thrash at the ice with her leaf-shaped light-blade to free herself.

I would not be controlled by the Lightguard. My people had been under their yoke for generations— and I wasn't going to take it anymore.

I was not their pawn to be killed in the name of their war. I was not their plaything to be tortured in their nets.

I looked into my core, and used the most purified Anima energy I could inside my chest. Into my hands issued shadows, forming the shapes of the two khopesh blades once more.

But they were stronger. I used up a huge dose of Anima, not caring how much I would be left with, and layered my weapons with coating upon coating of shadow, lined with flecks of blue.

And then I raised my blades and walked to my attackers, ready for another round.

The sister was enraged. For the last few heartbeats, she had been shouting at her brother.

It seemed like she wasn't used to being taken by surprise.

With a grunt, she swept her leaf-shaped light-blade across her feet, continuing to hack through the frozen surface of the pool. The gray sword sliced its way through a crackle of ice, creating a web of cracks around her feet.

Another hit would free them up entirely.

"You take the brother!" cried Tende. He was rushing forward, drawing water up from the surface into both hands and freezing it into long icicles the shape of spears. He began twirling his ice-weapons in a dance, glancing off the sister's swords.

I faced the brother. He created more crimson light-chains and started pounding them against the ice at his feet to free himself.

I didn't want to give him the chance to finish.

My blades arced through the dusk light, descending upon him.

He held up his light-chain tight between his hands, blocking my blows.

I shouted out, raining more and more khopesh strikes upon him. I swept my blades from one side to the other but I couldn't get any real damage done. His light-mail seemed to bulge and thicken when I came too close to piercing it. He also seemed able to thicken his armor ahead of my attacks.

I sped up, hitting him anywhere I could, until my blades managed to get through the mail. It only just pierced through the chainmail with its tip, but it was enough to make him gasp with pain.

I ducked under a swing of his chain and pitched forward, slashing down toward his leg with a khopesh, and swiping the other across his stomach. His armor writhed, coating the body parts I'd targeted.

My blades rang harmlessly against the light-mail. Nevertheless, I kept driving closer, head-butting my opponent in the jaw.

He howled, whipping his head back. Pain boiled through me, too.

But next to the light-net, the pain was nothing.

I looked for my next hit and saw his neck, where his mail did not reach.

I'd never killed a man. I'd barely even raised a weapon against anyone other than the monsters of the deep.

Had they shown some pity, I might not have made such a move. But my rage at being tortured, at my people having been slain and manipulated and used like pawns, carried me through.

I was ready to kill.

As if sensing my killing intent, I heard Tende's voice. I shot a look over to Tende. He was also struggling. His duel with the sister was a storm of blades and ice, their movements were acrobatic, almost too fast to follow. But it was clear: Tende was stepping backward, retreating.

The sister was winning the contest.

"Jason!" he cried. "Grant me a spray!"

I wasn't sure why he was asking for this, but I did as he asked. I took my blades, and hit the water, driving the flat of my swords into the surface.

And then Tende darted back. He summoned the droplets in the air into his hand— and used them to freeze the siblings' limbs together.

The sister raised a sword to cut the ice between them... but her brother barked at her to stop.

"Don't you dare... knowing you, you'll end up cutting my bloody fingers off!"

I took the opportunity to kick the brother, driving him forward with my foot. He toppled awkwardly, his feet still embedded in ice, and took his sister down with him.

Tende reacted immediately. Frost rippled through the water, creating shards of white, as if the world around me were sprouting teeth.

The ice enveloped the siblings, no longer just circlets around their feet or hands, but thick plates encasing their bodies. The siblings were trapped in a block of ice as thick as they were. Their heads were above the surface so they could breathe— but they were otherwise powerless, unable to move their limbs, frozen in a floating block of white.

I looked at the siblings as they spun gently in the water, shouting and blaming each other, now just laughable versions of their previous deadly selves.

I sought Tende, who was doubled-up and hyperventilating, completely depleted from all the Flow he had just performed.

"Tende, that was a*mazing*," I breathed.

Between his long breaths, Tende straightened and

answered. “It has bought us some more time. They will not break out of that for a little while.”

I looked at the center of the spiral. For a moment, I wondered whether we’d condemned the siblings to death by sending them into the sinkhole. But the hole was far too small. They would just float to the center, and then be stuck there like a beetle on its back.

“Still… I’m guessing our next move should be to get out of here.”

Tende nodded.

He motioned behind me, and I beheld that vast expanse of air. I’d almost forgotten, in the heat of battle, the enormity of the world, and it tugged at my insides once more.

“The Flow takes us that way,” Tende said. “Come with me.”

I gave one last look at the edge of the cliff, at the valley which had been my home for all my life. And I ran.

Chapter Four

We emerged out of the pool and kept running. The voices of the siblings were left in the distance.

...and I was still cowed by that massive sky.

Now that the sun had completely bled out, the sky was a uniform black. It was as black and impenetrably deep as any shadow I'd walked in, even in the underground tunnels of the Deep itself. It also contained swathes of uncountable stars, as numerous as cracks on a cliffside, or droplets in a river. I'd only ever gotten flashes of the stars before, now they looked close enough to touch, no matter how far away they really were.

I rushed ahead, keeping my head low and my shoulders hunched, and concentrating just on the rocks and streams that Tende strode across.

I desperately wanted to stop, to tell Tende to halt so he could explain everything to me. I needed him to tell me how he could possibly still be alive and so that he could tell me where he was going.

He was in no mood to slow down, so instead I paid attention to my aching legs and my protesting heart. Tende had grown up in his valley, just as I had grown up in mine. This was clearly more his domain than my own, so the best thing I could do was follow his lead.

After what felt like an impossibly long time, Tende finally slowed to a stop, and he knelt down to trail his fingers in a stream coursing at our feet.

While I caught my breath, he closed his eyes, and concentrated on the water. He did not seem anywhere near as out-of-breath as I was.

He used the Flow, Sensing the history of the water: where it had come from, what it had encountered on the way to his hands.

And then, all of a sudden, he straightened up.

"Our downstream is the water's upstream," he said, pointing towards the North-West where the water was gushing from.

Before he could explain, he started running again, his pace quickening. Even though I could barely catch my breath, I launched into a jog to keep up with him.

We traversed more streams, and ran over more rock, our wet sandals slapping against the ground. Before long, a dark shape loomed in front of us, a clump of trees.

With all the stars in the sky, it felt like I should be able to see as well as if I was under a burning sun, but the cleft of woodland only appeared in silhouette. I used what little Anima energy was still inside me and reached out with my Senses. Immediately, the darkness around the forest retreated, and the landscape revealed itself to me in colorless forms.

The trees were few, and they were short and stunted compared to the ones of the jungle of my home. They were gnarled and bent, subdued by the exposure to every impulse of the wind. Nothing like the proud trees of the Hollow.

At first, I wondered why Tende had made us follow this stream. What shelter did a few gnarled trees gathered around a stream give us?

But the moment I stepped underneath the cover of the branches, I felt a weight come off me.

Surrounded by something like shelter, suddenly the sky felt less oppressive. I realized that I had not stood up straight in hours, that I had barely raised my head.

My neck cracked in relief as I straightened, standing somewhat close to how I used to.

"Thank you," I breathed to Tende.

He nodded. "We can rest here for a while, but only a short while. Danger is spilling towards us with every moment."

"It's been one hell of a day," I answered. I raised an eyebrow, inviting him to explain himself.

He held up his hand.

"We need to rest and replenish our Anima. We can discuss how we got here after."

I nodded. As much as I wanted to find out what happened to him and tell him what I'd found out— I wasn't sure my body could keep up.

Tende was right, we needed rest.

I curled up under a bent tree and lay on my side in order to not face the sky.

The last thing I heard, before sleep raced towards me, was a sniff.

I glanced over at Tende, who was sitting upright in a lotus position. He was meditating before settling down or at least he was trying to.

Tears were gliding down his otherwise serene face.

Of all the things I had learned today, the fact that I'd looked an opponent in the eyes and gone to kill them was not earth-shattering. After all, I'd killed Echo the Endless with no regret.

But the fact that Tende had broken his oath of pacifism was clearly wreaking havoc on his emotions.

Tears dripped over his kaftan, and Tende did nothing to brush them away.

I drifted off to a more restless sleep than I'd expected.

* * *

It was still dark when I woke, and there was an overwhelming number of stars in the vast sky.

I turned, and got up, stretching my stiff muscles, ignoring

the heavens. I peeked over at the east horizon— and saw a blade of light, heralding the morning.

It was time to get moving.

I turned and saw Tende standing in the stream, eyes closed, breathing deeply. He was cycling, drawing in his energy from the water.

I did the same. While he drew his power from the Anima in the water, I pulled mine from the shadows. While he stood there, I sat down, cross-legged, at the foot of a tree and cycled. I welcomed in the energy infusing the darkness around me, the Anima of Dark, and let it permeate my body.

I felt the refreshing injection of energy, the sensation of my blood being renewed, as the Anima coursed through the channels of my body. It soothed my aches and nursed the cuts and bruises about me.

And then, when my channels were full, I then directed the Anima into the veins leading to my core, where the energy wouldn't leak out.

This took a little while: it required intense concentration, and absolute mastery over the body and mind. And my mind was still reeling from everything that had happened over the last day.

Still, I had, in the last few weeks, become good at calming my mind and cycling whenever I could. I managed to fill my core with a charge of Anima, which I infused with shadows.

Tende finished at about the same time as I did.

Soundlessly, we sat opposite each other, and I fished out a few meager nuts and dried fruit from my pockets. The parents of my friend Emilian had given me what they had as thanks for saving their son's life, and I shared the rations between us. Tende created two bowls out of ice and passed me one full of water from the stream.

As a dim glow of morning burgeoned in the east, we ate.

It did not take long for us to get through the nuts. We were both ravenous after the efforts of the previous day.

And then there was nothing else to do but ask the question.

I had many. More than a day’s worth of talking.

But the first thing I said came straight from my gut. The more I’d thought about it in my sleep, the more urgent my question had become.

“Why did you lie to me, Tende?”

Chapter Five

Tende took a breath, contemplating the light of the morning before he answered.

"I never lied. Not once."

"You let me believe that there were gods in the sky, barring us from ever leaving the valley!" A surge of anger flared up inside me. I had told myself that I would not let the emotions get the better of me.

This was a bad start.

He had saved my life, but I still felt a feeling of betrayal. A feeling that he, for all the good he had done, had colluded in a scheme to delude and brainwash me.

Tende nodded, acknowledging my words and my emotions. His movements were slow and deliberate, cool water to balance my fire.

"I never countered your beliefs," he agreed.

"My delusions, you mean. My whole faith was a lie, to keep me trapped in the Hollow, where the Lightguard could test their monstrous creations on us!"

"We Riverkind are nomads. We travel across the Canyonlands. We visit different kinds of tribes with different religions and faiths. It is in our nature to be tolerant, to ingratiate ourselves. How do you think we would fare if, every time we encountered a new tribe, we denigrated their traditions and beliefs?"

I shook my head. "Traditions. Beliefs. Words to make everything sound high and mighty. But that isn't what is happening in the Hollow. They're *lies,* Tende. Lies told to keep us in our little corner of the Canyonlands so they can test their Void on us. Lies to keep us fighting, and dying, until there is nothing of us left."

"And yet, you held those lies close to your heart. You lived and died by them. How do you think it would have gone, if, when you had stumbled into our valley, we had told you the truth? Your people barely trusted us. Your Commander would have drawn swords on us if we'd even *tried* to tell you the truth."

I gritted my teeth. He was right about Commander Helton. He'd spent his whole life serving our faith and had been unable to process anything which countered it.

"Tende, you know that I'm not like Commander Helton. I accepted the truth. I was able to handle it."

Tende turned to me. "I wish you all the shadows on the mountainside, Jason. I do. But I cannot agree. You are far from handling anything."

I blinked. "What do you mean?"

"You tried to kill a man, Jason. In fact, you almost succeeded. Had I not arrived with a different plan to defeat those warriors, had I not diverted the current… how would the fight have ended?"

Tende's eyes shimmered, the pain of thinking of what he had done returning to him.

"You are angry, and rash," he continued. "That is what the truth has done to you. It has made you into a violent man. Forgive me, but I wanted to spare you the truth until you were ready."

I paused at this. I did not consider myself a violent person at all. I had scaled the cliffs of the valley not to fight, but to save my father. If I was truly honest with myself, could I say that my father had been on my mind when I had encountered the sibling warriors? Or had the sight of the Lightguard, the tyrants of the Canyonlands, filled me with fury?

I shook the thought away. "You do not get to choose when I am ready for the truth. That's a matter of right and wrong, Tende. Not a matter of your condescension."

Tende nodded, in that contemplative way of his.

"And as for those warriors, they were also a matter of right and wrong. The inaction of your people just amounts to letting bad people get away with bad things! Sometimes you have to fight!" Frustration made my words harsher, and I could feel my emotions get away from me.

Tende shook his head in the most forceful way I had seen yet. Of all the things I had said, this challenge to the Riverkind's way of life seemed to strike his core. "My people would never call what we do *inaction*. We, in our own small way, by gathering knowledge and wisdom, are the force for peace your clenched fist can never be. You're too angry to see it right now."

I grabbed his arm. In the Hollow, we rarely touched each other. But I knew for the Riverkind, such gestures were normal to get someone's attention, or to emphasize a point. "You cannot treat me as a child, Tende. I will not be patronized. I have spent all my life being talked down to, and I won't have it come from you, now."

Tende took this in. Finally, he offered his hand. It was a Riverkind handshake, where you take each other's wrist until you feel the other's pulse.

I took it, and a faint echo of Tende's habitual smile came to his lips.

"So, shall we break the ice?" he said. "Tell each other everything?"

I agreed.

Tende brought us water from the stream and froze it into two large shards. We took turns holding them. This was the tradition of the Riverkind. To improve rapport, you had to tell everything in the most honest way you could, even down to your darkest feelings. If you did this before the ice melted, the listener was not allowed to judge or punish you for it.

I started. I told Tende everything that had happened. I told him that most of my tribe had been wiped out by the last attacks on the valley, and that I had faced and defeated our false prophet and leader. I told him about my father, and his illness and how that made me feel. And I told him about what it was like, for me, to sit under the weight of the cosmos. I said that having the whole sky above my head was like waiting for a blanket to fall and smother me.

When it was his turn, he spoke about how he survived the fight with the Void, when I thought that he'd perished. The fight had been in an underground river, and I'd been swallowed by a sinkhole. Tende told me that he, too, had entered it but due to his attuned Senses in the water, he could tell that the water had then gushed down different forks. Tende had been flung down a different one than mine.

By freezing himself to the rock, he'd managed to avoid being cast deeper into the earth. Then he'd slowly climb back up the rock, freezing his hands into ice holds in order to ascend, until he'd emerged at the top of the cliff.

"I was proud to have protected you and fought off the monsters of the Void to allow you to escape," Tende said, the thinning ice shard dripping from his fingers. "But on that slow climb, I also experienced regret. I was sad that we'd parted ways before I could tell you the truth. The Riverkind say the past is our guide. It is hard to choose the true path when you have journeyed on a false one."

In the palms of our hand lay a few thin triangles of ice. Not much left.

"Anything else you want to ask me?" Tende said.

I did. "How, given that you don't fight, are you so good at fighting?"

Tende smiled. "The peoples of the Canyonlands may not have to contend with the Void like your people do," he said. "But there are other beasts which roam the canyons. Many evils spill out of the Underworld. We Riverkind may not wage war, but we do protect ourselves."

"Well, skies if you're not the best warrior around, pacifist or not," I admitted. "You're so malleable, and can form so many different shapes, even with just ice. Those Lightguard, untrained as they were, could reform shapes of steel and nets, flitting from one form to another. What chance do I have against true warriors when I am stumped against novices like them?"

Tende contemplated this. "You have only just learned to use your imagination. The more trained your mind becomes, the more your Weaves will follow suit. But that takes time. In the meantime, it takes power and energy to change one Weave into another. You have Anima stored in your core, rotating and purifying. You can speed up this process by spinning it faster. That will make you regain your energy more quickly, for when your mind is ready."

There was so much to learn. I felt like I neither knew a single thing about the world around me, nor how my body functioned. "Will you help me, Tende? I don't know whether I'll be able to save my father without you."

Tende shook his head, sadness taking him. I was reminded of the tears he'd shed. "I'm sorry, Jason, but it's not in my Flow. After what I have done against those warriors, I must return home. I need to meditate with my Elders and learn how I can avoid doing what I have done ever again."

I was crestfallen.

Tende's decision meant I'd be on my own in a dangerous, strange world.

"But, perhaps I can point you in the right direction," said Tende.

I breathed a small sigh of relief. That was a start, at least.

I looked down at the small piece of ice in my cold palm, liquefying under my very eyes. "I've got one last thing to say, Tende," I said, steeling myself. "Is there anything else I should know? Anything that you've not told me? I am ready. Nothing you can say can surprise me now."

Tende's eyes grew sad. "I do not believe you are ready," he said. "But I will tell you nonetheless."

My stomach lurched at his words, but I tried to keep my composure.

"Say it," I said.

Tended breathed, contemplating how best to express himself. He looked over towards the East, where the sun was now showing its crown, washing the stars away and turning the sky purple.

"Your valley is not *the* test site. It is *a* test site."

His words turned my insides cold.

"What do you mean?" I asked, although my heart already knew the answer.

"Your people are not the only ones being used to test the Lightguard's creations. There are other tribes of Shade users going through the same thing as the Hollow, in a string of valleys across the Canyonlands."

My breath caught in my throat. I had not even imagined this possibility.

Now that he said it, I could hardly say I was surprised. After all, if the Lightguard were cruel enough to do it to us, they were cruel enough to do it to others too. I had a hard time imagining there were other people who'd suffered what we had endured. How many more of us were there who'd fought all their lives, and seen their loved ones die, without knowing that it was all in service to false gods?

I opened my lips to ask more, but Tende caught my hand. "We will talk about this another time. We need to go. *Now.* Fast as waterfalls."

"Why?" I asked, as we stood.

Instead of answering, Tende pointed towards the sky. There were two trails of gold light, crossing the sunrise hues and speeding from the horizon.

"Because of the birds?" I blinked.

Tende's response was heavy with worry.

He replied simply: "Those aren't birds."

Chapter Six

Tende ran and I sped after him.

He needed no time to build up his speed. From the moment he started, his strides were long and quick, allowing him to bound from rock to rock.

I could barely keep up with him. My mind became entirely focused on following his trail, on conserving my energy long enough to survive whatever was flying in the sky.

I had no time to consider the implications of what he'd said. All I could do was run.

We sprinted across the plain, heading east. Tende looked with growing concern at the sky whenever he paused so I could catch up.

I did the same when I could, snatching glimpses of the horizon. The gold, scorching light trails across the sky were getting thicker. Whatever was up there was getting closer.

Given that we were the only people around for leagues, we were easy to spot from the sky. We were black spots against the red rock, like beetles ready to be trampled underfoot.

"Are they Lightguard?" I asked Tende breathlessly as we sped along the rock.

"Yes, scouts of the sky."

This made sense. After studying the forms of the Void

monsters, I had once managed to recreate wings of shadow in order to clumsily glide my way to relative safety.

From all I had witnessed from the Lightguard, they were agile and creative with their Essence in ways I had never seen. If I'd been able to recreate wings, some of them would be able to do it a hundred times better. If there were people among the Lightguard who'd dedicated their lives to this form, they could scour the sky, gazing down upon their kingdom and reporting to their overlords.

"We've got to get undercover!" I cried. I looked back, seeing the light-trails curl and arch in the sky. "They'll see us in no time at all!"

"Do you see anywhere to hide?" replied Tende.

I scanned the rock spanning in front of us. I was not used to looking this far, of peering so intently, unless I was in the dark.

I'd studied the shadows from the moment I was born. I intimately knew the shape of them and what lay within.

I pointed ahead.

"Maybe there!" I cried, pointing to a spot where there was a large black line standing out among the cracks in the plain ahead of us. It was thicker, like a scribble of ink on the scroll of the world, tracing a long vein of shadow across the rock floor.

From here, it was impossible to see how deep or wide the crevasse was. But when it came to shadows I didn't need to see.

"Can you summon from here?" asked Tende.

"While running for my life?" I retorted. "I suppose we'll find out."

I continued to run, trying to let my mind fall into a balanced state. It wasn't easy, not while I was being pursued by enemies from the heavens.

A small part of me wondered whether I would ever get used to being in danger. Would it ever feel ordinary enough for me to maintain the focus I needed to practice my best cultivation while running for my life?

All I knew was that I'd never been chased by creatures on wings of light, where the threat of danger sent javelins of fear into my gut. I'd also never run across terrain like this, the largesse of the universe made me feel as small as dust motes.

Still, I did my best and tried to let my feet fall automatically, following Tende as I went into enough of a trance to do the task at hand.

Sweat poured over me and I started to feel short of breath.

I ignored the protests of my body, and held up a hand, focusing all of my thoughts and energy on that sliver of black ahead of me.

There were false starts, moments where a trail of black started to sail towards me, then retreat back to the crevasse, but finally, it happened. I loosened a line of shadows, no thicker than a few plumes of smoke from a dwindling fire and beckoned it to me.

The shadow traced its way through the air, picking its way across the plains like a snake until it came to my hand.

As it twirled its way around my body, I Sensed into it, picking up on anything the shadows could tell me, examining its history.

A vision came to me of a slim but deep crack in the ground, a narrow corridor where the sun could barely reach.

The vision was indistinct, wavering, but it would have to do.

I released the trail, letting the shadow dart back across the rock to its home. "Follow the shadow!" I said, and Tende and I poured new energy into our run.

I dared to look back. The lines of gold, shooting across the sunrise, were almost overhead. If they hadn't seen us already, they would soon.

"No looking back, Jason," warned Tende. "Quick as the rainfall, run!"

I didn't think I could run any faster. My lungs were already bursting. But with a fresh burst of speed from my companion, I forced my body to push harder. Ahead, Tende's legs were in constant motion, his long strides throwing his clothes this way and that, his arms swinging, driving himself forward. I grunted and urged my body to do the same.

The crevasse in the plain, dark crack started to loom closer, showing its width of no more than an arm's length. Yesterday, we'd jumped over a few crevasses while escaping from the guards. I hoped that my Senses were right and that this crack would be deep enough to hide us from the scouts' gaze.

I snatched another look behind us, and fear snatched right back at me.

It seemed like the trails of gold in the sky weren't circling aimlessly anymore.

They were arcing towards us.

I turned and saw Tende leap into the black, dropping into the crevasse and disappearing from view.

I followed suit, jumping before I could even stop to see what was awaiting me.

I dropped into the narrow slit of rock.

I battered into the crevasse, my arms and legs punished as I bounced against the far side. A lifetime of climbing in and out of tunnels told me to thrust out my hands and feet: I reached out on both sides, trying to grip the walls and allay my fall.

I succeeded, but only partly. I slowed my descent, but only by very little, with accompanying shoots of pain bruising my hands.

Luckily, the fall was not far. I tumbled down about two heights of a man before finding the bottom of the crevasse, almost landing on Tende himself.

Clattering into the narrow wedge at the bottom, I wanted to cry out in pain. Tende clamped his hand over my mouth, and his face loomed over mine, a finger to his lips.

Both breathing heavily and pouring sweat, we didn't move, waiting for whatever was going to happen.

There was a sickening moment of nothing but our breathing, of us starting at the slit of sky above us, dreading what it would reveal.

And then, white light sliced through the red dawn above us.

Two figures, elongated with golden light-wings, speared across the heavens, firing across the air above us like shooting stars.

They scorched across the corridor of sky and passed out of view once more.

I let out a breath I didn't realize I'd been holding.

"That was close," I grimaced, nursing my stinging knees, elbows, and hands.

"We can't see far enough downstream yet," cautioned Tende as he did the same, patting his clothes and ridding them of the dust we'd accumulated in the fall. "They did not attack us, and that is a blessing. But it does not follow that they did not see us. They could be alerting the Lightguard to our position."

I nodded wearily. "It's one thing after the other up here, isn't it?" I moaned.

"It would appear so. Or, at least, it is if you cross the Lightguard."

He gave a long sigh.

"What happened to your sunny disposition, Tende? You used to mock me for my moaning and groaning."

Tende shook his head. "I have not been myself since I raised my hand against those siblings. I will admit it. I cannot trust myself to see the Flow like I could. Everything is in flux."

"Welcome to my world," I muttered to myself, picking myself up.

"It is disorienting. No longer being in the safety of home." Tende spoke with utter calm, hardly sounding disoriented at all.

I remembered what Tende had told me, once. He'd said that the Riverkind are trained to fish, and to swim throughout underwater caves. They had to train themselves to be utterly in control of their emotions to not waste the air in their lungs when diving.

I looked down into the crevasse. The narrow corridor went

north, it looked like it was gouging deeper into the Canyonlands.

"I propose we try and make things as much like home as possible, then," I proposed. "Let's stick to what I do best, keeping to the shadows and seeing where they'll lead. Who knows— maybe it'll bring us to a river for you."

Tende gave a weak smile. "Here's hoping," he said.

And we started to crawl along the crevasse.

Chapter Seven

The cleft in the rock was not an easy path to follow. There was no flat floor to walk upon, and so we were constantly spanning two sides of the wedge with our feet and hands, splayed out like spiders.

Still, it felt good to once again be between walls and not be overwhelmed by the sky. No matter how hard the going was, clambering through rocks and shadows was in my comfort zone. This felt like something I could master.

I could have followed this rift for hours, even days.

But then, we had no idea where it would take us. The crevasse seemed to be bending and winding in a disorienting way.

"Do you have any idea where this goes, Tende?" I asked.

Tende paused. "Without a stream to give me information, I cannot tell for sure." He gazed up at the line of sky above us, and the direction of the sunlight. "But it seems to me that we're bending northeast, which, if I'm not mistaken, will bring us to the River's Greeting."

I'd never heard the term before. "What's that?"

"I have never been. I have only ever stayed in my valley, where you met me, and the plains surrounding it. I have only ever heard rumors of it..."

Tende paused.

"Well, what are the rumors?" I asked. "I've got nothing, Tende. I've been in the Hollow my entire life. This world above is more impenetrable than any tunnel I've ever been in."

"My reluctance to speak is not because I want to hide anything from you. It is because I am concerned of the idea of going there at all." He swallowed. "You and I have always lived in our closed valleys. In our homes, the rivers come from the plains above, carve their ways through, then continue on their path into the Underfolds. Everything is contained." Reluctance and trepidation slowed his words. "But the River's Greeting is where lots of different streams, rivers and valleys meet. That is where most of the peoples of the Canyonlands live. At its head, ruling above all that network of valleys, is the biggest city in all the lands. The Citadel of Light."

I hated the sound of the place, I hated how big and dominating it sounded. Most of all, I hated how fearful Tende sounded when he spoke of it.

But I pushed down a rise of feelings and spoke. "Well then, that's exactly where I need to be. If that's where this crevasse heads, then that's a good thing."

Tende shook his head. "But I can't go there. My tribe have avoided that place for hundreds of years. Ever since the Wars of the Levelling, when we knew that we needed to separate ourselves from the destruction and chaos."

"Even if it were the most dangerous place in the world," I pursued, "I would still need to go. If that's where the Lightguard are, then that's the place where I can find someone to help my father."

"Jason, the Lightguard would sooner kill you than help you. They have no regard for Shaders like you."

"They can't all be warriors. There must be healers, teachers, farmers. Someone whose first instinct isn't just to strike me down."

Tende contemplated this. "Perhaps you are right. Such people must exist. And yet... nothing Elder Lembta says makes me think that we will find them."

"Then I recommend not thinking too much and continue following this crevasse."

Tende stopped. I turned and saw that he had his eyebrow arched. "You are happier, here in the dust and the rock, aren't you?" he asked.

"There's entirely too much sky, and too much choice, up there. Down here is where I belong."

"You're about to face a bigger world than either of us can fathom, Jason. If you're going to take it on, you're going to have to outgrow your shadows."

He was right. I nodded, before adding: "But it would make it easier if you were to come with me."

"I can't do what you ask. Need brings me home, just as need spurs you on. I will take you to the River's Greeting, but no further."

"This isn't your fight," I said, trying to mask my disappointment. "But there might come a day when your kind will have to stand up to the Lightguard, Tende. And then you'll have to outgrow your valley, just as I have had to outgrow mine. The Flow can't divert you away from the fight forever. Not if you want justice in the Canyonlands."

And with that, I turned back to the crevasse, and continued walking.

We strode across the rock all day.

Just as Tende had thought, it bent more and more toward the northeast.

Luckily, it also got wider, enough that Tende and I could walk beside each other for stretches at a time. At such moments, we had to monitor the sky, and be careful that we were not seen. But the streaks of gold had gone, leaving the heavens unblemished. We managed to push on, tracing the crevasse like we were the river gushing down its floor.

After a while, much to Tende's relief, a stream spilled into the bottom of the fissure, spilling down from the plains, and joining us at the bottom of the ravine. We quenched our thirst and splashed our faces. We also took the opportunity to cycle, finding a place with shadows and water where we couldn't be seen from the scouts above.

Picking our way forward, we also came across some bushes with some berries that Tende said were good to eat. We hungrily picked them and popped the small fruits into our mouths. It didn't do much to fill our stomachs, but the sweetness was pleasant enough.

As we strode forward, we spoke.

I tried to glean as much information as I could from Tende about the world I was entering.

Unfortunately, our conversations never led into nearly enough detail as I wanted, leaving my curiosity as unsatisfied as my stomach. After all, Tende had been secluded almost as much I had been, having barely ever left his valley, which lay just next to mine. All he could relate to me was what he had heard from his elders in the village. Everything was second hand, a reflection of a reflection.

But at least I got some sense of how the Canyonlands were arranged.

Towards the northeast was the River's Greeting, and north of that, upstream of the mighty river of Aniene, stood the Citadel of Light, the epicenter of all the peoples of the Canyonlands. That was where Emperor Lucian lived, and where he organized the Lightguard. The closer we got to the city, the more people we would encounter.

Tende also spoke of things which my mind struggled to wrap itself around. Beyond the citadel lay the peaks I had seen on the plains, heaps of rock climbing toward the heavens.

The other confusing thing which Tende mentioned to me was that the Canyonlands also, towards the west, came to an end. I found this baffling. For me, all that existed were the canyons, the plains, and the skies. But he said that his people, the Riverkind, originated in a place called the Sea, where there was an expanse of water as great as the plains upon which we'd walked.

Such things were as distant as dreams, and I struggled to believe them. The idea of another world, made up entirely of water, seemed as fictional as my people's religion of deities living in the clouds. Despite my best efforts, I could never do more than half-believe him.

Instead, I asked him about the powers which I would encounter in this world. I had a taste of the Lightguard and knew about the Riverkind, but Tende had told me, when we'd first met, that there were other Essences that people used to Weave. He spoke to me of many kinds of warriors, who used their Anima to Weave forms out of rock, or earth. I listened to him and asked questions until my mind was fit to burst.

"I don't know much about them, I had never met any other kind of Essence User until I met you," Tende pointed out to me. "But I hear that it is easy to recognize those who Weave rock and earth with no problem, I am sure."

"Why is that?"

"You have noticed, perhaps, that my people are lithe, thin, flexible. Fluid, almost."

I had. In contrast, the people I knew seemed stocky and ungainly.

"Well," Tende continued, "that is because your Essence affects you. Light and Shadow are such ephemeral, intangible things that we don't see the effect so much. After all, we are already made up of light and shadow; we are already made up of water. But rock and earth are something else. You will see it in their skin and faces, I think. Something... different."

As with all my lines of questioning, once I pushed for more details Tende revealed that he didn't know much beyond what he had already said.

But it was enough for my imagination to be unleashed. What, I thought, could be stranger than to have your body become *rock-like*? How did it feel? How did it *look*?

"If what I heard is correct, we will meet Stonekind before long," Tende said. "They maintain bridges and steps and towers, allowing people to travel across the Canyonlands. All under the command of the Lightguard, of course."

My thoughts were occupied until the ridge curved and met

another crevasse. This one was much wider, and more open, with a larger stream running down its middle.

And, even more importantly, it had been used by men. A clear path, a trail evened out by footfalls, now followed the edges of the stream.

"What do we do now?" I wondered out loud.

Tende put his fingers into the new stream, Sensing its history. "This water has not met anything of note. It comes from the plains above." Getting up, he pointed downstream. "If we follow the trail of the riverbank, though, we are heading in the direction of the Rivers' Greeting as we thought. I've been told that just about any path in the Canyonlands, one way or another, leads there."

"Which is where we want to go..." I didn't finish my sentence.

"But the closer we get," said Tende, picking up on my thoughts, "the more likely we will encounter others and get noticed. We'll have to be careful, find a place to hide, and travel by night."

The path was a much easier route, and we found ourselves picking up speed. The path was on a gentle decline, which meant that we very slowly wound our way deeper through corridors of rock.

The way was completely silent: this was not a path that was used frequently; a blessing. At first, I imagined an opponent behind every corner, but as an hour went by I started to feel a little more comfortable in my walk. Still, the path was more open than I wanted it to be. The sky was wide above me and weighed upon my soul, and both of us constantly scanned it for the tracks of Light scouts.

"I wonder who uses this path?" I said.

"Herders, probably," replied Tende.

"Who are they?"

"Most of the plains are dry, for the water drains into the valleys. But some of the terrain is good enough to bring animals to graze. That is one of the main occupations of the Riverkind. It suits our nomadic lifestyle to raise animals, and travel through the canyons to sell them in the villages and cities."

"Not many herders now," I said.

"War will do that. Most Riverkind did as we did. Fled the war. Got as far away from cities and people and violence."

And fled from responsibility, came an angry, unwanted thought inside me. But I did not voice it.

"Those who didn't flee ended up serving the Lightguard, in one way or another. They are manipulators. Everyone in their orbit tends to end up serving them. That is what Elder Lembta says."

We walked the rest of the day and stopped at a place where the streams formed a pool. It made for a creek where there were bushes and trees in which to rest unseen from the eyes of the sky. It had probably been used as rest for herders, Tende informed me, who had taken care to plant fruit trees for sustenance. We gorged on the fruit and cycled, then rested until night fell.

As the stars revealed themselves in the deepening black, we got to our feet, preparing to continue on our path.

I stared up at the canvas above me as Tende stretched, readying himself for travel, contemplating the infinite.

There, in the forever of the universe, one last question came to me.

"Are there any more Essences, Tende? The world is so wide… surely there must be many, many more."

Tende raised his arms to the sky in a long stretch, elongating his body until he seemed a head taller than usual. Lowering them, he let out a long sigh, and looked at me.

"There is rumor of many more, beyond the mountains and out to sea."

"And here? In the Canyonlands?"

"Perhaps one more," Tende's eyes caught the starlight. "They call it the Lost Essence; a power no one remembers but was at the birth of civilization. A power more ancient than either of us could fathom. The only problem is no one knows anything about it."

I thought about this for a moment, my mind teeming with ideas and imagination.

"One path at a time, Shadowman," recommended Tende. "For now, you'll have to make do with the one in front of us."

And with that, under the jewelry of the night sky, we continued down the valley, heading ever closer to the Rivers' Greeting.

Chapter Eight

It felt more reassuring to walk at night. There was less of a sense that we would be spied on or come across an unfriendly presence.

Tende warned me that for every position of the Lightguard in the sun, there was another for the moon and stars, and that I needed to keep an eye out for any scouts darting across the sky. But none came, and I was confident that even if they did come, it would be difficult for them to spot us in the black.

We did, however, walk slower. The starlight coated the world in silver, but often, if the valley narrowed, we did not get enough light from above to see where we were going. In such cases, I used my Senses to see the world around me and Tende picked his way through the stream, Sensing in the water where to place his feet.

We traveled in this way across three nights, trying to cover as much ground as possible under cover of darkness, and hid away during the day. When walking, we rested only briefly at intervals, and took the opportunity to replenish our channels regularly so that we might be prepared for any encounter.

It was at such times in the night that I asked Tende how to spin the Anima inside my core, purifying the energy so that it could become more potent. With all the running, we'd not worked on my skills of Essence like he'd promised on the plains.

We were sitting on a ledge, out of sight of the path. The sky was a little overcast, and it made me feel a little more at ease, and the world was quiet. For once, it did not seem as if harm was about to spring upon us.

It was the right time to center myself and learn something new.

We sat cross-legged, and Tende spoke in slow, soft tones.

"To improve your Essence, you must know your core," Tende instructed. "Your center of energy."

I frowned. "My core?" I said, pointing to my chest. "I know it. I found it ages ago. It's where my anima goes to be purified. I direct energy into it."

"You know where it is," replied Tende with patience. "That is not the same as knowing *what* it is."

I was going to argue, but immediately found that I couldn't. He was right. I knew where it lay in my body but I'd never truly been able to conceptualize what it was. I could feel it filling and bursting with energy, I could feel the energy it radiated through the channels of my body. But it was still a mysterious force, something unknown and unimagined.

"Your core can fill and purify. But it can do more if you can guide it. It can pulse, like your heart, and send Anima circling around its chambers, purifying it at many times the speed it would do otherwise. To do that, you must reacquaint yourself with it. Find its edges. Massage them with your mind, so that the Anima spins within."

It was slow, and awkward, at first. But Tende's description of the currents of energy in my body helped me visualize what was happening inside my chest. I found the edges of the core; what had once been just a ball of energy taking shape in my mind.

"I feel it," I said.

"Good," said Tende. "You've taken the first step."

When I walked, I fell into a trance, my aching feet moved by themselves, plodding along. This made the time pass more quickly. My mind was not encumbered with worries about my family and friends I'd left behind or the uncertainty of my future.

In those moments, I was able to look into myself and train my mind to gently pulse my core. When we channeled, I did so again, with more focus, and felt the Anima churn inside my chest.

The effects were not immediate. I was disappointed at first, at how imperceptible the difference was. As more days went by, I found that my body was being charged faster; that the whole cycling process was quicker and more efficient. I felt that I had more powers of Shade at my fingertips than ever before.

On the fourth day, when the valley's cliffs became lipped with dawn's light once more, something new came into sight.

Ahead of us, the path ended abruptly. All that existed beyond it was air.

I approached the edge and peered out.

Before us lay a gaping chasm, with a steep drop down to rocks and a river below. The stream we had followed tripped down in the air to meet it, darkening the boulders below with moisture.

The gorge was not wide: the opposite cliff was not twenty paces away. And yet the cliffs were so sheer that there was no way to get across— not without a climb that would risk our lives.

The morning sunlight slanted into the gorge, dipping one side of the ravine in red, while we contemplated the sight.

"Look," said Tende, pointing straight ahead.

I followed his gaze and saw what he was getting at. Directly opposite, in the cliff facing us across the gulf, was a path mirroring ours. It seemed like a continuation: like it had once been one single, unbroken path until a goddess had pushed her fingers into the plains and created a chasm to interrupt its course.

"There must have been a bridge before," I said. I looked around, looking for evidence of wood and rope. But there was none, nothing to indicate that people used to travel across.

"Of course..." Tende breathed. "I did not expect to see them so soon..."

"Who?" I asked, frowning.

"The people who channel the Essence of Rock and Mineral. The Stonekind."

"But there's no one here," I began to say.

And then stopped myself.

There were people here. I just hadn't noticed them.

On either side of us, perched on the edges of our path among the rocks, were a man and a woman. Both sat, cross legged, barely moving, staring.

The two were barely distinguishable from the rock.

I had to pause for a moment, studying them to make sure that they were really bone and flesh. They seemed more statue than person. Their skin and clothes were gray and dusty. Their faces and arms were pockmarked with edges, like the contours of a boulder: lumped and cracked.

They were exactly as Tende had described. A merging between man and mineral, between flesh and earth.

They were so rock-like that they camouflaged into the canyons.

"They're not moving," I pointed out. It seemed strange to speak about them as if they could not hear me, and yet they were so unmoving, so still, it was like they did not inhabit the same reality as us.

"They take no notice," said Tende. His eyes were wide: I saw in him the enthusiasm and boyish sense of wonder which had always endeared him to me. "They've lived for so long, the world holds no surprises for them. I'm told they barely react to the events of the world. They care not for people who will live and die in such short times, just as we would barely take notice of insects buzzing in the air."

I walked toward one of them. "Hello?" I tried, approaching the woman.

Everything about her seemed... well, *eroded*. Hair had

clumped into bunches, spreading out from her scalp in disarray. It didn't just look like she hadn't washed her hair in months: it looked like she hadn't even ran her hand through it in that time either.

The rest of her was more of the same. Her visage was craggy and dusty, and resembled more the face of a cliff than that of a person, and her robes were patchy and hole-ridden, eaten away by time.

"Can you hear me?" I said.

She turned her head ever so slightly, and I swore that I could hear the grinding of stone in the turn of her neck. Her eyes were dark, and sunken underneath the protrusions of rock-like lumps in her skin.

She looked at me with no expression whatsoever, a blank indifference which made me feel as insignificant as a passing cloud.

"I hear you..." she said, her voice cracked and unused. Her words came out slowly, like echoes emerging out of a cave.

"Will you speak with me?"

A slight frown came over her features. Again, I felt like I could hear a weak sound of rocks grinding and rasping.

This seemed to be her response to my question. Through her frown, the only emotion I could pick out was... *why?*

And indeed, why? If you could learn the history of the universe by channeling rock, then what did I matter? Why waste her breath upon the likes of me?

I had questions for her. I wanted to know her name, and her life. I wanted to know the history left under the layers of the rocks and cliffs. Since being trained by ghosts, I cherished history and knew it was the ultimate teacher. I could only imagine what it would be like to have the knowledge of both past people and the history of the land too.

Looking upon those eyes, I didn't see wisdom. Instead, I saw lethargy. I bored her. There was an unwillingness to engage with the world, a look which said that anything her eyes could behold was dwarfed by the enormity of time.

Could there be such a thing as *too much knowledge?* I thought.

"We need help to get across," I said, dismissing the questions in my mind.

"It...is...not...time," the woman responded. She then turned back to her original position, and it was like she had never moved at all. Like the last minute had been a delusion, and I had stood in front of a statue all this time.

I turned back to Tende, who was standing nearby.

"What does she mean?" I asked. "What time?"

"Maybe..." Tende's eyebrows raised. "Maybe there is a bridge here, linking the paths. But only at certain times of the day."

"What on earth does that mean—"

My question was interrupted by its answer.

All of a sudden, a flash of light lanced through the sky, like a shoot of gold. But this was not a pursuer or flyer— it was too thick. It was like the shadow-blast I'd seen commanders at home perform, but writ large over the sky, a thousand times more powerful.

Then, soundlessly the blast divided, sprouting into six different shoots, streaking the dawn-lit sky, until they converged again in a pattern I did not recognize. It was like a deity scribbled across the heavens signing a scroll. Although the whole thing only lasted a few moments, I was dumbfounded, staring like someone lost in the haze of stars.

The shoots disappeared, and it was like they'd never existed at all, winking out of existence, and leaving the canvas of the dawn unblemished once more.

"What was that?" I wondered out loud.

"It...is... time..." the Stonekind woman said.

As if the canyons themselves were awakening, a cracking sound ripped across the air and a miracle occurred.

Chapter Nine

Tende and I stood frozen, as still as the Stonekind herself.

The boulders at the bottom of the ravine shifted, as if awake. They trembled and bumped against each other, as if floating on top of boiling water. If the pathway I stood on hadn't been so still, I would have said that there was an earthquake rippling through the Canyonlands.

I turned back to the gray woman, and although she hadn't moved and her demeanor was unchanged, I saw that her sunken eyes were closed in concentration. I looked over at the other Stonekind and saw that he was doing the same.

They were moving the rocks below.

Before I could point it out, the boulders stilled. Instead, they rose into the air from the ravine in a slow but steady unbroken movement, picked into the air by invisible giants. Thick lines of Anima were around them not just in jagged streaks, but in strange patterns and glyphs.

Many boulders, and many other, smaller stones too, rose in conjunction, rotating as they floated up towards us. It was impossible to tell which Stonekind was raising what, everything lifted at the same time in a practiced ritual.

They rose and rose until they were at our level, and here was the biggest marvel. The boulders gathered and interlocked, fitting into each other like puzzle pieces, until there was a stone bridge at our feet. It was a feat of engineering: although the bottom of the bridge was lumpy and misshapen, the walkway in front of me was smoother than I could possibly have expected. Every boulder and rock had been meticulously chosen in order to expose its flattest side on top, giving the easiest passage to those traversing the valleys.

It was all over in less than a minute. Suddenly, at our feet was a stone bridge as wide as a man was tall, and it looked like it had been there for a hundred years. Indeed, it was almost as if it *belonged* to the canyon in front of me. Like the gap which had been there previously was an anomaly, a missing tooth in the mouth of the landscape.

I was still reeling from this when Tende spoke. "I have heard of such walkways. The Lightguard are the dictators of time. Those beams in the sky are markers. The amount of shoots dictates the hour for the entire Canyonlands. There are many Stonekind around the world creating or dismantling bridges and walkways according to the hour. This is a fool-proof system against slowing invasions of the Demons of the Underworlds."

"They control time, thereby controlling movement," I said, voicing my thoughts out loud. "The more I find out about this world, the more I see how much the Lightguard have mastered it."

"Perhaps you understand, then, why my tribe decided to leave their chokehold."

"Is there any way of knowing how long this bridge is supposed to stay...well... *afloat*? I can't think of a better word."

"You may ask, but I do not think that the Stonekind will answer."

I sighed. "We'll be exposed, crossing that bridge. We can hardly wait until nightfall to cross it, though— it won't even be there!"

Tende looked at the sky. "No scouts at the moment," he said.

"Then let's go."

The first step was the worst. I hesitated and looked over at the Stonekind who I'd spoken to, but she remained just as immovable and stone-still as she'd ever been. Would she, or any other of the Stonekind, have the will to collapse a stone underfoot, and send me plunging to my death?

I held on to the fact that she hadn't cared what I did. I imagined the Stonekind held the history of the lands in their thoughts and did not trouble themselves with the petty squabbles of the present.

And I stepped forward, off the safety of the path and onto the stone bridge.

I don't know what I expected. Perhaps I wondered if the mosaic stone bridge would buckle, perhaps lower a little under my weight.

It felt as strong and stable as any bridge I'd ever walked across.

So I took another step, and then another.

Tende joined me, his patter of feet on rock joining my own.

Silence reigned for a moment. Our ears were primed for any cracking or grinding of rock, our feet ready to leap in case the boulder underneath us buckled.

My breaths were shot, my mouth dry.

I was ready, at any moment, for the plunge.

Tende and I both stepped gingerly, taking small, darting steps from one piece of rock to another until we made it to the midpoint between the cliffs. I tried not to think of the chasm below, and the jagged rocks that would welcome our fall.

At any moment, it felt like death would come and chase us once more.

And then, it did.

"Jason!" Tende exhaled, getting my attention.

I turned around, my friend had his neck craned, looking upwards. Following his gaze, I saw immediately what had made him pause.

A scout, soaring across the sky. But they were flying low, sweeping down from the heavens.

With startling speed, they rocketed toward us, coming to a stop just above our heads, out of reach.

It was a woman with long golden hair, curled and tousled by the winds. Her figure was slim and long, with thin limbs. Despite how tall she looked, it looked like she weighed no more than a collection of twigs. Perhaps that was the point—that she would be as light as possible, so she was barely a burden on her wings.

The golden appendages growing out of her shoulder-blades were beautiful: there was no other way to say it. The light-wings were golden, gleaming like sunshine reflected on water, and, flapping in the air above us, they were both huge and intricate. They perfectly replicated the wings of a mighty bird, such as an eagle or a vulture. They were large enough to send gusts our way with each flap and had a majesty that could only have been designed from the natural world.

I grit my teeth, resolve burning within me.

I pulled energy from the purified Anima circling in my core, and shadows surged out of my palms, creating my shadow-staff with spears at its ends. I put my foot forward and waited for the Lightguard to swoop down upon me.

I'd spent enough of my time recently battling Void and fending off winged creatures. If I was going to battle the Lightguard, then at least this much was familiar.

But she didn't move. She just stayed there, hovering above us, her features expressionless.

"Come on, then," I snarled up at the golden figure above us.

"She's a scout, not a fighter," warned Tende.

For a heartbeat, I did not understand what he meant.

Then, with a twist inside my gut, his words hit home.

She may not be a fighter, but she could be a marker. A signal.

A way to guide others to their target.

As soon as the thought came to me, the canyon burst into motion. The silence broke, filling with cries and shouts. The path we'd been walking along sprouted six or seven warriors sliding down the rock from the surface above.

They charged with a surge of energy, rushing towards us, stepping upon the bridge upon which we stood.

I started to run in the other direction. I thought nothing could be worse than confronting them on this bridge, where I'd already felt vulnerable enough without pursuers.

But Tende's hand stopped me in my tracks, and I immediately saw why. More warriors were pouring in on the other side of the chasm and were also stepping onto the bridge.

The Lightguard were on both sides of the bridge, and above us.

We were trapped.

Nothing but death waited for us below.

Chapter Ten

We thought the scouts hadn't seen us. Clearly we'd been wrong.

The warriors moved with coordinated stealth and precision. They were united by purpose and discipline.

All were true members of the Lightguard— and clearly a cut above the guards I'd faced when leaving the Hollow.

Given that I'd struggled enough with just those two, my chances did not look good.

I chased the thought away and clenched my jaw as I frantically looked for a solution. A way out. Anything.

"I'm not sure how we're going to get through this one," I said to him. "But for the skies' sake, don't hesitate to send some off the sides, will you?"

"Fighting is not the answer," Tende muttered, almost as much of a mantra to himself as a response to me.

The warriors were getting ready to fight us as they advanced. They Wove weapons of sunlight and starlight, gold and silver molded into weaponry. "Tell *them* that," I hissed.

"They are not going to kill us," Tende pointed out. "They are not making Weaves of swords and javelins. They want to capture us, not harm us."

He was right, they were not coming at us with us with swords and spears, but more light-ropes and chains. It was just like the siblings I'd encountered—for some reason they wanted me alive.

I had no plans to be taken at all.

My mind raced, looking desperately for any means of escape. My eyes darted from one side of the bridge to the next, then to the sky, and finally the ravine below.

"I'm going to have to fly us down," I said.

I'd never heard Tende surprised, despite all the beasts and foes we'd encountered. But his tone was unmistakably shocked. "You can *fly?*"

It was a good question. I'd once managed to replicate the wings of a Void from shadow in order to glide across my valley, but I could hardly claim to have mastered the Weave and had narrowly avoided death.

"Maybe," I said, as truthfully as I could. "Do your best to keep them away, and I'll try to recreate the Weave!"

"I will *not* fight them..." retorted Tende.

The enemy was almost upon us, their footfalls on the floating rocks sounded louder and louder.

I couldn't waste another breath.

I did the only other thing I could think of and directed my hands towards the cliffs, beckoning the shadows. Darkness billowed up to me, drawn from the shade on either side of the canyon, sailing up to me on my command.

Then I set them free.

Shadow-flames tore out of my fingertips. I'd only recently learned to Weave the shape of fire erupting out of a dragon's snout. The form was uneven and imperfect. I hadn't had enough time to memorize the shape properly.

But I could let my imagination fill in the gaps.

Misshapen though it was, the black fire blasting out of my hands had the desired effect.

I strafed my flames along where Tende and I had stood, toward where the Stonekind woman sat.

It was too far for the flames to fully reach her: my shots were too imprecise and unwieldy. But the heat made her flinch all the same and her stillness finally broke as she tried to shield herself from the blaze.

Tende cried out in protest, but I did not listen, screaming for him to hang on.

The loss of the Stonekind's focus had an immediate effect on the bridge. Entire sections suddenly dropped out from underneath us, plummeting back down to the bridge below. Every rock she'd been lifting either plummeted or wavered. Entire sections of the puzzle-piece of the bridge turned back to ore, causing a rain of boulders to cascade into the ravine below.

It was impossible to predict which stone would fall, and which would continue hovering.

All I knew was that the stone I was currently standing on, mercifully, shook but held.

Others were not so lucky. A pocket of our attackers flailed and screamed as they plummeted down along with the rocks, tumbling down into the ravine. Others had perched across two boulders, and barely had time to throw themselves onto the rocks which remained floating. Some found themselves hanging onto stones for dear life.

"Jason…" Tende whispered behind me. I saw that he was staring, wide-eyed, down at the canyon floor, which was now the home of broken boulders and broken bodies. "What have you done?"

"What I had to!" I snarled.

But there was no time to talk further. What was left was no longer a bridge, but a scatter of steppingstones hovering in the air. And the Lightguard were, without missing a beat, barking orders to each other, gathering in the rocks surrounding us.

A light-net was flung through the air, cast from a nearby rock. Tende's ice-hooks materialized in his hands with a cracking sound, and he swatted it away, letting it drop down below before dissipating into sunlight once more.

"Keep going!" I said.

Tende obeyed, his lithe form leaping about me, batting off a hail of nets and ropes, a storm of whirling movement. The crowd of enemies was implacable, relentless. If they'd wanted to kill us, we would have been dead within heartbeats.

I crouched behind Tende, and looked above, at the scout hovering above us. Trying my best to ignore my pounding heart, the shouts and cries about me, the dizzying plunge just a step away, and tried to focus.

I had only ever created shadow-wings once, in utter desperation. I hadn't thought about it since. I had not given my mind the time to recreate the shape in my mind and commit it to memory. It had ended in a very uneven, barely functional shape. But it had been enough to clumsily save me from death. I could only hope that here would be the same.

I used Anima from my core, and my dark Weave was flecked with streaks of pure blue. To use a Weave, I had to have a mold, a shape in my mind to recreate. This Weave was a mixture of half-memory, imagination, and a laughable mimicry of the scout hovering above me. It was unstable, immediately leaking trails of shadow as they formed about my shoulders.

I had no idea whether they would hold both me and Tende, but I also knew that there was no choice.

A hail of light-chains shot toward us from the surrounding rocks, ready to wrap themselves around mine and Tende's limbs. He would never get to all of them.

I took Tende by the shoulders, and he gasped in surprise as I ignored every instinct in my body as I threw myself off the rock and into the chasm.

Chapter Eleven

The air immediately yanked me down, plunging me and Tende towards the rocks below. Tende instinctively put his hands around my shoulders as I had thrown us off the ledge, allowing me to stretch my wings— but that didn't stop gravity from immediately taking effect.

My Weave was an ugly collage of shapes. It was made up of Void wings, the shape of the scout hovering above me, and my imagination. My wings did not even match each other, and my Weave was unstable, leaking shadows, leaving a trail of black lines in our wake.

Tende's weight pulled me down and threw me off balance.

It resulted in a few breathless moments of whirling and tumbling, spinning around in the nothing, the wings barely breaking our fall.

Death beckoned.

After a somersault of confusion and chaos, I felt my black wings at the ends of my arms take purchase on a current of air. We started a slow, broken arc, sailing along the canyon diagonally.

We were still falling, but now we were falling *sideways*.

My wings shook uncontrollably, the edges flailing and crumbling with the exertion, letting off more and more trails of shadows.

We were going to hit the ground *fast*.

The world blurred as our glide sped out of my control.

It was all I could do to try and straighten our trajectory—to aim it at the river.

I tried to cry out from the exertion, only to find the rushing air rip the sound from my mouth.

The water loomed underneath us— and Tende let go, crashing into the liquid beneath. I followed suit, letting what was left of my patchy, broken wings fade away.

The world spun and my senses rioted: I did not plunge into the surface, but rather bounced on it, skimming the surface like a tossed rock. My body was flung this way and that, my limbs thrashed in a demon's dance.

After being whipped by the water's surface a couple of times, the river allowed me in. The canyon disappeared, replaced by a world of fury-white froth.

I was thrust down deep, buried under water, going beneath the white and into the murky green, before floating back up to the surface.

That's when the pain finally hit me. I could not differentiate between the wounds of the fight on the bridge, or the impact of the fall, but it seemed like my flesh was aflame. It was not the concentrated, jabbing pain of a wound, instead it was like every inch of my skin had been whipped raw, like all the trolls of the Canyonlands had been twisting my flesh.

The stinging protest of my body was almost enough to stop me breathing in when I broke the surface.

I could not swim, I could barely move. All I could do was stay afloat, and try to take control of myself, as the water nudged me further downriver.

I had become somewhat talented at mastering pain and disassociating it from my thoughts. It was a necessary part of forming an energy core inside my chest. The pain I felt now was beyond anything I had experienced before, and it took me a while to stop my screaming body from overwhelming my reason.

I finally managed to begin to wade through the depths, feebly making my way to the rocky banks of the river.

I saw that Tende was doing the same.

For a moment, I did not understand what was wrong. I could only see that Tende, whose element was the water, was moving in a way which didn't seem right. His movements were slow and awkward, containing nothing of his usual grace.

Worry started to settle in long before we got to the bank.

We arrived at the same time. I dragged myself onto the rock, ignoring the howl of my muscles.

I turned and tried to take Tende's shoulder to help him up as well. But as soon as I touched him, he screamed.

I'd never heard him make such a guttural sound before, and it bounced back and forth between the canyon walls.

I retreated and let him emerge himself— on one arm.

His other flapped uselessly at his side, broken.

He collapsed onto the dampening rock, and faced the sky, cradling his arm.

I heard the flapping sound of the scout's wings approaching once more.

"Get up, Tende," I beckoned. I brought him up to his feet, and he groaned with the pain, cradling his broken arm as he did so. "We've got to go. They're coming for us."

It was true. I could hear the battle drawing closer, the shouts and cries of the warriors from above as they called to each other from one floating rock to another, discussing how to clamber down.

Tende took a sharp intake of breath and nodded. I offered him support, but he brushed me off, limping forward delicately.

We started to walk over the rocky bank in the direction downstream, but it was too slow. Above us, the hovering scout appeared, drawing the warriors to us. With every breath, my imagination was full of footsteps, coming closer and closer.

We were never going to be able to run away. Nor were we going to be able to hide, not with the scouts floating above us, highlighting our position to the enemy at every turn.

It was only a matter of time.

I reached out, Sensing the shadows, looking to see if I could find something— anything— which could help us.

"There," I said, pointing ahead.

Tende raised his head, which was coated in sweat, to see where I was motioning.

It was a small cave. An offshoot of the river, plunging down into the rock, digging its way downwards into the Underfold.

Skies knew where it led. All I knew was that we needed to get out of the light, away from that disturbing, hovering presence. If we could crawl into a place with darkness and water, then maybe we could lose our enemies in the sky.

Maybe.

Taking Tende's elbow, I brought him to the mouth, where a stream trickled away from the river poured down the throat of rock. The scout followed us as if it were our shadow.

It had not been far. Not more than a few hundred paces.

But it took us agonizingly long. The voices of our pursuers got clearer and clearer with every heartbeat.

Even if we entered into the maw, at the pace we were going, we wouldn't get very far.

"Tende, can you take the stream, block the hole with ice behind us?"

Tended winced at the thought. "If I can, it will take my last drop. There will be nothing left."

"Then do it. I'll do the rest."

I made Tende go first. He got on his stomach, and with a grimace of pain, started to squirm forward on his side, avoiding putting any weight on his hurt arm. He went head-first into the sinkhole, following the stream into the tunnel.

The sounds of men approaching grew louder, then I followed Tende. There was a moment of comfort as I slunk into the dark, damp, wet chamber. Away from the sun and sky, this was the home of the shadows. I'd be strongest here.

But then came the horrible realization that, of course, it wasn't good enough anymore. Not when facing the Lightguard.

We turned and looked through the opening. In that circle of sky was the enemy: the scout, hovering in the circle of sky in front of us. The sounds of feet slamming into rock sounded, getting louder and louder.

The water flowed around us in that narrow tunnel and I urged Tende on. I put my hand on his shoulder, encouraging him as best I could. "You can do this," I whispered.

He tried. He held his hand up and closed his eyes. His lips twitched, turning into a grimace of pain, but gradually he composed himself. He calmed enough to use his Essence, but couldn't manage to get rid of the shakes and the shivers racking his body.

The water, pouring in from the river outside, began to freeze. The forever-flowing water started to coalesce into opaque shards, spearing out from the border of rock, giving the cavern entrance a row of ice-teeth.

It was taking everything Tende had left, that was obvious. His breathing was not controlled, but short and unsteady and his body seemed to want to go into spasms of pain.

All this effort for a sheet of ice that would barely hold any time at all against a few strokes of an axe.

It was what I'd suspected. There was no hope that last, desperate acts could save us.

There was only one thing to do.

I spoke softly into Tende's ear. I knew that he was too distracted to pay too much attention to me, but I hoped that my words carried anyway.

"Keep going," I urged him. "Close it off. You're right, you don't belong here. The Flow doesn't want you. This is my fight. I've got to follow it alone."

"No..." grunted Tende.

" I'm the one who confronted the Lightguard back home. It's me they want. They won't chase you." Tende seemed like he was going to say something, but his body prevented him. His jaw was clenched, the veins in his neck bulged through the skin. "Just keep freezing, Tende. Look after yourself and follow the Flow. I'll see you again, one day. In one valley or the next."

I got up. I felt that I could hear a groan of protest. "I'm sorry for the pain I brought upon you," I whispered.

Then I clambered back outside, pushing through the gap of the tunnel. The shards were now reaching together, and almost touching. I had to push through them, cracking off some blades of ice as I went. Others did not break, and they raked through my tunic and skin.

It was painful but it didn't matter.

I'd made my choice.

I found myself back in the light, in the air. In the world of the Lightguard.

I looked up at the scout, she remained as stoic and as untouched as ever, hovering over me. A look of utter disregard. Even after all the pain my friend and I had gone through, she didn't have a speck of dust on her, and her demeanor had not changed.

I did my best to stand up straight and hold my head high.

Then the warriors descended upon me.

A net, like the ones we used back in the Hollow to catch fish, fell upon me. It was made of light, woven from the rays of the moon.

I tried to duck and swerve out of its way— but to no avail.

The moment it touched my skin, that strange feeling of confusion and agony bolted through me like there were blades in my blood. I gasped, and fell to my knees, unable to control my body anymore.

I had a few fleeting grasps of vision then. I saw warriors gathering around me, pointing their weapons at me.

As the pain of that net sent my body into spasms, I directed one last look at the cave. The net divided my vision into squares, but I saw Tende, with a look of utter dismay, peering from the other side of a sheet of ice.

I cried out, and darkness overcame me.

Chapter Twelve

When I woke up, nothing was the same.

The first thing I noticed was my body felt different. Even before I was able to take in my surroundings, when I still had one foot still in the world of dreams, I was aware of a yearning hunger at the center of my chest.

My chest, my core had been purged. I had no Anima left whatsoever.

This was a complete anomaly. Normally, ever since I'd been a child, I generally had *something*. Even when I was completely empty and did not have enough to even do the basic Sensing, there was generally a sliver of something passing around my channels.

But now that light-net had emptied me completely, drawing out my powers. I felt weak, almost sick. For a few moments, I didn't dare to open my eyes.

I heard the sounds of voices, and footsteps. I felt my body sway, this way and that. Like I was being carried.

I must be in some sort of cart, I thought.

I opened my eyes, fearing the worst.

I *was* in a cart, of sorts. But it was not like the hand-pulled cart that the farmers used in the Hollow. It was much larger, big enough that I could see the rolling tops of large wheels. It was big enough to hold the cage I'd been bundled into unceremoniously.

It wasn't big enough to carry me comfortably. I was bunched up, with my knees up against the bars on the far side. Every rock and bump on the path we traveled made the metal rods knock against my legs and the back of my head.

I shifted so that I could hug my knees, and not knock against the metal so much. It was a cramped, uncomfortable position. This was probably on purpose. While I was used to discomfort and pain, the inability to sit in a cross-legged, lotus pose would make it more difficult for me to cycle.

My mind finally raced through what had happened as I realized I couldn't cycle easily as they took me away.

The Lightguard— the puppet masters of the Canyonlands, had caught me.

I looked around.

The entire band of warriors was walking with me, following along a winding path. But they weren't pulling the cart. No one was. Instead, it was pulled by a creature bigger than almost any I had seen. The only thing I could compare it to was a cow, like the ones the farmers raised back home, but it was longer and sleeker with a long neck and antlers coming out of its head like branches of a great tree.

It wasn't the only one there. Two warriors, one at the front and one at the tail, rode on the backs of such creatures as well.

We were walking a path that followed a river which looked wide and deep. Around us, the water was fringed with greenery, with trees nestled in between the cliffs of the valley.

"He's awake, Sunguard Tulla!" someone cried out, sensing my movement.

The warrior at the front, riding her beast, turned and came to join me.

The warrior let the procession filter past until she was aligned with me. It was the same warrior who had threatened me on the stone bridge and ordered Tende's execution. I looked at her beast, which she controlled with ease. She had reigns wrapped around its mouth to direct it, but she also used a light-whip to slap the creature's rump.

I looked at the beast's eyes, wondering whether such treatment would give it distress, but it seemed docile and familiar with the situation.

"Never seen an achlis before?" the woman named Tulla sneered. "I suppose you wouldn't have. You've seen so little, cooped up in your little caves."

I ignored her jibe. "Where are we going?"

"Where do you think?" she answered. "To the Citadel, where the emperor will use you how he wishes."

I grimaced. My plan had been to find a Lightguard who would heal my father. I hardly thought that the Emperor, who had imprisoned my people in the first place, would be the best place to start.

Then again, I had no idea why he wished to see me—nor why the Lightguard had been ordered to keep me alive.

There was no way of knowing what awaited me, all I knew was I didn't want to be in the hands of these sadists. Perhaps there would be a way for me to cycle once the night fell and I could gather my forces enough to find a way to escape.

Tulla looked at me, a smile at the corner of her lips.

"Don't you have anything better to do?" I demanded finally. "Someone to torture, maybe?"

"It pleases me to see your brain turn. To see you try to think of options when you have none. You will be supervised all night, just so you know. My counterpart, Moonguard Marius, will watch over you."

"You can't stop me cycling, just as you can't stop me breathing," I muttered.

This seemed to amuse Tulla.

She held up her whip. "Do you know what the Moonguard use, instead of a whip, to move their creatures?" she asked.

I reluctantly shook my head.

"The commanders in the Moonguard all have the ability to charge their Weaves with starlight. You had a touch of the kind of pain and distress it causes with the light-net yesterday.

It comes in handy when it comes to spurring our beasts on. It's the perfect implement to jab between those cage bars, don't you think?"

I didn't want to flinch— I didn't want to give her the satisfaction— but my memory of that painful, searing sensation from the light-net stirred fear in me.

"Something to calm you down, should you get any ideas. I do love a multipurpose Weave. There's just something so efficient about it." She smirked in satisfaction. "If you so much as summon a *spot* of shadows, and you'll be sent straight back to the darkness you just woke from. Surely even a cave gnat like yourself can understand that."

I didn't answer.

With an unbearable smugness, Tulla winked, and prodded the backside of her beast. It yelped in pain, and trotted forward, drawing her back to the front of the procession.

She left me with nothing but an aching body, the bars of my prison, and a dark mood.

Chapter Thirteen

The next few days were a blur.

Cramps and discomfort spread from one part of my body to the next. I was almost never let out of my cage, and when I was it was with light-rods ready to prod into my flesh and whips ready to be cast across my back. Still, I treasured these moments as the only times where I had relief from the discomfort of those bars. I was able to dunk my head into the river and slake my thirst, and then have a bowl of broth.

Otherwise, there was no relief from that blasted cage, which I hated as if it were my worst enemy. It took all of my meditative power to try and keep my mind calm and overcome the complaints of my bruised and stiff limbs.

When I did, I spent my time observing my prison guards. If I could do nothing else, I reasoned, perhaps I could glean a little about how the culture of the Lightguard functioned. The more I learned, the better chance I had at navigating this new world and helping my father.

In some ways, it felt like the culture was not too foreign from the one that I knew. I remembered that when I'd first stumbled into Tende's valley, the difference in their way of life was shocking.

Here, in comparison, was a more recognizable structure. The Lightguard had commanders, and their ranks matched the ones of the Hollow. Tulla was clearly the one in charge. But she also had Binders following her, and then Weavers as well: their rank, just as in the Hollow, was determined by their ability to wield Light.

It was a mirror of the structure back home. This was surprising, at first. But then I reminded myself that that the Hollow had been designed in the same way as the society which had spawned it.

Exactly how the abilities matched up with the abilities of Shade Users was a little less clear, however. I was hardly seeing them at their fighting peak: I could only monitor their Essence when they cleared paths or cut down firewood. But I was able to witness that, in general, they seemed to have a far more fluid way of using light than the average Hollow tribesperson could use shadow. They came up with much sturdier and more intricate forms of Weaves, and they could all do a larger range of forms than my people, who tended to focus on perfecting just a handful of shapes.

What most fascinated me, however— and what was the biggest difference for me to account for— was how the troops seemed to operate in pairs. For every light-user who specialized with the sunlight, the others seemed to specialize in moon and starlight. In this way, the Lightguard seemed to separate into day and night divisions, called Sunguards and Moonguards. Every warrior had their counterpart in the other half of the company. The sun-users, who had a much more powerful resource at their disposal, seemed to hold the upper rank, this was reflected in the force and might of their Weaves. They made gigantic axes to hack down trees and thick swords the size of small men. Their counterparts, who stood guard at night, seemed to do more with less. They trained with shuriken, daggers, and katanas. But their forms were more intricate and beautiful, each Weave its own work of art. They moved with a stealth that was every bit as impressive as the force of the Sunguard.

Still, for all they seemed to match their daylight counterparts in terms of power and ability, the Moonguard took their orders from the other half—and their leader, Tulla.

She would give orders to scouts, who would fly to meet us and report back during the skies— but if she wanted the scout to return she would send a blast of light into the sky as a signal. It was an almighty blast—twenty times more than the efforts of Command Helton, the most powerful Shade user I knew. When she fired, it was like the earth was returning a lightning bolt to the sky.

Her counterpart, Marius, was able to do something similar. But while his bolts were thinner, they were beautifully intricate and more controlled. While Tulla's light forms sprayed into the air, Marius' blasts looked like they were made of patterns of stars, knit together in symmetrical knots of light. His Weaves were almost hypnotizing.

At first, it seemed clear that any escape attempt that I took would have a better chance at night. But I soon understood that the night faction was not to be taken lightly. While the sunlight users seemed to surpass the others in might, the starlight users seemed to have perfected their use of Essence with a control which was just as deadly.

However, I did get a clearer idea of how time worked in their society. There would be regular streaks across the sky, like the one we had seen from the bridge. The streak would then splinter into amounts of lines which displayed the hour. The company would follow this with an almost religious reverence. Almost every time the streak would cause a reaction, whether it was the sign to stop resting or to start a chore, there would always be an activity resulting from the streak.

It also determined how they navigated through the valley. While we generally followed the river bank, we often had to cross it, where, at certain hours, there would be Stonekind in position to construct stairs and bridges, or to remove boulders from paths. Everything ran according to a schedule that was dictated by the sky.

As time went on, we encountered more and more Stonekind— and more and more people. At first, we crossed groups of Riverkind, who seemed to live nomadic lifestyles, carrying their lives on caravans. We even crossed other tribes clustered in villages.

At those times, I would ignore all the aches and pains, and make sure that I scrutinized every detail that could. I had only ever seen how my own tribe operated, and that of Tende's. In both cases, there seemed to be communities formed out of one kind of Essence, shadow, or water.

However, in these conglomerations, the way in which they spoke to each other suggested a far more diverse collection of abilities lived together. I monitored these places in detail, searching for examples of people who used Essences which I had not yet encountered.

I did not glean much. On occasion, when she felt that I was being too curious, Tulla would command that I be put to sleep once more, where some rods of light from the Moonguard would be planted into my cage, and after a blaze of dizziness I would lose consciousness. She also did this whenever I tried to ask questions, such as when I tried to ask about Tende.

However, I still managed to glean some glimpses of strange people, here and there. Most villages seemed to be ruled by some Lightguard, who stood in the village center giving orders. There would also be solemn Stonekind living amongst them too, nearly always standing like gargoyles at the entrance of every village or community, ready to operate a bridge or walkway.

Among them would be poor, downtrodden people. Their backs were hunched and they wore dirty clothes. Some had black marks, patterns of ink, written on their skin. I wondered what it meant, until I witnessed one of them use shadow, and I grew excited that Shade Users existed out here in the world of the Canyonlands outside of the Hollow. I tried to catch their gaze, and reach out to them, but they avoided the Lightguard company like an illness, retreating to their homes and fields and avoided looking at us.

But there was also a faction of people I had not encountered before.

They seemed to populate the trees and fields: I would see them picking their way through foliage or peeking through long grass as the light procession passed. They had skin which at first I thought resembled that of the cracked Stonekind—but I soon saw the difference: vines lined their flesh like veins, sprouting foliage, and flaked visages with the red-brown curls of bark.

The gradual increase of people in the valleys were, for those days, the few indications that time was passing at all. I could feel my stomach shrinking, and my body getting weaker, as the days flowed from one day to the other. The journey became one uncomfortable, painful daydream. I never managed to fully sleep—and therefore fully managed to stay awake as a result.

The only indication of progress was the river we were following. I saw the river strengthening, getting more and more mighty with each passing day. Streams fed into it, thickening it, like blood flowing to the heart.

Until, finally, one day, the procession wound around a bend, and I sensed a mutter of excitement as we turned a corner.

"The River's Greeting!" someone cried, and the soldier spoke with the relief of someone returning home.

We were getting close to the city.

Chapter Fourteen

We emerged out of the narrow valleys and came into view of the River's Greeting.

The view was immense.

The valley we walked through was gargantuan. It stretched about twenty times the valley of the Hollow. The opposite cliff was so far away that the houses collected at its foot seemed too small to live in.

The whole expanse was almost entirely filled with water. It was fed by a hundred rivers and streams, some just trickles and sprays coming down from the surrounding cliffs, others more substantial rivers like the one we had been following. But it never felt like a river itself. The basin of water was so large that it seemed still, a lake with water as smooth as glass. I could only guess at its depths and what fish and creatures swam in its bowels.

The lake was home to a hub of activity. There were boats, all about twenty times the size of the little dinghies we used in the Hollow, decked out with triangular sails dyed almost every color I knew.

But human activity was not restricted to the water. Surrounding the lake on its bank was a strip of road with stone buildings and huts lining it. Some had wooden pontoons, and it was full of ships coming and going, with nets full of writhing fish. Others had a queue of carts unsettling the dust under their wheels, transporting piles of goods.

The line of traffic led to the city at the head of the lake.

The Citadel of Light was humongous. It was built around a semi-circle of cliffs, bisected by a waterfall cascading down its middle. You could barely see its cliffs, instead its rock was almost completely covered with stonework.

There were houses, towers, domes, arches, and walls. They all intersected and met across the cliff, forming roads and stairs and bridges. Looking over the city was like gazing at a jungle, with the chaos and riot of greenery replaced by the complex hive of habitations and constructions.

The city stood above the lake, its waterfall feeding the body of water, but as large as the lake was, it was dwarfed by the city itself. It seemed to swallow everything up. A multitude of boats lay anchored at its foot; all roads climbed up and lost themselves inside the labyrinth of stone, choked with human activity.

This was where the Canyonlands was run, I thought. Here was the seat of power.

Which meant that here sat my enemy, and hopefully, the key to saving my father.

If I could ever escape.

"A scout is sailing our way, Commander Tulla," a warrior announced, gesturing upwards.

I followed the warrior's gaze and looked up into the sky.

The sky was just as busy as the lake. Scouts crisscrossed the air above, leaving trails of light which formed a pattern across the horizons. One scout, however, seemed to be arching down in our direction. It slid into view, coming to a halt at the head of our procession.

It was the same scout I'd seen at the bridge. I felt a feeling of dread settle in my belly. My instincts told me that her presence would not mean anything good.

She and Tulla spoke to each other for a moment, Tulla on her beast, the scout hovering above her. Then they both turned to me.

The scout nodded, and then with a wave of her wings shot back up into the air, traveling so fast she soon seemed no bigger than a wandering leaf.

Tulla used her reins to turn and came back down the procession. She motioned towards me. "Get him out of the cage and get him ready," she ordered.

"Ready for what?" I asked.

I didn't get an answer. Instead, the warriors threw the cage open and pulled me out roughly. Those who were not manhandling me prepared light-weapons, ready to pounce on me if I were to make any unexpected movements.

They needn't have bothered. I was too weak and overwhelmed to resist.

I was dragged to the lake and submerged into its waters.

It was almost a relief. My skin was grateful at the opportunity to bathe in the water, cold as it was. I felt refreshed, and the shot of ice I felt was a welcome relief from the aches and pains of my imprisonment.

I soon realized that I wasn't just being put into the water. I was being scrubbed. Warriors about me used strigils, roughly scraping off the dirt and sweat.

I was being *cleaned.*

My skin felt raw, but also reawakened. Sitting in the cage, I'd started to feel less-than-human. I was content to let the warriors do what they wanted.

They stripped me down to my underclothes, ripping my tunic off of me. Once my limbs and torso were scoured, I felt hands rub an oil into my skin. It smelled strong and sweet, like wax.

I was handed a long, pure white tunic. It was of finer, softer fabric than I had ever worn before and hung loosely from my slim frame. A belt was circled around me, snugly holding the garment around my waist. With the folds it created, it gave the impression that I was not wearing one tunic, but two. I wondered if that was the fashion here, to act as if you had so many clothes that you wore two at a time.

I wondered why I was being prepared like this? It felt

pleasant to be rid of the grime of my old clothes. Indeed, I felt lighter because of it, but I doubted that this meant anything good in the long run.

"Well, well, well," said Tulla, looking down at me from her beast, smirking at my new look. "You almost look respectable. That's what spending time with the Lightguard does to you..."

She turned to the warriors about her.

"Now chain him up," she commanded. "He's to be brought straight to the palace."

"The palace?" I repeated.

She grinned. "You've been given the *honor,* prisoner, of being invited straight to the top of the Citadel. The Emperor wishes to see you."

I looked up at the towering Citadel, and its crest— a stretch of magnificent domes and arches, gathered about the shoot of the waterfall.

The palace.

So that's where I was headed.

Straight into the heart of the enemy.

Chapter Fifteen

It was a long journey to the palace with hours of navigating streets and a labyrinth of alleyways and gates and doors.

It should have given me the time to contemplate and theorize why the Emperor wanted to see me. It was a complete mystery to me why I had been captured, why I hadn't been killed the moment I had first encountered the Lightguard. In all the journey, I'd yet to find an answer to this question. And now, with the Emperor requesting my presence the moment I walked through the door, my sense of confusion doubled. Surely, with all this power at his fingertips, there was nothing my life could offer him. What could he want from me?

I didn't have the time to fully think these questions through, however. I was too awestruck by the city.

It began simply enough. I was placed on the horse which had drawn the cart with my cage. It was surprisingly comfortable, with its wide girth-- although I supposed that anything compared to the cage would seem like the height of luxury. With light-chains on my ankles and wrists, we set off.

As we headed around the lake, on the path circling around it, there were versions of things which were already familiar to me, only amplified to a larger scale. There were tanneries, which stunk to high heaven due to the process of sinking skins in urine. Next to them were large pens of animals and beasts, and meat markets where people loaded carts of meat and clusters of people bartered for goods. Nearby, there were stretches where cliffs were chipped away and hammered for stone, the results of their efforts piled by the road in to be carried back to the city.

All of those sights, which at least reminded me of similar processes at home, faded away as we neared the city gates.

Everyone stepped to the side and let us pass, thronging the sides of the paths, instead of making us wait in line. The people pointed at me with curiosity, gossiping to each other.

The road became paved, sturdy, and immaculately designed. It climbed up from the lake, traveling through a patch of woodland. Beyond all the people lining the sides of the road, I could see many more in the trees and undergrowth, nearly all of them had the flaked, bark-like the skin of the Earthkind.

We entered through large gates, with humongous wooden doors embroidered with steel, and light-warriors on both sides. The whole city was a stone fortress, surrounded by thick walls. It isolated the city from the outside world, separating it from the woodlands and lakes, and the people outside.

And then we were inside.

Immediately, the bustle of all of the men and women rose to a deafening level. All the chattering and bartering and arguing and scuffling. It overwhelmed my senses in a way which my jungle home never could.

How do people think in this place?

Clamping my hands over my ears, I peered at my surroundings.

The streets were like arteries, constantly pumping lines of people from one area to the next. I saw more people there than the entire population of the Hollow within minutes, all going about their days, carrying amphorae, sitting at tables, and drinking, selling, or buying produce, playing at dice. The alleys were choked with life, teeming with laughs and grunts and tussles and orders and protests.

Thousands of lives, all living their lives, going about their business.

I felt a flare of disgust. How could they be leading their lives like normal? Didn't they know that their lives depended on the slavery of people like me?

I tried to keep my emotions in check. The Lightguard were the enemy, but these men and women thronging the streets? I had no idea how much power they wielded, or how much they *knew*.

They seemed like ordinary people.

Perhaps, if there were ordinary people here, there would be good people too. People who could train me, people who could help me cure my father. Down here, in the first neighborhoods, there were certainly plenty of people with ink-marks on their faces, possible Shade Users who might be sympathetic to my plight.

As we walked, people began to gather around us, making our walk into a procession. Lots of people pointed at my face, discussing how I lacked a tattoo, or mark of my Essence.

"He comes from the Experiments!" I heard a child exclaim.

The Experiments? Was that what they called places like the Hollow? Did they know what went on there?

We climbed upwards through the city and through a labyrinth of streets more disorienting than any network of caves I had ever explored. We went through another set of gates, indicating that there were inner rings in the Citadel, city walls within city walls.

The higher we got, the less dense the roads were. They spread out with more space, and fewer people. Once we passed two gates, the population seemed wealthier, wearing pristine clothes with colorful rims, and they walked with a swagger of satisfaction. The excitement at my arrival died down, instead replaced with a more subdued curiosity.

With fewer people in this higher level, my senses were less crowded, and I could discern more of the architecture. There were long halls of stone, spearing out from the cliff wall, reaching towards the waterfall and the sun: here, people sat in baths of glowing water, brought down in stone canals, talking to each other in the sunlight, or they sat in rows of meditations, taking in the warmth of the sun.

Finally, we came to a gate even more mighty than the others. Here, warriors wearing white togas with blue pallas shaped into cloaks over their heads, looked perfectly still, trained not to move a muscle. They did not react when we approached, waiting for Tulla to clamber down from her beast and to make an intricate form of light in her hands, impossibly complicated, with several interlocking, moving forms inside it. Only once they had inspected this form were they satisfied, and formed a light-key, which was also impossibly complicated, then unbolted the gate.

"I'd recommend you be on your best behavior, Hollowman," Tulla said as my light-chains vanished, and I was left to clamber down my beast and enter on foot. "He may be an Emperor of the People— but Lucian is no sufferer of fools. You are alive now only because he wills it. One false breath, and you'll be picked up and dropped into the Demon's Lock."

"No idea what that is. But it doesn't sound like he's much of an Emperor of *my* people."

Tulla cracked a smile. "Say that in front of him, upstart. I'll wager you'd be executed within ten heartbeats."

We walked through the gates, and came into a vast courtyard, bathed in sunlight.

Water gushed from the lip of the cliff just above us, pouring into canals built in round patterns around the rocks, decorating the square with an exquisite pattern. Around it, flowers and trees grew in plots of earth: but they did not look like anything from the woodlands in which I'd grown up. Instead, the flowers were twice as large, and were blooming in colors brighter than any dye I knew.

I looked closer at the water, and saw that it, too, was not the normal translucent hue I was used to. No, swirling about in the liquid were plumes of purple, red and green. I had only ever seen such colored water in one place before, the cave which gave birth to the monsters of the Void.

The water was charged with power and energy. In the Hollow, we had a weakened version of this liquid flowing through the Jade River. Some ate Jade Roots, which enabled better cycling. Here, it was more concentrated and would enhance whatever Essence was channeled.

I tucked this thought into my mind to consider for later and studied my surroundings further.

The courtyard was busy with people, but they all seemed to be performing some act of servitude. There were Riverkind, standing by the canals of water, forming beautiful sculptures of ice, or directing water here or there to certain plants. One was raising the water into a mist, allowing us to walk through of its cooling moisture.

Some Earthkind were at the foot of the trees and flowers, their hands on the bark, seemingly shaping the flowers and bushes into ever-shifting, ever more beautiful shapes. Stonekind were on the sides, forming sculptures of a mighty warrior. The sculptures were twice the size of normal men, looking down on us with stern grandeur.

"Can they…" I wondered aloud.

"Oh yes. They are ready to step off their pedestal and crush you at any time. Anything here which is a symbol of beauty is also a symbol of might. Just in case you were thinking of doing something rash."

I noticed that every statue seemed to have similar features, a kind but striking face, with a perfectly groomed head of curly hair, surrounding the top of his head to his even beard.

I wondered who these statues were based on.

Until, in front of me, was the answer.

Sitting on a throne in the center of the courtyard was my enemy.

The Emperor.

Chapter Sixteen

The Emperor sat in the middle of the courtyard, bathed in, well, *everything*.

He was the center of all things. The canals of water, in their swirling pattern, led to a pool at his feet, and then rose in a cool mist, wreathing him, catching the sunlight, and making his aura sparkle gold. Flowers and branches curved above him, slowly moving through the air, twisting and turning, revealing a constantly weaving, changing pattern of bright colors while also providing shade. His throne was a stone chair which seemed to be molded to suit his slumped position, and when he moved, it moved to support him.

If there was ever a more extravagant position to be in, I could not imagine it. I sensed that this was rehearsed, that the first image he'd wanted to present to me was him sitting on his throne, a symbol of decadence and power.

My first thought was that it was all theatrics.

And my second thought was that there's no way in all the Canyonlands it would work on me.

I could see through him. The Emperor was a big man, in all senses of the term. He had bulk and muscle, and his limbs were thick. And yet it was apparent that his fighting days were long over. He no longer resembled the figure which the statues replicated. Years of lounging on the throne had filled out a considerable gut. His clothes, layers of thin, exquisitely patterned gold on a long purple chiton, could not hide it.

I saw through all the pomp, all the theatrics, and saw only my enemy. A coward. A weak man who was content for my tribes to die just so he could bathe in his pools of luxury.

Hatred and a pure, unstoppable anger, burned with fury inside my gut. My fists tightened. I knew that I could not fight him, that I could not raise my hands.

Every part of me wanted to launch forward and tear the man apart.

The emperor eyed me for a moment, chewing on something, his mouth flapped open and closed, before he leaned across on the armrest of his throne and barked out: "Who's this?" His voice was deep, the kind I could imagine giving orders and making speeches. There was a cracked, wheezing edge to it, like it had lost some of its strength.

Tulla, now devoid of all her confidence, rushed over, and whispered something in his ear.

"This is the boy from that blasted valley?" the Emperor barked. He looked me up and down again. "This is him? The one who caused all the trouble?"

I did not respond. I could barely even look at him, for fear that I would lash out.

"Can you speak?" he barked at me, in that wheezing voice. "Have your people forgotten how to conduct yourselves entirely? You're in front of the savior of the Canyonlands, boy. Bow."

He sat back, contemplating me. Waiting for me to respond.

"I suppose that I have some illuminating to do." His tone was one of annoyance, like I had bothered him in his time of relaxation.

He took his feet out of the pool, where someone rushed to me to place his sandals on. Then he rose out of his throne. There was a halo of people attending to him, two guards and a handful of Weavers maintaining the mist and flowers about him. They all mirrored his movement, stepping in line with him, rendering his steps a procession.

A shadow of sycophants.

The sandals he wore creaked as he stepped toward me. All I could think about was the smell of urine from the tanning buildings by the lake. The memory kept the smell in my nostrils.

He approached me, stepping near enough for his cooling mist of water to tickle my skin.

I noticed he was swaying a little, and his breathing was heavy, just from getting out of his seat.

"Now..." he said, standing in front of me. His breath smelled odd. Sour, even. "You will bow, boy. You can clench your fists all you want, but everyone bows."

My words blurted out. "I won't. Not after what you've done to me. To my valley."

He snorted with annoyance and waved an instruction at Tulla. "Give this boy a drink. I'm already tired of his petulance."

Tulla and a guard grabbed me. A kick to the back of my legs dropped me to my knees, and as I shouted in surprise fingers grabbed my face, prying my mouth open.

Before I could protest, the emperor had a gourd in his hand, and was pouring a red liquid down my throat.

I gagged. The liquid tasted rancid, reminiscent of his breath.

"You will bow, and you will drink my wine, and you will be grateful. I am the savior of the Canyonlands, boy, and you live every second only because of my grace. You will kiss my feet if I tell you to, and bow and thank me. You will do so every day until you grow to mean it. Such is the way of the Citadel."

He nodded at Tulla, and she pulled me to my feet, while I spat out what I could of that revolting liquid. But already it seemed to be having a strange effect on me, my brain felt light-headed, and the world seemed to be swaying a little, like I was on a raft on the Jade river.

The emperor's lips curled into a mocking smile. He drained what was left of the gourd into his own throat, demonstrating how little it affected him.

"This way," he said. His words were not stern, they did not need to be. Even a whisper from his lips carried a weight which no other voice could. He walked, and his guards and servants trailed him.

With dizziness stopping me from protesting, I found myself being led by Tulla, pushed ahead so that I could keep apace.

My rage was urging me to fight, to protest, but I was in no position to do anything. My vision was lurching, no matter how much I tried to stabilize it.

"Now that you've loosened up a little," Emperor Lucian observed. "You will listen better."

"What did you give me?" I spluttered, with none of the certainty and strength I'd had just moments before.

"A delicacy, far superior to what you and your people could ever appreciate, from the vines of valleys far from here. Now be quiet, child, you speak too much when you should listen."

We entered a wide, open space. In the middle was a grand structure, a pointed sculpture of steel, in the form of a shard which pointed into the air. It stood upon a flat circle of stone with symbols on it. Surrounding the impressive structure were two decorative moats of enchanted liquid. One spun one way, the bottom layer rushed in another. Two Riverkind were sitting by the sculpture, willing the waters to flow in a circle around the sculpture.

"Do you know what this is?" asked the Emperor, pointing at the design.

I shook my head.

"Of course you don't. It's so easy to forget, you are basically a newborn, aren't you? Blinking in the sun. Compared to me, you are still taking your first breaths. Which, of course, is what this is all about. It's the Sundial. It measures time. Time, of course, is a marker of sunlight, something we Lightguard know quite a bit about. We can feel the strength and weakness of the sun. As a result, the whole of the Canyonlands look to us to organize them. They work in the allotments of time we dictate."

I looked more closely at the structure. The pointed bar created a shadow on the plinth at its foot, tracing a black line among numerals.

"In order to keep everyone protected, we run this valley on timeslots. All dictated from here. Here is the word of time. Everyone here marches to our beat. Just now, with the shadowing nearing the next hour, a ray will blast into the sky, announcing the next phase of the day, and the entire Canyonlands will shift and adapt accordingly. A world, dancing to the tune of my making. I even have the signet ring here—" the emperor pointed to a ring of metal encircling a prism of crystal pointed to the sky— "to project orders and instructions onto the heavens above when I want to. Everyone is under my yoke. And you, you will dance along too."

I tried to form words, even though my tongue did not seem to be fully obeying my will, slurring my speech. "I will not."

The emperor snorted. "Your defiance is as boring as it will be short-lived. Once you have heard my terms, you will do as you're told, and you will cease your whining." He clapped his hands, and a servant appeared with a platter of meat. Clearly, my anger was not having any impact on him whatsoever, unless it was making him hungry.

He bit off the meat of a thigh, tossing the bone behind him for another servant to sweep. "Where was I?" he said. He belched and continued. "Ah yes. Dancing. You see, the reason people obey me is because I was the warrior who kept the demons from the underworld at bay. The hero of the Wars of the Levelling. And now, the people are scared once more. There's all these rumors that the Wars are starting up again. It's nonsense, but I must be seen to be acting, so they can go back to their sorry little lives. Which brings us to you."

"Me?" I blurted.

"Indeed. My people don't know much about the Experiments. All they know is that the Shade Users betrayed me and tried to rise against me. As a sign of my mercy, I did not crush them, but sent them to work in far-away lands, atoning for their treachery by helping the Lightguard prepare for the wars against the demons. Word has traveled that you have escaped, that something has happened in a valley on the other side of the Cayonlands. The city is full of gossip, wondering whether the Shade Users have risen up again, wondering what has actually been happening over there. Word has even travelled of a particularly skilled warrior, one different from all the others. Which brings me to you. You will placate the city. You will tell them why you're really here. You will tell them that I've selected you out of everyone in the Experiments…to *help us*."

My head spun. "What are you talking about?"

'We have been monitoring you, Jason. We know of your particular skill, through our spy creatures. You commune with ghosts, you can Sense the past like no one else. Even the highest masters of the Lightguard cannot understand it yet. Which means you are… *useful*."

Anxiety twisted in my gut.

"All the people are talking about how the Demons, led by Cizin, are going to rise up from below and invade us once again," the emperor said, imitating the people with the city with a whining voice. "They are about to unleash their hordes, and attempt an invasion of the surface, apparently, they have concocted some scheme to do so. It's ridiculous, I defeated Cizin long ago. But there are only so many tongues I can remove. Word gets around."

"What's that got to do with my ghosts?" I found the last words difficult: my words slurred once more.

The Emperor paused for a second, before speaking to me in slow, deliberate tones.

"I will be sending you to infiltrate the Underworld with a team of my warriors. You will observe the ghosts there. You will Sense the past, and what the demons have been preparing."

I shook my head, despite the slight dizziness it seemed to create. "I'll die."

"Does it look like I care? The demons have prepared nothing! I defeated them centuries ago! There is nothing to investigate, boy. What matters is that you show everyone in the city that it looks like I am taking this seriously. You'll be trained, in full view of everyone, you'll speak about your skill in Sensing the past, then lead a parade of warriors down into the Underworld. Everyone will think that I have done my part."

I spat on the ground. "If you think that I'll lift a finger for you, you're mad."

"I'm a persuasive man."

There was something sinister in his tone I didn't like. "What do you mean?"

"There's only a few left of your tribe at this point. My warriors are ready to slay what's left of your family and friends. All I have to do is say the word, and the order will be painted across the sky. All the people you love would be dead within hours."

This hit me like a rock to the chest. I could barely stand; the wine, and the words, combined to make my legs feel weak. The idea of my people— of my sister and father, of Emilian and Yennenga—attacked by Lightguard, it was enough to make me sick.

I tried to say something, but I felt like my legs could not hold my weight anymore.

The Emperor grinned and helped himself to another greasy piece of meat. He turned away from me, watched as someone observed the sundial, and blasted a streak of light in the sky.

The valleys around us groaned with movement, with stone grinding into new forms, bridges forming or disbanding, walls shaping and dismantling.

The Emperor put his greasy hands on his protruding stomach, the grease leaving a mark on his chiton and barked with delight.

His orders were written in the sky and followed to the letter.

Chapter Seventeen

A guard escorted me out of the palace, through a winding alley. I barely paid attention to where I was going, or who was leading me. My mind was elsewhere, focused on my family and friends.

What the Emperor had just proposed was in the realms of fantasy. I had no idea what the Underworld was, not even a vague concept of what it could be. In the Hollow, we used that term to speak of a hell in the bowels of the earth where your soul descended if you died without glory or dignity. The term evoked flashes of fire, torture, and damnation.

Could the reality of the actual place, home to some army of demons, be close to the myths of my childhood?

The idea that I would descend down there and survive was absurd, even if a shred of the legends were true.

And yet, if I did not brave this lair, if I did not do the Emperor's bidding, then all of the people I knew or cared about would die. All of our struggles, and my journey, would be for nothing. My tribe would be exterminated.

It didn't bear thinking about.

All I had to hang on to was the idea that I was going to be trained. I hoped that this would grant me enough abilities and powers to find a way out of this mess, to keep my people alive, and save my father.

It was a thin hope, but it was all I had.

I was led through a door, flanked by a guard, into a building. The door I walked through locked behind me.

There was a lounging chair in the first chamber, and this was enough for me. My mind could not handle any more information, any more stimulus.

I lay on that couch, stretching out my aching body. Perhaps it was because I had been staying in a cage for so many nights. Perhaps it was because the couch was made of a kind of soft material which I'd never felt before in my life.

In any case, my body succumbed to its comfort immediately, and a deep sleep came upon me the moment I closed my eyes.

* * *

I'm not sure how long I slept. It was the kind of deep sleep which came about from a body in exhaustion and a mind in shock.

When I opened my eyes, the evening was upon me. I looked out of the window of the living room, the sun was retreating over the cliffs, coating the rooftops in a color of vermilion.

The network of buildings took me back once more. The cluster of habitations in this vast network of alleyways would take some time before I was able to regard it as normal.

It was a world I was going to have to face, one way or another. I'd have to make it my own. Right now, the city felt like a prison. But I would make it my battleground.

First, I had to prepare.

I sat cross-legged on the floor, where the shadows had started to darken the room, and cycled.

It was not pure darkness. I would be able to replenish my channels with far more ease a little later, in the fuller gloom of the evening.

I didn't want to wait that long. I did not trust this place, and needed to be prepared in any way I could.

I deepened my breaths, first focusing on taking in my environments. Details of the room around me, which I had not noticed before falling asleep, grabbed my attention. Despite being my prison, this room spoke of a house more extravagant than anywhere I'd ever lived. The couch I had slept on was upholstered in light tan leather, and stood on spindled bronze legs. A low table by the couch was a deep brown which spoke of good quality wood, polished enough to shine.

It was yet another indication of the strangeness of this world. Immaculate appearances, masking dubious morals. The thought was enough to bring back my anxieties; for my friends and family, for my mission down into the Underworld.

After a minute, I found the details of surroundings left my mind as I focused inward. I closed my eyes, and opened up my body, letting my channels be infused with the darkness around me. I let the shadows circle around me and infuse my core. Then I started to gently spin the Anima, as Tende had taught me. The memory of Tende threatened to throw me out of my focus, but I managed to hold it together, controlling my every breath and the movement of energy around my core.

It felt better to feel my body become replenished with energy and strength, to feel the Anima inside me purify inside my spinning core.

I started to feel a little like myself again.

Once I'd had my fill, I rose to my feet and started to explore. Beside my chamber was another, which seemed to be used as a study. There was a box in the corner, which was encased in metal strips as some kind of complicated locking system, as well as an oak desk. There was a line of scrolls on the shelf above it, which surprised me too. Scrolls were the preserve of the library back in the Hollow. Here, they seemed to sit there as an ornamental, everyday object.

I walked through an open door into a kind of courtyard at the center of the building. It contained two rows of earth, with decorative flowers providing some color in the paved surroundings. Amongst them were busts of people I didn't recognize. One statue, however, in a statue that was wax-white, was a depiction of the Emperor back in the days of his physical prime.

In the center of this courtyard was a fountain of water, coming out of a well. It had the glow of the magic-infused liquid.

A man waited by the fountain.

My heart made leapt. I thought I was good at Sensing the presence of someone. I didn't think that anyone would be able to be in my surroundings without my being aware of it.

It was clear, with every passing moment, that I knew nothing of this world.

The man was perched on a stone bench by the well.

"I thought you would never emerge," he said. He motioned to a small seat across from him at a table with two goblets. "We have much to discuss, and work to do."

"Who are you?" I demanded.

There was a gleam of teeth, which were as white as the marble busts I'd passed.

"I'm the face of the Empire," he replied. "The Emperor's counterpart."

Chapter Eighteen

He was the most immaculately dressed person I'd ever seen.

He had long, dark hair, but it was tied and pinned neatly so that it dropped in straight lines behind his ears. He had a long black overcoat, adorned with gleaming silver buttons, perfectly fit to his slim, tall frame. Its edges were decorated with seams and cuffs lined with flashing gold filigree.

He reached into the fountain with both goblets on the table and filled them with water. He took a sip of his and proffered the other.

"What is that stuff?" I grunted.

"We call it Elixir. The Stonekind find it in pockets of the earth, stored, condensed power of ancient Essence. The Riverkind bring it to the surface, and into our goblets." He smiled a smooth smile as he took a long drink.

I didn't move, nor take the offered goblet.

"You're a friend of the Emperor, then?" I said.

"I've mirrored him for centuries. Nothing he does is a surprise to me anymore. I am, what we call here, his *reflection*. The night to his day. His counterpart."

He sat down, leaving my goblet on the table, content that I would sit beside him eventually.

"But that does not mean that we are similar, or share the same methods," he continued. "I imagine the Emperor gave you wine. Instead, I offer you Elixir. The water of revitalization. The lifeblood of the Citadel."

"The liquid used to create the Void," I said, as pointedly as I could.

"Indeed. And also the liquid used in the Jade Roots, which you took in order to defeat them. Dislike it all you want, but if you're going to be as powerful as you wish, you will need to adopt our ways. We have a regular diet of the Source. It flows through our atria and our baths, directed by the Riverkind, so we can consume it on a twice-daily basis. Think of what chewing on a Jade Root every day would do for your forces, and you will get an idea of what effect this could give your abilities."

I reluctantly took a seat, inspecting the goblet before taking a sip.

He was right. I hadn't felt anything like it since I'd chewed on a Jade Root. I knew it would take a moment to take effect, but I could already feel my channels expand, getting ready to increase the amount of Anima around my body. It brought a jolt of energy around my body, making me feel twice as powerful as before. The fact that I had a ready source of this, inside my quarters, was incredible.

A gilded prison, indeed.

"You see? Your development is my priority," the man said.

"I don't even know who you are," I returned.

"My name is Cleander." His voice was smooth and unhurried, his diction perfect. Every syllable completed rounded, appreciated. "I'm the head of the Moonguard. As you have probably understood by now, we are a government for whom safety and security is our responsibility. This city is the cork on a bottle of foul of demons. To maintain security at all times, we have doubled every role in the Senate and ministry, one for the night, and one for the day."

"And so you're the Emperor's right hand man."

He smiled. "I will not deny it. The Sunguard contingent have always had the prosperity and the glory, and the larger share of the power. After all, there will always be more sunlight to fuel their abilities than we will have star and moonlight. But without us, the Empire would crumble. If Emperor Lucian makes all the big calls... well, I'm the one making sure they happen."

"Sounds a lot like you're a minion, rather than a reflection."

This did not affect him in the slightest. "You may have realized, Jason, that our beloved leader is not a detail-oriented man. So, the details are left to me. But all the details, over all the decisions made across all the Empire, amount to more power than you would think at first. Just like the Elixir you are drinking."

I contemplated this. I wondered whether there was something to it. The users of Starlight, if he was to be believed, had to do everything that the Daylight users did, with only a fraction of their Essence. Presumably, it forced them to be stealthier, more intelligent, less of a blunt instrument.

Perhaps, in some ways, they made for a dangerous proposition.

The Emperor Lucian's message had been clear. He, in all his power, would use me for whatever he wanted. He was ready to kill me if I didn't comply. A conversation with him had consisted of a display of power.

As for this Cleander character, there was something more elusive about him. I could not grasp his character, nor what he wanted from me. Even his introduction was odd. In clear contrast to the Emperor's pomp, Cleander had waited, patiently, in my own quarters.

Was he trying to ingratiate himself with me? In the warrior troops back home, there was always a Commander making the difficult decisions, and then a second-in-command who had a better rapport with the warriors and supported them to make the decisions happen.

Was this dynamic replicated in this duo of leaders?

"I can see that your mind is whirling," said Cleander. "I imagine that all of this is a lot to take in. But, given all your progress, I would dare to say that you'll take it all in stride in no time. Now, it is time to go."

He got up, straightening his overcoat.

"Go where?"

"To show off my city."

I grimaced. "The Emperor made it very clear that he does not care whether I live or die. And yet you're going to take the time to show me around?"

"The Emperor may have made it seem like you're not important. But I can tell you, *everything* is important to me. That's what it takes to be the head of the Moonguard. Now come."

I drained my drink and stepped forward. As much as I did not trust Cleander, I needed a guide through this infernal place.

Until someone better came along, he would have to do.

Chapter Nineteen

Cleander strode with long strides through the courtyard and out of the chambers. Although he wore long leather boots, he had delicate footfalls, the kind which somehow made no noise on the paved floors.

With a flick of his fingers, a silver form created a key in his fingertips which he inserted into the front door, letting us both out.

A guard nodded at his exit. It was not the same person that had let me in, presumably the shift had changed at dusk, and the Moonguard had taken over.

I followed Cleander through the streets, his soft footfalls barely a whisper compared to the clunking sounds of my footfalls.

"Where are we going?" I asked.

"The most important place in the city. Its epicenter."

"What happens there?"

"You'll see."

We headed down streets and stairs, with barely a word passing between us. There was still a considerable amount of bustle. I'd assumed, wrongly, that things would quiet down during the night. But there seemed to be a fresh, new populace thronging the streets, breaking up any conversation we might have had.

It struck me just how anonymous Cleander seemed to be. He wove his way through people without a notice. He might have been one of the most powerful people in the Empire, but it didn't show here in the alleyways. Many nodded at him, a gesture which he returned, but just as many flitted by without paying him any attention at all.

Which, presumably, was how he wanted it.

If Cleander and the Emperor were meant to be counterparts, they operated completely differently. If the Emperor was a blunt instrument, this Cleander figure seemed to be a sharp, precise knife. Everything was calculated.

We broke out of the alleyways into a large square. "This is Navona Place," informed Cleander. "The heart of the Citadel."

I could see what he meant. There were three aspects to the square, each entirely individual and unique.

First was a bustling market. It had three lines of stalls, with many people filling in between them, perusing what was on the other. Then, a little further on, were three large fountains with connecting canals, where people were sitting, bathing in Elixir.

The square ended in a platform which speared out over the gorge, creating an outcrop into the air, away from the clutter of the city. Here there were lines of people basking in the light from above, soaking in the silver rays of the stars and moon, cycling the magic of the heavens into their bodies.

There must have been hundreds, possibly even thousands of people in the square. It was more people than I had ever seen at once. If I had witnessed the center of power in the Citadel, this, it seemed, was the heart of its culture.

I did not have time to dwell on it much, however. The heartbeat I took to take in the sight was enough for me to almost lose Cleander, and I had to rush to catch up. He was already among the stalls, weaving through the throngs of people. I cursed my short frame as I followed him, trying desperately to peek through the endless bodies to see what was being sold.

I only caught snatches, here and there.

It was enough to tell me something very clearly, this was not the kind of market I was used to from home.

Instead of food and tools, what seemed to be on offer were scrolls, or little statuettes of objects. At times, people seemed to be haggling over Weaves, forms made of silver moonlight.

"What is being exchanged?" I tried to talk through the mass of people over to Cleander.

"Forms, of course. We are not like you in the Hollow. We cultivate our minds as well as our bodies, from when we are very small. As long as our Mind's Eye is developed enough, we can become experts at creating many different objects. If your friends and family can typically only make a handful of patterns out of their shadows, we can make five times that out of light. This is where we exchange our forms, either the blueprints on scrolls, or statues out of marble, which are much easier to study and recreate. For the most privileged members of the Citadel, they can purchase the form itself, the Weaver will maintain its structure for days, allowing the buyer to recreate it themselves."

The idea of an entire currency was made of exchanges of forms was baffling to me. I was the only one from my valley who could make a variety of Weaves, using my imagination to supplement whatever I could not memorize entirely. But the other members were bound to just a few forms. Was it because they hadn't developed their "Mind's Eye," whatever that was?

If that was the case, how could they develop it? How could we catch up, in order to hold our own against the Lightguard?

"How many forms can you create?" I asked.

"I specialize in being an Imagist. This means that I can create everything which I can imagine or remember, but only in thin images, only as thick as smoke. This may not be ideal for battle— although I can of course create my fair share of real weapons, just as anyone can in the Lightguard. My specialty is ideal for messages, for showing people what they need to see. You saw the signet ring in the palace. This allows me to project images into the sky and show the people the pictures of our glorious Empire and its illustrious history. The prophet of the Hollow, Erebus, was the same, to be an Imagist appeals to the intellectuals of the Lightguard. I curate the messaging of the Emperor and his Senate, if you will, that is why I am called the Emperor's Poet."

Before I could ask any further questions, we emerged from the stalls, heading past the fountains. The waters of the Elixir, managed and directed by Riverkind planted at different ends of the square, seemed to come from bridges from above, transporting water throughout the city.

"We call them aqueducts," commented Cleander. "Nothing is more important to our strength than water from the Source. We all take in as much Elixir as we can, to be ready for the next war against the demons of the Underworld."

I noted that many people bathing in the line of water between the fountains did not seem too concerned with maintaining their strength, though. For every warrior in peak physical shape sitting in the channels, methodically scooping up the liquid in goblets to drain them into their throats, others seemed to luxuriate in it, sitting there with friends, laughing and cackling, taking up space with spread legs and prominent guts. Such people were not warrior elites. They were taking in the waters, not because they had to, but because they could. It was a statement of power.

I noticed a line of people at the end of the channels. They were taking it in turns to dip amphorae into the waters before placing the heavy receptacles onto their shoulders. It seemed like such people were of a different class than the others surrounding me; rather than the spotless chitons and jewels of those bathing, these had worn and faded clothes, and less manicured hair and skin. Many of them were not Lightguard, and there were patches of earth and stone-like crusts on their flesh, or tattoos.

"Do they not have channels of water going to their courtyards and houses?" I asked.

"No. Not in the Lower Levels on the other side of the gate. The Source is precious, infused with charged minerals which we unearth from ancient rock. We do not have enough to carry the water around to the whole Citadel."

I contemplated the fountains, and the vast baths of water in which people were socializing. "Doesn't seem like it's so precious to me. Seems more like you want to deprive the others of your power."

I thought that this would engender anger. There was something about Cleander that was altogether too calculated for me. I wanted to see whether I could pierce that cool demeanor of his.

But his reaction was not what I'd expected. It was not of anger, or irritation. Instead, he stopped his stride for a moment, and looked at me. A curl formed on one side of his lips. Instead, he was interested, delighted, even. There was something subversive about his smile. Something playful and dangerous.

He enjoyed being challenged.

Suddenly, I was left with the notion that Cleander was contemplating using me in his own, particular way. Something separate from the orders of the Emperor.

"Here," Cleander said, walking on again. "I will show you why we prioritize the Lightguard with the Source. You can tell me, then, if it is really as self-serving as you make it sound."

We walked along the outcrop, the platform with rows of people cycling in the moon and starlight. Sitting crossed-legged, with their eyes closed, poised. Beckoning the power of the light into their channels.

We continued around the outside, leaving all those cycling in the middle, until we were at the very tip of the spear.

It commanded a look down the valley of the Citadel. In the moonlight, we could see the entire city, stretching down all the way to the foot of the lake below. The shape of the cliffs was choked with stonework, buildings, and roads, with bridges carrying streams of people or water.

The lake was now far away, with the odd gray boat shifting

about its waters like wandering ghosts. The waterfall, coursing down the middle of valley, rushed to meet it, feeding its hungry depths.

"What is this supposed to prove?" I asked, gazing at the sight.

"For all of your attuned senses, your observation could do with some refining, Jason, Son of Ventos," said Cleander. "Look directly below us."

There was, underneath the outcrop, a honeycomb of platforms in which warriors were training in the night light, Weaving grey weapons to spar with.

This series of training platforms led far below, connected by a series of winding stairs.

And it finished in a round, stone amphitheater at the foot of the city, far below. There were people posted all around it, guarding it like sentinels.

"The Demons of the Underworld are pure, malefic beings, Jason. Should they take over the surface, the Canyonlands would be swamped with torture and agony, with death. As the Lightguard, we must take the larger share of the power, frankly, because we are the only ones who can stop them. That, below, is a range of Stonekind. They maintain layers of rock in that circle, blocking a hole which leads straight down below into the Underworld. Into the territory of the enemy."

I considered this for a moment. Cleander stared down too at that circle of rock, guarded by warriors and Stonekind, his eyes lost in its implications.

"We say," he said in his smooth tones, "that the Canyonlands rest upon lakes of malignance. We are the safeguard. We take power, in order to wield it. To keep the Canyonlands alive."

I swallowed. Underneath that stone was a hole which led directly into the bowels of the Earth. To the Demons.

And that was where the Emperor wanted to send me.

"The Emperor spoke of rumors that the Demons were planning another uprising. What were they?" I asked. "What are the signs? He did not seem to think it was worth worrying about."

Cleander straightened, retreating from the hypnotizing look of the hole at the bottom of the valley.

"I am not as optimistic as the Emperor. That is, in many ways, my job. To be as suspicious as he is boastful. I make people safe, he makes people feel safe. It's the reason why our rule has worked." I tried to detect a sense of jealousy, but Cleander continued, not betraying his emotions. "It is true that our best companies have been attacked. Ambushed. Which isn't new. But the way the attacks have been done is... curious."

The way in which he said the last word sent a shudder through me. "Curious how?"

"They did not kill and maim in the way in which they normally do. No, instead they took *pieces* of people. Some warriors, our best, in fact, disappeared completely. For others, the Demons took their heads, their arms, their feet, then disregarded the rest. Almost like they were not fighting us but *collecting* us. Whatever it means, it is a portent of war."

"So, I'm supposed to sneak into the world of these collectors? Monsters? And hope that somehow they won't take parts of me too?"

Cleander turned away from the amphitheater below. "Not without training, you won't. Which brings me to the real reason why you're here. Your trainer will finish her cycling in just a few moments. Then she will start."

"Is she here?" I asked, turning to all the people sitting cross-legged behind us.

"Oh no. She doesn't cycle here, in the light. She's like you, she uses the shadows. It's normally outlawed for all Shade Users who aren't part of the Experiments, it's been that way since their failed attempt to overthrow the Emperor. They are all tattooed with the mark of Shade, a sign that they may not use Essence. But Aelia is an exception. She is my protégé, someone I convinced our leader would ensure the goodwill of the masses."

"And I'm going to start training now?" Much as I was eager to begin, I was still aching from days of imprisonment in that cage, and lack of sleep.

"Now, indeed," said a voice below.

It came from a training platform.

Chapter Twenty

I looked down from the ledge.

"May I introduce to you to Aelia," announced Cleander. "She is the only Shade User trusted by the Lightguard in all of the Canyonlands. And certainly the most powerful. You'll need her, and her lessons, to live. So I'd recommend that you—*pay attention* seems like too small a phrase—*Listen for dear life* would be perhaps more appropriate."

With that, Cleander turned and whisked away, his long strides taking him away from the jutting platform and back into the throngs of the market.

Leaving me with *her*.

Aelia was looking up at me.

Generally, from such a distance, people seem small and powerless.

But not her.

She was on one of the many semi-circles of paved stone protruding from the cliff wall below me. All the platforms were of equal size, yet hers seemed smaller. And that was because of how much space she took on it.

She had a look which made even the hardiest of warriors back home seem thin and reedy. It was not just her tall frame and broad shoulders, but the netting of ink patterns on her face, darkening her features. It was the scars, bruises, and blood stains on her bare arms and legs. Her hair was golden, lighter in color than I was used to, but this did not soften her appearance, it was tied back in lines of plaits, tightened so much it seemed to be pulling her scalp back.

"Are you going to come down, or do I have to come and throw you down?" she said. She glowered at me, tapping a shadow-staff impatiently at the stone under her feet.

Snapping out of my reverie, I found the stairs to the platform she stood on.

"I'm..." I started to introduce myself.

"I don't care. Stand there and take a stance. Show me what you have."

I was taken aback by this. "I'm here because of the Emperor," I protested, a little weakly. "I'm serving him on a secret mission."

"You and half the Lightguard," scoffed Aelia. 'We've all got special missions, upstart. That's the way this place works. Lots of pies with the Emperor's fingers in all of them. And the pies mostly rot and die."

I frowned at the analogy.

Before I could act— Aelia was on me. She leapt with a whirl of movement from the other side of the platform, sweeping my right leg with her staff. I was thrown down onto the stones, flailing clumsily flat on my stomach.

"Is preparing not a thing where you come from?" she commented.

I clambered to my fight. "You have no idea what things are like where I'm from," I muttered, despite myself.

"Maybe enemies in your canyons announce themselves. Here, Demons will strip you of all your breath before you can Weave a quill if you're not alert."

"Is that my first lesson?"

"No. That's just a threat. Now get up and Weave."

I did as I was told and straightened my shoulders, composing myself. Then I focused on the Anima inside my body, the energy inside.

I hadn't prepared for combat. But if this was the moment

to prove myself, then I was going to do my best.

Using the Anima spinning in my core, I conjured shadows into my fingertips, creating my own shadow-staff. The bar materialized in my hands, a stretch flecked by lightning blue with spearheads at both ends.

With this in my hands, I bent my knees, bouncing on them a little, ready to pounce at whatever came next.

Aelia did not move. She eyed my shadow-staff, an eyebrow raised. Out of mockery, or because she was impressed, I could not tell. It was possible, I thought, that my spearheads gave me some sort of edge. After all, she had only made a long stick, with nothing at her ends.

But it didn't matter—she was already advancing on me.

The weapons hummed as shadow met shadow, and staff met staff.

Aelia moved with grace, as broad as she was, she was still able to maneuver with stealth and precision. She made everything seem easy as she charged me and struck in what seemed like five directions at once.

I barely had time to make my own offensive moves. Between parries, I jabbed with one end, aiming high. But she waved her head from one side to the other as if she was just irritated by a fly.

Then, if anything, the sparring got quicker. Aelia was an expert at handling her staff, tossing it from one hand to another to jab, or grabbing it with both hands for strength when clashing with my own, even using her shoulders and arms to balance the weapon in a way I'd never seen before. At one point, she even spun it in front of her, creating a whirl of black between us which seemed every bit as impenetrable as a shield.

I was out of my depth.

As if to emphasize that point, Aelia started to hurt me.

I was circling on the outside of the semi-circular platform, stepping sideways to find a better angle of attack. She turned in the middle, barely moving a muscle, keeping her eyes locked on mine.

Then she sprang towards me, her staff aimed at my chest.

I caught the movement with my own shadow-staff, deflecting her stick upward by holding up my own, leaving my middle exposed.

Then, Aelia's left hand did something I did not think was possible, it snapped off part of her staff, and with the now short end, she jabbed at my ribs.

A blade cut through my tunic, grazing my stomach.

I retreated, right up to the edge of the platform.

I'd never seen a shadow user change and morph their Weaves like that before. It used so much concentration to create a shape out of shadows, it seemed unthinkable to transform your weapon in such a way *in the middle of a fight.*

That was what the Lightguard did. Here, though, was proof that I could do it too, only with shadows.

I flailed, swiping my staff in front of me, trying to keep her at bay. It didn't work.

She pounced again, waiting for the right time between my clumsy hits. Her staff was now whole again, making one long bar, her shadows leaping from one form to another.

It struck me, her staff was not just a staff. It was a blank scroll on which she could draw whatever she needed. For all I knew, she could turn it into anything at any time. A spear, a hook, a sword. If she could morph it into something else during the fight, then there were myriad possibilities, and none of them were good for me.

She slipped her staff forward, toward my head, proving it. A mesh of shadows which ensnared my face sprouted from its end, sneaking into my hair like a nest of snakes, blinding me.

It threw me off balance, and I toppled back off the edge, my shadow-staff immediately dissipating. My hands no longer belonged to a warrior—but were those of a panicking child.

It was a long drop down into the chasm below.

I cried out, but just as I began to tumble a shadow-rope whipped underneath my armpits, stopping my trajectory.

I was pulled back onto the platform, where I collapsed on

my hands and knees. I looked up and saw the rope and net melt back into the shape of Aelia's staff.

"You have some talent for Weaving," she commented, looking down on me as I caught my breath on the floor, my heart still pounding. "But your thoughts are untrained."

"Is *that* my first lesson?" I gasped.

"No. This was a lesson for me. I have now learned all I need to know about you. Tomorrow, at first starlight, we start your training to develop your Mind's Eye. In the meantime, get some rest. You're no good to anyone half-dead."

She turned and started to walk.

"Wait," I said, before she stepped off the platform.

She turned, eyebrow arched.

"What will you teach me?" I said. "What will I be able to do?"

"That depends entirely on you, upstart. But if you're going to survive a minute in the Underworld, you're going to need to Weave ten times as fast, and with ten times as many forms. You're going to need to go from one form to another, so that you have all of your arsenal at your fingertips."

I got to my feet. "What about the *amount* of shadows, though? I've seen Stonekind raise entire bridges. Can we control a mass that big, too? Can we move that amount of shadows?"

"The Stonekind have been practicing their craft for their whole lives, as long and old as stone, longer than any lifetimes a young boy like you can imagine," dismissed Aelia. "Don't let your dreams run away from themselves, upstart."

There was something in her tone, though, which made me feel as if she wasn't telling the whole truth.

She walked off, leaving me with a heaving chest, and a tumult of thoughts.

There was power here, in this city.

The kind that Aelia would teach me, and the kind that she wouldn't.

I was determined, then and there, to learn both.

Whatever she didn't tell me, I told myself, *the ghosts would.*

Chapter Twenty-One

When Aelia walked away, I half-expected a guard to manifest themselves, or for Cleander to return. But there was no one, I was left to my own purposes.

I looked around for a moment, doubting whether this could be true.

Then, I realized I was a prisoner in this city, whether I had an escort with me or not. Even on the other side of the Canyonlands, when I was in the Hollow, I had been monitored all the time, Erebus had used the bird-like mazots to spy on me. It would be naive of me to think that someone like Cleander didn't have people checking on me.

If I was going to pursue my own objectives, away from my orders, I would need to tread carefully.

I stepped back onto the platform where even more Lightguard were meditating, taking in the starlight from above. I scanned the surroundings, looking for anyone who might be monitoring me.

But it was impossible to pick one out. There were at least a half-dozen people who were pointing at me, discussing me, or just looking at me. They whispered about who I was, and how I had fared in the training. I heard someone mention *the boy from the Experiments.*

So, no matter what I did, I was being watched.

I sat down, taking my place on the platform, among the Lightguard. But instead of cycling starlight, I cycled shadows.

I spent an hour there, opening my body, welcoming in the Anima of Dark, filling my channels, and then infusing the core in the center of my chest too. I found an abandoned gourd floating in the waters of the Elixir and filled it, in case I needed it for later. It was odd to think that the Lightguard, who had become my sworn enemy the very moment I'd heard of their existence, were now surrounding me. Indeed, it was almost as if I was entering into their lifestyle, partaking in their habit of communal cycling.

Still, I knew I would never be one of them. I would never take such riches for granted, not while people suffered and died in other canyons.

They might look at me and be cycling like me, but they lived in an entirely separate world.

When I was done, I got to my feet and looked around. The moon had risen, and my surroundings were lighter. Most people didn't bother to look at me anymore, and I took it as a sign to explore.

I had to find the healers of this city if I was going to help my father. That, or find out as much as I could. Knowledge was power, that much I'd learned in the last few weeks.

I threaded through the people of the market, all the while staying wary of my surroundings, noting whoever seemed to be taking special notice of me.

There were a few. It was hard to discern who might be spying on me, and who was just genuinely curious to see someone from outside the city. Either way, I felt uncomfortable, and quickened my pace, sliding down into narrow alleys whenever I could to get away from gazes and whispers.

I strode deeper and deeper into the bowels of the city. There were a mess of steps and throngs of people, creating a labyrinth for me to navigate. The further I explored, the more alleyways opened up, going this way and that. Whatever looked the most forlorn, and the most unexpected route to take, I took, thinking that this was the best way to lose anyone trying to follow me.

After a while, I managed to flit into an alleyway which was completely empty. But before I could rejoice that I had lost any followers, I saw the reason for this, it was a dead end.

I muttered under my breath, before the realization came to me, this might be a dead end to most people, but not to me.

In fact, this might be my best chance to truly lose anyone on my tail.

I grabbed some shadows out of the thin air, extending my fingers with black until they curved into claws.

Then I did what I do best and climbed.

I scaled the walls, clambering up the stonework, digging my claws into the cracks between the walls, scaling up the balconies and the window ledges, until I was perched on the roof. I looked back down: it didn't seem like anyone had noticed my ascension.

I looked around and saw from my elevation a patchwork of rooftops around me, tumbling down to the bottom of the valley.

For the very first time, I was not in awe of it. I could scale the buildings, get away from the throngs of people and find moments of peace in this place. As long as there weren't any scouts in the sky looking for me, this would be my way of investigating the city. The way of making the place my own.

I had two objectives. First was to learn Lightguard healing and see how it could help my father. The other was to uncover any hidden secrets of the city, the sort of thing people didn't want me to know. Such insights would, with any luck, be the key to my survival.

To gain access to the secrets, I needed to consult the deepest and darkest shadows I could find.

I didn't know how to find healers, but I knew how to find shadows.

I paced from one rooftop to another, then clambered down into the heart of the city.

If there was any place which seemed of prime importance,

it was down there, underneath all the training platforms and far from the palace.

The Underworld's opening.

Chapter Twenty-Two

It did not take me long to get down there. For the first time in many days, I felt like I was in something approaching my element. But navigating the city, leaping from one roof and balcony to the next while staying hidden, was no small feat. The buildings were all clumped together, which meant that jumping from one to the other was not difficult. The streets below were often choked with people, and I had to avoid such areas.

I also learned the gates, separating one level of the city from another—what people called the Upper Levels and the Lower Levels— led to long walls which stretched across the whole metropolis, dividing it in half. In those places, I needed to get down to street level and immerse myself in the bottleneck of people passing through the gates, doing my best to not be noticed before I once again took to the rooftops.

It was an hour before I got close to the circle of rock, the stopgap from the Underworld. I realized, from the conversations I overheard on the way, that everyone called that place the Demon's Lock.

As it turned out, it was a meeting place of its own, just like the piazza had been up top. Around its edges people gathered and bartered and drank. Only here, the people did not have the luxuries of the class above. Most of the people here had earthy features or tattoos, appearing to be Earthkind or perhaps Shadowkind. There were Riverkind too, but they seemed to be slaves of the Lightguard above, carrying amphorae of Elixirs about, continuously rushing.

I wondered if I should approach other Shadowkind like myself. Perhaps they would help me in some way: after all, surely they would take pity on the plight of our people in places like the Hollow?

I could not assume anything. Nothing was certain in this city.

I put the idea aside. Before I tried to make connections, I had to find out how this place worked.

That meant finding out about places like Demon's Lock.

It was literally at the bottom of the city, on an outcrop on the cliff. Beyond it, just a street down, was the city wall, on the other side lay the forests and the lake.

It was a jagged circle, and there were many people around its edges. There were three Stonekind, meditating and cycling like I'd seen on the bridge. They were maintaining the stone layer blocking the hole. Accompanying them were three guards, all Lightguard warriors standing bolt upright.

The stretch of rock covering the hole was entirely untouched. People milled around on the outskirts, doing their business, but no one walked onto the stone. There was almost an air of suspicion about it. Even though the rock seemed sturdy, ensuring that no demon could emerge from below the surface, people avoided it.

There were a few statues overlooking the hole, all depicting Emperor Lucian in his time of glory, and I sat behind the plinth of one. I tried to drown out all the activity behind me and access the shadows. I used up some Anima in my channels and reached out.

In the past, this had allowed me to access how the past was imprinted in the darkness; how it carried a history of light and dark. I had used it to see how other tribes used their Essence and copied their forms, allowing me to emulate the Weaves of the people of yesteryear.

What I Sensed from the past had always been an amalgamation of all the movements and events in history. The more often a shape or movement had occurred in that darkness, the more distinct it became, and I had to unpick those more stable and detailed shapes within the whirl of ghosts. I'd assumed that Sensing into the history of such a busy place as the citadel would reproduce a cacophony of spirits something that would take me hours to unpick.

But when I reached out with my Senses here, there was something entirely different.

It was one event.

One ghost.

It was embossed onto the shadows, permanently marked like the ink-patterns on Aelia's brow.

I was immediately taken aback by the force of a gigantic ghostly presence, so distinct, so huge, rising to meet me, that I gasped and instinctively deactivated my Senses.

It disappeared as soon as it had come.

I turned around. The ghost's roar and overpowering presence distorted all of the blackness, becoming imprinted in the history of this air. It felt so loud that everyone should have heard it. My heart was still pounding because of it.

No one did. No one could use their Essence to Sense the past like I could. They were carrying about their nightly travels, talking, haggling, selling, unaware of the inferno of the past.

I shook my head, almost regretful for a moment. All my life, I'd had to contend with the weight of the past. With the voices of ghosts, whispering in my ear. For a moment, I fantasized what it would be like to use one's Essence without inviting previous eras in, how blissful and calm that would be.

I shook that idea away, centering myself again.

All I had achieved was because of the lessons of the past. The ghosts were my blade, and without it I would have perished many times over.

So I calmed myself, took a deep breath, and reached out, plunging back into the nightmare of the old.

It was just as overwhelming, but this time I was prepared for it. I Sensed out and felt a tornado of shadows, of the blackness around me being completely distorted and rent out of shape.

There was no other way to say it. It felt... *unnatural.* Like the laws of light and dark were being torn apart, creating chaos instead.

By peering into history, all I could Sense was a storm of ghosts, of people and bodies and stone flying through the air, of streaks of light-forms and shadow-forms hailing in a battle that could barely be made out. I winced, as if this cataclysmic event were happening to me in the present and I'd be carried away in the tornado.

I lost focus, shocked by the violence of my Senses, and was left hyperventilating and sweating.

What happened here?

There was only one thing for it. I took out the gourd, full of Elixir, and drained it in one gulp.

The impact on my body was almost instantaneous. I'd felt something like it when I'd eaten a Jade Root back home, but this was a hundred times more potent. It was like my body was frothing and fizzing with energy, like all my currents of energy were moving twice as quickly. I felt like I was suddenly bursting with life.

I tried once more, my mind diving into the past.

It was difficult, and the task pulled at my energy levels; and yet still the past was blurred and indistinct.

But finally I began to make out what was happening. What seemed like a storm was not a storm at all.

It was a person.

Or at least the shape of one.

Rising up among the rocks was what looked like a man, with a human shape, arms, legs, feet, and a torso.

And yet he was also *in*human. It wasn't just his demeanor, which had a mad savagery.

No, it was his size. He was huge, as tall as five men, and he was growing bigger.

Shadows were flinging themselves at him, making every limb and muscle distort and magnify, coating almost every inch of his body with bulging boils of blackness. The blackness whirled into him, creating the storm which had warped my visions of the past.

He was growing, getting ever thicker and bigger. A demonstration of power, and of Shadow Essence manipulation beyond anything I had ever dreamed possible. It was equal to how the Stonekind formed bridges and roadblocks, it seemed.

Yet the huge man did not seem to be in control of it. He was howling and screaming and laughing, in the depths of what I could only describe as mania, as more and more shadows poured into him, and his body became more elongated and misshapen.

It was just a ghost, this event was ancient history. I knew that, but it didn't stop my blood from running cold. This was how we used to describe the devils who lived below the earth, back in the Hollow. This was power without control, and power without control could only end in destruction.

I tried to peer further back, beyond the cackling madman, and the chaos of shadows sweeping about him. Two figures came into focus, beyond the humongous figure. They were Lightguard of some sort, hurling blasts of light at the monster, one threw silver lances, threaded from starlight, the other thew bolts of sun-gold.

I Sensed further, using up more Anima. The ghosts of the two figures were rendered in further detail, and I saw that the two warriors were younger versions of Cleander and Lucian. The two faces of the power of the Citadel, working together to defeat the shadow-figure.

This surprised me for a moment. To see the ghosts of people who were still alive was disorienting. I had to remind myself of how long the Lightguard lived, their time in the Canyonlands spanned centuries.

The vision showed me the two when they were in their prime, at their most powerful. Their Weaves were impressive in scale, but adaptable and ever-changing. They morphed, becoming the exact weapon needed to pierce the monster's side, so much so that the fight was like witnessing the very elements of the world clashing against each other. I could barely keep up with their dance of light and dark.

But, despite all their best efforts, the shadow-giant barely seemed phased by the attacks of the warriors. More and more weapons were flung at it, even piercing through its shadows, and finding flesh. Underneath the chaos of shadows, the giant was bleeding profusely. Despite all the injuries it was taking, it didn't seem to care. Every few blows, the giant stumbled, and lost control of a flurry of shadows. Still the colossus laughed its maniacal laugh, even as more and more weapons hit it. Indeed, it seemed to laugh *more*.

Until finally, after this exchange, the ghost of Cleander's past made an audacious move. Leaping off of a platform, he sprayed a net of silver across the shadow's shoulders. Lucian then created a streak of light like a golden lightning bolt, blasting the energy directly at the madman's head. The energy seared through the flesh of his face, rippling across his jaw.

The giant howled, closed his eyes, and clutched his face, and yet the howl turned once again into maniacal cackling, even through his blindness and pain.

Cleander took advantage of a moment of weakness and dove down, pulling at the net and throwing the giant off balance.

The madman fell, losing his footing—and dropped out of my sight. I realized that, during the time of this fight, the chasm had not been covered by rock. The Stonekind had not yet sealed it with stone and created the Demon's Lock.

Back then, it had been a gaping hole, leading into the bowels of the earth.

The ghost of the mad giant passed out of sight, disappearing into the chasm, still howling its insane laugh. With it, the tornado of shadows whipped about his falling body, shredding the sides of the hole, making boulders cascade down after it. The earth rippled and cracked, and the ground shook as layers of stone were caught in the destruction.

The tornado of shadows finally stopped, and the past reality settled.

I was left with the ghost of the young Lucian gazing down into a chasm which I could not see, his shoulders heaving with the efforts of the fight, his face a mess of dust and blood. His eyes seemed lost in it for a moment. Then they focused again, and I saw in his ghostly features a hint of the arrogance and confidence I'd seen when we'd met.

He spoke.

The past had never been so present, so tangible. Normally, all I heard were echoes and chants. Here, even though his voice was distorted, as if heard through a storm, I could still hear him.

There was something about this event which was monumental, something which had made its mark through eternity. It was the only reason I could Sense it now, that and a body full of Anima and Elixir.

I held on to the vision, and kept my focus, peering in on the ghosts of the past.

"He's done," said Lucian. "If the fall didn't kill him, the falling rocks did."

Cleander was still getting his breath back. "I wouldn't be so sure. He was so powerful. So unlike anything we've encountered in the past."

"Then get me the best Stonekind we can find," Lucian replied. "Get them to seal this over with rock. This is to be Cizin's tomb. He can never return again, for the good of the Canyonlands. This must remain locked." Cleander nodded and began to turn. "Cleander," Lucian said, stopping him. "You do realize, we are heroes now. Or we could be, if we paint this in the right light. You're good at that sort of thing."

Cleander contemplated this. "Good at what, exactly?"

"Painting the right sort of picture."

Cleander shook his head in exasperation. "We just saved the city from Cizin's madness. Who knows what would have happened if he'd continued to gather shadows like that..."

"Your point is?"

“I see ruin, and you see opportunity. There’s something disturbing about that.”

“This could be our first step towards something bigger, Cleander,” Lucian grinned. “There’s *nothing* disturbing about that.”

Chapter Twenty-Three

The events of the past which I had seen echoed through my mind for many hours afterward. The nightmarish image of Cizin, and Lucian's actions, all had repercussions, of that I was sure.

What I didn't know was how it changed anything for me, or how to use that insight.

All I knew was that it was possible to marshal massive amounts of shadow, to manipulate the darkness the same way the Stonekind manipulated entire boulders of stone.

However, it also seemed like it might have made the user mad, like Cizin. Perhaps my father's mind had been affected by the overuse of shadows for the same reason.

I decided that I had done enough exploring for the time being. I slipped back into the alleyways, climbed back onto the roofs of the city, making my way back up through the different levels, traversing the city walls and heading up to my quarters near Lucian's palace. At this point, many people saw me, but I didn't care.

They didn't know what I had seen.

I soon came back to my quarters, and after cycling for an hour, I rested.

I fell into a deep sleep and slumbered well into the next day.

When I arose and ventured into the courtyard to have a drink from the well, I saw a streak of light rising into the sky well above dispersing into many plumes, telling me that I had rested well into the evening.

Food had been left on a table, an amalgamation of fruit with cold meats on a platter. It was delicious. Even the most basic meals in the Citadel were more luxurious and varied than anything we ate in the Hollow.

With that, I left my quarters, trying to get more of a sense of the city before night fell, and I would once again be training.

I felt eyes on me the moment I left the building.

As the sun set, spraying the stone buildings in crimson hues, the heat still rose from the paved streets. It was during this transition period, I noticed, that the city was actually at its emptiest. The ones who made use of daylight were heading back to their quarters, while their night-dwelling counterparts had not yet risen.

Still, there were many people still throning the streets. Many people looked in my direction, either to gossip or with malice.

I descended into the bowels of the valley, to the bottom rungs of the city again. Partly, I wanted to get away from all of the Lightguard and rich people who lived near the palace.

In the lower rungs though, near the lake and the Demon's Lock, where the fishermen and the tradesmen were, it seemed like more familiar territory to me. I roamed there, observing.

I approached someone with a similar tattoo as Aelia, gutting fish with a rusty dagger. He had worn, dirty skin and hair that had thinned into patches.

"Are you a Shade User?" I asked. He didn't respond, eying me with suspicion. "Shadowkind?" I persevered.

He grunted. "I'm a Shadowkind all right," he said, indicating his tattoo. "Like my father before me, and my father before him. But no one's a Shade User. No one actually uses it. Not in public, in any case."

"What do you mean, not in public?"

"There's an underground movement. Haven't you heard of it? The Uprising? They train to use shadows. Cause riots, and trouble, every once in a while. Nearly all of them end up in prison or dead, though, so you'll excuse me if I don't place too much hope in those vagabonds."

He hunched back over his fish. His posture belied a lifetime of servitude, hunched and asymmetrical.

I, however, stayed there for a moment.

"Struck dumb? Is this your first time in the Citadel or something?" Understanding dawned on his features. "You're the man who was brought in yesterday?" he finally said. His eyes narrowed in suspicion. "What do you want?"

"A friend," I said. "I've come from a valley far from here. From the Experiments, I think you call it."

"I don't want to hear about it," he answered. Anxiety flickered across his features, and he looked from side to side. "Where you come and how you've been treated is none of my business. No one wants to hear about the Experiments." He shifted uncomfortably, his eyes gazing around us, looking up and down the streets as if two Lightguard were about to leap upon him.

I wasn't going to convince him to help me, to be my guide to this place. I could tell that.

"What happened to us?" I said, despair creeping into my tone. "We're warriors, where I come from."

"Good for you. We don't have the freedom to Weave a wisp in the city. We used to, before Cizin. Then everyone thought we were going to turn mad like him, they imposed all kinds of limits on what we could or couldn't do. When we fought back, we were cruelly punished, stripped of our possessions, murdered, or made part of the Experiments. Only the very misguided would fight again, after that. It takes a fool to reopen a wound twice."

"Wasn't that generations ago?" I asked.

"Aren't you the one who's supposed to hear ghosts?" the old man spat bitterly. "The past lives with us. Especially the oppression. That lingers the longest. Now get out of here, I don't want to be seen with the likes of you."

"Tell me one last thing, then," I said. "I know a Shade User who is being swallowed up by the past. His mind is stretching further and further back, and there's nothing he can do to stop it. I heard there might be someone in the Citadel who could help him."

"No one gets help for that sort of thing here."

"Please." I came close, in desperation. "This person, he's my father. There must be someone who can advise on such illnesses?"

"Illnesses of the mind? The only ones who get treatment for that sort of thing are in the Senate class, in the Upper Levels," he said, his eyes flicking upwards to the top of the city.

"Why are they such good healers?"

He squinted. "The Lightguard? They're not good healers, they just pretend to be. The Earthkind are. But the Lightguard steal the best Earthkind and make them work for them. Whoever told you otherwise didn't know what they were talking about," He scowled. "You've got me started, now. I've spoken too much."

And with that, he waved his shadow-blade, bidding me to leave.

I did, but as I left, I saw him grab another person emerging from the house next door, and immediately start talking about me.

It was odd. The people in the Lower Levels seemed to be scared of even talking about those in power, they had contempt for them but couldn't articulate why. Everyone spoke about me as *the one from the Experiments*, but I never heard anyone mention the Hollow, or the Void.

It's like they knew that *something* was happening to people like me, in faraway canyons, but they didn't know what. They didn't want to know either, they were too scared.

With my explorations of the city done, and night starting

to blacken the sky, I traveled to the main square, where I cycled to the fullest extent that my body could take.

I was ready for when Aelia arrived on the platform where we had fought below, to make a better impression.

She stood there, as implacable as yesterday.

"Drink this," she said, pointing at a gourd of the Source.

She was not one for hellos and goodbyes, apparently.

I picked up the gourd. "I've had many today." It was true. I had been steadily drinking throughout the day, and feeling the effects on my body, which was fizzing with energy.

"I'm told you've been in the Lower Levels," she responded. "The aqueducts don't lead that far. So you've spent at least a few hours without a regular drink, that will stop your progress."

"Why isn't it brought down to the Lower Levels of the city?" I asked.

"I'm not here to be your guide," she responded. "Now, show me all of your Weaves. Today, I must see the contents of your Mind's Eye."

I noticed something in the way she dismissed my question, did she not care to answer my questions, or did she not want to? It struck me again that she was the only Shade user permitted to use her skills of Essence in this society. Surely, she cared about the subjugation of her people? The fact that the others seemed to be in the lower classes, or even worse, killed off in valleys beyond, like the Hollow?

I didn't know her well enough to judge, but I made note of it anyway.

I acquiesced and went through my Weaves. The daggers, the khopeshes, the claws, the vines, the flames, and the staff. Each time, it took something out of me, and I had to take a breath or two to move onto the next form, during this time, she tapped her foot impatiently. Only a plume of shadow-flames seemed to raise her eyebrow in surprise, but she masked her reaction by quickly returning to her frown.

"This is all that is contained in your Mind's Eye?" she asked.

"I don't even know what the Mind's Eye is," I said. "But if you mean my memory, then yes. I have used other forms too, like wings or the tail of an ahuizotl, but they are not fully formed in my mind. I have to have it fresh in my thoughts, and then I still have to invent the parts I do not know. I can hardly retain their form for any length of time."

"So you do use creation? Imagination?"

I nodded. "I'm the only one in my community who can do that," I added, hoping that this would explain my level as well as impress her a little.

If it did make the desired impact, Aelia did not show it. Questions about her filled my mind. Why was she the only one to be allowed to use the Shade? Did she know how Cizin had managed to summon such a vast mass of shadows?

"Come," she said, gesturing to the edge of the platform.

"Why?" I asked cagily. "I don't much want to be dangling off the precipice again, if it's all the same to you."

She sat at the edge, her feet dangling over the edge before crossing into a lotus pose. "It's easier to work on your Mind's Eye when there's nothing in front of you."

I joined her, sitting at the lip. Before us, the city tumbled down the cliffside, accompanied by the waterfall to our left, all the way down to the Demon's Lock, the forest on the valley floor, and the lake.

"Now," she said, taking a long drink from her gourd as I sat, "tell me about this memory of yours. Say you were to form the shape of your khopesh. Where do you see it when you recreate it? What is the picture formed in your mind?"

I thought about this for a moment. "I suppose I've never really thought about it before. It just comes to me," I turned this over in my mind for a moment. "I guess I remember the first time I learnt the shape. Ghosts showed it to me. They used it, and I studied the shape. It's like the ghosts put the weapons into my hand."

She nodded. "We're going to take it out of that memory and put the form into your Mind's Eye. Right now, you can only associate the weapon with one particular fighting style.

But if we put it into your Mind's Eye, it will become more adaptable. You can combine it with other forms. That way, your staff can become khopeshes, your khopeshes could turn into flames."

I pictured my staff shooting shadow-flames or throwing a vine with a blade at its end.

That sure sounds useful, I thought, my excitement picking up a little.

"But I don't know how to do that. How can I 'put' a memory somewhere?"

"That's where your imagination comes in. The first lesson is this, constructing a place in your thoughts which makes sense to you, which you can navigate like the rooms in your quarters. Riverkind tend to imagine a stream with interconnecting pools and tributaries. Lightguard spend all their time in their large houses, so they imagine a set of rooms."

"And you?"

"Never mind me," she said, a little sharply. Again, I got the sense that she was holding something back.

"I'll go for a network of tunnels," I said.

She nodded. "Now, I need you to meditate, and then think, and then meditate more, and think more. This could take hours or days. Take the same focus you have when you study the form and shape of a weapon and apply it to your imagination. You must create tunnels in your mind which are solid and stable. They have to seem real to you, as real as the tunnels you spent your youth in. Then you can put your forms in different chambers of your mind... and then, tomorrow, we can start to make the connections between them."

I set to work. It was a strange task, to try and construct something completely out of thoughts. With Aelia's instruction, I built a place in my mind, rock by rock and wall by wall. She coaxed me through it, telling me how to color the space with detail, to add moisture and texture to the rock, to imagine the smell in the air. Then we would take a break, and drink some of the Elixir, before starting again, until the first chamber started to become consolidated in my mind.

We did this until dawn.

She seemed relatively satisfied with my progress.

The question of Cizin, and his powers with shadows, lingered in my mind.

There was a way to go much further than what she was instructing. To create huge Weaves like the most powerful did, like Cizin had.

If there was a way to perform that without going mad, I was determined to find it.

Chapter Twenty-Four

The next day was spent much like the last. I returned from training at dawn and found that more food had been laid out for me in my quarters. I was surprisingly hungry, taken aback by how exhausting it was to develop my Mind's Eye. I'd done it as much as I could, both under Aelia's instruction and on my own.

After I ate, I drank more Elixir, and tried to pore through the decorative scrolls placed in the study room.

I had never been a fast reader, not like my friend Emilian, who tore through texts like a hungry man tore through a plate of food. For me the process was slow.

But, unlike the scrolls in the Library of the Hollow, these seemed designed to peruse and flick through, rather than to study in detail. On almost every scroll there were detailed illustrations, giving me a sense of what was being described.

More often than not, they described Emperor Lucian. A lot of these texts were dedicated to his exploits as a younger man, when he still looked as chiseled as his statues.

There was even a moment which seemed to describe what I'd seen in the Demon's Lock, with the mad Cizin being cast down into the underworld as a cone of shadows swirled into him from the sky.

It seemed like this was the start of Lucian's rise to power.

I put these thoughts and questions to one side as if sheathing a knife. Knowledge was the sharpest weaponry, I didn't know much, but I knew that much.

I slept for a few hours, until the morning had waned and the afternoon sun was dipping.

I meditated and cycled in the garden, doing as Aelia had asked to construct my Mind's Eye in my imagination, making it seem more detailed and real than before.

Then it was time to go back out and explore the city. To arm myself with more knowledge.

There were eyes on me again the moment I stepped out onto the paved streets just as there always was. This had been a constant feeling whenever I stepped out in public, the idea that Cleander had people keeping tabs on my every movement I hated having Cleander's men follow me, even though I had no plans to do anything out of the ordinary, I lost them, sprouting shadow-claws and making my way to the rooftops to explore the Citadel at my leisure.

My knowledge of the place grew.

I became more aware of how time worked within the city. For every hour, when a shot was fired into the sky from the palace, I saw a ripple through the city. For one thing, many statues of Emperor Lucian changed position. It seemed that there were, on every level, Stonekind whose only job was to shift the stone figures in accordance with the time. This had the effect of making the whole city groan, as stone shifted. It also, I noticed with a scoff of derision, ensured that the statues of the Emperor were always in the most striking position according to the angles of the sunlight.

With a new hour announced in such a way, there were repercussions across the alleyways and the streets. I noticed this as I climbed down, where the changing times seemed to have the most effect. It seemed that sellers had specific time slots in which to sell and enter different parts of the city. With a new streak of light in the sky, and a new grind of stone, there was a flurry of movement as people packed up their stalls and hurried somewhere new.

I studied this throughout the day, it seemed to account for the stress and nervousness of the people in the lower levels. They lived in absolute fear of time, which could leap upon them, chase them in and out of various parts of the city, and determine their livelihood for the day. For every changing hour, there were bottlenecks of people queuing at the gates to leave or enter another slice of the Citadel.

They were slaves to time, and time was a cruel master.

I kept to myself and saw how their lives were dictated by the Emperor's whims. The people in the Upper Levels, the people of the Senate, were not concerned. The timestamps did not seem to put any pressure on their works. The people below were forced to blindly scrabble with what time was being parsed out for them.

It seemed like madness that they did not protest against this blatant unfairness. But then, I had to tell myself that I too had followed unjust orders, back in the Hollow.

Still, I explored the city, looking for some kind of resistance, some kind of gesture to show acknowledgment of how time was being wielded against the lower levels.

And I saw something, of a sort.

At one gate, I saw a man trying to get into the Lower Levels of the Citadel. He had a cart filled with amphorae. Presumably he'd filled it with the Elixir in order to sell it to the people below.

But a guard was having none of it. A tall Lightguard, with a long thin mustache and an implacable smirk, stood barring his way, impervious to the pleas of the man who'd missed his timeslot to pass through the gate into the other neighborhood.

The seller begged, and even got frustrated and angry, shouting about how he'd not had enough time to make his sales. I could not hear what he was saying but guessed that he was cursing how impossibly short the time he'd been given had seemed.

The reaction was instantaneous. The mustachioed Lightguard snapped his fingers. In the next moment, another Lightguard stepped in, wove a light-net, and cast it over the man. It was clearly the type of weave that was charged with those bolts of pain, and it sent the seller, crying, onto the slabbed floor. While he convulsed, the mustachioed Lightguard nodded to a warrior to his left, who proceeded to clamber onto the seller's cart and throw the amphorae off the side.

The pavements were filled with shards of pottery, the contents of the amphorae, the Elixir, channeled down towards the Lower Levels, accessing where the seller could not, gleaming in the crevasses of the stonework.

The liquid pooled and coursed at people's feet as they paced around the streets, but no one stirred or even stopped to look at the seller's torture and misfortune. This kind of violence and abuse was clearly a common occurrence, common enough for it to not draw attention.

My mood darkened. My fists clenched, and my body made as if to leap down and address the situation.

For a moment, I was ready to do it.

Then logic took hold, and I turned away. It was not up to me to save the man. I was likely to lose a fight with powerful Light warriors. I was like an infant here in this world, blinking in its first light. I did not know enough to take on the burden of responsibility.

Anything I did which didn't contribute to my mission of helping my people, and my father, would make things more difficult for me.

I turned away and picked out a rooftop to leap to, anything to get away from the screams.

Chapter Twenty-Five

"So you think your Mind's Eye is ready, do you?"

I nodded.

Aelia's lips pursed in annoyance. "People spend years developing their Mind's Eye. It's a key part of being a youth in the Lightguard. And you, who have never cultivated your imagination, claim to have built your foundations in a matter of days."

We were both crossed-legged on the platform once more. A few days had passed, and I'd regularly been using the tools Aelia had given me in order to construct this imaginary place in my mind. She'd guided me through numerous meditations, and as a result the space in my mind had started to feel like a real place I'd visited, as vivid as a memory.

I gazed down the valley, at the edifices of stone losing themselves in the lake and forest below, the light of human activity merging into the gloom of nature.

"I would argue," I chose my words carefully, "that I have cultivated my imagination for longer than a few days. Think of what it would be like to have unseen people whisper in your ear your whole life. Think of what it would be like to be surrounded by ghosts of people you have never met, down in the pitch-black tunnels. My imagination has been doing heavy lifting for years."

Aelia shook her head slightly. "We will see, I suppose. If you're lucky, your confidence will be punished in training, rather than down in the Underworld."

Her mood and words had remained sour in tone since the first night of training, but I had begun to feel comfortable with it. Her negativity was so relentless that it had lost its potency.

All I cared about were results and I was confident that she could help me obtain them. Aelia was powerful. Her ease with Weaving, with creating intricate, solid forms and passing from one shape to the other, matched anything that I had ever seen in the Shadowfront. And I was certain she was capable of much more, even if she did not show it.

"All right," she said. "Get to your feet."

I obeyed.

"We are going to put your forms, or rather the idea of your forms, in certain chambers of your Mind's Eye. To do this, you will have to categorize them. Once we find links between your forms, then we can begin to expand your mind so that you can pass from one to the other."

I nodded, mentally going through all my shapes. "How do you categorize yours?" I asked.

Aelia shook her head. "The labels must be yours. It must make sense to your mind and thoughts. That is how ideas anchor themselves properly in our imagination. Now, start with your first form."

I created shadow-claws, borrowing from the night's gloom.

"Describe the shape at your fingertips," Aelia ordered.

"They are… sharp?" I ventured.

"More. Anything which comes to your mind. Anything which you associate with this Weave."

I threw more words out. *Appendage. Nature. Claw. Movement. Climbing. Scuttler.*

Then we passed onto the next form, where I did the same with my shadow-vines.

Eventually, I started to form groupings of the different Weaves in my mind. I found that I put shapes born out of nature into one category, claws, vines, a dragon's breath. Aelia instructed me to imagine these forms all belonging in one chamber in my Mind's Eye, then I spent an hour ensuring that they all resided in that particular cave of my thoughts.

The threat of dawn was in the sky by the time I had finished.

"We have established that there is some resemblance between all these Weaves. They are all shapes based on your observations of nature."

I nodded. "How will that help?"

"The fact that you have established a link between these forms, in this case, their origin in nature, means that your mind can more easily transform one into another. Your vine can more easily be reshaped into a claw. Your claw can more easily be reshaped into a vine. Your shadows can flit from one shape to another. That flexibility will let you become more creative: attaching a claw to the end of a vine, for example. But that's for another time."

"What if I wanted to combine Weaves from different categories? Add flames to my khopesh, for example?"

"That will need more serious training. That's when you start eroding the walls between your chambers. That's when you dig tunnels from one cave to another, and form connections between your chambers."

I nodded. This would have seemed impossible until a few days ago. But now, in this vast Citadel with people and cultures and abilities I had never seen nor imagined, *impossible* did not hold much meaning.

"What about...adding the shapes together? Making bigger shapes, like how the Stonekind make bridges of stone, or the Lightguard create arcs in the sky?"

Aelia's look turned even sterner than usual. "Shadowkind don't do that. We do not build beyond ourselves."

"Cizin did," I said. My words were quiet and tentative. Unsure of her reaction.

"My, my," Aelia said, a scowl spreading across her tattooed features. "You *have* been doing some digging, haven't you?"

I shrugged. "I grew up in a valley of lies and misinformation. When I think that something is being held back from me, I Sense it. There are things you aren't telling me. Like why you were selected to be the only one who could use the Shade. What your abilities are, and what I can learn from you. I've seen our people get slaughtered in the Experiments and serve as a frightened underclass in the city. It seems to me our people need to be able to build beyond themselves. You could be the key to that."

I realized that, as always, I had spoken too much.

Her brow knotted into concern. "You ask too many questions, upstart," she said, in hushed, urgent tones. "This training session is over."

She set off, leaving the training platform.

I, however, was not satisfied. There had been something in her look when I'd uttered those words. But there hadn't been outrage, or anger.

It made me think that at least some part of her agreed. But she couldn't say so. There was something she was keeping from me, and after all I'd lived through in the Hollow, I wasn't going to let that stand.

If she had secrets, then I would do my best to uncover them.

On that instinct, I followed her, from a distance, as she made her way through the city. At the first opportunity, I scaled the walls, and crawled over the rooftops, keeping an eye on her as she made her way through the city below.

It took a while. For a time she mingled, and spoke to people in the Lightguard, and I was tempted to walk away without learning anything new.

After an hour had passed, I saw her behavior change. She cast her eyes about, before going into an empty alleyway. I crouched low, and made sure she couldn't see me, before I followed her from above, trailing her through narrow, empty streets, far from the bustle of the crowd.

She took a few turns, casting her eye about once more, checking that the streets behind and in front of her were empty, not thinking to look above and catch me observing her.

She waited there for a moment.

Before ten minutes had passed, two men emerged, the other side of the valley. They wore cloaks and had hoods, but I noticed that there was the ink-mark of the Shadowkind on their faces.

My mind rang with questions. I wondered what clandestine meeting this could be, and why they were being so secretive. Aelia and the two men faced each other for a moment, sizing each other up, before they put out their hands in greeting.

For a moment, I could hardly believe my eyes. I thought that I must be mistaken.

But there was no mistaking it, the men were creating a Weave out of shadows, just as Aelia was. Their greeting was an illegal act, banned throughout the city. It could lead to their imprisonment.

But it was more. Their greeting was to create a symbol out of shadows, about as large as a hand. It was something I recognized. It was the symbol which had marked forbidden scrolls in my home valley, and the ones used by the Riverkind. Three lines, ending in a circle.

I had no idea what it meant, but I could guess. If this was the greeting of Shadowkind using the Shade against the rules of the emperor, then this was also a sign of resistance,

I gasped. I had barely made more sound than a whisper, but it was enough. Aelia's head snapped up, and her eyes met mine with a look as cold as steel.

Before I could react or protest, her order came through.

She pointed up at me, and said, *"Get him!* I want him *dead*!"

Chapter Twenty-Six

I ran, leaping from rooftop to rooftop, trying to put as much distance between myself and those men as possible.

Once I had jumped over a few buildings, I created shadow-vines and rappelled down to the streets below, before entering into the crowds of a marketplace.

I had to lose them in the thick of the city.

I kept low, and threaded through the crowds, trying to make myself inconspicuous by surrounding myself with other citizens. I constantly had to look around to see whether the Shadowkind had found me.

They were nowhere to be seen. For a few moments, I thought that I'd managed to escape them.

Looking around, I saw Aelia's cold look once more, piercing through the throngs. The two men were with her.

They immediately started pushing through the crowds, coming after me.

Get going. Pick up the pace.

I spurred myself forward. I dove through any opening I could find through people and tried to zig-zag in a way which would make things difficult for those who were chasing me. I sprinted down side streets, sometimes launching myself up on stalls and leaping over obstacles.

This carried on for a few breathless minutes, me picking

my route at random, hoping the random nature of my path would help me shake off my pursuers.

The only problem was that I still did not know the city well enough to navigate it properly. So I came to a long street which ran alongside the ring of a city wall, barring the way down to another part of the city. I had to follow the foot of the wall all the way round to get to the gate, before I could escape into the Lower Levels.

It wasn't possible, I saw the commotion of people pushing through behind and in front of me, and then, sure enough, on either side of the throng, were the Shadowkind.

They were shoving their way through the masses from opposite directions. Soon they would spot me and be upon me.

I needed to get out of there, fast.

I looked up. The thought came to me to Weave some shadow-claws and go up the city wall. But that felt slow, surely there was another way?

I centered myself as crowds tore around me. I reached out, not into the darkness but into myself. I peered inside my Mind's Eye, to see what I could use. I went from the chamber of weapons to the chamber of natural forms, seeing the form of vines, claws and fire. Could I use any of those?

Or, could I use a combination? Use the category into which I'd placed them, and the link I needed to merge two forms together?

I activated the Anima spinning around my core, reaching deep inside myself.

Then I raised my hands skyward and shot.

Anima-inflected shadows sprouted from my hands and tore upwards, climbing the wall, giving the stone a pattern of back veins. They climbed and climbed, snaking up the monument.

I heard my pursuers getting closer. They'd seen me but I took no notice. Every ounce of my energy, every speck of concentration, was on my Weave above.

There was nowhere for my vines to wrap around, nor lash onto, nowhere for them to take hold.

Not unless I managed to form one Weave at the end of another. I cried out with the exertion, trying to shut out all the movement and confusion around me as I felt a hand clap upon my shoulder.

Then I managed it. At the end of the vines, shadow-claws formed and dug into the parapet. Form upon form. Shadow upon shadow.

I had woven a kind of grappling hook out of shadows, it had taken hold at the top of the wall.

I pulled, and with a great heave, I tore out of the grasp of the shade-users, scrambling away from the crowds below and going up the wall as quickly as I could.

Aided by my shadow-hook, I pulled myself over the ramparts, and onto the wall.

I expected to have a moment's relief, just to catch my breath while my Weave unfurled back to the shadows.

But instead I found myself in danger once more. Aelia was on the ramparts as well, running toward me.

I held up my hand, creating a shadow-khopesh in my wrist, but a feeling of dread knotted my stomach. She'd demonstrated in training just how much of a superior warrior she was, I didn't have a chance.

A shadow-trident sprouted into existence from her fingertips. She charged at me with it, and I clutched at my khopesh with both hands to stop its teeth piercing into my stomach. Aelia twisted her trident, and I was thrown onto the wall of the rampart.

I clattered to the floor, and she kicked away the shadow-khopesh from my grasp. It unspooled into black.

"Why are you doing this?" I croaked. "I'm Shadowkind, like you!"

"You'll never know," hissed Aelia, aiming for my neck with her trident. Ready to execute me.

I closed my eyes— waiting for my execution. A dozen half-thoughts raced through my mind, all centered on everything I'd wanted to do, everything I hadn't accomplished.

A voice stole across the ramparts.

Cleander loomed tall over everyone, his immaculate robes and posture granted him his usual poise. He seemed to come out of nowhere, walking along the city wall, his hands behind his back. That was the impression he'd given me since the first minute I'd met him. In this city, he was nowhere, and everywhere, like he was a part of the very walls, the gates.

"I would recommend you compose yourself, Aelia," he said in his silky voice. "Before we get ourselves into *real* trouble."

Chapter Twenty-Seven

The trident left my neck. Aelia backed away with alarming reluctance. She'd been ready to kill me, that much was certain.

I got to my feet, a little shaky.

"What is going *on*?" I muttered.

Aelia's eyes brightened with even more fury; something which I had not thought possible. "Not another word," she glared.

"Aelia is right," said Cleander as he approached us, his cloak brushing the stone floor. "You should listen to your trainer, Jason. This is not the place for such discussions."

I shot a look behind him, there were Lightguard who had noticed the commotion, clustered not a little further along the ramparts.

Cleander came to Aelia and spoke quietly in her ear. "We will take him down the Well. But we will take him as a prisoner."

What?

I was so confused. Nothing made sense anymore. I was *already* their prisoner, trapped in this sky-forsaken city. And what on earth was the Well?

Aelia brusquely took me by the shoulders and turned me around. I heard the hum of blackness being woven together and felt a shadow-lash wrap itself around my wrists. "Will someone tell me what is going on?" I cursed.

I felt Aelia come close, her lips whispering directly into my ear. "I am still itching to kill you, Jason. So when I said *not another word,* I meant it. Unless you want a sharp shadow in your spine, you'll be quiet."

I held my tongue. Whatever was happening, I just hoped I'd get answers soon.

I was pushed forward roughly. I heard Cleander inform the Lightguard that he and Aelia would be taking me away for questioning, and no further guard was needed.

I was led down a flight of stairs into the city, and then taken through the busy streets once more. The moon had fully risen by now and was peeking through into the narrowest of alleyways, and I could make out many people looking curiously at us.

Within a few minutes, Cleander unlocked a door to the side of a nondescript building. It opened into a narrow hallway going down into the earth.

I expected it to be the basement of someone's quarters, but I soon realized that this was a secret passageway, tunneled into the cliffside. Aelia and I activated our Senses in order to make the darkness visible, while Cleander seemed to know the passageways so well that he did not need to.

We stepped through and found ourselves in a larger tunnel which led steeply down. In the middle of the tunnel was a canal of water, racing down the rock.

"What's this place?" I breathed.

"These are the sewers. Where dirty water drains from the city, and feeds into the lake below," explained Cleander. "There used to be a whole network of tunnels underneath the city, where the Shadowkind cycled the Anima of Dark. After Cizin, when the Shadowkind were banned from using Shade, the tunnels were all closed. Only this one is still in use."

Cleander made a motion. I realized that there was a Stonekind standing completely still there, next to the passageway we had just come through. The man, at Cleander's motion, held up his hand and there was a grinding sound once more. My Senses picked up on a flurry of shadows, I noticed that the tunnel morphed, disguising the fact that a passageway had ever existed.

With another nod from Cleander, Aelia let her shadows disperse, and I was no longer restrained.

"I know you have questions, Jason," said Cleander, as if he could peek into my thoughts. "And I have answers for you, but first we must descend."

He continued ahead, and we all followed, accompanying the gushing water down into the earth. Aelia and Cleander had iron-shod sandals, unlike mine, but I noted that they did not ring in the tunnel as expected. They had light feet, experienced in walking undetected.

I had less of a feeling that I was going deep into the city, more that I was plunging into a world of secrets.

We followed the steps alongside the tumbling water for a few minutes. It was a steep, downhill walk without any variation, so much so that I started to feel my calves. When we had sunk down far below the streets, there was another Stonekind, standing in the gloom, waiting for us.

Cleander nodded to her, and the Stonekind lifted her hand, and the rock wall behind her rearranged itself, revealing another hidden door.

The door swung open, and we entered a separate chamber, hearing the rock cloak the entrance again behind us, sealing us in with the secrets of the room.

And the room *was* one of secrets.

The chamber was round, and there were people sitting in circles around stone chairs. It was almost completely silent, reminding me of the religious caves of home. A reverent, deep silence, one befitting the solemn and dark surroundings.

There were about twelve people in total, some Earthkind, some Stonekind, some with black scars on their cheeks, and even some Lightguard, by the looks of it. One of the latter had their palms open and seemed to be scattering motes of starlight around the chamber, lighting the chamber. It made the room look like it was an encapsulation of the night sky.

There were two chairs available, Aelia and Cleander took their places. Cleander motioned to a Stonekind. He put out his hand and rocks drew up from the floor, creating another chair for me.

I sat down, uncertain of where to look. I was aware of people's eyes on me, there in the gloom, piercing through the floating stars.

Cleander placed his hands deliberately on his hand rests and leaned forward in his seat a little. It was a small gesture, but it commanded attention. Everyone turned to him, edging their gazes away from me.

"So begins the meeting," Cleander announced.

It was then that I saw a design on the floor. There were thin canals of glowing Elixir water, spiraling around the stone at our floor, shining a bluish glow at our feet.

It was the same pattern, the spiral on the librarian's hidden documents. The sign that Aelia had made to the Shadowkind before chasing me across the city.

"There is a new member among us, as you will have noticed," Cleander said. He turned to me. "Welcome, Jason. We are rebels, here in this room. Dedicated to the overthrow of Emperor Lucian. We are the Uprising."

Chapter Twenty-Eight

So this was it. An alliance, meeting in secret, to rebel against the status quo. And, in the middle of trying to find my own feet in the city, I'd stumbled right into it.

But I still didn't understand why. Why had they brought me here? I had seen Aelia meet with rebels. I could have reported her to the Emperor. In fact, it would have been in my interest to do so. After all, with him threatening to wipe out my entire people, I needed to do anything I could to remain in his good graces.

That was why Aelia had tried to kill me. To ensure my silence.

But the question remained. Why wasn't I dead? Why had Cleander spared me?

I'd only met him once. It didn't make sense that I had been invited to such a secret ceremony, after such little time spent in the city. I had yet to earn anyone's trust.

I felt concern grow in the pit of my stomach.

Cleander wasn't someone to trust. He used people. If I was here, it was because I was going to serve a purpose of some kind.

Cleander was the city, and the city was nothing but lies and exploitation.

I shifted in my newly sculpted rock seat, awaiting whatever happened next.

"Fellow rebels," Cleander said in his smooth voice. "You may be wondering why our newest member, a stranger to most of us, is here. Jason, Son of Ventos, a warrior from the Experiments, is wondering the same. You will excuse me while I explain to him what our goal is."

He turned to me. "I promised you answers, Jason. And really, there is only one place to begin. We must begin with the end."

His words hung in the air, shifting with the glowing stars, making everyone's face go grave.

"The end of what?" I said in a quiet voice.

"Of everything," came the answer. Cleander put out a hand, and silver forms wove into the air in the center of the circle.

"Emperor Lucian is blinded by his own arrogance. He has become lazy and careless, too busy drinking wine and partying with the Senate to fully appreciate that the Wars of the Levelling are upon us once more. The Demons of the Underworld are getting ready to rise again from below and take dominion of the surface world. Their invasion is closer than he will ever admit."

The silver form morphed into a replication of the citadel. There were paths, then, stretching out from the city, creating a web of lines expanding from the city, showing trails and walkways expanding into the hills and valleys beyond. "Aelia, please explain what you found in your expeditions from the city."

I turned to Aelia. She still had a scowl on her face, etched onto her features since I had cut her.

"To what purpose, Cleander?" she said. "Why are we revealing all of this to a newcomer? This stranger strolls in from the valleys and suddenly you place him within our inner circle? Just by bringing him into this fold, he now knows more about me than my last half-dozen lovers."

"All in good time, Aelia. I promise you, I have my reasons.

Trust comes first from honesty, the Riverkind taught me that, with their ritual of breaking the ice. Is that not true, Fealta?"

A Riverkind, dressed in a kaftan, nodded solemnly.

"So we must first be honest. And then we can trust. Tell us all what you found out, Aelia. It will be new for Jason, and a timely reminder for the rest of us."

Aelia held up her hands. "So be it. If a mess comes of this, then don't come to me to clean it up. Cleaning up *your* mess tends to be a dirty affair." She sighed and started. She didn't even look at me while she explained in a quick, impatient voice.

"Over the last few months, I took out a patrol with Stonekind, Earthkind and Shadowkind alike. We found entire canyons where the Essences were disturbed. The earth was uprooted, the shadows morphed. The very stone trembled, as if nervous. Nothing that could be seen with the naked eye, but we could feel it. There was something wrong. Something uncanny. The Lightguard with us saw nothing, they were too arrogant. The light, coming from the skies above was the same as ever. Everything below our feet was like a broth getting ready to boil.

"I reported this to Emperor Lucian, but he would have none of it. He trusts only himself, and his judgment. He laughed me out of the gardens, even as I told him of the forthcoming devastation."

Cleander intervened here. "The trembling of the earth, Jason, is said to herald the final invasion. They say that the Canyonlands will be rent in two with an almighty crack in the Earth, and the dark hordes unleash all their might from the Underfolds. Soon the ground will shake for good, and the last phase of the war will have begun. We are woefully unprepared. The emperor only knows how to subjugate and control his people, he does not remember how to wage war."

Cleander turned his fingers, and the light-form of the Citadel loomed larger, becoming more detailed as he enlarged it. I could make out the different levels, the gates, and the Demon's Lock. In his Weave, the lock burst open, and creatures of every shape and size erupted out of it, swarming the city, buildings crumbling in their wake.

A figure, larger than all the others, led the charge. I recognized them immediately.

"Cizin," I whispered.

Cleander nodded. He waved his hand, and the shape of the city dispersed. "Lucian and I cast him down into the Demon's Lock, but he survived. He continued experimenting with the shadows, down there in the Underworld, becoming a leader of the demons. We don't know much for sure, all of it is rumor, whispered from the bowels of the earth, and the odd skirmish with demons when they attack the surface. But we have reason to believe that Cizin's return is imminent. The emperor will not accept this, his entire image is based upon being the one who slew Cizin in the first place."

Cleander took a breath.

"You see, Jason, my role is not just to mind the city at night. I am not supposed to just be Lucian's right-hand man. As his counterpart, I am supposed to keep him in check, too. That is what I intend to do. For the good of the Canyonlands, I will depose him. It is the only way that we can be ready for the coming war. Lucian is now just a sad reflection of what he once was. I must, for the good of all the surface people of the Canyonlands, take the throne so that we can meet the hordes of Cizin."

"Who is Cizin?" I asked.

Someone tutted in the black. Presumably this was an obvious question, one which exposed my complete ignorance. I didn't care. Cizin, it seemed to me, was the key to everything, he was the enemy of the Citadel, and the most powerful user of the Shade I'd ever seen.

Cleander ignited the air once more, filling it with his light-sculptures. It morphed, light inter-knit into the form of the giant figure I had Sensed at the Demon's Lock. herein Cleander's projection, he was calm, noble even, not the madman I had witnessed.

"Cizin was a warrior like us, in the early days of the

Citadel. In those days, we had regular elections, where leaders were appointed by the people. Cizin was an almighty fighter. The very best, in fact. He proclaimed that, one day, he would be able to make fortresses and mountains just out of shadow. His ambition was second to none.

"He experimented on using his Essence, pushing it, and pushing it. He kept on trying to invite more Anima of Dark into his core, so that he could create grander and grander Weaves. Until, one day, he pushed too far."

The light-image changed to show the raving, cackling figure I had seen before, his hands raised, the air about him a swirling mass of chaos. The mere shape of him, formed in Cleander's silver Weaves, was enough to make me shudder.

"The darkness overwhelmed him, taking over his body. Darkness is an absence, if you welcome too much into you, it will obliterate who you are. He lost control, and darkness swept across the valley. He almost brought the night sky onto our heads."

I tensed at Cleander's last words. It wasn't just that I didn't believe his description of darkness as simply an absence, I knew, as every Shade User did, that darkness was full and rich, thick with history and meaning. It showed that Cleander, for all his desire to be the head of a diverse community of rebels, still saw things very much as a Light-User. He was like the Emperor in that regard, someone who saw the Essence of Light as the only Essence worth considering.

More importantly, his words about being overwhelmed by darkness had a sad connotation for me. That was what had happened to my father, that was the main reason I was here. My father was swamped by darkness, it had taken him over, wiping out his control of his own mind.

Cleander got up, dismissing the light-forms, and pacing around the chamber. "The reason why there are two leaders is not just to cover the time periods of both day and night, Jason. It is also to ensure that one man does not have too much power. Lucian does not listen, he does not hear me. He has become enamored with his own power, his own riches. The world grows weaker and more divided as a result of his rule and the people close to him in the Senate. We must stage an uprising."

"With what army?" I asked. "The people seem afraid. Just like my people were. They don't even dare question the Lightguard, or what is happening with the Experiments. And why would they? You whip them for it!"

"The people are more ready for a new era than you think," Aelia intervened. "The Shade Users have been punished enough. Cizin gave us a bad name, and we were shunned and punished just for using the same Essence as Cizin. We weren't allowed to use our Shade to the fullest of its extent. When we protested, we were punished, our people were banished from the city or sent to be used in the Experiments. We have been made an underclass. Servants to the rich in the higher levels. All it will take is a spark, and the fire of the revolution will ignite. We are not brainwashed like your people are."

This stung, for some reason. I was put on the defensive. "The city runs like the turning wheels of a cart. Lucian shoots a flare into the sky, and the whole place turns over to follow his whim. Your people are just as brainwashed as mine ever were."

A Riverkind stood up, the woman in the kaftan I had noticed upon entering. Cleander had called her Fealta. She knelt on the floor and made a goblet of ice out of her core. She scooped up the glowing liquid from the canals on the floor and handed it to me. "Drink it," she said, in a kind but direct voice.

I peered into the cup. "What is it?"

She smiled. "The run of water you walked down is supposed to be sewage water. Waste, runoff from baths and toilets. But it isn't, is it?"

I frowned, and at her request, sipped at the goblet. "It's the Elixir," I said.

"Exactly. We have so much Elixir that the city flings it down to the lake unused. They would rather it be wasted than distributed to the people of the lower levels, where the Elixir can only be procured in amphorae. The people know that they are being subjugated. Underneath every citizen of the city is an undercurrent of rage. We only need to show them, to give them the taste of injustice like the goblet you just sipped from. Then, they will rise up, like we have."

"My people will too," An Earthkind rose. His face was wreathed in vines and foliage, his scalp carpeted in moss. "We live in the Canopy outside the city walls, and no one minds us. With the help of the Riverkind, we have made a tributary to this Elixir, and channeled it into the forest with no one knowing. We have roots and flowers charged with the stuff, and secret Elixir supplies. We have spread the power as best we can. If the rebellion is on our doorstep, we will redouble our efforts, and smuggle more Elixir to the people."

"Thank you, Kauri," said Cleander.

I squirmed a little in my seat. The inevitable question, the one I'd been trying to avoid, came to my lips. "What does this have to do with me?"

Cleander faced me, his lips curled with self-satisfaction. Whatever his plan was, he clearly thought it was a creation of genius.

"My people have been watching you, Jason. You interest me greatly. You will be the face of the revolution. The promise of something new. The heroic underdog from the valleys beyond, surviving the Experiments and coming to bring change to the Canyonlands. The spark, as it were."

He paused for a moment, while my thoughts reeled in shock.

"You will be given a name, to inspire the downtrodden populace," Cleander continued. "You will be the Blade of Rebels."

Chapter Twenty-Nine

I shifted in my seat. I didn't know what Cleander's words meant, but upon hearing them a sense of dread spread through me. I looked about and noticed Aelia on her chair. She was shaking her head, clearly opposed to the idea.

"The Blade of Rebels? What on earth is that?" I said.

Cleander leaned back on his stone chair, satisfied with himself. "I may be the ruler the empire needs right now. But I am no poster child. I keep to the shadows, the people at large do not know me other than as part of the old establishment. We need a symbol to inspire the people. A hero to fight for their cause. That person is you. You are, after all, someone who followed in the footsteps of the Therians, a community of Shadowkind who were the main fighters in the last rebellion. The Therians were the ones who were at the vanguard of the struggle against the oppressive rule of the Lightguard."

My mind fired in a hundred directions at his words. Of course. The Therians were a people who had died out, but I'd encountered their ghosts in the caverns of my home. It was only when I'd adopted their way of fighting that I'd developed any fighting ability at all. I used to go to where they lived, the tower of Babel, and Sensed their ghosts, figuring out how they used forms from nature, and the past, in order to create their Weaves. Then I'd followed suit.

I'd always wondered what had happened to their civilization. Now I knew. They had been wiped out for being part of a revolution against the Lightguard.

"The Therians had a leader," Cleander continued. "They called her the Swallow, a bird who was adaptable, who could make a home anywhere. If it weren't for her, the people would not have fought so hard. You need to be the new Swallow, the focal point of the revolution."

My mind reeled. In my valley, the ghosts of the Therians had whispered many incomprehensible things to me. One of them had stayed imprinted on my mind.

Beyond the Babel, within the dirt
There flies the swallow, there contains the world.

The "swallow" in that mantra had been a person. A hero, who had carried the world and the culture of the Therians.

They wanted me to carry the Uprising in the same way.

A feeling of revolt, of intense discomfort, made me squirm in my seat.

"Aelia does not trust you. She think that I am putting too much in your hands," Cleander continued. "But I am confident that you can work together to ruffle the feathers of the Lightguard. Inspire the people to take arms."

"Work with Aelia?" I blurted out. "She was going to kill me!"

"I trust that is your way of thanking me for saving your life?" Cleander smiled a little at his own joke before his features regained their former seriousness. "It did force my hand a little. I'd hoped Aelia would trust you more by the time I revealed this all to you, but I was already convinced. You are too valuable to the Uprising to die. We have been spreading rumors of a warrior, someone from the lower levels who has been training in secret and will be the focal point of the resistance. We knew we needed a symbol. But you are more powerful than anyone we have been training. You are the symbol, made flesh. You are exactly what we need."

"But, even if I wanted to, I *can't* do what you ask." I couldn't help but let a note of distress leak into my voice. "I can't move a muscle against the Emperor. He is holding my tribe hostage."

A few of the members nodded sympathetically.

Aelia nodded. "You see?" she pointed out to the other members of the chamber. "The Emperor has too firm a grip on him. He'll sell us all out to Lucian!"

Cleander barely tried to hide his impatience with Aelia. "That's precisely what makes Jason perfect for the role. You see? You become a symbol in secret. You wear a mask, become a symbol. Adopt a name, the Blade of Rebels. Then, on the day of the revolution, we storm the palace. You reveal your identity to the world and tell your story. Everyone suspects, deep down, that the Experiments are cruel, even if the Emperor claims that they are not. When you tell your story, they will listen to your every word. The Emperor's lies and cruelty will be exposed. When you have enraptured the people, and captured their sympathy, you will endorse me as the new Emperor. There will be no going back, then. The change of power will be irreversible."

I could feel my heartbeat rising. "But you're not listening to me. I *can't*. You are asking me to take a risk which I can't afford to take, even if I hide my identity. Get someone else to be the Blade of Rebels!"

Cleander waited for me to finish with the calm of someone used to getting their way. "There can be no one else. There have been many Shadowkind training in secret, instructed by Aelia, but they do not have your level of the Shade. Only Aelia does, and she has a different part to play. Only you can send the message that Lucian can be defeated. We will give you time to think about it. In the meantime, I will give Aelia your cowl, your full costume will arrive smuggled in a statue, to be installed in your quarters. Just remember this, with me in power, your people will be safe. Much safer than any promise the Emperor makes to spare them. You wouldn't be doing this for us. You'd be doing it for the Hollow. Isn't that why you came? To protect them? Just think, if we bring about a coup, you will not have to go on a suicidal mission into the Underworld."

Another figure rose, holding a hand to speak. It was the Earthkind, his hands had tufts of greenery poking out of his sleeve. "My name is Kauri," the man said. Even his voice sounded, well, earthy. He had the low tones of hollow wood in some words, the whisper of rustling leaves in others. "The Earthkind lends their support to Jason, Son of Ventos. With our roots in the city, none of us know what it is like to be part of the Experiments. We know that you and your people have sacrificed much already. I only wish to say this. We Earthkind are in balance with the greenery. It is this balance which helps people find peace when their minds are troubled. The Lightguard took our best mind-healers for their own, to treat their soldiers. But in the Canopy—the woods outside the city walls—there are still many who could look after your father."

A memory came to me, of speaking to the Shadowkind in the Lower Levels. The one who'd gutted the fish. He must have passed on the word to someone in the Uprising about my father's condition.

This revolutionary network clearly had connections all over the city.

Kauri sat back down.

At that point, the chamber went silent. I felt everyone's gaze on me, a sudden weight of expectation pinning me to the back of my chair.

As if I didn't carry a large enough burden already.

Unable to process my feelings, I felt an outburst of anger rising in my stomach. "You know everything about me, but I know nothing of you. You use my father and my people against me. Manipulating me. Playing me."

I looked around. Everyone's look was blank. Only Kauri, the Earthkind, seemed to have sympathy in his expression.

"I can't do this," I said, directing my gaze at Cleander. "I will not be a pawn for you when I am already a pawn of the Emperor. You speak smoothly, but your promises are just threats dressed in different clothing. You are not offering me a choice. You will not allow me to say no. You're just another Lucian, another liar in a city of lies."

Cleander's eyes narrowed. "Whether you take on the mantle of the Blade of Rebels or not, you are now a part of the Uprising. You have seen this chamber. You know who we are. You are in the gutter of lies with the rest of us, whether you like it or not. The choice you face is if you will help us. Your only real chance of saving your tribes, and all the other people in the Experiments, is to help us overthrow the Emperor. Your father's only chance is with Kauri."

Cleander sat back in his chair, a look of satisfaction on his face.

"So, what's do you choose?" He asked.

Chapter Thirty

I left the meeting with darkness in my heart.

Aelia escorted me, but I ignored her. As I left the room and climbed up the side of the efflux, my thoughts and feelings overwhelmed me. I tried to work them out by striding up, working a sweat, replicating how I used to deal with my feelings in the Hollow by climbing walls and exploring the valley.

At the top, I finally turned to her. "Why are you following me? What, are we going to train now or something?"

Aelia tilted her head in frustration at my sarcastic outburst. I could tell that she was unhappy too, but I didn't care. She'd been only too ready to kill me earlier, and I wasn't going to let her forget it.

We went back out into the city. In the crowds, it was easier to ignore one another, and I felt my feelings settle a little. I was able to turn over the proposition with a bit more distance and start to consider what I'd agreed to.

I'd told the Uprising that I would be the Blade of Rebels. I hadn't been given a choice, despite Cleander's smooth words, that much was clear.

What I couldn't figure out yet was whether I *wanted* to be the Blade.

The Uprising promised me a less cruel world, my people

spared, and treatment for my father's condition. They would also spare me the trip down into the Underworld.

It was everything I wanted.

However, carrying out their plan carried a huge risk. It meant wearing a mask and hoping no one would recognize me. It meant I'd be gambling the safety of my family and friends.

Could I take that risk?

It seemed like too much to take on. I was still the boy who cowed under the vision of the sky. The boy who'd failed to win against two clumsy guards at the top of my valley.

I didn't feel like I could take on the whole Empire and win. If I didn't win, and the coup failed, my people would be executed. Everything would be lost.

"Here," ordered Aelia.

I had been so deep in my thoughts that I hadn't realized we were back at the training platforms. We found a free stretch, but instead of taking on a fighting stance Aelia just sat on the edge, facing the valley.

I did the same, and for a stretch we just contemplated the waterfall, and the city, and the lake below reflecting the stars. Aelia started breathing in a rhythmic, meditative way, and I found that I naturally fell in with her rhythm.

After a moment, I spoke. "What are we doing, Aelia?"

"Thinking."

"I would have your thoughts."

Aelia looked around. The warriors on other platforms around us were sparring, no one was paying attention to us. Still, I sensed that she wanted to speak in a veiled manner.

For a moment, it felt like I was back at home in the Hollow. When my father and I used to speak, it was always in such a manner. Contemplating the valley and not looking one another in the eye. It tended to bring out more honest conversations.

I felt a pang of grief at the thought of my father.

I hoped he was doing all right. I hoped it wasn't too difficult for Rana to look after him.

I hoped, without ever believing that my hopes could come true.

"My thoughts are complicated," admitted Aelia. "But it boils down to one thing. I don't know if I can trust you."

"And if you can't? Will you kill me?

"Of course. There's too much at stake."

I snorted in derision. "More threats. My people's lives are being threatened on one side, and my own being threatened on the other. You really think this is the way to conduct a revolution?"

"It's not about threats. It's about security. If we don't overthrow Lucian, then the entire Canyonlands are at stake."

"Is that what Cleander told you, then? *If Jason doesn't go ahead with the plan, slit his throat?"*

"He didn't have to. But he would. Cleander has been the heart of the Uprising for a long time, without him, we'd be nowhere."

I turned to Aelia. "Let's just be honest, for a moment. Let's act like we're Riverkind, breaking the ice. What makes you so angry about me becoming the Blade? Do you want the role for yourself, or something?"

Aelia shrugged. "*Want* is the wrong word. But I have given everything for the cause. I was raised a Shadowkind in the dirtiest streets of the Lower Levels, stealing and fighting and scrapping my way through life. It was Cleander who saw my potential and mentored me through the ranks. It was not easy. I had to do terrible things to prove my worth and earn the Emperor's trust. I had to fight twice as hard, kill twice as many. That's why I can't be the Blade, most people in the city hate me. They think I'm a traitor who sold her soul to the Emperor. I give my life to the people, and those people would gladly watch me bleed onto the cobbles. This is my life, Jason. I have no one. No family, no friends. They've all died or disowned me. I have nothing except this city and what I would do for it."

A silence settled between us then, while I contemplated these thoughts.

"Do you think I could do it, then? Be the figurehead they want me to be?" I said.

Aelia made a grim face. "You don't know a thing about this city or its people. You came out of nowhere, caring only for your tribe, and suddenly you're the heart of the revolution? I, and many other good people besides me, have spent our lives bleeding for this city, and the Shadowkind as a whole. Is it any wonder I have my doubts?"

I swallowed, taking in her words. They rang true, and my anger at her dissipated.

"It's like the sky," I finally said.

Aelia grunted. "What is that supposed to mean?"

"It's too much at once. I come from a small place, Aelia. A month ago, I didn't even know other people existed outside of my tribe. When I first came here, it was all too much. Emperors and demons and propaganda and revolutions, it's overwhelming. All I could think about was my family. My father, and my sister, and my people."

"Well, you're going to have to look beyond yourself. The Canyonlands are vast. Out there," she gestured at the horizon, "there are countless dying fathers and orphaned young girls. I know because my family was one of them. If you play your part, Kauri will heal your father. He's the best there is. You need to think about the rest of the families out there. All of them are suffering under the rule of the Emperor."

It felt strange to pity someone as large and as powerful as Aelia, but I did. Feelings of sadness rippled through me.

"How about this," I said. "You try to kill me a little bit less, and I'll do the best I can. For my father, and my tribe, and everyone else too. If I can look beyond myself a little more, then you can look into your heart and see whether you can't give me a chance. How does that sound?"

Aelia pursed her lips, and finally made a grunt of approval.

"As my sister always likes to say, *it's a deal,*" I said, before immediately regretting it. Just mentioning Rana made me miss her. "But if we're going to do this, let's do it properly," I continued, ignoring a wave of homesickness.

She wasn't expecting this. "What do you mean, upstart?"

"I mean putting the rebellion in my hands. I mean training me *properly.* Not just to use the Mind's Eye and make a variety of weapons. But to make forms of real size and strength. Something that will help us paint the world in shadow. Something close to what Cizin did, but without the madness and destruction."

Aelia nodded, slowly at first, while she contemplated my words... and then in agreement. "Now you're talking."

She stood up.

"Let's get started."

Chapter Thirty-One

We returned to my quarters, so we could train in the atrium. Aelia said that we had to hide what we were doing, if we were going to do some proper summoning.

We cycled for a full hour, ensuring that our cores were completely filled. Then Aelia told me what we were going to do.

"If you're to be the Blade of Rebels, you're going to have to deal with symbols and emblems. You're eventually going to use the Staff of Half-Moon Blades. It is an ancient weapon, and the one that the Swallow used. You wielding her weapon would send a clear message to the people that you are following in her footsteps. You also need to train with *this*."

She took out of her knapsack a long dark cowl, decorated with a hood with beautiful streaks of gold and a scarf to place over the mouth and nose.

"Why the gold? Wouldn't it be better camouflaged if it was completely dark?"

"You want to represent the people of the shadows, but you want to be *seen*. You are a symbol, remember? You are the rebellion. Your image must spread through the hearts and minds of the people. Gold is a color which only the Lightguard are permitted to wear, and they can only have patterns. The Emperor is the sole person in the city permitted to have gold clothes. You wearing gold is a statement, that power also resides with the people."

I turned the cowl around. On the back was that pattern of circles in gold. "So this is the insignia of the Uprising?"

Aelia nodded. "It is an old sign. The circles meeting each other represents a lack of hierarchy. No one is more powerful or more influential than the other. Your librarian in the Hollow was a plant, a spy from the Uprising. He smuggled in scrolls with that sign. When the time was right, he was supposed to show them to your people and seed doubt among the brainwashed people of the Experiments."

I considered this. I'd asked my friend Emilian to look through those documents marked with the insignia when I'd left. Hopefully he'd gleaned something from them.

"After every piece of resistance, you must create that pattern in shadow form. That will be your mark. It is simple enough to be replicated, hopefully, everyone will start using that insignia, and it will become a way for sympathizers of the Uprising to show their support. Do you know what graffiti is?"

I shook my head.

"Well, if tonight goes well, you will soon find out."

"What do you mean? What happens tonight?"

"The first appearance of the Blade of Rebels, of course."

"What? Already?"

"We have been waiting and preparing for the Blade to be among us for a while. Now we have found him, there is no time to waste. Practice the sign."

I learned how to replicate the insignia in the air. It was simple, just a few lines circling each other.

Next, we trained to use my Mind's Eye more, making my transitions from one weapon to another, trying to find connections between my forms so I could pair them like I had with the vine and claws.

After this, we cycled again, and filled our cores once more. At this point, the sun was rising.

We each drank a goblet of Elixir, and with it came the feeling of our chests expanding, of Anima rushing around our bodies twice as fast. As we did this, Aelia explained how we could go further.

"The structure of the Hollow was created by people from the Lightguard," explained Aelia. "They have the same terms for the different stages: Sensors, Binders, Weavers. But the Lightguard go one step further, once they get to what would be a Commander in your valley, they reach for the next level."

"And that is?"

"To become an Elite. This is what we have to become if we want to control forms which are both large and intricate. Which is what the Stonekind do when they move huge amounts of rock. This is what the Lightguard do when they create light-blasts, explosions with devastating, destructive impacts."

My eyes widened at the proposition. "How do you do that?"

"I've never done it myself. You have to go through a process called Essence-Gathering. It is a process which is difficult, and only a few manage to do it. Do it wrong, and it is extremely dangerous, as Cizin showed. This is why it is the preserve of the Elite, and why it is banned for us Shadowkind."

"For now," I said. "But when we learn it and show people that we can do it safely, that will change."

Aelia held up her hand. "One step at a time, upstart. The reason why it is difficult, as far as I can tell, is because it goes against all the tenets of our training. Normally, we enter the harmony of the universe. We borrow light, or shadow, then return it. But to Essence-Gather is to break the world, and hope it mends on the other side. To do it, you must carry a certain kind of self-belief. You must have the strength of conviction that what you are about to do is worth breaking the harmony of the world for."

It was such a strange concept. It was no wonder that my people had never tried it themselves; it went against everything I'd been taught about the Shade.

I noted that, for someone who claimed never to have tried it, Aelia seemed to know a *lot* about the process.

"Stand," she instructed.

I did.

"When you create a shadow-form, does it create a shadow itself?"

I shook my head. "No. We are just rearranging shadows that already exist. They cannot create *more* shadows themselves."

"And yet, that is what you are going to do. Distort and break the world, so that your shadows create shadows. Your form must feed itself. In fact, think of it as less of a form, and more like you are creating another warrior, with another core, attracting shadows and Anima."

My thoughts spun at the idea. "How do I do that?"

"You know how to spin Anima inside your core?"

I nodded.

"Well, now you must learn to spin it the other way. The *wrong* way."

I considered this for a moment. I'd never even thought about which way I'd spun it, the direction had come naturally, like being right-handed. "But the spinning invites Anima inside my body."

"Exactly. When you create a form, you want to *eject* Anima into it. Normally, when you form a Weave from the shadows inside your core, they are infused with Anima. You can see that, as they have those blue streaks. Elites take it one step further. When they spin your core the other way, they can eject Anima itself. Pure energy. It comes in hard, thick lines. It is then possible, if you train hard enough, to shape them into a Core Glyph, the sign of the Therians."

I remembered. On the walls of the Babel Tower, where I'd first encountered the ghosts of the Therians, I'd seen a representation of a core, a circle with lines towards the middle, representing the different channels.

"You can Weave Anima…" I said, wondering aloud at the thought.

"Just about. And if you can shape it into that glyph onto a Weave of shadow, then that Weave will attract more shadows. Then your shape will get exponentially bigger, thicker."

"I've *got* to try this."

"First things first. Try to spin the Anima in your core the other way."

Aelia was right to warn me. I was getting ahead of myself.

It became abundantly clear within minutes. It took all of my concentration just to find my core and to try and spin the Anima the wrong way. I started sweating, shaking, and barely made it shift.

I took a rest, then tried again.

This time, I managed a little, the Anima crawled slowly in the other direction. It felt so odd, and my body protested. It felt about as natural as seeing with my ears or hearing with my eyes, it was like my insides weren't suited for this purpose.

With a groan of exertion, I tried to shape a shadow-weave. Something simple that I knew well, like my khopesh.

I felt heartened when some thick lines of Anima appeared with the shadows—but they dispersed immediately, the shape completely unstable.

I gave up, and immediately felt dizzy. Aelia grabbed me.

"That's enough for today," she said. "We have to rest before tonight. The arrival of the Blade of Rebels has to be exactly right."

"What will his first act be?" I asked, hyperventilating.

A gleam of excitement appeared in Aelia's eye. "To throw open the gate between the Upper and Lower Levels."

Chapter Thirty-Two

"Break the gates?" I echoed out loud, wondering at the ramifications of such an act.

Aelia nodded. "The gates were originally put in place as an extra protection against invading forces like the demons. Over time, they have become symbols of oppression, subjugating the people of the Lower Levels. If we want this coup to work, then we have to communicate to the people a promise of a fairer city. The gates will be rebuilt, but to be used against the demons. The people of the citadel will roam free, welcome in any street, as equals. As a united front, we can beat the demons, otherwise we're doomed to fail."

"United?" I asked.

Aelia nodded. "Everyone training. Everyone having access to Elixir. If the demons are coming to the surface to wage war, they will come up through places like the Demon's Lock. We will need everybody there to stop the enemy from surging up to the surface, every member of the city, ready to fight. Lucian has forgotten the core tenet of warfare, to have as much as you can in the hands of the warriors. By keeping all the power to a select few, we've weakened ourselves. But in order to get started, we have work to do. I need to organize tonight, you need to prepare."

We spent the day resting, and training, and resting, and

training. Throughout the day, when I needed to recuperate, Aelia would head out into the city, preparing what we would do in the evening.

When the dusk came again, I donned the cowl. Aelia created her own shadow-cloak, masking her from head to toe. It was a spectacular form, one that was flexible, moving with her.

Again, I had the sense that she was more powerful than she was letting on. Aelia knew a lot about the abilities of the Lightguard, and she'd clearly tried her hand at replicating them herself, but with shadows.

Instead of going out of the door, we climbed out of the atrium, and clambered along the rooftops. That way, the guard posted outside my door would hopefully swear that we hadn't left, and we wouldn't be suspected of whatever happened in the city that night.

We snuck onto the city wall dividing the Upper and Lower Levels. It was suspiciously empty.

"Cleander organizes the Moonguard," Aelia explained. "I mean, he basically organizes all of the Lightguard, including the Sun divisions, as the Emperor drinks too much to do any work anymore, but I digress. He has ensured that the wall is mostly unguarded tonight. Come."

We ran across the battlements, the city teeming with life on either side, until we reached the square of the city gate.

The battlements stretched across the gate, topping it with a flank of stone and a statue of the Emperor. On the battlements on the other side, there was a Lightguard, I recognized him from the council of the Uprising. He was deep in concentration, but I couldn't quite see what he was focused on. Most of his body was blocked from view.

However, once I activated my Senses in order to better make him out, there was something I noticed, slivers of moonlight, snaking their way toward him in the air. He wasn't summoning from a particular direction, trails of light seemed to be drawn towards him, like water drawn to a sinkhole.

I'd only seen something similar once before, in the ghosts of the past, around the mad, cackling figure of Cizin.

"Is he...?" I whispered out loud.

"Yes," Aelia answered. "He is Essence-Gathering. Making a concentrated light, which in turn is gathering more light together. He will use it in a light-blast."

I nodded. I had been told this would happen, it was part of the plan, but I hadn't prepared myself for how hypnotizing and fascinating the process was. All I could see was light radiating toward someone, and all I wanted to do was cross the flank of stone and observe how it was done.

I didn't have time.

A flare of light tore through the air, scarring the night sky.

Marking the end of one hour, and the beginning of the next.

It was our cue, but also the cue for the rest of the Citadel. With sudden urgency, even as the statues across the street groaned, changing position, there was a rush toward the gates below us.

People from the Lower Levels were trying to get back home.

The guards did not wait for them to hustle through. No, the main guard, a man with white hair the color of moonlight, barked an order, telling two others with him to close the gates.

There was a flood, as a mass of people bottlenecked into the already swinging gates, accompanied by a shriek of protest as the crowd contemplated the prospect of being cut off.

I didn't know what the exact laws were for being in the wrong part of the city, but from what I'd seen of the Lightguard I knew that it wasn't pretty. Jail, beatings, losing all the profits you'd made in the market during the day, I'd seen all kinds of punishments meted out.

The injustice of it all stung, like an old wound. I was ready to start doing something about it.

"Let's do this," I said to Aelia.

She nodded. There was something in her eyes. Excitement, wonder even. This was the true Aelia. Not the grumpy, ill-tempered teacher, this was the warrior who fought for her people.

She glanced at me. "Don't fail me," she said, although there was joy in her voice. "Remember, let me do the heavy lifting. You're not powerful enough to take anyone on from the Moonguard yet. You just do the easy bit and be a symbol." She steeled herself. "Once we start this, we don't stop until the Emperor's gone, and justice is returned to the city. This is our chance. Got it?"

I nodded.

With that, I wove shadow-claws, and launched myself over the parapet. I scratched down the wall, using the claws to slow my descent, and landed in a throng of people, my cloak pooling in a satisfying, dramatic fashion about me as I landed.

There was a hush, and the throng of people backed away, giving me space. There was a murmur of confusion, a pause in the rush towards the gate, as everyone contemplated my cloaked, black image.

"Who are you?" snarled the main guard with white hair. "No Shadowkind is permitted on the parapet!"

At these words, the moment froze, no one knew what to do. The crowd separated, like cracks in the earth, as the guard advanced towards me.

"I am no one," I answered. The cowl muffled my voice, making it sound throatier and deeper than usual.

The white-haired guard stood in front of me, moonlight gathering into a grey blade with a thickened middle, the shape of a teardrop. He did not respond for a second, confusion writ upon his face.

It was like no one had ever spoken to him like this before.

"I'll ask you that very same question," I said. "Who are you to block these people from returning to their homes? Who are you to beat the citizens of this city, when all they are doing is trying to make a living?"

The people about me physically cowed, as if a whip had been cracked over their heads. No one talked back to the Lightguard.

Shock paralyzed the guard's expression, and I felt a sense of pleasure tingle through me. Through this mask, I could do what I wanted and not risk the lives of the Hollow. I could point out the lies of the Citadel, and not face any consequence.

It felt good.

"You will answer for this in the palace dungeons," the guard finally said, when he had regathered his senses.

"Not before you answer for the subjugation of the Shadowkind, and all other segregated peoples of the Canyonlands," I held out my hand, creating a shadow-staff. "The gate is open and it will remain open. The people will come and go as they wish."

The guard turned to the two other Lightguard at his command. "Close the gates!" he barked at them. "I will deal with this criminal."

"The gate…is…*open.*" I repeated. I launched forward.

It had all been calculated. I was not trained enough yet to take on the Lightguard, perhaps. Tonight was about making a statement, and that statement had to announce a new hero for the downtrodden.

Aelia's role was to do the fighting. But I had to be inspiring, and I could not make a single mistake.

A heavy shadow-net fell from above, dropping onto the guard's arms, just as I rushed towards him. Perfect timing by Aelia.

The guard blabbered something and started tearing away at the net with his arm and sword.

I made a wheeling motion, letting my cloak lift into the air. I wheeled my shadow-staff and cracked it across his face. There was a hard thudding sound, and the man collapsed into a netted heap on the stones.

I stepped over him and watched the gates. At this point, the people around us had retreated away from the fight.

There was no one at the gates but the guards who had closed it.

Surely now was the time.

I looked up at the Lightguard who had been Essence-Gathering on the wall above. He'd noticed the same opening and dropped a light-blast.

A ball, an orb of moonlight, almost as white as the moon itself, dropped down and fell upon the floor at the side of the gate's hinges.

The world turned white.

Nothing could have prepared me for the intensity of the charge, or the power of Essence-Gathering. The orb belched out light, silver exploding in all directions, as if a star itself had fallen among our feet. It made the sound of a furnace, and it was like nothing I had felt since I'd confronted the Kukulkan.

Light flew through us, cowing the throngs, rushing back to its natural place in the world.

The orb died out, and although my blinking eyes were still dazzled as if I'd looked directly at the sun, I saw what had been accomplished. The guards standing at the gates had been thrown onto the pebbles by the blast onto the floor, incapacitated.

The gate was mine.

I threw out a vine of shadows, streaming through the night, tipped with claws. It latched itself upon the gate door, and I grabbed hold of my shadow-shape with both hands and heaved.

The gate swung, and still I pulled, wrenching it all the way open.

I held my fist in the air, turning to the shocked throngs behind me.

"The gate... is....open," I said, one last time.

One beat passed, then another. The people stared down at me with suspicion, terror.

All it took was for one person to step forward, and then another, and then another before everyone was running through the gate. Drops of water, becoming a stream, then a river.

Then all the throngs charged ahead, ignoring the wounded guards, crossing back into the Lower Levels. Glee and excitement made them run with jubilance as they crossed the boundary without being challenged.

It was an explosion of joy, following the explosion of light.

With the freed people streaming past me, I lifted my arms, and made one final weave. The symbol of the rebellion, the swirls of lines, materialized over the charging crowd, hovered in the air in the opening between the two levels of the city. More shadows, sent down by Aelia, came to join the sign, thickening it, and then the Lightguard who had thrown the orb sent moonlight too, underlining the dark with the light.

The symbol was the size of two statues, and stayed there, making its mark.

The people noticed it and spoke about it in shrieks of excitement as they rushed through the gate.

The plan had worked.

The uprising had begun.

I turned and ran, pacing through the streets, climbing walls, and leaping over roofs, the promise of the future giving me more energy than any charge of Anima could.

We had taken our first step.

Chapter Thirty-Three

The effect on the city could be felt within days.

As we walked through the streets, the sign was everywhere. Overnight, there was the sign scribbled in chalk, or carved into stone on buildings. I'd even seen people with the shadow-mark do the sign to each other in quiet, hidden alleyways, weaving the mark to each other in solidarity and talking of the exploits of the Blade of Rebels.

The gates had only been opened for a few minutes before the Lightguard had taken control of it again. But those few minutes, when the people of the Lower Levels could pass from one part of the city to another with complete freedom, was all anyone could talk about.

The mechanics of the city, which had run for so long, had been broken.

The Blade of Rebels had made a good start.

It was something to be celebrated. I'd certainly taken a lot of satisfaction from it. I also saw how the presence of the Lightguard was doubled, and it was a cruel reminder of the Emperor's power.

"Are you sure they won't trace it back to me?" I asked Aelia, when we were roaming the streets, the levels of noise from the crowds around us allowing us to speak freely.

Aelia held up a hand, detecting my note of anxiety. "Don't

start having a moment or anything." She held up fingers, counting off arguments. "We weren't seen leaving your quarters, so the guards should vouch for the fact that we were here training and couldn't be the Blade. You've got to remember that we've been spreading rumors around about a new warrior for a long time, long before you arrived. Everyone is going to think it's one of the warriors of the Uprising. Plus, remember that Cleander is there, giving advice to the Emperor. He should be steering any suspicion away from you, and onto the underground shade-users in the Lower Levels."

"Still, I should have been more careful. I can't use any of my normal weaves, no one can link the Blade with me. I have got to train… *hard.*"

"Which is what I have been saying since we first met. Today, though, you're going to start using the weapon the Swallow was best known for. No more khopeshes, no more staffs. Today, we start preparing with the staff of half-moon blades. Come—the form should have been delivered to your quarters by now."

I nodded. I wasn't going to let the role get to me anymore, I would use the half-moon blades, whatever that was, and other new forms, and nothing else. I wouldn't be so stupid anymore.

A thought occurred to me as we turned towards the alleyways climbing back up towards the Higher Levels and the palace.

"Hang on," I said. "You said *preparing with* the half-moon blades. I'm presuming that you have something specific in mind?"

"Yes. The other night was just a beginning. We have made a statement that we are willing to stand up against the Lightguard. That has already won us some hearts in the city, for sure. What we haven't said yet… is that we will stand up against the Lightguard *and win.*"

"How are we going to do that?"

"We have to start taking out some powerful players, and you need to win in combat. You need to go toe-to-toe with one of the most hated Lightguard out there and defeat him. That will tip the balance and lay the groundwork for the coup."

"And who will this powerful, hateful opponent be? I'm hating this line of thought already."

"Hate away, you're taking him on in three days, regardless."

"But who—" We turned around the street corner, and came to the gate.

I didn't bother finishing the sentence.

The Quaester, the man with the mustache who cruelly beat passersby, was now in charge of manning the gates. He was there, spitting out orders, cracking shadow-whips at the crowds jeering at him.

Aelia motioned in his direction. "He's the most unpopular man in the Citadel. Everyone from the Lower Levels despises him. We are taught to fear the sight of him from the moment we are old enough to walk the streets. They say in the Senate that when people do not respect the law, then the law must be strengthened through punishment. The Quaester is that punishment."

"We're going to have to step up the theatrics," I answered. "There's no way I can beat him on my own."

"Of course not," answered Aelia, far too quickly for my taste. "The Uprising will be there to aid you, as we did last night. Still, we're going to need to ramp things up over the next couple of days."

I arched an eyebrow. "Next couple of days?"

"In exactly three nights, the Quaester will be on night duty. That's when we'll take him down. Lucian is going to want to send you on your mission into the Underworld soon, so we must have our coup before that happens."

I gulped.

"Well then, let's get training," I said.

We returned to my quarters.

Inside, I saw that a new statue had been delivered. However, with Aelia's help, we saw that it was hollow, and inside was all the equipment that we had ordered. There was the rest of my costume, fitted to my size.

More importantly, there was the marble form of the Staff of Half-Moon Blades, a weapon with circular blades at its ends.

Once we had meditated and filled our bodies with Anima and Elixir, we started training. I learned the form of the new staff, which did not take long. Having the shape in front of me, I could run my fingers over it, committing the shape to memory. It was not altogether unlike the shadow-staff I normally used, usually placing spearheads at its ends. Aelia taught me that instead of memorizing the shape of the entire weapon from scratch, I could just memorize the semi-circular heads, and put them in the same chamber of my Mind's Eye as the staff. That way, I would link the two items together, and using the staff as a common link my mind could replace the spearheads with the half-moon blades.

Before long, I was in the atrium, with a black form of the Swallow's favored weapon in my hands. I tried twirling it, and found it ideally weighted. It was surprisingly easy to handle.

Aelia studied my movements and instructed me on how best to use it. "It was designed so that the warrior could fight people coming from all sides. The 'sweep' was the legendary movement of the Swallow, whereby she could do low spins, and cut at the feet of everyone surrounding her."

I tried it, spinning, and found that without even wanting to, the weapon cut through blades of grass growing between the slabs on the ground, sending tufts of green in the air. "It's so sharp," I said, incredulously.

"Well, you've mastered how to use it in garden maintenance," Aelia jibed. "Now let's see how well you can use it against an opponent. First, we establish some moves, then we spar. You can practice fighting people on different sides."

"How can I do that? There's only one of you, I can hardly spar against two people at a time."

Aelia went to the newly acquired statue, the hollow form of Lucian the equipment had been smuggled in. "I'd say giving this a few scars wouldn't go amiss. Judging by how much you enjoyed being the Blade the other night, I'm guessing you need to let out some anger."

I grinned. "You guessed right."

"Then give him hell."

I did. I learned how to place my hands in order to wheel the half-moon blades, slicing at the statue of the Emperor, biting at the form until it was lined with cuts and looked like it had been mauled by an animal.

Aelia then sparred with me from an opposite side, and I learned how to use the blades while defending myself against her while also cutting into the statue at the same time. I found out the weapon it wasn't ideal for parrying, and that my opponent's sword could slide off the half-moon shapes and still be dangerous to me. Instead, we decided that the weapon was very much an offensive one, to counter its weakness I had to be in constant movement, swiping everything to the side with force to keep attackers at bay.

We also quickly saw that it had become the Swallow's weapon of choice for its aesthetics as much as its practicality. The constant circling made for a spectacle, and as I became faster and faster with it, it almost felt like the weapon was dancing in my hands.

I hoped that I would provide a good enough show to incite further rebellion.

We fought until sweat was pouring down our faces, and we'd had enough. I then gave myself a break by having some food, meditating some more, and refilling my Anima.

I then returned to the other exercise we'd started yesterday, Essence-Gathering. I found that the rush of excitement from being the Blade of Rebels gave my mind a focus that improved my practice. Before, I had been wracked by self-doubt and the fact that I was working for my enemy.

Now, however, I found that my body was more responsive. I could go deeper into myself, letting my mind go to my core, and will the Anima spinning within to circle the other way, expelling the energy out of my body when I wove. The Anima came out in an ice blue which I could barely control and dispersed immediately.

"Well, it's some improvement," said Aelia, although her tone countered any positivity in her words. "But it's not enough. If you're going to master this, we're going to have to spend all day, every day working on it."

Which was what we did.

* * *

Weeks passed, every day was spent in rigorous training. We drank Elixir, meditated, cycled, and worked on using my Mind's Eye and Essence-Gathering. In the former, I started to have more and more success, being able to reshape my Weaves easily. It was satisfying to pass from one form to another, and also to see what variety of weapons I could make simply by pairing certain forms together, like when I had attached claws to the end of the vine.

With Essence-Gathering, however, I was less successful. Aelia was keen to remind me that very few managed it, across all Essences, and next to no one did it with shadows. But that didn't stop me from trying, and feeling the disappointment when I did not progress. Nearly every time, I would prepare for a long time before trying to eject Anima into a stable shape of the Core, and it would come out a sharp glowing blue before fizzling out almost immediately. It was hard not to feel that I was putting in a lot of work for very little result.

In the meantime, the conversation around the Blade of Rebels was growing. Sometimes Aelia and I would head out and project the sign of the rebellion from city walls, blasting them into the sky from rooftops. On other occasions, Aelia would do it without me, and I without her, ensuring that we both had alibis in case suspicion fell upon us.

It never did. All everyone talked about was the groundswell of the revolutionary movement of the Uprising, and its base in the Lower Levels. No one suspected that the Blade of Rebels lived next door to the palace.

We were helped by the fact that the actual Uprising was making their presence felt more and more. Shadowkind caused riots and fighting against guards, crying out the name of the Blade as they launched into a skirmish, gave the impression that their hero was one of them, a rebel born in the Lower Levels. Such skirmishes tended to end badly, with members of the Uprising sent to prison, and yet the fact that people were on the streets, using the Shade, was further evidence that the Emperor was losing his grip on the city.

The groundwork for the coup was being laid, bit by bit. Aelia and I monitored it closely, sensing the desire for change in the streets, sensing the hope for a fairer society.

One day, as we were training in my atrium, we spoke about what was to come next.

"There are still a few steps to take before the coup," Aelia said. "The Lower Levels are showing their dissatisfaction and causing more chaos. This is good. It makes the Emperor look weaker. But it's not enough. We need to show that the Senate is inept, that they cannot protect us. If we show how vulnerable they truly are, it will be the ultimate sign that they are not fit to wage war against Cizin."

"How do we do that?" I asked.

"We strike at the Senate itself," she answered simply. "We show that they are drunk fools who've forgotten how to lead their people."

A worry gnawed at me. "How much longer is this going to take? Lucian is surely going to send me down into the Underworld at some point, isn't he? If I want to escape that fate, we need to act fast."

Aelia nodded. "Agreed. What's more, the demons could start a war at any time. We don't know when Cizin will come knocking. But we'll only get one chance to depose the Emperor. We have to sit tight and do it right. The only chance we'll ever get to defeat Cizin is as a united people, with Cleander on the throne."

She was about to say more, but we were interrupted.

The door for my quarters was roughly pushed open. We

had hidden the form of the blades and my costume, they were out of sight and we were doing nothing wrong, yet my heart still hammered like it was in the hands of a blacksmith.

Two Lightguard came in, filtering into the atrium. I had the distinct feeling of being surrounded. These quarters had come to feel like a safe space, almost a home.

Now that feeling was ruined in an instant.

"You are summoned to see the Emperor," one of them said.

Before I could even acquiesce, two others grabbed me by the arms, leading me out.

Just as I left, I saw the guard's eyes rest on the statue of the emperor, noting how scarred and disfigured it was.

A thought lodged itself in my mind.

This is not going to be good.

Chapter Thirty-Four

I was dragged to the palace, my dread intensifying like growing hunger inside my body. Aelia accompanied us, walking to the side. She played her part well, as if she did not care one jot about me or my welfare. She did not meet my eye.

She must be concerned, I thought. If they'd learned something about me, then surely that could put her in danger too?

If it wasn't so devastating, if the lives of the Hollow weren't on the line, then it would have been sickly funny. Our great revolution finished after only a handful of riots and the opening of a gate. It was a neat encapsulation of the balance of power in the Canyonlands, nothing survived the light's glare.

I did my best to follow Aelia's lead, and not betray my emotions. I walked steadily, even though my mind was a storm of anxiety.

We entered the Palace and the courtyard. The canals and the flowers were a burst of color, and the opulent luxury hit me. Now that I knew how the city operated, it was even more disgusting how much space, light, and Elixir there was in this place. It was a direct contrast to the hovels in the Lower Levels, where the less fortunate people were crammed into small buildings.

The Emperor, however, was not on his throne, like the last time I had seen him. Instead, he was pacing back and forth, a face of barely concealed fury on his features. A Riverkind, creating a cooling mist of water, could barely keep up with him as he paced through the courtyard. Even before we approached him, the tone of his voice could be heard, a series of grunts and childish sulking noises.

I realized, once I got past a grouping of foliage, that he was speaking to Cleander.

As I approached, I dared to shoot a look at Cleander, trying to assess what was going on. I was for a sign or clue, anything which could reveal my fate, and that of my people. But he didn't even meet my eye or even acknowledge my arrival.

A good act? Or did he truly not care?

A cruel thought sprung to mind. What if this whole rebellion had been a set-up? A way to root out those who would oppose the Emperor, and his right hand man?

I tried to calm my thoughts. There was no reason to rush to such conclusions, I was being paranoid.

But the thought nested in my mind, nonetheless. I still didn't trust Cleander. He wanted power even though he already had a lot. His hand wielded influence like no one else, save the Emperor himself. He was not like Aelia or myself, coming from a community of the segregated. He was closest to the throne, and I could not put my faith in someone like that.

The Emperor turned to me, a glare of anger on his face. "What took you so long?" he spat in my direction. It was unclear as to whether he was accusing me, Aelia, or the guard who had come to collect me for my tardiness. It didn't matter who deserved blame, only that he was unhappy.

He then pointed to the ground in front of him. I did not know what that meant, but I soon found out.

Hands surged to grab me and strong-armed me forward, and then to my knees. Suddenly I was on the floor, prostrate before the Emperor.

I looked up, and saw that a Stonekind had come at the Emperor's request, and was weaving a stone chair where the Emperor stood. Lucian sat down, barely waiting for the form to solidify behind him as he lorded over me.

"I trust," he said, leaning over to me and rasping, "that you have heard of what has been happening to my city?"

I didn't know what to answer to this, I just wanted whatever was going to happen to be over with.

"A man attacked my guards," the emperor continued, with a voice so full of fury I could imagine him lashing out at any point, "Opened *my* gate to let people from the Lower Levels through. Since then, he has been spreading chaos and treachery through the streets."

Panic swelled inside me. *He knows.*

"This man *deigned* to go against the tenets of the Citadel," the emperor said. "To undermine the traditions of a city which has kept the Canyonlands safe for thousands of years. Would you know anything about this... *Jason*?"

I looked to Aelia, then to Cleander. They were not moving.

Of course they weren't. They had no loyalty to me. Loyalty means nothing, I thought. Not here in the Citadel.

"Cleander informs me," came the Emperor's seething voice, "that you are the catalyst. That your presence has incited the masses, that people are openly discussing the rumors of the Experiments, and of a new war with Cizin. Disobedience is on everyone's lips. Is this true?"

I shook my head and tried to keep my voice calm. "I don't know anything about the public's mood..."

This made the Emperor's anger boil even further. "Cleander tells me the Shadowkind think you're some kind of inspiration. That everyone is speaking of you because you survived the Experiments."

Cleander said this? I almost exclaimed.

What was he thinking?

I stared at him again. There was just the slightest movement in his eyes, barely perceptible.

Indicating that everything was under control.

I picked my words carefully when answering the Emperor. "If that was the case, then it was no fault of my own. I have spent my time doing as you asked, training with Aelia. I have spoken to no one. I wouldn't do that, not when my people are under threat."

Cleander intervened at this point, stepping forward. "This is true, my lord. My spies tell me that he has been made an emblem of the rebellion, but through no contact with the rebels themselves. He has been training with Aelia, as you have asked. His presence is but a source of inspiration. He reminds them of the Therian rebellion and the Swallow."

"I *wonder*," the Emperor spat, his presence looming over, blocking out the sun. "Are you innocent...or have you gone behind my back, after the chance I've given you? Have you connived with criminals, and become the heart of the rebellion?"

"You think I would risk the lives of my people, when you've threatened to wipe them out?" I exclaimed without thinking. My voice wavered. All my doubts, all the times when I'd feared for my family and friends made my words raw. "You think that I would go against a world I've only just stepped into? I may be from the valleys beyond, but I'm not a madman."

I raised my head and looked the Emperor in the eye, he was leering over me, leaning in close, as if he was trying to sniff out the truth.

I didn't care and stared right back at him, at his huge face and jowls. We were close enough for his cooling mist to tickle my skin, and in that moment we were in a world of our own.

Testing each other.

I saw the veins in his forehead looking like they were going to burst, like rivers in spring. I saw the hatred in his eyes.

I kept up the act of an ignorant child, one who knew nothing of coups and uprisings, staying silent.

A low growl, like the guttural warnings of an animal, escaped from the Emperor's lips. His face turned into a scowl sour enough to poison a well.

I continued to give my look of obedience.

Then, nothing. The emperor leaned back, distancing himself from me.

I chanced a glance at Cleander. What in all the skies did this mean? But the man remained blank, unreadable.

The Emperor held out a hand, and a servant rushed over, putting a goblet in his hand. It was an interminable silence as this happened, the only sound the pattering of the servant's feet. The emperor's eyes never left me.

Finally, when he had taken a large gulp of his goblet, the Emperor spoke again. "Well then. It seems like our stranger may be telling the truth after all. You have convinced me, for now."

I exhaled, unable to mask my relief. He didn't know that I was the Blade of Rebels. Me, and my people, might survive this day. I had hardly breathed in the last minute, and my chest now heaved in order to replenish my lungs with air.

"It's a pity," said the Emperor, twirling his goblet in his fingers. His voice was calm again: there was something sick, conniving in it.

All my instincts were awake once more.

"What is a pity, my lord?" asked Cleander. His voice, smooth as the surface of the lake, made it sound as if he was speaking out of simple curiosity.

"I truly thought that this Jason could help us. But now, it seems to me that the solution to the rebellion is clear. There is no other option. If Jason is the emblem of the rebels—why, we must take their emblem and destroy it." He turned to a guard nearby. "I will be using the crystal. Ready it."

Confusion tore through me. *Destroy it?* What did that mean? And what use would the signet prism be?

I could not utter a word: a storm of hands were placed upon me once more, suddenly lifting me to my feet. The guards who had been accompanying me were now pushing me to the dial from which the hour-lights were shot into the sky.

The Emperor got to his feet as well. "You probably don't know how we do public executions, here in the Citadel. But I promise you, it makes the impression. Your death will make quite the mark."

I could barely process what he was saying. All I wanted to

do was tear away, to run, to somehow get out of the grip of the guards holding me.

But nothing was happening: the word *execution* paralyzing me.

The Emperor pointed upwards. “My scouts will raise you up into the sky, and drop you, plunging down, in full view of the city. You’ll be dropped all the way down into the Demon’s Lock, which will be temporarily opened for you. You’ve shown a talent for falling and surviving, so you’ll have to be mangled a bit first. But don’t worry…”

The Emperor smiled before finishing.

“They’ll remember you.”

Chapter Thirty-Five

I was marched past the Sundial, my mind spinning. The crystal prism sat, framed by steel, and pointing to the sky at the sundial's feet.

Lucian shot a look at Cleander. "Well?"

"Would you like me to do the honors, Emperor?"

"Well, it can only be one of us, can't it? It's not going to be me!"

At the Emperor's behest, Cleander strode forward, and created a silver dagger, drawing from his core. He drew the dagger across his palm, and blood dripped from his hand. He placed it on the ring at the bottom of the prism, and the sheen of crystal rock shimmered inside it, infusing it with magic.

Aelia had told me about this. The crystal, found buried deep underground, magnified images. Here, the Emperor could inform an Imagist to write a message or send an image. Sent through the crystal prism, it would then be projected in the sky.

For security it had been locked, only Cleander and the Emperor could use it, by activating it with their blood.

A Lightguard sent a flare of light into the ether at the Emperor's request. This was shown to be an order, and the moment it was sent into the clouds, two scouts with wings of light descended, landing in front of us.

They were going to take me into the air, then fling me to my death.

I imagined them taking me by the shoulders, hoisting me up over the city, over the Canyonlands, into that terrifying sky.

Then, I would be dropped, mangled and bleeding for the Emperor, my body a plummeting rock.

I would not even hit the city, nor grass, nor the surface of the lake.

Instead, my body would be swallowed up in that darkness of demons. The home of Cizin.

My senses were dulled, numb, the thought of my death rendered my body virtually useless. I heard the Emperor order the Stonekind at the Demon's Lock to be ready to open up their rocky lid in order to let my body fall down into the earth, but the words did not seem to make sense to me.

The Emperor turned to an Imagist, standing by the prism. "Project my body into the sky, I have an announcement to make. But first... we must bleed the boy, make sure he cannot survive the fall." He looked around for a suitable warrior, choosing Aelia. "You'll do. Do some damage, I just need him alive enough to scream as he falls."

The words would have stung if they'd had any meaning. But now it was as if he were talking about somebody else. I was not going to be bled or injured. Surely that was happening to someone else.

I felt Aelia come closer, standing in front of me. In her hand, slowly, as if reluctant, a blade materialized, shadows knotting into shape.

I looked up at her face, her features were cold, unforgiving. Hard. I saw something in her eyes.

Something akin to...*regret.*

She raised her blade, and I closed my eyes, wincing in anticipation.

"One moment," a voice intervened. It was Cleander, approaching the Emperor. "Lucian, this may be a mistake."

The Emperor did not take this kindly. "You will never cease to be *clever*, will you Cleander? Clever Cleander, always coming up with better ideas! What mistake am I supposed to be making this time?"

Cleander spread his arms, his palms open. "If what I am about to say does not please you, then I welcome your decision. But first, lend me your ear. I have saved you from enough rash decisions in the past to warrant that, yes?"

The Emperor growled. "Fine. But you will refer to me as *your lord* in front of company, Cleander. I have been reminding you of that for centuries now."

Cleander nodded. "Of course, my lord."

Even though I could barely stop shaking, and my death was still imminent, I could see through Cleander's façade. Not referring to him officially had been no mistake: Cleander knew when to refer to the Emperor with the pomp of official etiquette, and when to approach him as a friend.

Cleander continued. "If you slay Jason now, then of course it will deal a blow to the rebellion. But will it have the effect you desire? Will it take the wind out of their sails? Or… will it stoke their fire further?"

"Get to the point, Cleander," the Emperor rasped bluntly.

"If we execute Jason, it'll make him a martyr. The rebellion might swell in his name, even more people might join their cause, having pity as they do for Jason."

The Emperor contemplated this for a moment. "What do you suggest instead?"

"Fear is not the only way to control the people. At times, love must accompany fear. Love, in this case, might be the best way to steer the hearts of the Citadel." Cleander turned to me. "What if we took this boy, so beloved by the rebels, and showed that he is not to be pitied at all? What if we showed that he was working for you, collaborating with you? What if he showed his support for you? Then all the respect they showed for him would spread to you. The emblem for the uprising would become *your* emblem of power."

The Emperor contemplated this for a moment.

Cleander continued. "What you do with Jason will either sharpen the blade of the rebellion or blunt it. The choice is yours." With that, Cleander took a few steps backward, withdrawing to let Lucian turn his words over in his mind.

It must have only been a few breaths, but for me it seemed like eternity. I could not breathe, it was as if my heart was clogging up my throat, not allowing air to pass.

"So be it," the Emperor said. "Jason will not be killed but turned. *Very* publicly." My relief was short-lived. He came to me and grabbed me by the scruff of my tunic. "You will pledge your loyalty and support for me. Anything less will result in the death of you and yours. I will not hesitate. I trust I've made that clear."

I grimaced to have his wine-breath waft over me, to have that wide face so close to mine. Suddenly, my fear was immediately replaced by anger.

"You've shown your colors, Emperor," I whispered. "There's no getting any clearer than that."

The Emperor brought me even closer. "If you love your family, you're going to have to put on the performance of a lifetime." The Emperor dropped me, and then barked at the Imagist by the signet. "Get ready to project our images into the sky!"

The Imagist, a wide-eyed woman in a simple chiton, looked at me, studying me carefully for a moment. She circled me, taking in my shape and size, it felt like I was being dissected with her eyes.

She nodded at the Emperor when she was ready.

"Let's begin," said the Emperor, smoothing his clothes and gathering himself.

What I saw next was extraordinary. The Imagist took the image of the Emperor, standing before her, and wove a picture of him in beams of light. This was their role: to specialize in Weaving to communicate, to deliver images. Their Weaves were, presumably, fleeting, not thick and sturdy like the weapons created in their hands, yet they could replicate what they saw and reflect it instantly with their Essence.

She made a replica of the image of the Emperor, projecting

it in light, then made it go through the crystal. The prism magnified the light, no, *charged it,* and sent it into the sky.

Among the clouds, there was a rippling image of the Emperor. It was a gigantic image, one of a god looking down upon his people.

"I speak to you, my people, at an urgent hour," said Lucian.

The imagist wove her hands, and the image of the Emperor in the sky moved as he did, like a reflection in still water. As he opened his arms, beckoning to the people, so did his image, with barely a moment's delay.

Another Imagist, a man in a similar chiton, closed his eyes, and wove light too, sending shapes through the magnifying ring. There, underneath the image of the leader, words formed in light, gold lettering scribbled across the sky as if the heavens were the parchment of a deity.

I speak to you, my people, at an urgent hour, the lettering said, transcribing the Emperor's words.

I stood in awe as the message was written in the sky, broadcast to the Citadel below. I imagined the whole city stopping its bustle, everyone craning their necks to witness the likeness of their leader carved into the sky.

For the Emperor, however, this seemed to be nothing at all, he continued speaking at a fast pace, not giving the imagists a single second in order to catch up as he delivered his monologue.

"My people of the Cayonlands," he said. "I hear that you are afraid. I have heard of fearmongering, false rumors of war. I do not wish you to be scared. Myself, and the Lightguard have kept you safe for hundreds of years, and we will continue to do so."

The Emperor gave a dramatic pause. "It is also unfortunate, that at this time, a few criminals have decided to seed disquiet and violence. They have taken advantage of your fears. They will be met with the full force of the guard, I cannot let such people create havoc when it threatens the security of the Canyonlands."

He then smiled, a huge smile that I thought seemed impossibly overblown and insincere, until I saw it translated into the sky, where it seemed perfectly judged. The Emperor was in his element.

"But I am generous. I hear your fears, and I act to assuage them. I have a new warrior, an ally that will provide hope to everyone, from the farmers and shepherds in the farthest reaches to the senators in the palace. Some of you in the city know of whom I speak. He is a man who came from the Experiments, having shown his worth there. He came to the city and offered his services to me. A man who may not seem much, but whose powers will be able to let you sleep better at night. I am speaking of Jason, Son of Ventos, the Unmarked."

The moment he said those words, his image in the sky disappeared.

Replaced by me.

I was there, an image in light, there among the clouds and sky; a clearer picture of myself than perhaps I had ever seen. I moved my arm, as an experiment, the light-painting of me moved it in accord. I was a puppet-master and a puppet, all at once.

"Tell them, boy," spat the Emperor. "Tell them of my glory, and our mission, or I will have the Hollow cut at the throat."

I tried to compose myself; to smile like the Emperor had—but seeing myself there, painted upon the heavens, rendered me awkward. I could not stop staring at myself.

The Emperor spoke once more. "Speak now, boy, or you'll never get the chance to speak again. Tell them of our project."

"I am Jason, Son of Ventos," I said, my voice a little uncertain. It did not help that my words were immediately whipped into forms of light and flung into the sky. "I...am from The Experiments. I have braved many dangers in my homeland. And now, I have come here to aid the Emperor, and you. I may not seem like much, next to the might of the Lightguard. But I have an ability which they do not. I can see into the history of light and darkness, and Sense so far back that I can listen to ghosts. At the Emperor's request, I will be traveling into the Underworld, with the mighty warriors of the Citadel. I will see, there, if there is any danger or if there have been any preparations for war."

I felt a hand on my shoulder. The Emperor was now at my side, beaming. I tried my best not to flinch as I saw the image of the two of us in the sky, side by side.

"Jason is our new hope," said the Emperor. "He will see what we cannot. With his Senses, he will be able to see for good that there is no danger facing us here in the Citadel. Jason's force will go through the Demon's Lock, and into the Underworld, the day after tomorrow at dusk. I welcome everyone in the Citadel to gather there and wish him well in his venture. Citizens of the Citadel, where the light resides. I bid you farewell."

Our images vanished, and our words with them. I looked back at the prism and saw that Cleander was finally able to withdraw his bloody hand from the crystal.

The Emperor was already walking away, his work done, his gathering amassing around him.

"The day after tomorrow?" I asked, I called after him. "But I'm not trained…"

"You will leave the day after next," said the Emperor, tossing his words over his shoulder.

Anger got the better of me. "I'm not ready! I'll die!"

The Emperor stopped and turned. "You're right, you'll probably die. But you're clearly a bad influence on the city, and I will be glad to be rid of you." He turned to Cleander. "You have one day to get the excursion prepared. Then he goes into the black."

Chapter Thirty-Six

The day after next?

The seeds of rebellion had just been sown. There was no way we could engineer an uprising before then.

I would actually have to go into the Demon's Lock after all, to do the Emperor's bidding. I'd probably die in his service.

The thought echoed cruelly through my mind.

How am I going to get out of this?

I was accompanied back to my quarters by Aelia. We went to the atrium, and sat for a moment, contemplating our predicament.

"So, just how dead *are* we?" I asked her.

"Just be quiet, will you? Stop pestering me for once, and let me think," she said, pacing.

"Oh, I'm sorry, I'm a little on edge. Perhaps it's because you were about to *execute me. Again.*"

Aelia rolled her eyes. "You know the score, or at least you should, by now. I've done far worse to rise up the ranks. One man's death means nothing next to the Uprising.."

"What Uprising? What can we do in one day?"

"All it takes is one spark to ignite the fire. We must cause many sparks, and hope they catch. If we can cause widespread protests, and keep the Lightguard busy, then we can infiltrate the palace and use the crystal to show everyone the true identity of the Blade of Rebels. The Emperor's reputation will be in tatters, and Cleander can take over."

I nodded. "Sparks it is. But where do we start?"

A voice came from behind us. "With the Senate."

It was Cleander. His tall, slim frame entered the courtyard so smoothly, so at ease, it was like we were in his quarters instead of mine.

"Cleander, I didn't hear you approach," said Aelia.

"Of course you didn't. You were too busy despairing," Cleander said, taking a cup of Elixir from the fountain. "Which, by the way, you were doing *incredibly loudly*. Not really respecting the spirit of a secret rebellion, now, are we?"

"Why did you say that the riots were because of me?" I burst out. I had been meaning to ask. "That nearly led to my execution!"

"The city has not seen revolt and rebellion in many a year. And now it begins, just days after you arrive? The Emperor may be brash and arrogant, but underneath all that bluster is no fool. If I didn't make the connection, he would have, and my silence would have been suspicious."

He sipped at the goblet, brushing off my furious glare.

"You're no expert at lying, Jason. I am. And I can tell you this: the best lies are the ones laced with truth." He sat down at a chair. "Besides, I got you out of your execution easily enough."

"Easy to remain so calm when the blade isn't hovering over your neck," I started.

"The blade is *always* hovering over my neck. I have been a hair's breadth away from execution for longer than you have been alive. The only difference is, I'm used to it."

I closed my eyes and swallowed down my anger. The man made the hairs on my neck stand up, but this verbal match was getting us nowhere.

"You mentioned the Senate?" said Aelia. "We weren't supposed to target them for days yet. Jason isn't ready."

Cleander nodded. “I have called a Senate meeting tonight, at twilight. They will all meet there, becoming targets. Our hand has been forced. We must incite the rebellion quicker than I’d planned. This means that we launch the next phase.”

“And what does the Blade of Rebels do in this last phase?” I interjected.

“Kidnap members of the Senate. We remove some of the most hateful people in power, and that sends a message as clear as the one the Emperor sent into the sky today. We show them that we are capable of anything.”

“And then?”

“Tomorrow we take on the Quaester. With key members of the Senate gone, and the key figure in charge of maintaining the city defeated, the coup can occur. With the Lightguard of the city in disarray, there will be chaos. And chaos is just violent energy in need of direction. We’ll direct it toward the palace, then storm it.”

Aelia shook her head. “It all seems so soon. The rebellion was supposed to simmer far longer before it reached a boil.”

Cleander finished his goblet. “If the fire underneath is hot enough… we’ll reach the boiling point regardless. So we all need to get to work and light a fire underneath the city. Make sure that the Blade of Rebels does his bit, and we’ll get our uprising.”

“You sound so sure,” I said.

“We have no other choice but to proceed.” His features darkened. “Even if the Emperor wasn’t forcing our hand by sending you into the Underworld, the reports from the Stonekind in the valleys are getting more and more concerning. The ground is trembling beneath us. Every week, I’m told the ground is behaving more and more strangely, even though we may not sense it yet. Something is happening, deep below the surface. It means war. I thought we had months before the demons came to invade, now I suspect it may be a matter of weeks, if not less.”

Cleander was quiet for a moment, gazing into the distance.

For the first time I thought that I saw past the mask and the poise, and heard sincerity in his voice. "To think of the demons breaking through the Demon's Lock, and spreading into our streets, it is unconscionable. Unless we have every warrior trained, drinking Elixir, and ready to do their part to help stop them from emerging from the Lock, we are dead."

Cleander shook his head, and the façade of confidence returned to his features.

"Do your part," he instructed. "I will do the rest."

With that, he took his leave.

Leaving Aelia and I to plan and train.

After meditating and trying to settle our minds as best we could, attempted to do some Essence-Gathering. To my regret, I failed to master it. I was able to spin the Anima in my core in the different direction, and therefore, upon creating a form, it had cool, hard lines of blue.

But this took such an effort that my form dispersed immediately, creating a thin mist which disappeared as quickly as smoke from a spent candle. I was no closer to forming a Core Glyph with my Anima, and therefore no closer to gathering a larger mass of shadows.

Aelia barely hid her frustration, and I could see where her mind was going. Was there even any point trying to get me to learn something new at this late hour?

"You're wondering whether to give up," I said.

Aelia pursed her lips, considering her words.

"I always imagined the Blade of Rebels to be powerful. For that to be part of their appeal. To be inspiring, they had to convince us that the Lightguard could be defeated, and that therefore, they would be better than the rest of us. You have, I'll admit, become more adept at the Shade than I thought you would, but you will still need my help in the face of the Lightguard. Perhaps we should leave Essence-Gathering to focus on what we *can* do. The wielding of the Half-Moon blades, the development of the Mind's Eye."

I shook my head. "We can do that, but I'm not giving up. It

took me years just to Weave, I'm not going to be put off Essence-Gathering because I didn't manage after a few days."

Aelia did not move for a second, but then slowly nodded. "I can respect that. Maybe you can't do Essence-Gathering now, but when the time comes, you'll be ready."

Training then moved on to my Mind's Eye. Aelia got me to practice going from one form to the other and using the half-moon blades.

We focused on the most difficult pairings, which involved finding a link between forms in different categories of my Mind's Eye. There was no connection between the half-moon blades and vines. Often, when I tried to pair the spears with claws, or blades with fire, the forms spluttered to nothing.

Aelia counseled patience, the most infuriating piece of advice one could hear.

With my frustration, and my fear, and my anger, I stood in front of the statue of the Emperor.

And I absolutely let rip at it.

Something about the fact that I had just been in the Emperor's presence, and the fact that he had almost killed me and my family, made me hit the target with increased fury.

I hit at the shape with the half-moon blades and gave the statue of the Emperor a new net of scars. All of my outrage was vented into the damage I inflicted on the statue, and as a result I learned to use my weapons more and more interchangeably, giving in to my every impulse to carve the marble with all the blades at my disposal.

I breathed, meditated, then started again.

I stood in front of that smug, self-satisfied face and disfigured it.

Here, though, I managed to combine my weapons in different ways. I thought of the ancient warriors of the Therians, and how they'd been punished for standing up to the Emperor. The reminder of their ancient techniques, mimicking the forms of nature, allowed me to form a mental tunnel, linking the chamber of blades to the chamber of natural forms.

The link was the past. The link was the Therians, who used both shadow-steel and shadow-vines.

The link was the Swallow.

With this in mind, I could damage the statue even further. I slashed at the statue with my staff blades, then combined it with flames and vines. I even experimented with merging the half-moon blades and the claws, seeing if I could have the circular steel shape wrap around my knuckles for close combat.

None of it made for particularly stable forms. I was trying to do too much at once. But whenever the Weaves became stable, even if it was only for mere moments, I scarred the statue.

"You know, it occurs to me that perhaps Essence-Gathering simply requires just readjusting our approach," said Aelia, contemplating the scarred visage of the Emperor before us. "The people who gather Essence do so out of greed. Out of self-interest. It goes beyond the natural balance of light and dark, like wolfing down an entire feast by yourself, just to sate your own hunger. Perhaps that is why Cizin managed to do it, and why it drove him mad."

"But the Lightguard manage it."

"Because they are taught to be entitled. To wolf down the feast."

"What are you getting at?"

She shrugged. "We focus so much on balance, on calm, on meditation and control. Perhaps we should borrow from the Lightguard, and address that hunger, there at the pit of our stomach. Our outrage."

"Our emotions?' I frowned. "I was always taught that emotions simply make us lose control. That they are no good for Weaving. I mean, Cizin certainly had that want, that desire. Look where it got him."

"Yet he could gather Essence, and shadows, like no one before or since. If we are going to follow in his footsteps, perhaps we need to borrow a little from him. We can't let our emotions get away from us, but perhaps we can try to harness them."

I looked at the decimated form of the Emperor in front of me. "I definitely have some rage to spare."

Aelia nodded. "My thoughts exactly. It seemed to give you clarity, somehow."

She turned away, leaving the Atrium. "Now get some rest. Tonight, we rebel."

Chapter Thirty-Seven

Dusk seemed to come early that day. It felt like I'd barely rested at all.

I meditated, cycled, and got dressed. For the first time, I donned the full cloak of the Blade of Rebels which Cleander had commissioned for me.

I had spent my entire life in loose, ill-fitting tunics, stitched together from hand-me-downs and rags taken from the fallen. Nothing I'd ever worn compared to the material which clung to my sides and limbs now. They were comfortable, and allowed for all the movements I would need for my deeds that night, but also dramatic, making me feel bigger than I was. Strips of tight-fitting metal followed the contours of my body, armoring me without impeding my movements. Flecks of gold nodded at the power I was supposed to embody. It was directly to spite the Citadel's custom, that only the Emperor wore gold.

Once I'd pulled on the cowl, hiding my face, I climbed out of the atrium. The clothes made me feel like a predator looking for prey.

The city itself was my prey.

With the memory of my near execution still burning in my heart, I prowled across the rooftops as the last embers of sunlight burned out and the dark inched across the heavens.

Unlike the last appearance of the Blade of Rebels, tonight I did not have to go far. Right next to the palace, there was a wide street leading to a building with a large entrance, propped up by columns large enough to hold cliffsides.

Aelia said it was called the Curia, or the Senate House.

Large fires, with pans of burning coal and oils, lit up the entrance, sending long shadows of the columns across the city; the black forms radiating out in the shape of spears. Aqueducts arching across the buildings, sending Elixir down from the cliffside above, onto the building's roof, and then spilling down into the streets below.

The whole thing looked impenetrable—and indeed, in some ways, it was. There were Lightguard posted at every column, keeping watch on the street leading up to it.

Luckily, I had not come by road, but by rooftop and cliff. As the Curia was near the top of the city, it hugged the cliff. I'd be meeting with Aelia and a group of warriors in a cleft to the building's left.

"Well met, Blade," said Aelia. She scanned me up and down. "So, the costume fits."

"I suppose so." I suddenly felt a bit embarrassed about my grand, theatrical robes. But then, as I peered behind Aelia to the group which accompanied her, I saw that the entire company was clothed in black, hiding their features.

We all were walking, fighting secrets, even to each other.

Even in the midst of a rebellion, even as we put our lives into one another's hands, we refused to trust each other.

The suspicion angered me before I realized that it was all for the best. If the people got wind of my identity, that would put my people in danger. I didn't want to show my face, even to them.

Perhaps that's part of the problem, came the thought. But I pushed it aside. This was Cleander's rebellion to organize, not mine. If it had been down to me, I would have done it differently, with less subterfuge and manipulation. I probably would not have lasted a minute.

Aelia got me close, and we huddled together in the cleft of

the cliff. She outlined her plan, as detailed by Cleander. To me, the it seemed risky. But, as all the hooded figures nodded their heads, I followed suit.

I didn't have a choice.

I had to make the first move. After checking that there were no scouts in the sky, I crept to the edge, and looked out at the temple, another rebel climbed down. I waited for them to create a diversion, and it soon came.

A rebel snaked along an aqueduct, creeping along the edge of the canal as it bridged across the street leading to the Curia. They made a light-hammer, and with great weight slammed it into the side of the canal.

Immediately, some Elixir spewed out of the side where the stone had crumbled, cascading down onto the slabs below and glistening on the streets.

There were shouts at this strange incident, and Senate guards rushed forward to see what was happening. The warrior, however, was nowhere to be seen, only where we were, at our higher elevation, could we see them floating down the aqueduct, borne by the liquid which had not splashed into the streets below.

With the attention of the guards looking at the leaking aqueduct, trying to judge whether the cascading liquid was the result of a crumbling old stone construction or subterfuge, I made my move.

I gathered a string of shadows and turned them into a shadow-hook, which I then threw across the air and onto the roof of the Curia. Satisfied that the claws had taken hold on the far side, I hooked the vine on the cliff. As soon as this was done, the rebels lowered themselves onto the vine, and pulled themselves along by hooking their knees over the rope.

I maintained the vine until everyone was across, then went ahead. I made my way across, back in the company of the Uprising. I let the form fade away, and it was like it had never been there, the shadows retreating back their homes.

I caught my breath before we continued the mission. Soundlessly, the group of rebels communicated through a look, and we inched across the rooftop. Walking silently, we peered over a parapet into the atrium below.

The space was about fifty times the size of the atrium in my quarters. It stretched across a large square, so wide that one would have to shout to make themselves heard from one end to another.

What I saw disgusted me.

The sight made me feel sick to my stomach, a revolting example of why the rebellion was needed.

It was, simply put, the most decadent thing I had ever witnessed.

I had expected a sober political gathering, with people sat around debating issues. Which, in some way, I supposed they were. There *were* about fifty people sitting in an amphitheater, talking to each other in their finery.

But that was where the similarity ended.

They barely seemed to even pay lip-service to the idea of a political union. The men and women gathered below lounged about, with enormous platters of food at their side, more than they could ever be able to eat. They glugged huge goblets of wine, staining their extravagant clothes. The atmosphere was one of festivity and debauchery, not debate. People were cheerily talking over each other, burping as they laughed, and some seemed completely inebriated. As I scanned the atrium, I saw one person vomiting in the corner, and this seemed to surprise absolutely no one.

Amongst the Senators were a whole host of servers, lining the walls of the room. There were some guards, but mostly the Senators were surrounded by dancers, musicians, and poets. A lot of them were in various states of undress, men and women showing enough of their perfect forms that it felt wrong to look at them.

"This is the seat of power for all of the Canyonlands?" I muttered under my breath. I needn't have bothered: in all the merriment beneath, no one would have heard me.

Aelia nodded gravely. Even though I could only see her eyes, I saw that she too held the sight with the same disgust as I did. "It's gotten worse, over the years. They care less and less. This is the problem with people who live too long, they stop caring."

"How were these people elected?"

Aelia shrugged. "They all, in their prime, were impressive in some way. But they all have lost whatever they had. They barely even train or cycle anymore. That would be too much effort. They just let their servants and guards do everything for them."

I looked at the center of their circle, at the epicenter of it all was the Emperor. He seemed to be enjoying himself more than the others, roaring with laughter at some crass story a senator was recounting. Clearly enjoying the reaction, the senator continued, shouting louder and louder until her words were accompanied by wine-colored spit.

"Why doesn't he get rid of them? Find new people to run the lands?" I said, although I didn't truly need a response. The answer was right in front of me.

"They're his friends. He enjoys their company. That way, he can drink and eat himself into oblivion with others like him."

I shook my head. "In my valley, we also had a hierarchy where the important people lived high up, looking down upon the others. But at least they had the decency to pretend that they were *honorable*. At least they acted like they *deserved* that power."

Aelia nodded. "We need fresh blood. The world needs the Uprising. This lot down here aren't capable of waging wars or defending us against the threat of the Demons. Maybe they were, many years ago. But not anymore."

"Silence!" the Emperor suddenly barked below, getting all of the senators to quiet down, along with the music. There was a roar of disapproval among his audience, who wanted to continue the festivities. "Now, now, my counterpart has called for a meeting, you drunkards. You know how much he loves a meeting!"

Lucian gestured to Cleander, who was sitting to his side.

Truth be told, I hadn't noticed him before, he didn't seem to take up the space of everyone else. He was quietly sipping at his goblet. I guessed that he had barely touched the liquid inside.

"Well, come out with it!" the Emperor shouted. "What is it, Cleander, that you must discuss, and interrupt our revelry?"

Cleander stood up, his slim frame and perfectly tailored clothes coming to the fore as he took up the speaker's position by the Emperor at the center of the amphitheater.

"We need," he said in his dulcet tones, "to talk about the potential enemy of the state. The person whom the rebels are rallying around. While the Emperor wisely brought him on his side in the announcement this morning, but more needs to be done. He could still be a thorn in our side."

He paused for effect.

"I am speaking, of course, of Jason, Son of Ventos."

Chapter Thirty-Eight

My throat went dry.

"Why is he talking about me?" I grunted to Aelia.

"Who else is he supposed to talk about? You're the talk of the town," Aelia said. "All of this is just a pretext to get them here, remember? You're the best pretext Cleander has."

My brows furrowed. "Seems like he never seems to miss a chance to bring me up." Aelia was about to say something before I cut her off. "I get it, I'm supposed to leave the politics to others. It would be easier if I wasn't constantly being put in the center of things, though."

Aelia eyed me curiously. "Have you ever considered that he might be doing it on purpose? The more he talks about you as a problem, the more influential you seem. We will need the senate on our side when Cleander takes over. It would help if they already respected you."

I made a face like I had swallowed a sour piece of fruit. I pointed downwards. "*They're* going to *remain* in power? This sorry lot? I thought we were aiming for a clean slate!'

"There's never a completely clean slate. Not when it comes to matters of government."

I shook my head. "Whatever, keep your rotten senate. As long as my people are safe, your city can eat itself for all I care."

I made a point of looking down, cutting off the conversation to listen to what Cleander was saying to the members of the Senate.

Aelia made to do the same, but then decided against it, turning to me once more.

"I don't believe you, just so you know."

I frowned. I wasn't sure what she meant.

"You're not just the man fighting for himself and his kin anymore," she said. "I can see it, especially when you wear the cloak. You're not just a warrior for the Hollow. You're a rebel of the Canyonlands. Much as you would like to just focus on your family and friends, you've seen too much for that now. You're fighting for everyone."

I paused for a moment, wondering if she was right about me. Aelia had told me that I had to look beyond myself and see the bigger picture. But I wasn't entirely sure how much I'd done it. On the one hand, my thoughts were constantly focused on my home, my sister, my father, my friends.

Yet I couldn't say that I didn't care about the city as well. Perhaps it was the time I'd spent on the rooftops, observing how poorly the Lower Levels were treated. Perhaps it was the interactions with people on the streets like the fishmonger who'd told me he was too afraid to use the Shade.

If I was honest, most of all I thought of Aelia. She'd lost all her family and friends due to the Emperor, an orphan who'd dedicated her life to infiltrating the enemy and was hated for it.

Her words lodged inside me. They made me uncomfortable, somehow. Yennenga's words used to do the same. I'd learnt, a long time ago, to realize that it probably meant that there was a ring of truth in them.

I didn't like it. Whenever the task before me seemed insurmountable, whenever the city seemed to be swallowing me up, I'd always reassured myself by focusing on the singular goal of returning to the Hollow and keeping what was left of my village safe.

If Aelia was right, and I was invested in something bigger

than the Hollow, then would I ever truly be able to go back? How would I spend my days in a valley on the other side of the world, waiting out wars and not getting involved?

"Quiet, you lot!" shouted the Emperor, the clamor of the Senators had risen again. "Let's listen to what my clever counterpart has to say."

Cleander nodded in appreciation as the Senate quietened. "Thank you, my lord," he said, bowing his head. "I have called this meeting because we still have work to do. The Emperor was wise to present Jason as an ally for all to see today. But Jason is no performer, he was not convincing enough. My informants tell me the rabble still see him as their hero. They think that he is playing us, and merely pretending to obey."

The emperor grunted with irritation. "Is there no end to the idiocy of the Lower Levels? I have Jason in my pocket!"

One member of the senate cried out. "Is it true, though? Could he be a part of the rebellion?"

Lucian belly laughed, putting his greasy hands on his stomach as he tipped his head back and cackled up towards the sky. "He would love to be, I'm sure. But I have all he holds dear hostage. He is under our heel, I can guarantee you that."

"The question then," Cleander intervened, regaining control of the conversation, " is this. What do we do? How can we quell his part, intentional or not, in the rebellion?' He turned to a woman with a heap of hair, tressed into intricate patterns. "Lady Livilla has a solution to propose to you all."

"Who's she?" I whispered to Aelia.

"She's the Senator for the Experiments," responded Aelia. "She manages them for the Emperor."

Aelia's words were tossed aside as nothing, but they hit me differently. This woman's job, day to day, was to ensure the exploitation of Shadowkind across the lands. Hate boiled in me as I watched her rise, smoothing down her wine-stained chiton, a proud, gleeful look on her features.

"Dear Senators," she said, the toothiness of her smile suggesting falsehood. The pomp of the words did not seem appropriate, it was returned with cheers, and someone making some joke which I could not make out. I sensed that she liked the veneer of decorum and the power she believed it reflected on her. "It struck me that we don't need to manage the image of Jason, but that of the Experiments. All the rabble know is that the Emperor's enemies, many years ago, were moved to valleys across the land to aid with the secret projects as penance. But word has travelled across the city, over the years. They sense, even if they do not know, that the Experiments are no frolic in the lakes."

"Get to your point, Livilla!" ordered the Emperor.

"Well, why not show to the people how much of a success it has been? Why not show the results of our hard work? We can sway everyone if we demonstrate that Jason's people have not been the victims of a punishment, but key collaborators in the creation of what could save us. The people are scared about a war, right? Well, let's show them how protected they are. How we have developed the perfect weapon to fight the demons. Of course, they don't need to know *how* they were developed."

The Emperor frowned and gulped down his drink. "You mean… the Void? Or whatever they're called?"

Whatever they're called.

Rage boiled within me. He'd set up the Experiments when he'd still been a warrior who was concerned about protecting his people. Echo the Endless had shown that to me. But it was clear, now, that the Emperor didn't care one jot about the Experiments, or the results of them. He'd been happy to just let them happen, a means of control, nothing more.

Which meant that my people had suffered and died, and the Emperor hadn't even noticed.

"Quite, my lord," Senator Livilla said, the delight of holding her audience all too visible in her eyes. "We show them the Void."

There was a grumble among the Senators. "We have kept our work with the Void secret for centuries!" someone cried. "The people will be even more ready to revolt if they see this! Are you mad?"

Livilla took delight in this. "I just think it's time for a change of strategy. The people don't need to be told how the creatures were made, but they do need to see them." She shot a quizzical look at Cleander, who nodded back at her. At his acquiescence, she put up her hands, stretching her fingers up to the sky.

Streams of light shot out of her palms, streaking across the air, and forming a gigantic shape.

"She's an imagist?" I asked Aelia, who nodded.

"Many of the inventors are."

The light beams Wove together until there was a picture hovering over the Senate. The moment it took shape, I felt my heart leap in shock.

Displayed before me, was an image of the Void—the monsters which had plagued my home. The beast was how I recognized it, with its outstretched wings, its long skull with spear-head teeth, its claws as sharp as swords.

I heard Aelia breathe in sharply. "That's what your people were fighting?"

My jaw clenched. "They sent waves upon waves of these creatures. They weren't all like this one. They were tweaking it as they went, making it more and more deadly, measuring its success by how well it killed us."

"Skies above..." The reality of my former life hit Aelia hard.

"This one's different again," I muttered.

It was true. It wasn't just the monster I knew and loathed. It was distinct in significant, and horrifying, ways.

For a start, it was larger than any Void that I was used to confronting, far larger. The image, if it reflected the accurate size of the monster, was that of a beast that took up a huge portion of the amphitheater, at least twice the size of the ones I'd slain in the Hollow. Its size brought the details of the creature into horrible detail, its black veins, the translucent grey skin in its wings, the dirt layering its claws.

The image of the creature looked this way and that or at least it seemed to. Its head swayed back and forth, as if taking in its audience. Although it couldn't, of course, even if it was really here, it had no eyes.

"Last I reported," said Livilla, "we had improved upon the creatures by increasing their abilities to travel through underwater channels. We thought that we had reached the heights of our creation. But, with an experiment in the South, we managed to give the creature one more quality."

She flicked some fingers, and the image morphed.

Suddenly, the image was covered in the shape of flames, leaping off its back, trailing the lines of its neck and wings. It made the shadow-form of the creature seem even bigger, even more indomitable.

"The Void we created before were brittle, and quick to flame. But now they have a coating of substance, coming from their pores, which makes them impervious to heat and flame. They can travel through the hellfire of the Underworld, and never stop in their slaughter. I give you, my Emperor, the Void Enflamed."

There was a roar of appreciation amongst the senators. I had the opposite reaction. My main defense against the Void had been shooting black flames at them, copying the breath of a dragon. Now, it seemed that this would make no difference to them whatsoever.

"Well, well, well," said the Emperor. "This will certainly silence the naysayers. Who would have thought, the Experiments, provided something worthwhile after all. Let's see the Uprising tell us we're not prepared for war now!" He raised his goblet, demanding more drink. "I think this calls for celebration!"

Livilla cleared her throat. "I should say, Emperor, that the Void Enflamed are still in development. There are only a few of them in existence, and they have been somewhat, shall we say, difficult to tame. Should there actually be a war with Cizin…"

Emperor waved his hand, dismissing her. "There *is* no war!" he barked with impatience. "How many times do I have to say it? I defeated Cizin years ago—he's dead! It's all in the minds of the rabble in the Lower Levels! All we need to do is show them that we have the weapons should there ever be a threat again, then tell them to get back to work!"

This got a big reaction, the crowd barked out their appreciation, and they all sank into their wine, some spilling it down their chins. With the goblets drained, some even threw them in the air, causing a flurry of servants to tidy up after them.

Cleander whispered in the Emperor's ear, and he nodded.

The emperor held out a hand, beckoning everyone listen once more. "I think a demonstration is in order. Before Jason and a company go down into the Underworld, he will travel the streets with the image of this improved Void, claiming that it is the result of the hard work of the Experiments. He still has too much tongue for my liking, let's see him prostrate before our labor, and introduce our new killing machine to the people. That will remind him who's in control here, while further cementing his status as an ally. If the people need reminding of the worth of the Experiments, well then, let the man from the Experiments himself, tell them. He can tell them how many lives the Void will save and teach them to love their Emperor once more."

A wave of nausea passed through me. Surely, this was one cruelty too far. I was going to have to *celebrate* the Void, the very creatures who had almost killed everyone in the Hollow? I was going to have to parade through the city, and sing its praises?

I felt like I was going to throw up. My skin, my insides—everything felt like it was twisting in discomfort. It wasn't just that I didn't want to do it, I didn't think that I was even capable of it. How could I praise the Experiments, the very enslavement of the Shadowkind?

And even if I managed, how would I ever sleep again? How would I be able to look into the eyes of my sister, of Yen, and not want to drop dead in shame?

I felt a hand on my arm. It was Aelia.

"That anger," she hissed. "Don't let it take over it. Channel it, allow it to sharpen your blade."

I nodded, trying to calm myself, doing my best to recover, and slow my breathing.

"Good," she said. "It's almost time."

I grit my teeth.

Aelia looked down, and noticed something that Cleander was doing, he was tapping the fingers of one hand on the knuckles of another. "That's the sign," she said. She turned to the other rebels. "Weaves at the ready, warriors. It's time to break up the party."

Chapter Thirty-Nine

Three things happened at once.

I'd been informed about them. Aelia had told me exactly what would happen.

That didn't make them any less incredible.

In quick succession, worthy of the discipline of the Shadowfront, the rebels turned the Senate room into a maelstrom of chaos.

First, a light-blast was lobbed into the center of the room, one of the rebels had been Essence-Gathering while we observed their discussion. The orb of light plunged down into the atrium, and the very moment it hit the floor, it was as if lightning was in the room. White light blazed through the air, and with it came an eruption of surprised screams and shouts.

With the people in the room in a daze, scrabbling over one another to escape, another light-blast was dropped down onto a nest of furniture. Tables and chairs erupted into flame, immediately spewing smoke. Some Riverkind also created steam, directing water toward the flames.

As a result, while the Senators were crawling, and hands and arms pressed to their eyes while recovering from the flash of light, a swamp of smoke and steam flowed around them, veiling the entire room.

Into the chaos, I rappelled down on a shadow vine, dropping into the fog. The other rebels followed me, sliding down my vine and leaping into the mist. The few who had created the steam fog continued to do so, a stream of essence sprouting from their fingers and thickening the smokescreen, while everyone else wove weapons of light, shadow, and ice in their hands.

The warriors merged with the smoke as the fighting started.

Even though we had not been dazed by the explosion, our visibility was as clouded as our enemies'. We had the advantage of surprise, and it was a potent one. As I traveled through the smoke, the forms were vague, silhouettes against mist, shadows among shadows. Sometimes I only saw the light-weapons clashing, as if light was battling itself, swords floated in the air, clashing against each other, accompanied by the hum of their formations and the disembodied cries of battle.

I, in turn, created my own weapon, the half-moon blades at the ends of a staff. The moment the shadows interlocked, hardening into place, a guard emerged from the fog in front of me, and I immediately put it to use.

My training with Aelia kicked in, and I was immediately grateful for how much she had trained me. The Lightguard in front of me was wielding a large light-scimitar with a long and thick curved blade. The way it cut through the mist was like the smoke was fleeing its presence.

I spun on my heels, wheeling the half-moon blade in an arc. It carved through the smoke and whacked away the scimitar, beating back the attack with decisive power. This, Aelia had told me, was the advantage of my staff's size. Fighting with the staff was a rhythm of building up momentum with the swing, then letting the momentum drive it into my opponent.

The guard grunted, and I saw a glimpse of my opponent's face through the whorls of shadow and steam: a man with a square jaw, and an ugly look in his eye.

I pounced, driving my staff low to swing at his knees. He

leapt back, swiping as he did, but he was off balance, and I dodged his attack easily.

I darted about, twirling, my cloak billowing the mist, and screamed as I swung my half-moon in another circle.

I let the momentum do the work for me, and barely felt my weapon's bite as it slashed across his midriff, making my opponent double up and crumple on the floor. I left him groaning there and pushed further into the clouds of shadow.

My feet bumped into bodies, not just guards, but senators too. My body pumped with adrenaline and hate, I did not stop to mourn them. Our mission had been to remove the senators, kidnapping them. This, Cleander had decided, would both make for good hostages, hamper the running of the Empire, and also show morality by keeping the death rate down.

Yet a dead senator was still a senator removed from power, one person fewer to clog up the canyons with injustice and misery.

I had been uncomfortable with it before, but after seeing the Senators at work, and in the heat of battle, I did not care.

They had lived for longer than I could ever imagine, far longer than they deserved. They'd had their time and had used it to poison the world.

A sweep of movement came into sight, just to my right, a rebel battling a Lightguard. I surged forward to help them but came to a halt as the Lightguard bested them, plunging a light-spear into their chest.

Spinning, I looked to go somewhere else, and find a senator to take for my own.

Or—better yet—the Emperor himself.

I heard a cry, someone shouting "Swallow's flock!"

That was the signal, so I activated my Senses to better make my way through the wisps of shadow. It became a confusing mosaic of light, dark and mist, but through the haze I could discern a group amassing in the far corner.

We were gathering to make our exit.

I dismissed my Senses, to get a better sense of detail of what was around me as I ran after them.

Within a few leaps across the amphitheater, the clouds dispersed, and the group of rebels were there. A few were missing, but many had accomplished their goal, they had Senators in front of them, daggers at their throats, and were dragging their hostages toward a set of stairs. The politicians looked frozen in fear, their eyes bulging at the blades touching their throats, crying out in distress.

There was a thickening line of Lightguards in front of them, advancing, waiting their time to pounce, shouting threats at the rebels. Their advance was stayed by Cleander, who was screaming out orders on the sideline.

"Lower your blades! They will kill the senators!"

I ran, hoping to go around the line of Lightguard and join the rebels with their hostages. But I didn't get far, something wrapped around my foot, and I was flung to the floor.

A light-whip.

I twisted to try and avoid it, but not in enough time before a light-net, charged with pain, was flung over me. I swiped at it with my staff, but its edge caught my elbow, pulsing a charge of agony through my entire right side.

I cried out, and for a moment I was debilitated, unable to move. Above me a figure emerged from the mists, a Lightguard with a coil of hair tightened into a bun, and a look that was thirsty for blood.

She held her hands, reusing the light from her net to create a wholly new one, ready to cast it down on me.

I moaned, willing myself to move, but found my movements sluggish. The net was held high, then flung down, spreading enough to spill all over the top half of my body.

Until it wasn't. A blade pierced through the smoke and intervened, batting the net straight back into the guard's unsuspecting torso. The guard shrieked as she collapsed, convulsing on the steps of the amphitheater.

A hand hauled me to my feet. Aelia.

"Thanks," I murmured.

"Don't thank me, return the favor," she grunted.

I looked around and saw what she was hinting at. The

company of rebels was withdrawing up the set of stairs, as planned. We couldn't join them, there were Lightguard blocking us. Aelia and I were by ourselves in the Senate room, with no company but enemies and a smokescreen that was dispersing more and more with each heartbeat.

the more it dispersed, the more guards it revealed. All of them were thirsty for blood, and all were looking our way.

There was only one way out, and it was the way we came.

As guards began to sprint in our direction, I looked up and, letting my half-moon blades disperse, shot up a shadow-hook to the roof we had fallen from earlier.

Aelia and I barely waited for the black cord to fully materialize before we grabbed it, hauling ourselves up to freedom, adrenaline making us wrench ourselves faster than we thought possible.

It was not a moment too soon. The guards around us started throwing projectiles in our direction. I narrowly missed a spear entering my foot as I pulled myself higher on the vine into the rising mist. Luckily, there was still just enough smoke wafting up to give us some cover, although some light-spear and arrows whistled past our ears and brushed my cloak on my ascent.

We clambered to the top, swinging onto the roof.

I peered back down at the vine dropping down into the fog, and saw that some warriors had followed us, pulling themselves up on the same cord we had.

I prepared to let my shadows disperse, to get the cord to de-materialize, dropping the guards back down.

But I was in a vengeful mood, and eager to put my training to use.

Using my Mind's Eye, I paired the vine in front of me with the flames of a dragon, I gathered more shadows, and infused them into the form of the vine, until the whole of the cord sprouted black flames. The climbers howled as the flames seared their hands, and one by one they let go, toppling from the shadow-cord and disappearing into the mist.

Serves them right.

"Time to exit, Jason," Aelia urged.

I followed her lead. Leaving the sight of the Senate room, I raced along the roof.

As we ran, the rebels in our company emerged from the stairway—about eight of them. They'd managed to bring three hostages. Lightguard chased after them, pointing their swords and spears at them, waiting for them to make a wrong move.

The rebels backed to the edge, next to it, an aqueduct flowed Elixir down into the city. This was to be our escape route.

But in order to escape, they needed time, a rebel was Essence-Gathering, creating an orb of light which was essential to get everyone out safely.

Escaping wouldn't be easy. Around the rebels, a mass of Lightguard were gathering in front of them, bearing their arms. No matter how much the rebels screamed at them to stay back, threatening to kill the hostages, the Lightguard were undeterred, advancing. Above them, lines of light gathered across the sky, showing some scouts were coming our way.

We would have to move fast.

"Jason, I've got an idea," said Aelia.

Chapter Forty

"Can you weave a vine of fire like that again?" Aelia asked.

I nodded.

"Give me one end, and then ignite it when I give the signal!"

I did as I was told, a gout of shadows came to my hands, and I knotted them into a vine.

"Tie it to my blade!" she instructed, a dagger materializing in her fist. I did as I was told, she made it easier by creating a hilt to knot around it in a figure eight.

I had hardly even begun when Aelia threw herself forward, her strides so long that it seemed more like she was flying. Her figure, cloaked in black, tore across the roof, with me following behind her. The vine trailed longer and longer as it stretched from Aelia's dagger and my hands.

She tore across the line dividing the rebels and the Lightguard, the boundary tightened between two snarling hordes. There were weapons, made of gold and silver light as well as shadow and ice lining that divide but it did not deter Aelia. She stayed close to the rebels, who gave her cover by throwing projectiles at the Lightguard and got them to take a step back.

When the clamor of weaponry was too thick, she cried out... and threw herself down, skidding across the tiles and passing under the spikes. Rolling, she made it to the far side of the corner of the roof. Leaping up again, she curled behind a Lightguard and dug her dagger into his shoulders.

There was now a shadow-cord stretching from a guard's shoulders on the far side of the battle, to me.

"Ignite!" Aelia bellowed.

I obeyed. Using my Mind's Eye, I combined the dragon's flames with the vine, until black flames overlined it, leaping from the streak of shadows.

It created a dark, midnight fire between the rebels and the guards.

The Lightguard retreated, stepping away from the black glare of the fire. It caused a ripple of shock, and I realized that these soldiers might not have ever seen the Shade used in such a way, or at such a grand scale.

It gave the rebels the time they needed.

"Go!" Aelia ordered. The first rebel turned away from the fight and went to the edge of the roof. The chute carrying Elixir down into the city was almost directly below them, the river held in the air by stone. They leapt and landed in the water, getting whisked away into the city.

The rest of the rebels followed, wrestling their hostages with them, plunging them into the waters, and getting carried off too, a stream of black figures pouring off the roof and plunging into the moving waters of the Elixir.

Some guards tried to leap over the line of black flames or stamp it down. It was wrenched from my grasp, and the cord dissipated.

Chaos broke out across the roof. The Lightguard went to pursue the rebels, getting to the chute, and it was all Aelia could do to hold them off. Her daggers back in her hands, she parried and danced, doing her best to hold them back.

She screamed at me to get out of there and jumped off into the aqueduct.

She was right. I had no chance against the amount of guards now on the roof. I started to run, charging to the edge of the roof where I could jump into the aqueduct.

I was not far from the edge, only a few footsteps away. Still, it was enough time for some guards to try and pounce on me. I Wove a staff of half-moon blades and wheeled it side to side, knocking the blades away as they came toward me. I didn't even look, all I did was run. I felt blades rip through my cloak and punch into my armor, stopping the blades from piercing my skin. At other times I was not so lucky, as spears scraped across my limbs or shoulders in ways that nicked my skin and made me howl.

Still, I did not stop.

I ran to the edge, and jumped off, and for a moment the world blurred into spinning night.

I landed on my side in an awkward dive, immediately immersed in Elixir. The liquid was like a broth, frothing with movement. It was like being in the clouds of a lightning storm.

My face emerged, and I saw that the water was carrying me down at considerable speed. The sides of the aqueduct were charging fast enough that the current was carrying me away from the Senate House.

Light-spears hummed into the rocky sides of the aqueduct around me, and some fizzled in the froth of the Elixir, but I was speeding down the chute too fast. None hit me.

I managed to turn in the speeding liquid and look back at the roof of the Senate House, many of the Lightguard were jumping into the aqueduct after me, trying to pursue me, while the scouts coming from the sky were closer now, hovering above the city and trying to follow my course down into the metropolis.

We had planned for this. I was relieved as I passed by a rebel warrior who was perched on the canal, here was where we had blasted a hole in the aqueduct earlier. I, along with all the other rebels, should have been spat back onto the streets in front of the building we had just invaded. But instead a Riverkind had stayed there, creating a sheet of ice to momentarily repair the damage we'd done.

As it was, I shot across the hole like it had never existed, the gap plugged by a stretch of ice. Behind me, I heard the ice crack as the rebel destroyed it and leapt into the chute behind me.

Satisfied, I heard the surprise as all the Lightguard who had followed us were suddenly thrown out of the aqueduct, with the gap no longer bridged by Woven ice.

The aqueduct bore me down through a twisting trail into the city, weaving between one building and the next, the stars spun above me. I entered a tunnel, and the Elixir writhed through the cliff, before emerging again in an aqueduct which traveled over the roofs of a different street. There started to be many turnoffs, leading into various atria and different parts of the city, but a Riverkind rebel had done their job well, creating ice-walls which funneled me in the right direction.

Soon, I could not see the scout above, and although I was still diving along in a miasma of Elixir, I allowed myself to breathe a sigh of relief.

We'd invaded the site of the elite of the city and made it out intact.

But my breath of relief came too soon.

A figure loomed ahead blocking the chute. Someone clutched to the side of the canal, their legs still in the flow of water, trying to drag themselves out.

I didn't have time to react before the current drove me into them, knocking them off their perch, dragging them down back into the flow.

The moment it happened, I spun, and my surroundings became a dance of stars and froth. The Elixir stung my eyes and made everything mash together in a vague world. I barely made out the white robes of a chiton, marking the body as one of a hostage senator, before I felt hands on me, driving me down into the water, nails on my face.

What followed was a tumble, a scramble, as I was tossed this way and that. The liquid sprang into my nose and stung my eyes, and I had to tear off my cowl to get air. My breaths came in short bursts whenever I was able to put my lips above the surface, and the air was often accompanied by enough liquid to make me cough and splutter.

There was no fight here, no battle. No focus for perfect weaves and forms, no duels. No, this was a panicked scrap, not far from the tussles of children. I clutched at hair and clothes and threw my fists at whatever seemed near. I tried to tear their hands from my face as it tried to push me underneath the water, tried to hold them far away, but they kept coming, digging into my cheeks, prying at my face.

I could tell that this person was as panicked as I was. I could sense it in their motions, which were as frantic and uncoordinated as my own. But I could tell, also, that they were determined to kill me, to get rid of me. Fear had driven this person into a bloodlust. If I wanted to survive, I would have to kill them.

We wrestled as we tumbled through the network of aqueducts, tossed this way and that, interlocked as we plunged through the Citadel.

When an unexpected turn threw my legs to one side, I hit my head on the wall of the aqueduct, pain howling through my skull. My vision was even more blurred than it had been before.

My enemy seized the opportunity to wrestle on top of me, and, putting their hands around my neck and driving me down into the Elixir. My head was plunged into the boil, so deep that it hit the bottom of the canal, bouncing painfully against the bottom. Liquid poured into my airways.

I couldn't see or hear anything. The only thing that existed was the churn of the Elixir and the insistent hands on my throat. I coughed, but it still felt like my lungs were filling with water.

I tried to scramble and tear myself out, to turn and make my way to the surface, but the villain's hold on me was cruel and stubborn.

With nothing to see or hear, and barely any air, I did what my instincts told me to. I found my opponent's face with my fingers, and pushed, trying to tear my assailant off me. I pushed at what felt like their jaw, but my reach wasn't far enough, even though I thrust the jaw away, their grip on my neck did not lessen.

All that I'd done was push their face further out of the water, high up in the air. Away from danger.

While I continued to drown.

Then everything went black, all of a sudden. We'd been diverted into a tunnel.

And my assailant's grip on me immediately went limp. They collapsed on top of me as if they had been struck by an arrow.

I shoved them off, and put my head out for air, spluttering as I coughed out the liquid in my throat.

The current slowed, and I was able to calm myself. The senator who'd almost drowned me floated, unmoving, beside me. I fumbled enough to grab some part of their chiton and tried to lift them up: if they were unconscious, I could save them from drowning.

With enough focus to activate my Senses, I made the tunnel turn in shapes and lines, making the darkness penetrable. I looked over, and gasped, evacuating the last bits of Elixir from my mouth.

Two things were inescapably true about my assailant.

The first was that I recognized her, she was the senator in charge of the Experiments. The one who'd proudly come up with the new Void and demonstrated it to the Emperor just earlier.

She was dead.

When I'd pushed at her face, I'd lifted her head to a degree that her head had smashed into the low entrance of the tunnel. In any case, now that we were in a slower current, a huge amount of blood was darkening the liquid around us, and when I felt the back of her head, bits felt missing in a way which made me sick to my stomach.

By the time I arrived, floating, into a channel where the rebels were gathered, fishing everyone out of the water, I was retching.

Chapter Forty-One

I did not know yet what to make of it all. When Aelia's hand came, guiding me out of the pool, and the world was still spinning, like I was still in the froth. I could just about make out that we were in the tunnel where I'd met the meeting of the Uprising a few nights ago. I could also make out the other rebels, who were thrusting gags to muffle the senators before picking and shoving them down the tunnel.

I couldn't react that fast. My emotions were too raw for me to do anything but get out of the water and sit on my knees there, dripping, looking down at the pool in front of me, and the body of that senator.

"We knew we weren't going to get them all alive," sneered Aelia, recognizing the body. "Good riddance, I say. She can be washed down into the lake without ceremony, for all the suffering she's caused to our people."

With that, Aelia Wove a shadow-mace and knocked at the barrier of ice which had brought me to a stop. Now all the liquid gushed away again, joining the main tunnel bringing all the Elixir down into the depths of the city.

The body was taken away, then dropped mercilessly into the shoot, falling away from sight with the pool of her blood.

The floating body stayed in my eyes, circling in my thoughts, almost as if she was still there before me.

A part of me agreed with Aelia. Killing the one who had designed the exploitation of our people should have given me gratification. Just the memory of what they had said in the Senate had filled me with bloodlust: a bloodlust which should have had me sated.

There was another part of me, too. One that couldn't believe that I had just caved in another human being's skull. A part which couldn't believe that all that training and fighting had led to a dirty scrap in the sewage, and a completely unnecessary death. It felt different from all the fights I'd been in, and the deaths I had caused. They had always been indirect, the people falling from a bridge, or the Void killing Echo the Endless.

I had never killed someone with my bare hands. I had never witnessed a body float in front of me afterwards.

I looked down at my hands, but they didn't have blood on them. My mind told they should be stained. It shouldn't have been washed away, and replaced by this valuable, sparkling Elixir.

I was truly part of the city now, I thought grimly. Smelling clean yet steeped in blood.

"We're going to report back at the..." Aelia started to say.

"Report away," I replied gruffly. "I'm having none of it."

Aelia's eyebrow arched in surprise. "What do you mean? Just because it was a success, doesn't mean we get a rest..."

"I've had enough of the taste of success for one night," I grunted. "In the Citadel, success tastes as sour as failure."

Her lips pursed in frustration. "If you want your people to be freed..."

"For one second, for one minute, I'm not going to play your city games!" I bellowed. I ripped off the cloak, freeing my face, so I could stare back at her.

"This is not a game. This is a rebellion. It's *your* rebellion as much as my own."

I went up to her, pointing at her. "This is a *game*, Aelia, and we are being played. We're dancing to Cleander's tune while we're not dancing to Lucian's. Maybe you've all been in the city too long to realize that. But I need to be free of it, even if it's for an hour."

With that, I turned, and started heading upwards, to the stairs going up the sides.

"Careful, Jason," said Aelia after me, her words laced with anger. "You and your *morals* are in danger of getting a lot of people killed. Remember, your sense of duty and honor were created by the city, too. And it was a way to subjugate you."

I didn't answer. I didn't even look back.

Instead I made my way back up the tunnel and through the city. I crept up into the rooftops, as the city was swarming with guards, filling the streets, it was a tense, sharp atmosphere, with soldiers ready to beat and whip anyone at the drop of a hat, and people whispering to each other in hushed tones about what had happened in the Senate house.

None of it had made an impression on me. I was stuck in my own thoughts and preoccupations. I went back to my quarters, where I took some time to process what I had seen and done.

That was the problem with this city, it was always clogged with *people,* all of them demanding something. I had spent my youth by myself, climbing walls and training. I was used to having time to myself, and silence. But in this city, everything was constantly screaming at me.

I dropped into my atrium, and sat down in its center, drowning out the noises of the city and focusing on my channels.

I couldn't fully calm myself down. My heart continued to hammer, my emotions fluctuated, any meditation interrupted by the thought of that Senator, floating in the pool of Elixir.

In the end, I gave up. I got to my feet, and paced around the atrium, drinking Elixir as I did. I thought about the Senate and the fact that a new Void creature had been created. I thought about how the Emperor had decided to make me parade through the city to praise their hellish new creation. I thought about the fact that Aelia had almost executed me at the Emperor's orders.

I thought about what they had made me. I'd been an honest person, almost to a fault, back in the valley. Now I was someone who crept around the city in a mask and cloak. I'd become a killer who broke skulls.

I stopped in front of the statue of the Emperor, and its net of scratches and scrapes, its lines where I had swiped at its marble form in training.

I felt a new pulse of hatred course through me like the water running through the city. The hate and fury were almost physical, less of an emotion, more a charge of energy running through me, from the insides of my brain to the trembling in my fingertips.

The thought came to me: *Aelia told me to use my emotions.*

I tried, with a disdain and the absolute certainty of failure, to gather Essence. I was hardly in the right mood to do anything difficult or mentally taxing: I was a wreck, physically and emotionally. But I still felt the need to do something with my energy, with the drive inside me.

I stood in front of the statue, with its disgusting look of arrogance and pride, and reached inside myself and to my core. I made the Anima inside spin in the other direction, and few trails of lightning blue energy expelled out of my body alongside a clutch of shadows. Just like all of the other times, it did not remain, instead unspooling into the air and dispersing.

I was surprised, however, that I had managed even that. The anger was still shuddering through me, something that would, in normal circumstances, disrupt my use of the Shade. So I tried again but found that the results were the same.

My emotions *could* make me focus, sharpen the blade of my mind. That was what Aelia had said. But she had not known herself, she could have been wrong.

Or, the thought occurred to me, perhaps she had been *half right*.

The spasms of fury, the flashes of the body of that Senator, the thought of celebrating the Void, perhaps they caused too many emotions at once. Perhaps it was this contradictory, unfocussed, mess of emotions that could never lead anywhere.

For something to sharpen a blade, it had to be *precise.*

I looked at the statue once more, taking in its disfigured arrogance, and the overinflated muscles. And the idea came to me just to take the strongest of all my emotions and center myself on it. To discard the rest, and direct that feeling all in one direction, so that it could purge itself in shadows.

The answer lay in the statue before me.

I found that it wasn't my feeling of guilt, or my insecurities, or doubts, which came out the strongest. It wasn't even the dislike of my enemy.

It was my sense of injustice. Of right and wrong, and how much the leaders of the Canyonlands did not care about it. Even my mightiest enemies in the Hollow, even Commander Helton, who had tried to kill me multiple times, were fighting for a cause.

The Emperor, and his Senators, had none.

It was this fundamental sense of grievance, not for me, but for all of the people in these lands, that I harnessed. I felt it rise to the top of all the churn of my thoughts and feelings, and I took it as if by the hand, and let it grow until it was all my mind could dwell on. I let it expand until it felt like this sense of *wrongness* was there in every part of my clenched muscles.

I tried, again, to Essence Gather.

The results were immediately different.

The spinning of the Anima in my core gathered speed almost by itself, whirling about in my chest, gathering momentum as it my emotion itself was spinning a wheel inside it. When I created a shadow, I ejected Anima out of my core, and cords of blue were as thick as vines.

My hands shook and sweat started to drip down my brow. I clenched my teeth and ignored the sweat. My feelings, my emotions, were still charging ahead, they still wanted me to carry on, so I held on to that instinct, even as my brain told me that my body was overextending itself.

The blue Anima lines slowly and reluctantly curled. It took all of my willpower to make them take shape.

And then, in the cloud of black around me, they did. They took the shape of the Core Glyph, the circle with lines running into the center.

The moment the lines formed the shape, it was like there was a force acting upon my body which was bigger and stronger than my own. Shadows tore from their perch and raced to me, rushing to my hands to join the black clouds, and with them came other shadows. Blackness upon blackness, turning the air in front of me as dark as ink.

I could barely move, my body felt like someone was reaching into it and ripping away at its insides. My energy was burning out, and I barely felt like I could stop. Everything rushed toward that floating Core-shape made out of blue Anima.

It was a taste of what Cizin had done. To invite too many shadows, and to lose control over them.

The dark wrapped itself about me, becoming as thick as midnight.

The bigger it got, the more it seemed to attract shadows. Here was a process that seemed to run itself.

That was a terrifying thought.

The moment it occurred to me, all my sense of righteousness was replaced by fear and panic. I cried out, cutting off the channels of energy running riot in the air. I broke the Core Rune and let the Anima disperse.

There was an explosion of shadows as the air about me morphed and distorted, as a roomful of blackness tore back to its place all at once.

I was knocked off my feet and landed hard, pain flared through my forearm as I landed on my elbow. I lay there, breathless, as the last of the shadows dispersed above me, like a sped-up vision of clouds parting.

Dazed, I picked myself up gingerly, my chest burning, barely able to comprehend what had just happened.

It had felt dangerous, that was for sure. I had never felt

that before. In all the use of the Shade in the Hollow, the ability depended on complete control and mastery of everything in your body. This Essence-Gathering, on the other hand, felt like courting chaos.

It was terrifying, and yet exhilarating too. The sheer quantity of shadows which had leapt to my fingers was unlike anything I had done before. The possibilities of what I could do with such forms were an intoxicating thought.

All I needed was training, time to master this new version of the Shade. A moment to not just invite that cloud of shadows in, but to shape them too.

Getting to my feet in the atrium in a daze, and looking ahead, I knew exactly what shape I could make.

Chapter Forty-Two

"Jason, what are you doing?!"

The shout dragged me out of my unconscious mind. I was still in the atrium, I had collapsed on the stones, my body giving up.

I had been training too hard and had fallen flat on my back.

My eyes blinked, taking in Aelia's form over me. Overhead was the first promise of morning in the sky, the black canopy beginning its slow retreat.

How long was I out? I wondered. The training had been addictive; I had been learning to Essence-gather for hours into the depth of the night.

But if it was morning, then I'd been out for a few hours at least.

"What's going on?" I grumbled. I hadn't rested enough to go into deep sleep, but I was a still a little groggy; I tried to get up, but felt my balance sway as I rose, and I grasped Aelia to steady myself.

"Haven't you heard? Where have you been?" Aelia seethed at me in exasperation.

"Heard what?' I said, rubbing my eyes.

"The city is in turmoil. Somehow, people learned about the kidnapping of the Senators in the night, and an impromptu protest happened. Everyone from the Lower Levels took to the streets. The Lightguard are everywhere, quelling it. It's messy."

"Uh... well, that's... good?" I shook my head to wake myself up. "That's what we wanted, right?" There was a note in her voice which told me that I was reading the situation wrong.

She shook her head. "It was too soon. It wasn't coordinated, none of the Uprising were involved to lead the people in the right direction. What's happening now, it's just sprawling masses, destroying whatever they find. Punching walls and getting themselves hurt."

"So it's natural. Not something managed by Cleander. Sounds to me like it could be a good thing."

Bitterness glinted in Aelia's eye. "I have been waiting my entire life for this, Jason. It gives me no pleasure to tell you this, but it's happening all wrong. The crowds didn't get to the palace. They didn't get anywhere near. Without a leader, it was just a series of scuffles with the Lightguard. This isn't the uprising we wanted."

I sighed. "Nothing is ever simple in the Citadel, is it?"

"Never."

"Can we salvage it? Give the crowds our support, and make it work?"

"With the Blade of Rebels there? Maybe. It's a long shot. You *should* have been there earlier, Jason." There was anger in her, a tightening in her lips. "You should have been with us. Where were you?"

Aelia waved a hand away, dismissing my answer before I could even speak. "In fact, I don't want to know. There's no time. Get yourself ready, cycle, and get your cloak back on. The people need their symbol. If not, the empire lives another day—which means you get to parade a new version of the Void, and we head down into the Underworld tomorrow."

My thoughts came into focus the moment she said the words. "You're right," I said. "Let's go overthrow the government."

I got ready as quickly as I could, drained some Elixir,

wolfed down some bread, and filled my core with Anima as fast as humanly possible. I noticed that the sounds of revolution were now filling the air; the city was fighting, clashing, shouting.

It was too much to remain patient to fill my core completely, itching to join the fight, I half-filled my core before telling Aelia that I was ready.

We climbed up off the roof and went to join the rebellion. The clamor of the protests became louder and louder. It was like the metropolis was on fire with voices, alive with movement. There were scrolls of smoke, cloaking the stone facades in pockets across the city. The alleyways were clogged with people crying and shouting, rushing about the place, overrunning stalls, and crushing lines of Lightguard.

As we made our way across the rooftops, I had an impression of how many people actually lived in the city. The whole time I had been here, the population had been divided in half throughout the day, those of the night, and those of the day. Now, though, it was like the entire city was out in the streets. It was, in some ways, a surge of hope: there were more people from the Lower Levels than I'd imagined, and that meant more people rallying to our cause. I had the impression that a rebellion was more possible than I ever thought.

On the other hand, I could tell that Aelia was right. This was uncoordinated rage, just people spilling out on the streets and venting their anger. No one was grouping together or leading, no one was trying to march on the palace. It was not a coup, only chaos.

I noticed that Aelia wasn't even looking down as we made our way over the rooftops. I wondered whether it was too painful to finally see the people revolt, but not in a way that would bring about meaningful change.

"How did this happen?" I hissed as climbed down a wall, dropping down into the streets below.

"We'd planned to bring crowds together, and announce what had happened, and then bring them on a march to the palace ourselves. But we were still reconvening, locking up the senators, when riots started breaking out on the streets. The fights broke out in drips and drops, a small crowd here, another gang there. Never coming together into an organized whole."

"Wasn't Cleander supposed to be organizing everything? Couldn't he have pre-empted this?"

"Clearly, he underestimated how quickly events would turn."

We fell silent as we made our way across an aqueduct bridging one building to the next.

All of a sudden, a chant which had been indistinct before came into focus. "Is that..." I asked.

Aelia stopped, listening for the first time.

Our eyes met as we recognized what they were chanting.

Blade... Blade...Blade...

"They're calling for me!" I gasped. "But why?"

"I don't know,' Aelia replied grimly. "I guess we'd better find out."

I went forward, overtaking Aelia and following the sound. It led across the houses, and towards somewhere familiar.

The main square, the place with the baths and platforms, and the market of forms. That's where the crowds were gathered. The sound of the chant got stronger and stronger, like the chanting of priests back in the Hollow: it filled me with dread as I got closer, wondering what was awaiting me.

Finally, we got to a house which overlooked the square, and we beheld what was happening.

It wasn't pretty.

The square, normally a place of bustling markets, meditation, and bathing, was now a warzone. The stalls had been ripped apart and lay in tatters on the cobblestones. People were massed everywhere, with pockets of fighting and struggling opening and closing like bubbles among the crowds.

At the edges, people were trying to storm a line of Lightguards barring the way up to the Palace. The Lightguard were ruthless, tearing away at the frontlines of the people with blades and light-shields, keeping them at bay with sharp lashes of whips tipped with claws. Overhead, scouts circled like hungry Void, sometimes dropping down onto the crowds with daggers. Periodically, someone would launch an orb made out of essence-gathered light, and it would explode in the crowds, sending an explosion of people in the air.

I cast an eye over at Aelia and immediately regretted it. I could see the sadness in her eyes, she had pictured this scene for so long. Her dream had to have been different, with the leaders of the Uprising at the front, leading an organized people into a battle, breaking into the palace, or infiltrating it with quick efficiency. Not the people creating a storm of skirmishes and blood like this.

A surge of pity took me. "Come on," I said. "There might be a chance to salvage this yet. The people are there, and they need our help."

Aelia pointed at something. "You can say that again," she said. I followed the direction of her finger and saw what she was getting at.

The chant of people among the crowds was growing into a chorus.

Blade. Blade. Blade.

"They want you to lead them."

"Well then," I said. "I suppose I'd better give them what they want."

We went down into the crowds. At our presence, the people gave a deafening cheer, making space for us. The sound of their chanting was as loud as thunderclaps, everywhere around us people cheered.

Aelia and I stepped forward, urged on by the people's thirst for blood. Fists pumped in the air as the word *blade* was chanted over and over again, and people made space for us to go forward, creating a path through the sea of populace.

It was an overwhelming experience. Never had I been cheered on like this, not since I'd been a child winning competitions in the caves below our valley. Even my own people had rejected and banished me when I'd stepped outside their cultural norms.

And yet here, I was being embraced. Celebrated, even.

It was almost enough to bring a tear to my eye.

But the moment didn't last.

"Light-blast!" someone shouted.

Before I could move out of the way, an orb of light landed in front of my feet.

The world blazed white, and Aelia and I were flung to the ground. Pain ripped through me, and my ears rang.

My head spinning, I got to my feet, and saw that some Lightguard had thrown themselves upon us. Aelia immediately leapt to her feet to take them on, while I gathered myself, my head feeling like it was about to split in two.

Then I saw it.

At the end of the path of people was the Quaester. He was grinning with an evil grin, his eyes hungry.

The light around his hands stitched together into weapons.

He wanted to fight me in a duel.

Chapter Forty-Three

We circled each other for a moment. I tried to blur everything out and focus on my opponent. Around us, the crowd gathered in excitement, while Aelia fought guards behind me. Above us, a scout was wheeling in the air, presumably to see who would win the fight.

I tried to ignore it all. I stepped along the borders of the people. There was all kinds of racket around us, chanting and shouting and cheering, but I ignored it. Everything that mattered was right in front of me.

The light and shadows jostled with each other as the morning sun was starting to the conquer the sky. The Anima, brimming inside me, waited to be used.

My opponent was right in front of me.

The Quaester seemed ready to get into the fight, he was like a caged animal, unable to stand still. While my footwork was deliberate and cautious so that I faced my enemy at all times, he would turn on his heels, striding from one end of the circle to another. He did not seem to be studying me, as I was studying him. No, he was riling up the crowds, jeering at them, daring them to come at them, before turning back to me with the face of someone savoring the look of a hearty meal.

"So you're the hero, are you? The one who's launched this little operation?" His voice was wet, spittle coming out his lips and decorating his beard. He wiped his face with huge, plate-sized hands, to little effect. In his other hands, some intricate wire of light was forming, something cruel and deadly, I had no doubt.

"The people started this. And they did so because of your cruelty," I said. My words were lightly goading, I needed time to come up with a strategy with which to defeat this brute.

It was not going to be easy, he was one of the biggest men I'd ever seen, and his muscles seemed to want to pop out of his armor. He was a mass of hair and strength.

"Strong words, for one so short," the Quaester jeered. His words came with a flash of crooked, broken teeth. "You're *stalling*," the Quaester breathed, before exploding into a guttural laugh. "So much for the fearless warrior!" His laughter died, and either side of his broken, ill-shaped nose his black eyes narrowed. "No more waiting. You and your petty rebellion are to be punished and killed. So speaks the might of the Lightguard."

Then, the Quaester burst into action. His hands let fly a whip, made out of gold light it arched across the morning air, glinting in the young light, before clawing at me.

I ducked, rolling out of its way. The whip did not have just one end, but many, it spread out into a web of dagger-like claws, grasping like claws of a beast. The whip dug into the cloak at my back, planting itself into the cloth about my shoulders.

The Quaester stepped back, pulling at the whip, and I was pulled to the stone before there was a tearing sound, and my cloak was ripped off my back. Luckily, the hood and scarf masking my face remained, the cowl was still intact up to the shoulders.

But, this was not a good start. I leapt to my feet, ready for the next attack. The whip came once more, its trajectory as straight as a plummeting rock, by this time I had grabbed at the shadows and formed them into my staff with half-moon blades. I batted the whip away, swatting the gold claws with the flat of the blade.

I couldn't let him have another chance. I charged at him, screaming as I did, the roar of the audience behind me. Discarding his whip, the Quaester simply reformed another one, light writhing into place, and in a mere second he was throwing it at me.

I once again batted away at the oncoming flash of light; this time, I was less successful. A few tendrils of light-blades still scraped me, some clunked ineffectually off my armor, tearing at nothing but the clothing around it. One claw dug into my arm, just below my elbow.

Pain erupted through my body, causing me to stagger, and clumsily go onto my knee. My breath was taken from me, and all I could do was croak.

But I recovered, mastering myself, in order to tear it out—only to find it *changing form inside my flesh.* I howled, and looked at my opponent in disbelief, as the claw became a hook, digging into me, sending more shoots of pain across my forearm.

The Quaester was grinning, as he walked towards me in a sadistic reverie. One hand held the whip, while the other was outstretched, weaving the light-form so that it drove deeper and deeper inside.

"You know what they say about me, rebel?" he breathed. "All I need to do is lay one finger upon you. One finger is all I need. Because *I never let go.*"

I shouted with exertion, before ignoring all the agony, the protest of my body. I got to my feet, my balance was uncertain, my vision blurry with pain-induced tears.

But I wasn't going to give this man the satisfaction of killing me on my knees.

My staff had been unraveling due to my lack of concentration. There was still a bit of a dark, circular blade left in my hand. I hacked at the whip connecting to my arm, dragging the claw out. It emerged out of my flesh with a lashing of blood, but I didn't care, not having that *thing* in me was a blessed relief.

The Quaester looked disappointed, but not for long. He

lashed out again, and I didn't move quick enough, my side-step didn't stop a few claws hitching into the side of my neck, biting in.

I howled once more and tried to pry them out like I had with the previous whip. But the Quaester did not pause this time to enjoy hitting his target. He pulled at the whip, and I was dragged forward.

He pulled again, and the pain hauled me forward once more. He was bringing me closer to him, and the light-sword forming in his left hand.

He was bringing me close in order to execute me.

I did the only thing I could, the only thing which I thought he would not expect. I did not try to pull back but rushed at him instead.

He was taken aback as I rushed forward, my armor grazing his semi-formed sword. I ran and bowled into him, pushing him back. Taken by surprise, he stumbled, and we both tumbled in a bath of Elixir.

This was where the people of the Upper Levels bathed in opulence, looking down upon the city. But with the Quaester and me fighting inside it, it became an eruption of violent color.

The Quaester unwove his form, and my neck was freed. With this, we both got to our feet in the water.

The huge man loomed over me, his face one of fury. He did not like being harmed, not one bit. Especially not in public. Glowering in anger, he Wove another whip. Only this one was silver, made from threads of gray.

I gasped in surprise.

"That's right, rebel," He spat. "I can harness the sun *and* the stars, see. Not many can do that. I like the brute strength of the sun, but when it comes to really causing pain, there's nothing like a bit of starlight. So I keep some handy in my core for special occasions."

He raised his whip, ready to strike.

He brought his hand down, whipping his moon-claws towards me. I caught his claws with a hastily made shadow-staff. I'd barely had time to make a form more intricate than a stick. But it didn't matter; it was enough.

I simultaneously leapt out of the bath and drove the stick down. I plunged it into the liquid, submerging the claws wrapped around it too.

The Elixir was a conduit for that charge of energy, it rippled across the liquid and made it churn once more. The man howled, the whip now a conductor for that charge, and fell over into the water.

It gave me the time I needed. A few breaths, a few seconds.

While the Quaester recovered from the charge, I decided to do what I had been training for. It was a gamble, it was going to take a lot of energy, all the Anima I had, in fact. If it didn't work, then it would be the death of me.

But if it *did* work, then it might be just what I, and the people, needed.

I started to Essence-Gather.

Chapter Forty-Four

I had just a few seconds while the Quaester got back up, gritting his teeth while the last shocks passed through his body.

I did it all within heartbeats. I coupled my urge to rid the pain from my body with the urge to rid this city of injustice. I channeled that feeling of anger that men such as the Quaester were allowed to punish people with his whip of pain.

I let my emotions take over. I did not harness the balance of the world. No: I wanted to *change* it. To bend the universe closer to my will.

I wove shadows, fueling them with my desire to change the world, and expelled lines of pure Anima from my core. The cloud of black in front of me was filled with tendrils of blue, climbing into the smoke like ivy up bark.

I wove that blue into the core symbol.

There was a hush in the crowds around us, a sense of shock. It was understandable. I was doing what Cizin had done, Shadow-Gathering.

Fear was there in the people, in their faces and their cowering. They'd been told that to gather shadows like this would lead to madness, like it had for Cizin. The Lightkind had convinced the world that they had the monopoly on power.

They'd lied.

The Quaester was in shock, dumbstruck that I was using the same power as Cizin.

It gave me a few more precious seconds. The glyph locked into place, the blue sign gleamed in the cloud of black, imbuing the shadows with light. The rune of the core.

And then, immediately, shadows were attracted to it. The rune harvested black from all around us, like insects to light, like a horde of Void unto a victim. They wound away from people's feet, they ribboned across the air from the shade of a nearby building.

They painted the air in front of me like a wall.

I felt that wrench inside of me, that panicking feeling of losing control, of enslaving myself to the depths of black around me. I held on to that emotion, that sense of injustice, that sense of a world being so wrong and out of kilter that it had to transform.

I Wove.

I had not mastered the practice. It was not precise, yet I could still broadly control the strokes of darkness swelling about me. I directed it into a rough form, and it wrapped around me, making me the center of a storm of shadows.

The shadows started to settle in the place I wanted. They knotted about my arms, about my legs. I seemed to grow, as all parts of me were extended in shadow, with cords of black bulging arms, lifting the bottom of my feet, thickening my shoulders.

The shadows around me were not stable. Still they attracted more, gulping up more blackness from their surroundings, and yet they leaked out too from my unstable form, making me a large, black figure in a black cloud of moving darkness.

The Quaester was upright and facing me but he did not move for a moment, like he was still struggling to understand what was happening in front of him.

As he was looking up, not at my normal shape, but the shape of a scarred, disfigured shape of the Emperor.

I took on the form of the statue I had been training on,

built out of darkness and fueled by my sense of injustice. The shadow-armor was wrapped around me, making a layer of scarred marble.

"I am the world your Lightguard created," I announced. "A scarred, angry world, gone rotten. I am the world you created, I am the world fighting back."

I stepped forward, shadows writhing around me. I felt huge, and frightening, over my face was the face of the Emperor's statue I had scarred so much.

It didn't matter. I had become a symbol of a world gone wrong, of the ugliness beneath the veneer of the Citadel.

I could feel my presence become more powerful than it ever had before. I could feel people take a step back. I could even see the Quaester swallow, a sign of nervousness that I had never seen in him before.

It didn't take long for him to recompose himself and take a stance. His hands held his whip, which he then threw towards me.

I didn't care anymore. The teeth of his whip buried themselves in the coating of shadow-marble without penetrating my skin. I was encased in black, black which was imitating a statue. And it was a better armor than anything in the Canyonlands.

I stepped forward again, bringing all of my shadow-mass with me. More shadows were plundered from my surroundings, surging toward me, and they joined my armor just as much as my form leaked, scudding black into the air like smoke.

I stepped forward, and it was like I was in a different body, one of a giant. My movement was slow, and with every movement my Weave had to change and adapt, taking more from the blackness around me to keep me swaddled in black marble. It was a huge amount of power, and the effort pulled at my chest.

But I didn't care. All that I needed was to get through this duel and demonstrate to the people of the Lower Levels what we could do.

I grabbed the Quaester by the neck with my thickened fingers. I closed my marble-hardened fingers around his throat and drove him back.

The Quaester snarled, and a curved light-sword took shape in his hand. He croaked and grunted, slashing at my face.

I flinched, but I didn't have to. The sword planted itself into the black mask over my face, thudding close to my eyes but never touching flesh. I was swathed in shadows, and although layers leaked, more came to replace them.

I kept on driving forward, pushing the Quaester back further and further, ignoring his wild movements. I was dimly aware of the crowd parting, giving us room. But the duel was now in the center of a whirlwind of black, and their presence seemed to belong to another world.

In the eye of the storm, nothing existed but me and my enemy.

The Quaester morphed his sword into a huge light-hammer and started to bring it down upon my arms. I felt the blows vibrating through my body, but it did not hurt. Shards of shadow-marble crumpled off my arms, and as they dropped off me they turned into amorphous black.

He would not get through all the layers, not before I had achieved my goal.

I kept on walking, kept on driving. I thought that I would have arrived at my destination by now, but still I had to push and walk. My body screamed in protest, and my chest started to feel like it was a chest plate hammered out of shape.

I started to howl with the exertion, and it joined the hum of the shade and the Quaester's protest in a cacophony of sound.

Finally I found the lip of the platform which jutted out into the valley. Below was the honeycomb of training platforms.

I kept on pushing, holding the Quaester as close to me as possible, and launched us off the edge.

We dropped, falling through the air, leaving a column of black behind us as shadows steamed off me.

And then we landed *hard* on a training platform below. The

Quaester landed before the full force of my weight bore down upon him.

There was a sickening noise as I crashed into him, my shadows hurtling into his body like a wall of marble. His chest armor caved in—the only thing which stopped him from dying immediately. The shock of the collision was enough to make his eyes go wide and unfocused, and for his mouth to flop open, agape.

I moved off of him, finally letting go of the shadows. My body gratefully unwound the symbol of core magic, and the blackness radiated away from me, returning to their place in a flooding of darkness.

We both lay there a moment, sprawled on our backs, hyperventilating. The Quaester was hurt, wheezing. I was exhausted from my Shade. I had been emptied of Anima and couldn't do anything further.

I was dimly aware of the crowds gathering to look down from where we had dropped; of them looking and pointing. I was also aware of the strange shapes in the sky, which was netted in lines of light, some of which were getting thicker and thicker.

The scout, who'd been waiting to see what was happening with the dual, was now heading towards me.

I willed myself to move. I rolled onto my front and got to my knees. I shot a look at the Quaester, lying beside me. He was groaning, making the sounds of deep, unmasked pain, but I had to be sure that he would not attack me again.

He could not move an inch, that much was clear. His whole body looked limp, unmoving. He had been winded, or injured, in a way from which he would not recover any time soon.

Something in his eyes made me pause. He was looking at me, but not in anger, or pain, but surprise. His gaze poured over my face, darting back and forth like fish in rivers.

"You..." he wheezed.

My hands darted to my head, and I understood. In all the commotion, and all the writhing of shadows, my cowl had slipped off, revealing my face. I quickly tucked it back over and lifted the cloth up to my nose.

I glanced up to the people above, watching us. A swelling sense of panic and helplessness took over me. Had they seen me? It was impossible to tell, they were all chattering excitedly to one another, but also cheering, and making weapons so they, too, could join the rebellion.

It did not look like someone had noticed my face. But that was not the case for the Quaester. He would tell the Emperor who the Blade of Rebels was.

The Emperor would retaliate by ordering the execution of the Hollow.

A thought, unwanted but insistent, shuddered through me. I had to kill the Quaester, finish him off. Dead, he would keep my secret. It was the only way.

I just had to throttle him, there on the platform.

I tried to Weave a dagger, anything at all, but nothing happened. My reserves were depleted. I had no Anima to speak of. And the scout was swooping down in my direction.

I had no time.

Shouting out loud and cursing myself, I left the Quaester's side. I tore away from his weakened form, and leapt down the platforms, running away from the approaching Lightguard.

I kept on running, even as regret burned inside of me.

Chapter Forty-Five

The world was dark. I was alone.

The chamber did not feel empty, because my thoughts themselves were running wild. Emotions and thoughts swayed, this way and that, and with them came thoughts pilling upon each other. It made the walls feel close, it made the air feel sparse.

As I sat there, listening to the flow of Elixir beside me, the more my thoughts began to slowly disentangle. The more I calmed myself, the more my emotions unknotted, unbraiding and drifting away like shadows released from a Weave.

It brought a sense of certainty, just beginning to pierce through.

It was not long before I heard the sound of footsteps ringing through the tunnel. I got up, straightening.

Aelia stood in front of me.

"I thought you'd be here," she said.

We were at the meeting point from the previous night, where I'd ended up with the floating body of the senator. I'd made my way through the aqueducts; there was no way I'd ever forget the path I'd taken with her, no matter how quickly I'd taken it.

"You've got to come with me," she said.

I noticed, from Sensing, that there was a black streak of blood coming from her brow. "How is the Uprising?"

Her voice wavered; it offset her strong, battle-hardened demeanor. "Dying. Your duel with the Quaester reinvigorated their hopes, and we charged against the palace gates, but we did not get far. We were too few by then, our numbers too dispersed across the city."

I paused before continuing. Her words were full of sadness and regret. Aelia had waited her whole life for the chance to overthrow the established order. Now it had happened but had been bungled.

"I revealed my identity," she said. "I thought that it might give everyone more hope, to see an insider of the palace be at their sides. So now I am wanted. The Lightguard will kill me if they get a chance."

I nodded. If we'd been closer, I would have tried to embrace her, or take her hand. Tende had shown me how much a friendly touch can accomplish. But even in the darkness, I could tell that Aelia would not let me approach. She was reeling from too much to let me in.

"What will you do?" I said.

"Go into hiding in the woods outside the city. When I get a chance, smuggle in a boat, and try to regroup. The Uprising is not dead," she said, with a note of insistence which suggested that she was trying to convince herself rather than me.

"Aelia," I said quietly, hoping that a calm voice would best find her among the rage of her emotions. "The Uprising is not dead. But it needs a rebirth."

Her response was bitter. "You've been in this city for a month or so. Now you're an expert, are you?" she lashed out.

"Not an expert. But an outsider. Maybe that's just the angle we've been missing."

Aelia's first reaction was a defensive one. I could hear her trying to breathe out her anger. "Go on. I'm listening. I might hurt you, but I'll listen first."

"The Quaester saw me, Aelia. The Emperor knows that I'm the Blade of Rebels. Right now, he might be ordering the execution of what is left of my people. I have to go back to them. To help them any way I can."

Aelia tensed at this. "You're talking to me about a rebirth, while all I'm hearing is that we have to abandon the fight."

"That's just the thing. We're trying to fight the Emperor from within. But there's a people who have been raised to fight, who have been taught all their lives to follow orders and coordinate. That's the army of the Uprising we need. The Shadowfront."

Aelia shifted her weight.

"All this time, the Senators have been making honed weapons with the Experiments. That's the Void. But they've also been making honed weapons out of our people. If we release them, they will rally to our cause. They have more reason to oust the Emperor than anyone."

I took a step forward. "What I'm saying is, come with me. Help me save my people. Do this for me, and in return, we can start an Uprising anew. Starting with the Hollow."

"Weren't most of your warriors killed?"

"Every single one of my people is a warrior, one way or another. You'll see that once you come with me. Besides, the whole plan was to infiltrate the palace, and use the crystal to announce the identity of the Blade, right?"

"Right..."

"Well, isn't there an underground tunnel leading up there? Cleander said that there used to be a whole network of tunnels where the Shadowkind used to train and cycle before it was made illegal. Couldn't there be a way to the palace underground?"

Aelia thought about it for a moment. "No one has explored those tunnels in years. They were blocked off, forgotten. I honestly don't know if there's a way through..."

I held up my hand. "In the Hollow, spending time in forgotten tunnels is part of our lives. We have developed Senses like no one in the city from it. If there's even a trace of an underground passage to the palace, then I can find it and use it again. Worth a try, no?"

Aelia contemplated this for a moment. "All this time, you've been torn in two," commented Aelia. "Torn between fighting for your people, and the city. Now you've found a way to put it all together."

There was something in that. Aelia had been so purpose-driven, so single-minded. I'd never heard her be so insightful.

"Will you help me?" I said. "There isn't much time, I've got to get back to Hollow as soon as I can. My people depend on it."

Aelia breathed. The silence weighed down among us; it was long and drawn out.

"There might be a quicker way than you think."

I almost couldn't breathe. "Does that mean yes?"

"I've been doing my best to help the people of the Shade my whole life. Your people need help more than anyone right now." Aelia shrugged. "Plus, if I stop fighting now, I won't know what to do with myself."

I raised my hand, inviting her to slap her palm into mine.

"What's that?" she asked.

"We call this a Hollow handshake, where I'm from." Tears of gratitude pricked my eyes, but I swallowed them down. "You're one of us, now."

Chapter Forty-Six

We made our way down the tunnel, following the channel of Elixir. The main course flowed out to the city, but Aelia led me to the secret meeting place of the Well and in the catacombs she fished out a scroll which she then sprawled out on the table.

"This is a map which few people have ever set eyes on. This is a vision of the Canyonlands normally only granted to the palace."

I frowned. I'd never seen a map of the entirety of the Canyonlands, and just the intricacy of the scrolls was unlike anything I'd ever seen. The page had other pages which unfolded, growing to make it spread over a space four times bigger than any other map I'd ever seen. The amount of detail was hypnotizing, and if it wasn't for the pressure of wanting to get back to the Hollow as soon as possible I could have lost myself in its sprawl. Swathes of valleys stretched from one side of the page to the other, each with its climbs and hollows and rivers.

Across the entire map was a network of lines, stretching from one corner to the other. They were in a variety of colors, peppered with symbols which meant nothing to me. "The palace wants to keep information of space in the same way they want to keep information of time," Aelia explained. "But the Lightguard need Riverkind, Stonekind, and Earthkind to best know the contours of the Canyonlands. They rely on us to map the world, to create bridges and pathways and passages. So one of the projects of the Uprising was to create, bit by bit, our own version of the map. A more complete one."

I pointed to a valley with a familiar-looking shape, off to the corner of the map. "That's the Hollow," I breathed.

Aelia nodded, and then followed a pattern of lines to get there from the valley of the Citadel. "A legion of Lightguard will be following this path to get there, it's the quickest way. But we can take some of these secret paths, and with our head start we will get there before them."

I was left reeling. The entire world, which had felt so disorienting and sprawling and endless, now seemed so much smaller and manageable. "It sounds so easy," I said.

"It isn't."

She bundled up the map, folding it back into place and then tucking it under her arm.

* * *

We left the tunnels, which led across a passage which then emerged into the woodland outside the city walls.

It was altogether unlike the jungle of my home. There was the same thick closeness, the same volume of undergrowth.

But the woods of the Canopy, as they called it here, was an explosion of color. Flowers and fungi, growing over each other, with every different kind of flora I could imagine taking up every corner of space. While the jungle of my home felt uniform, a collection of similar trees desperately reaching for sunlight, the Canopy was a vibrant, magical ecosystem, brimming with health and variety.

Aelia informed me that it was because of the tending of the Earthkind, who knew about plants and soil more than any other community in the universe. But it was also because of the Elixir they siphoned off, it seeped into the soil, giving the plant life a boost of energy which brought about the range and flamboyance of the plants I could see before me.

The wind meandered here and there, and there was the usual clucking of birds and hum of insects. But apart from that there was a calm silence in the woods, one completely at odds with the violence of the rebellion that had occurred in the city this morning. The Earthkind seemed happy to ignore it all and focus on the vegetation about them. Some had their hands and ears to the trunks of trees, while others seemed to be whispering into flowers and brushes as if gossiping with the leaves.

As we hurried through the woods, we were wholly ignored. All the Earthkind seemed to be enraptured with the trees, the ivies, the flowers, and the brush, not even moving as we strode past.

"Don't they care?" I muttered to Aelia, conscious of the silence about me. "Does it mean nothing to them, that there was an attempted coup in the city? Judging by everyone here, you'd think that we were having a completely normal day."

"It's a mistake to take their calm for complacency," replied Aelia. "Here, among the woods of the Lakeside, are the foundations of the Uprising."

I arched an eyebrow. "Really? I couldn't imagine them organizing a rebellion."

"Of course. You know how flowers open and close every day to take in the sun, and yet you never see them moving?"

I nodded.

"The Earthkind are the same. They do things deliberately, carefully, and yet they move the world. For the Stonekind, the here and now is meaningless. It is hard to convince them to depart their routines, even if the routine is one dictated by the Lightguard. Given the millennia they see when peering into the rocks, everything we go through just comes across as petty squabbles. The Earthkind are different. They have a firm sense of balance, of how we are in a delicate dance with the forces of the world. Too much power in someone's hands, and the Earthkind can feel it in the soil."

"So what do they do? To help, I mean?"

"There's been many a rebel smuggled through these woods. Many enemies of the Lightguard have found sanctuary here. And what's more, they work with the Riverkind to direct some Elixir into pools across the woodland. The roots and plants they grow there are potent and are distributed to those in need in the Lower Levels."

I thought of the Jade Root, which had been made in exactly the same way in the Hollow. The extra power it had given me then had saved my life. If the Earthkind were distributing such boosts across the streets, it was a significant aid to the rebellion.

"You will have your time to discover the Earthkind," said Aelia. "Now, though, we must rush through the roots."

"The roots? What are you talking...?"

But before I could finish my question, the answer was given. Aelia had approached a tree, and then removed a flap of earth, revealing a passage underground. Using our Senses, we went in, and I found that it was a tunnel like no other I had ever been through. It was not a tunnel of rock or earth. Instead, it was a series of paths through the roots of trees, which created a wooden labyrinth among us. Here and there, there were arches of wood, stretching across the gloom, knotting the darkness together, as if we were in the center of a humungous spider's web.

"Is this on the Emperor's map?" I breathed.

"Not on the Emperor's. Here, among the roots of the forest, has been our main hiding place and smuggling route for decades."

Aelia looked grimly amused at my astonishment. "Still think that the Earthkind aren't a worth a damn?" she tossed over her shoulder she began to make her way through the gloom.

Chapter Forty-Seven

The journey home was exhausting. It pushed my levels of fatigue and made my muscles ache.

Yet I was grateful for every punishing moment, if I were left to my thoughts, I'd succumb to anxiety. I worried for my people whenever my brain was left to its own devices.

First we made our way along roots and soil, ducking under bridges of wood, clambering over others, for hours. It was a tiring passage, one where I could only focus on my Senses, and where to put my feet. My mind went blank as I picked my way across the earthwork, and it was almost blissful to forget about all of my worries.

The root tunnels did not last for long, however. It couldn't, not at the speed at which Aelia and I were travelling.

When we resurfaced, we were in woodland crop by the side of the lake. Peering out, we saw that no one would see us, and so we traveled out in the open air. We could not, however, forget the presence of the city. It loomed behind us on the other side of the lake, watching us like a predator. Thoughts of the Lightguard being sent to wipe out the Hollow, descending from the Upper Levels and making their way through the valleys, riding those strange beasts, was enough to make me quicken my pace threefold.

I turned my back on the city, part of me wishing to never set foot there again, and another part knowing that I had to.

"What are the chances that the Emperor will be too busy, and in too much need of the Lightguard, to make good on his threat to my people?" I asked Aelia as we wound our way around the lake, keeping off the paths and away from the sight of the fishing boats. Whenever possible, we kept to woodland, so that scouts passing overhead could not find us.

"Nil. If the news has travelled that you are the Blade of Rebels, then you will have been a source of humiliation for him. For that, and that alone, he will come down upon you and yours like a thousand hammers." My look darkened at her words. "You asked," she pointed out.

I made sure not to ask any further questions of the sort and focused just on keeping my pace.

At one point later that day, we departed from the lakeside, and Aelia had to consult the map to find a spot in the cliffs towering over the lake. She found a ridge which traveled diagonally upwards, hidden from view above by overhangs, and we made our way up it until reaching the higher plains.

We did not emerge fully onto the plains above, like I had with Tende. We kept to more inconspicuous terrain, traveling from valley to valley, never straying up into the flat landscapes that lay above. Still, in the visions that came to us from the tops of the valleys, I was reminded of the person I had been when I'd first emerged from the Hollow and seen the awe of the landscapes burning in the distance. Then, as now, the awe of the hanging skies, unbroken in the sky above, was enough to give me discomfort. And yet I felt like it didn't weigh upon me, and bow my head, quite as it had done before.

I had learned a lot about the world of the Canyonlands since then, and I had grown as a result. It was not that the world outside the Hollow was any less threatening, but now, at least, I knew what the threats were.

I could face the sky without cowering as I used to.

As the day's light began to decay, we took a little break by a pool. Aelia handed me a satchel, one which was permanently stashed in the catacombs of the root tunnels for people who needed to flee. It had a stash of food, and we gnawed on the dried fruit and meat, and caught our breath.

Even though my legs cried out for rest, my mind could not take it. I got to my feet again and told Aelia that we had to move on.

"You're no use to your people if you arrive half-dead," she noted.

"I can't stop, Aelia. I keep imagining a sword, hanging in the sky, waiting to drop onto the Hollow. I can't stop until I am with them again, not until they know what's coming."

Aelia got up. "Well, no one can fault your energy, Jason."

"I won't quit. Not when there's a chance."

"I know. And, perhaps, that's what I need right now. Someone who still dares to hope, in this day and age. After the botched uprising, I don't know if I've got it in me to look to the future anymore."

"I can hope for the both of us," I said. "But only if I've got my people by my side."

She nodded. Without looking at me, as if to hide her sadness, she looked up, beyond the cliffs, up into the sky, and its deepening layers of gloom, and the dim stars just starting to be unveiled.

"Where does it come from?" she asked suddenly. "Why don't we hold up our hands and give up? What is it that stirs us, along with all the Anima in the world, to continue the fight? I wonder sometimes. I've been pretending to work for the Emperor for years, all for a moment when I could see him fall. But it was all for nothing. He still sits on his throne, and we're still crawling in the dark. We should be finding a place to hide, we should be getting away as far as we can, across all the Canyons, even to the seas beyond. Instead we keep striving, we keep moving forward. Why, in all the skies, should we continue to fight? Is it because we know nothing different? Are we to die just because we couldn't find anything better to do?"

I pondered this. "Maybe," I said. "But then... I don't see it the way you do. If we were to die tomorrow, it wouldn't be for nothing."

Aelia shook her head. "If the Lightguard descended upon us now, and slaughtered us in a ditch, it does the Uprising no good at all. I'd hardly count us as heroes."

"You never know. I've seen what kind of footprint the past can leave. It can be bigger than you think."

"You mean the ghosts? Can you Sense them?"

"Louder and louder, the closer to home I get. There are ghosts everywhere, of course. But it didn't look or sound like anything in the city. It was all too crowded. But out here? This is Therian country. Their movements, their songs, their oaths, the air is tuning, like an instrument, to their song. It speaks to me. It tells me that there was once a world of Shade users who were prosperous, and strong. People who could stand up to the Lightguard." I put a hand on her shoulder. "It tells me that we can change the world, even through failure, even through death."

Aelia finally turned away from the stars. "I'd like to Sense these ghosts, like you do."

"Then you're coming to the right place."

I knew that Aelia would never admit such vulnerability. Her reaction was to get up and stride ahead, making us continue on our journey towards the Hollow.

The stars brought us further across the plains, and we didn't speak as we traveled. We rested and cycled in the morning, but not for long. We were compelled, and that compulsion made us drive on. We didn't need to encourage each other, nor even speak much. Our goal was all we discussed.

As with my journey with Tende, we had to keep a constant eye out for scouts, streaking across the skyline, and kept to places where we could hide and find cover. We yearned for nightfall every day, where we could cycle to our heart's content and walk freer knowing how much more difficult it would be to spot us.

The hours and days drained away, all a fog of aching muscles and anxious dreams.

Until the moment came where the Hollow was in sight.

I first noticed the place where Tende and I had sheltered, then the streams, where I'd encountered the first guards. My heart started to pound quick and heavy, until it was like boulders were falling off a cliff and landing on my chest.

It was early morning, and it was eerily quiet. The sky overhead was huge, monolithic, I kept my gaze steady, looking forward and not above. There was nothing before me to see.

When I'd first emerged from the valley, I'd stumbled across guards almost immediately. Here, I had the impression that no one was there, that the landscape was empty.

Many thoughts raced through my mind. *Was everyone dead already? Are we too late?* I tried to will away these thoughts, but I failed.

We approached the hut of the sibling guards, and silently got our Weaves ready to attack whoever was inside.

But it was empty.

"Aelia," I finally said, as I couldn't bear the thoughts burning in my mind. "Why would the guards not be here?"

"I don't know," she replied. It was an honest response, and yet there was a grim expression on her face which told me that her thoughts were just as dark as mine. "Let's take a look at the valley."

At that, I reemerged from the hut, and strode towards the edge of the cliff, ready to look down into the Hollow. Dread and fear grew with every step.

I walked to the edge of the cliff, and before me unrolled the sight of my home. The woods, following the river, which were still blackened since the struggle with the Kukulkan. The Half-Dome wall in the cliffs below my feet.

And, in the middle of it all, the Temple. This was where I'd told the survivors to live, in the ruins of the temple, where our leader Echo the Endless had reigned. The mountain was there, spearing up from the bottom of the canyon, reaching up towards us. The broken statues, the dilapidated walls, were all there, standing defiantly to the sky and winds.

Not a single person wandered among them. There was no habitation there. No sign of life.

"Aelia..." I spoke, my voice as weak as if I had just climbed a dozen cliff walls. "Where *is* everyone?"

Chapter Forty-Eight

There was no answer.

Aelia was mute, and the silence filled the air about us, as overpowering and dominating as the heavy sky.

I sat on the edge and beheld the valley of my home before me. I continued to stare, as if some resemblance of the life I had once known there would manifest. Troops of Shadowfront warriors patrolling. Farmers, taking around provisions in carts. People scaling trees.

But there wasn't a breath. The valley was, well, there was only one word for it.

Dead.

The forest was a stretch of scarred earth. The black corpses of trees like shadow-daggers ready to dematerialize. There were stretches of green, and the lush jungle life I recognized, but only in patches. Whatever remained looked vulnerable and naked.

This was not my home. This was a forgotten, abandoned place. The last time I had been here, it was still on fire. Since I had left, I had never fully acknowledged how disfigured the valley would look once the smoke had cleared. In my yearning for home, I had pictured visions of a valley untouched, the valley of my youth.

That place did not exist anymore.

But that didn't matter half as much as its people.

"They can't have been faster than us," said Aelia, decisively. "I've been thinking it over. Yes, the scouts can traverse the Canyonlands in no time at all. But a company of Lightguard? There's no way they got here first. Which means that your people left of their own accord."

"Or..." I started, but then realized that I couldn't finish my sentence. I didn't want my thought to be given the reality of spoken words.

"You're thinking that it might not have been the Lightguard," Aelia pointed out, so I didn't have to. "You're wondering whether the Void finished off what was left of you."

I shook my head, less as a disagreement, and more because I hated the idea. "It's true that there were few trained warriors left when I left. But my people are strong. And they were in capable hands. Corinthia, Yennenga, the best leaders I know. This can't be the end of them. They will have found a better place to go."

"Better than the temple?" asked Aelia, a puzzled look on her face. "The caves are full of the Void. From what you've told me, they're the plague of your people. Where else could they go to escape the darkness?"

I tried to answer but couldn't. My shoulders slumped. I simply didn't know.

I picked up a rock and tossed it into the dead valley. I followed it with my gaze, all the way down, hoping that once it hit the bottom, some sense of what had happened would come to me.

Nothing did.

Aelia roused me out of my thoughts. "Get in the hut!" she said, rising quickly to her feet, her eyes fixed on something on the horizon.

I followed her look and could not make out what she saw. But still, pushed by her sense of urgency, I raced behind her, until we were in the simple hut, peering out of the window. "What is it?!" I exclaimed.

"A scout," she said. "But it isn't moving." She pointed

ahead at the horizon, and I finally realized what she was looking at.

A scout, hung in the air, a league or so away. It did not have a streak of light, because the form was not moving. It just hovered, like a bird of prey before it drops on its meal.

"What are they doing?" I asked, but before I finished the answer I knew the answer. "It's a marker. It's there to guide the Lightguard to the right place."

Aelia nodded. "Which means that your people are probably over that way too, just underneath them. Any idea where that is?"

I took this in for a moment. The idea that my people were still alive gave me a rush of promise, as did the fact that Lightguard had not arrived to execute them yet. But it seemed mad for them to leave their home. They had spent their whole lives believing in their leader, Echo the Endless, who had told them that the valley was the safest place for them, and that they should never leave the valley.

What could have driven them out?

My mind raced, wondering where that place was, underneath that scout. I knew that they had not traveled in the plains—everyone at home had grown up with the faith that the gods would smite them forever for daring to scale the cliffs as I had.

But if that was the case, then they'd had to go through a cave, or tunnel. Which would have put them in the danger of the Void.

Unless…

Two thoughts came to me then, in quick succession.

The first was that the Hollow had escaped to the Excavation Tunnels. For all of the monsters and creatures down there in the deep, the Void had never emerged from there in my lifetime.

And the second came even quicker.

"The Tower of Babel," I breathed. "Emilian, you genius!"

"What's the Tower of Babel?" asked Aelia.

"It's where I first witnessed the ghosts of the Therians.

That was their capital, their training ground. It was the imprint of the past, of their fighting and sparring there, which allowed me to gain my abilities. Emilian showed them the way, he brought them there so they could all train like I did."

Aelia took this all in and nodded in admiration. "If all of them can Weave like Therians, we might not have been wrong to hope after all…" Her eyes then focused, taking on gravity once more. "Is there a way to get there without the scout noticing?"

"Isn't there just," I said, grinning despite it all. "I can't believe I'm going to say this, but I'm actually excited to say that we're going to go through the Excavation Caves."

Aelia balked slightly at my expression. "That pit of darkness where you spent your entire youth scrambling around your artifacts? I'm starting to get a sense that you Hollow people are *weirder* than I anticipated."

"Just you wait," I said. "I'll introduce you to my favorite ghosts on the way."

And with that, I did not wait. The thought that I would see my family again, that Yennenga was within a few hours' travel, gave me the energy I needed. I took shadows until they twined together into a vine, and used it to lower myself over the edge of the cliff.

I could barely wait for Aelia to follow me, such was the rush of anticipation of returning.

It wasn't the idea of returning back to the valley that had been important, after all.

Only its people.

Chapter Forty-Nine

The last time I had been here, the entire people had scaled to the very heights of the valley, in fear of the swarm of Void rising from the darkness beneath. Now, the trajectory was reversed, going from the endless skies of the plains into the bowels of the Earth.

We scaled down the Half-Dome onto the Last Ledge, and down the switchback trail into the woods. Here and there lay the detritus of my tribe's past: the charred bones of houses and bodies, the scorched vegetation in the wake of the dragon. But I chose not to dwell on such sights, indeed, not even to *look* if I could help it. I concentrated solely on finding my friends once more.

Aelia did not mention the sights either, out of respect for my silence. Not a word was spoken between us, but I felt a kinship with her for a moment. In the aftermath of the Uprising's failure, she too lived in a destroyed world.

I raced through the scarred jungle, and soon we crossed over to the entrance of the Excavation Caves. Here, we used our Senses to plunge into the gloom, leaving the sunlight behind us as we ventured through the black. I knew some of these caves like the back of my hand, having traveled through them almost every day of my youth, and so I barely needed to reach out with my Senses. My movements were more based upon muscle memory than anything else.

This seemed to surprise Aelia, who could not keep up with my bounding pace. Although she was a Shade User, she had never become acquainted with the subterranean worlds like I had. For all her time in the caverns of the Canyonlands, her universe was in the streets of the Citadel.

Still, we raced along, buoyed by desperation to be among my own again. Even the thought of my father, sick though he doubtless would still be, was going to grant me relief, even if I hadn't gotten nearly as far as I wanted in terms of getting him help.

We burrowed down into the gloom until we reached the chamber of the Temple of Therians, where I had learnt so much from the ghosts. Their voices came to me then, as they always had.

Beyond the Babel, within the dirt

There flies the swallow: there contains the world.

I had heard their words and riddles so many times, ringing in my head all through my youth. And yet now, upon returning to the Hollow, it felt like there was more sense to them than there ever had been before.

We arrived at the chasm, where we had to go down in order to get to the Tower. I felt a burst of warmth and vindication as I saw that a rope ladder had been cast down the edge. it had been made out of the ruin of other rope ladders, hastily tied together, and it led the way into the sightless cavern below our feet.

When I had first ventured down there, curious about the sound of ghosts below, I had been the first to travel there in years. Now it was a pathway for the Hollow, retracing the steps of the ancient Therians.

Nothing had changed, here in the caverns below the world. And yet, everything had.

We clambered down, and I marveled at how easy it was to scramble down now, and far less perilous than when I had downclimbed it during my training. Before long, our foot found a ledge which was affixed to the cliff, a pathway which clung to the sides of the cliff and would lead us to Babel.

Not long now. Just some walking, and then I would see my sister, father, and friends once more.

I took a step forward, and then another, before something grabbed my attention. A movement, there at the edge of my Senses, down deep below.

"What is it?" Aelia hissed. "My Senses aren't as attuned as yours!" she added impatiently when I didn't immediately respond.

"Movement," was all I said. "Down there, in the chasm."

"Is that normal?"

"No. There were always creatures down here, but they were mostly scuttlers and snakes. Nothing big. But here..."

I peered over the parapet. Using my Senses to decipher the darkness, everything was in monochrome, shades of grey and white. I reached out further, and more of the gloom morphed into shapes and lines. More rocks, more emptiness. The floor of the chasm was still out of reach, making the view underneath a lake of black.

But there was movement, there too. Eddies and currents of shadows dispersed, as if ripples were traveling across the surface of that midnight lake. Surging, twisting, twining. Spreading like echoes.

And with the disturbed shadows came the sounds I had heard all too often in recent weeks. Claws, sharp as swords, clacking on rock. The regular heartbeat of wings flapping.

There was no mistaking it.

Somewhere down there, in the emptiness were the Void. The monsters who had persecuted my people, the result of experiments to create a weapon to send against Cizin in the Underworld.

"It can't be, Void never came to the Excavation Tunnels," I breathed. Then my mind stepped in, and I was reminded of how the Void in our valleys have developed a way to travel through waterways. And then came a crueler thought, with the jungle in the valley empty, who was there to chase the Void back into their homes? They could spread to all the tunnels in the land now that they were unchecked. The thought occurred to me that the Void used to be controlled, at least to some degree, by Echo the Endless in our valley. Without her around, the Void would be untethered. Left to their own devices.

Would that make them more dangerous? Or less?

I couldn't know.

Nothing had changed, and everything had.

"Well, they're here now. I Sense them too," Aelia remarked. "Which means that the shadows are more and more disturbed.

I clenched my jaw. "They're getting closer," I agreed.

"How far to your tower?"

"Too far for comfort. But here on the ledge, we're nothing but prey. We've got to run as fast as we can, now!"

I started in a sprint, my Senses picking up on the shadows starting to boil below us, a centrifugal force winding the blackness. My calves and knees did not want to respond, my muscles worn from our travels, but I gave the pain no notice. I charged, running fast enough for the stale air that belonged to these subterranean lands to whip by me as if in the winds of the storm.

Aelia ran behind me, her iron-shod sandals hitting the rocks of the pathway like the sound of a pickaxe in a mine. We were making a lot of noise, which would attract the Void, but we had no choice. Our best chance of survival was to get out of there, and to do it fast.

All the while, the storm gathered from the chasm below. Clouds of shadows churned into a frenzy, shifts and trails of black shooting this way and that.

And then, a few minutes into our run, the first appeared. Shoots of elongated grey heads, emerging from the darkness like grotesque flowers emerging from soil. And then, as they rose out of the empty black, the long wings with the claws at the ends, the translucent skin drenching the thin, serpentine bodies, the tails...

The stuff of nightmares. For the first time in my life, when I'd been in the city, I hadn't had to dream of their violence.

But now it all came flooding back, as if the nightmares had never left.

Our pace somehow quickened: I'd thought that I could not run any faster, but some reserve of energy made me speedier still. My feet slammed against rock: my heart slammed against my chest. But no pain could stop me from putting as much distance as I could between myself and those killers emerging from the gloom.

The path wound as it clung to the side of the rock, scaling up the cliff. As we started to turn our back from the depths, I barely dared to turn back to see the ascension of the Void. But I heard them instead, as they started to screech, that unholy whine that grated the ears.

The sound could only mean one thing: they had seen us.

The horde would be heading straight for us.

"Faster!" I wheezed, as if the word would manifest a longer stride, or speedier footfall.

The path climbed into a tunnel, piercing through a ceiling of rock, and becoming a narrow passage. This, at least, was something: the Void could not swoop or fly through a shaft this small. I risked looking behind—

And immediately regretted it. The horde were howling through the air in the chasm behind us, a murmuration of nightmares ascending in a spiral, as if they were all running up an invisible staircase. The spool of monsters was bending, a line of creatures stopping their upward surge and heading towards us instead.

The screeches were becoming deafening.

I dove into the tunnel, followed immediately by Aelia, and we kept on running. I did not even try to slow down in order to create a Weave to protect myself, every ounce of energy went into my run.

I remembered that the tunnel was short, and that in a few

minutes we would be at the tower. But a few minutes was still long enough for us to get torn apart.

The shadows in the passageway swirled and tore, upset with the movement. I shot another look behind me and saw that the tunnel was filled with bone and teeth, with scraping claws and eyeless menaces. The monsters were almost scrabbling over one another to get at us, filling up the passageway like a flood.

The snapping and gnashing got closer, and closer.

And *closer*.

"We're not going to make it, we need to fight!" shouted Aelia.

She didn't know. She hadn't lived a life where Void lived in every shadow. She hadn't lived a life where your family and friends were in constant danger of succumbing to their ferocity.

She didn't know.

"No, keep running!" I barked, barely able to find the breath to shout.

There was some cry of protest, but I couldn't make it out. I didn't care. To stop was to die, I knew that as much as I knew anything.

The crunch and slobber of clapping teeth got closer, until I started to imagine the jaws of the monsters jabbing into my heels at any moment. A chorus of bone hitting bone.

There. Ahead. I could see the end of the tunnel.

And the tower beyond.

With a few more strides, I spilled out of the passageway, and the structure stretched out before me, spearing up from the ground about me for a league, climbing up all the way to a small ray of sunlight above. The chamber was fringed in light, spilling from above, but it only looked bright in comparison to the darkness from which we had emerged.

There was no direct sunlight here, and therefore the Void would still be upon us.

The previous times I had been here, I'd had to climb

through the window to enter the tower. But we did not have the time to do that now; the monsters would be upon us.

My only hope was that my people would be there to greet me, ready to fend off the oncoming wave of Void.

Only... they weren't. The chamber was empty, the tower was the lonely monolith it had always been.

"Now what!" shouted Aelia.

"There!" I pointed. The tall wooden doors at the foot of the tower; I had always known them to be blocked, but I could see that one was opening, allowing us to go in and get away from danger.

We charged ahead and heard the Void behind us clatter out of the passageway, screeching as they once more had the space to launch into the air.

I launched ahead, screaming with effort as I did. Aelia ran next to me, her hands a blur of movement as she sprinted.

Void-spittle sprayed onto the back of my neck. Their jaws snapped shut, just breaths away from my head and claws grabbed at what was left of my cloak.

My flesh would be next to be torn off.

I hurled myself through the door, spilling onto the floor beyond, and Aelia crashed on top of me. I rolled onto my back, my hands up in the air as if they would be sufficient to hold off the monster about to sink into my skin.

But no monster fell upon me. Instead, a spray of shadow-spears hummed across the air, battering back the first wave of monsters with screeches of pain. Then a shadow-vine, snaking across the air, pulled at the door, swinging it shut. The door crunched into a barrage of bone and teeth, blocking the Void out, and a lock fell into place, a huge metal bar sliding across both doors.

There was a medley of clawing and battering at the door. But the doors would hold for now. We were safe.

I rolled on my stomach once more, in order to witness who had saved me. The spears were one thing—but the only one I knew who created shadow-vines was myself.

There was a line of Shadowfront there, warriors from my home, in fighting stances.

And at their head, with shadow-vines uncoiling into the air around his face, was a familiar face.

"Emilian!?" I cried.

Chapter Fifty

I leapt to my feet, and rushed into my friend's embrace, even as his Shade forms were still collapsing about him. Touching was generally not done in the Hollow, but I could help it; there was something immensely comforting about seeing him. He seemed more tired, more haggard than before, but still his stocky frame and round face the same as ever before.

Slightly shocked, Emilian gasped "Skies above…" as I grabbed his shoulders. He returned my hug, but then pulled out, a little embarrassed, reddening.

"You can Weave now?! That's amazing!" I exclaimed.

"A lot has happened since you left," he said. "But, er… Jason." He stared behind me, pointing a finger. "Who's that?"

I hadn't thought of this, the fact that I had rushed here had stopped me from even thinking about the impact we would have by arriving unannounced. When I had left, many of the Hollow still thought that I had brought the curse of the gods through my different Weaves, and that no other human existed in the world outside of our tribe.

The presence of Aelia, standing up and dusting herself off in front of us, was enough to send ripples of shock in the line of warriors standing there. It was now that I understood, too, how incongruous she looked. Despite our long journey, she still had her clothing, armor, and chest plates of a quality unheard of in the Hollow. We both did, but Aelia also had lines of tattoos darkening the skin on her face.

To them, we looked like nothing that belonged on this Earth.

"This is Aelia," I told Emilian. "She will help us. A lot has happened to me, too, I'll explain everything. But, do they know the truth? If you can Weave like that..."

Emilian saw what I was hinting at and waved a hand of dismissal before I said anything further. "It's more complicated than that," he said in a low voice. Still, the warriors around us leaned in, trying to catch his words.

It struck me that Emilian's status had risen immeasurably since I had seen him last. He seemed now to be a leader of some sort. Everyone hung on to his every word.

My joy at seeing my friend dissipated, and the weight of the situation hammered back into my thoughts. "Emilian, I'm afraid we don't have time for complicated. We're all in danger. That's why I came back. To warn you, and fight for you. Aelia is the best Shade User I know, and she's here for the fight too."

Emilian's eyes darted to Aelia, who nodded in agreement, but otherwise kept silent, letting me navigate this strange encounter.

"You'd better come up and speak to everyone, then," said Emilian. "I can't make heads nor tails of what you're saying, but it doesn't sound good."

Aelia took a step forward, but some of the warriors raised their shadow-blades, which I now realized they had not dispersed.

Emilian put his hand out in a calming gesture, but it did not have too much of an effect. The energy amongst the warrior was one of deep suspicion. "Let her pass," Emilian said.

"Who is she?!" one exclaimed, still holding her blade up.

Aelia sighed. "I am two things," she said at the black forms pointed at her. "I am someone who could rip through your forms in heartbeats, and I am here to save you. Either way, I'd recommend that you put away your needles."

This did nothing to reassure the warrior. I stepped between them and looked into the warrior's eyes. She was young, not much older than myself, and her trembling blade was unsteady, leaking trails of shadows with every second. "I recognize you," I said. "You used to be a trainee priest, and a keen one, if I remember. You used to welcome people into the Chamber of the Purest Darkness with chants and prayers. Seems like you have put the same efforts into being a warrior now. I know that this is all a lot for you, but I promise you, with everything that I know, with everything under the skies above, the circumstances for our people are dire. We did not brave the Void for nothing. If you don't allow us through, then you risk everything. Every second counts."

The woman's eyes were suddenly coated with tears, as her confusion and fear got the better of her, and she let what was left of her blade uncoil into the shadows at the corner of the room.

"Quite the welcome," Aelia hissed at me as she was allowed to pass, and we followed Emilian up the stairs leading up the center of the tower.

"This is going to be trickier than I'd thought," I admitted in a glum tone. "But they accepted us, that's the first step."

"Acceptance is not trust," she responded. "If they are going to survive, they are going to need to trust us. And fast."

"Well, I'll have to think of something," I said. "Unless you've got any ideas...?"

I turned back to Emilian and took in our surroundings. Above us, the tower was pretty much as I'd left it. It was a humungous structure of stone, a cylindrical shape which climbed all the way to the plains above. Above us, there was layer upon layer of staircase, crisscrossing up like a switchback trail upwards, leading to a series of chambers dotted around its center. The stone, and stairs, were blackened from time, grayed with dust. The steps were held up by a network of corbels covered with cobwebs, and the stairs were worn into smooth grooves at their center, the structure abraded by age.

There were, however, signs of habitation and life. The doors and windows we passed were blocked and reinforced with wood and steel. My people had reinforced the barriers with leaning planks of wood and crisscrossed spears in the locks, preventing them from budging.

There was also sound. When I had been there by myself, the place had been teeming with ghosts, whispering in my ear. But here was a more vibrant, sharper sound. The sound of life. People emerging from chambers, people climbing the stairs and crying to each other across the tower. Torches, flaming from brackets, giving the black stone a golden hue.

This was a home.

"What happened? Give me the short version," I asked Emilian as we ascended. "Is my family all right? My father? Rana?"

"Your family is in much the same state as when you left them," answered Emilian, with a note of regret. "But before I explain, what happened to *you*? You're the one who went over the top in the Plains Above!" I heard the old excitement in his voice, buried underneath all the concern. Emilian had always been the curious one, the learner. I had learnt how to be that person, he had been born that way.

"I'll tell you everything, but time is of the essence," I said. "I need the broad sketches of the state of the Hollow, so we can decide together how to save it."

"I can see that your life has been just as dramatic as ever," responded Emilian. "Your father is...well, the same, I'm afraid. His mind has regressed more and more in time, so much that I can barely tell where his head is anymore. He's lucky that Rana is there, caring for him. You will be proud of your sister, she is a pillar here, amongst us. Her strength is the contagious kind.

"But more has changed. Yennenga, Corinthia and I have

tried to lead as best we can, but it has been no easy path. We sheltered in the ruins of Echo's temple, and we had far more sunlight. But still the Void attacked us, still they picked at our slim number. Within a few nights, we were desperate. Something had to change.

"I consulted the scrolls which the librarian had kept hidden. They were quite the eye-opener. It spoke of this tower. It was the kind of information which changed everything."

I nodded. "The librarian was not someone of the Hollow," I pointed out. "He was a member of what we call the Uprising. He was sitting on those scrolls for the right time, hoping to open the eyes of the community."

"Really?" Emilian's eyes widened. "Well, he could have said something sooner! But then, I suppose he has saved us, in a way..." His voice went quieter. "You know why we call it the Tower of Babel?"

"No. It's just what the ghosts told me."

"It comes from *babble.*"

"Babble? As in, speaking?"

Emilian nodded. "That's the whole point of this place. It was a place the Therians established as a place of training, when they decided that they would rebel against the Emperor. The whole point was to establish a place where generation after generation would come here and learn how to use the Shade. Each warrior would add a new layer of ghosts, and history, to these walls. Everyone would listen to the 'babble' of history and be guided by all the ghosts. Just as you did it."

"That's how I managed to progress so quickly," I said.

"Exactly. It's a short cut. Someone called the Swallow devised this as a place where anyone, no matter how lowly their ability in the Shade was, could pick up on the ghosts, and mimic the way in which they wove shadows. There's so many ghosts here, so many generations of people saying the same words, using the same fighting stances, using the same forms, everyone can sense it, even if it's only in their subconscious. Once I read that, I realized that we had to relocate here. Most of our warriors had died, we had a whole new host of people to train how to fight, and we had to do it fast."

"Based on what I saw you do, you made the right decision," I said. "I almost died back there, and it wasn't from the Void. It was seeing you weave that shadow-vine!"

Emilian winced. He wasn't used to being praised, especially not for his use of the Shade.

"It wasn't an easy decision. We're far from the valley here, so it means regular excursions through the tunnels, which are now full of Void, to get food. But it's true that you're not the only one waving khopeshes anymore."

We came to a chamber, and Emilian bade me to walk in first. "She's going to be very happy to see you," he said.

I walked in and recognized it immediately. It had been an old place of training, with little shrines along the side. It was the room where I had first seen the rune of Core Magic carved onto the walls and learned how to shape weapons such as khopeshes and shadow-staffs.

This was clearly now a central place for the community of the Hollow. People who I recognized from Pastfinding and agricultural communities were trying their hands at guiding shadows into weapons, created leaky, unstable forms such as daggers and khopeshes to spar with each other. The halls rang with the hum of Shade, and of people breathing hard as they concentrated on creating their weapons and using them.

At the other end, giving instructions, was Yennenga.

Something inside me made me freeze, made my footsteps stop. I had thought about my childhood friend every hour, and every day, since my departure. But now that I was in front of her it felt like my memories had intruded into real life.

Her eyes locked onto mine, and panic took me, as if she were a stranger.

She dropped what she was doing, and strode among all the sparring people, the new generation of the Shadowfront.

By the time she got to me, I could see a glint of tears in her eyes, reflecting the firelight of the nearest torch.

"Jason..." she said, as if about to say something meaningful. But after a pause, all that came out were the simple words. "You're back."

Somehow, it was enough to break the silence, and we inexplicably both broke into smiles.

"Yeah," I said, just as ineffectually. "I'm back."

Chapter Fifty-One

I wished that I could give everything up, and just be with Yennenga for a while. To talk to her, in that easy way that we were used to talking to each other. With her veneer of sarcasm which made me laugh, and her strength of moral conviction.

But that was not our lives anymore. We were burdened with responsibility, and The fate of our people now lay in our hands.

Our time was no longer ours.

"Yen," I said. "The Lightguard, the people who I told you about, the enemy who created the Void to then test them upon us, they're coming to annihilate us. We need to get ready."

"Annihilate?" a wave of shock passed through my friend then, and it was like something physically hit her. Her head went back, and her mass of ringleted hair shivered in the movement. "But, why?"

"Because I tried to help overthrow their seat of power. I thought that it would help us. But it didn't, I failed. And now they're coming for us as punishment."

Even after I spoke the words, their bitter taste lingered in my throat. A note of despair, of anger, passed through Yen's face, and I wondered whether it was aimed at me.

Aelia stepped in. "He did not condemn your people," she said. "The Lightguard did. Do not bear him any ill will."

Yennenga nodded. "I don't know who you are," she said. "But I assure you, I have known Jason longer than almost anyone. My anger is not at him. My anger is at the people who would kill and punish me when I have never even seen their faces, and they have never seen mine. My anger is at the stars, and everything that lies beneath them."

Aelia took this in. "My name is Aelia… and I rail at the stars too, as well as the world beneath them."

"Then you are a friend." Yennenga motioned us away from the eyes of all those training, as they had all stopped to gawp at us. "We need to know everything about what's coming, as soon as possible. I will get Corinthia, she is cycling right now."

Emilian, Aelia, and I followed Yennenga, until we were out of sight of all the other warriors and traveled up another flight of stairs until we were in a small chamber, lit weakly by a single torch. Yen went to get Corinthia and returned quickly, until we could close the door behind them and get some privacy.

It was a relief to see Corinthia, and she smiled when she saw me. A master warrior, and one of only two Commanders left from the Shadowfront, I was sure that she had been masterminding the defenses of the tower and ensuring the people's safety.

She was, however, also a family friend, someone who'd known my mother closely. We provided a link to each other of someone dear who'd passed away. We did the Hollow handshake, and touched our foreheads on our intermingled fingers, and it was good to get a chance to look into her eyes once more.

"Well met, Jason," she said. "Now, Yennenga tells me that there is danger afoot?"

"A company of Lightguard are marching from the capital of the Canyonlands, ready to wipe us out."

Corinthia nodded, her brow fixed. She had weathered much in her time in the Hollow, and was able to take bad news without flinching. "How much time do we have?"

"None, or close to none," said Aelia. "They could be here any moment. I'm surprised that they're taking so long, to be honest."

Corinthia's face went grim. "I am honored that a stranger such as yourself came. I can imagine you risked much to aid us. For that, we are grateful." She gave a bow of the head, and I sensed a note of appreciation in Aelia's nod in return.

This was what Corinthia was good for, I thought. Keeping a cool head and remembering to keep to rules of etiquette and discipline.

"Now, it seems to me that we have two options," Corinthia continued. "It sounds like the enemy knows where we are. We *could* leave the tower, we would have more of chance fighting Light warriors in our own territory in the tunnels. But it'll leave us exposed to the Void, which is a death sentence. Since the death of Echo, they are just wandering around, aimlessly killing. If anything, they're worse than before, they're certainly more unpredictable."

I shook my head at the idea. "What's the other option?"

"That would be to turn a danger into a defense. Right now, we have two enemies, the Lightguard and the Void. Why not make the Void an obstacle for the Lightguard? If we stay in the lower levels of the tower, where it's darkest, the warriors will have to contend with their monsters if they want to get to us."

Aelia grunted in approval. "It's a good plan for today. Not so sure it's a good plan for the days that follow. The more we barricade ourselves in, the more difficult it will be to get out. The Lightguard could besiege us until we starve."

"We have food and water to last for a few days, at least," said Yen. "By the time we run out..."

"We'll have thought of something," I said, trying to put a lighter note on Yen's bleak predictions.

"It'll have to be a pretty damn good *something*," Yen remarked. "But I agree. We stay put in the tower. Which just leaves us with one major problem."

Aelia's eyebrow arched in disbelief. "*Another* one?"

"Welcome to the Hollow. We collect problems like

gemstones, here. Don't worry, you'll fit right in." Yen sighed. "The issue is with our people. What do we tell them? What do we say about what is coming? We need to be united if we're going to survive."

"And we're not?" I asked.

Yen shook her head, and a note of sadness and regret passed in her eyes before she averted her gaze. "The problem was that, after you left, Jason, everyone was in shock. Everyone was grieving. We planned to give the people the truth, to gradually wean the Hollow off the lies about their faith. But we couldn't, it was the crutch that was keeping them going."

Exasperation took me, and I lifted my head skywards. "What do they believe, then? When I started coming here and learned the way of the Therians and another culture, it broadened my horizons. Allowed me to question my prior faith. Has it done the same for them."

"Well, that's the thing. I never lied to them, but I never told them the whole truth. We all thought that we would do it in time. We thought that it would better keep our people strong if they held on to the thoughts of the souls of their dead loved ones going to the heavens above in the realm of the gods. After all, it had always worked before!"

Emilian too, started to avert his gaze. He seemed to share Yennenga's shame for not getting this decision right.

"But when we came here to the Tower, it just caused confusion. Fraction. Mostly, people still believe in the gods in the sky above, and they believe that their Echo sacrificed herself to save us. They think that all of this is a further test of their moral strength and honor. Some have refused to use Therian ways of Shade. They think that it's cursed, that it's part of the test that we do not submit to the dark magic of weaving animal shapes like you do. No matter how much Emilian told them about the scrolls, and the history, they cling to their old superstitions like a tree in a storm. The skies only know what they will make of an invading battalion of Light-warriors."

"I see it's not just the city that deals with lies and half-truths," scoffed Aelia.

"These are lies we *inherited* from the city!" I said, suddenly feeling very defensive.

Yen placed a hand on my arm. Her touch was like a small, pleasant version of the punishing whip from the Quaester, sending charges around my body. "There's one person in particular who's been seeding dissent and confusion. One person, contradicting everything Corinthia, Emilian and I say." Yen breathed. "You're not going to like this, Jason," she warned.

I was about to ask who this person was, but as soon as I opened my mouth a furious knock sounded at the door of the chamber.

"Come out! We will not have you whisper your conspiracies in secret, sequestered from the rest of us!"

The voice was booming, and cruel. It brought memories of death, and abandonment, and murder.

"It's him, isn't it?" I breathed to Yen.

She nodded, and my fears were confirmed.

It was the only other Shadowfront commander left in the Hollow.

Yen's father.

Chapter Fifty-Two

I felt a surge of hate channel through me, prickling my flesh.

Commander Helton.

The murderer of my mother, and the man who had tried to kill me. The person who had left me for dead in a nest of Void. He had always been blind to the faith and devoted to our traditions; even though he had witnessed the Riverkind, and seen that there were other ways to live.

Last I had seen him, he had been imprisoned before he could do more harm, so that he could let Corinthia and Yennenga save the Hollow.

"You let him roam free?" I spat at Yen. "After all he's done?"

"You haven't been here, Jason," she replied. "I meant what I told you before you left, I'll never forgive him for what he did to your family. I wanted to have nothing to do with him, to let him *rot*. But..."

"He's your father?" I said, immediately regretting how bitter and immature I sounded.

"He's a warrior with experience. Especially in fighting the Void. We don't have too many of them left. In those early days, before we retreated to the tower, and on excursions to get food, he saved many lives. You *haven't been here*. You don't know what things have been like!"

"I order you, in the name of Echo the Endless, to come out and tell the truth!" came his barking voice from outside the door. "Otherwise, I will break this door down before you decide what lies you will peddle."

"He sounds *exactly* like the kind of problem we don't need right now," remarked Aelia. She limbered her shoulders. "I have no knife in this fight. I'm not his daughter, he didn't do anything to my family. I'm going to deal with this, *right now*."

"Wait!" called Yen as Aelia headed towards the door.

"Skies," said Emilian, retreating into the corner, clearly unhappy with the way this situation was going.

Aelia flung the door open and stepped out of the chamber. We followed.

Outside the chamber, throngs of people were on the stairs. Above and below, the people of the Hollow were gathered, waiting upon us to come out and tell them what was going on.

Standing in front of them was Commander Helton.

The sight of him made my insides twist, and my flesh crawl. He hadn't changed a bit. He was still just as imposing, with his long white hair, his netting of scars, and his tall presence. And yet, now that I knew who he truly was, I thought of him as small and weak. Someone whose mind was as small as their frame was large. Someone who clung to the past, where they felt comfortable... no matter how cruel that past was. Someone who did the bidding of Echo the Endless without question, even when it led to cold murder.

"Are you going to tell us what is happening" he snarled.

"It depends," Aelia snarled right back. "Are you going to listen?"

The two warriors, both huge in their own right, seemed to rise up to an even fuller height as they squared off against each other. "And who might you be?" Helton growled.

"Someone who's come to save you. And someone who won't mind beating you up to do it."

"Please, Aelia," Yennenga pulled her back. "This isn't helping."

Aelia kept her eyes fixed on Helton. "I did not venture

through the Void and risk my life to squabble with the likes of a simpleton. This insurrection needs to be cut off at the root. I'd be only too glad to do it for you."

"I said step back! You aren't doing our cause any favors!" said Yen.

Reluctantly, Aelia took a step back. Before her, Commander Helton stood strong. I realized that behind him, gathered on the stairs, was a row of people with evil stares. They seemed ready to pounce.

Helton, it seemed, had support. I recognized a few faces. Nearly all of them had been priests in the Hollow. I also noticed Feljax, the bully who'd managed to get me exiled.

Weak-minded people, all of them.

"Interesting," Helton said in a performative manner. He spoke as if he was merely thinking out loud, and yet his voice was loud enough to ring up and up the stairs, funneling up and down the tower. "It seems you and my daughter already have an accord." His eyes came to me. "And Jason is here too. The man who nearly brought about our downfall."

"Jason saved us!" Emilian squeaked, but then immediately regretted it and retreated further behind us.

"We'll see," said Helton, in a suggestive manner which I didn't like one bit.

"People of the Hollow," said Yen, talking to everyone gathered on the stairs, taking in all the eyes pouring over her. "Jason has returned and brought an ally with him. They have concerning news. There exists in the Canyonlands another people, a people who use light in the way we use shadows. They are coming to wage war against us."

There was a ripple of shock as the Hollow processed this; mutters and whispers filled the tower.

"And why should we believe you?!" cried Helton. "Is this another trick to try and convince us to do more of your accursed Darkshade?"

To listen to him repeat the lies of Echo the Endless, the superstitions which had restrained the Hollow, was unbearable. I could not hold my tongue any longer.

"There are ghosts, streaming all about you, even as you speak, Helton," I said. "Their presence is no lie. And they were more powerful than you, or I. They are not accursed."

"All of this is part of a test!" Helton cried to his people. "A test of the gods. Echo the Endless, our beloved leader, the prophet who died for us, she said this continuously. And yet, a few weeks later, it is like you have forgotten what she did for us all. Too many of us have already succumbed to temptation and used shadows in unnatural ways. You will not be welcomed into the skies upon your death, mark my words. You will wander the underworlds instead, like our *savior* Jason."

"You met the Riverkind!" I said to him. "You *know* that other tribes exist in the Canyonlands!"

"Godless people, all of them!" growled Helton.

"I will speak," said Yennenga, in a voice that matched her father in authority and gravitas. Her voice cut through the air. The shouting and the jeering stopped, and everyone went silent. The only thing making noise now was the spitting flames of the torches on the walls.

Yen walked to the edge of the stairs, placing one hand on the banister. She looked up and down the tower, taking in as many looks as she possibly could, before continuing.

"If the Riverkind were Godless, then the skies only know what to call the moral worth of the people attacking us now. If that is indeed our test, if that is what the deities are placing before us, then we must fight with *everything we have.* If they mean us to survive, then we will need all our skill, all our strength. They will have no regard for what can or cannot be done with their light. We must do the same with our shadows. Do not listen to my father, he speaks from fear."

I felt a flash of admiration. Yennenga had managed to walk the line exactly right, she had not confirmed the people's beliefs, and yet she had used language which would appeal to their faith, nonetheless.

This, I realized, must be her life. Weaving her words with

more intricacy than I wove shadows. Doing whatever needed to be done so our people could survive.

It was beyond me.

I felt the mood of the people change, her words having an impact.

"You would ask us to risk our afterlives," spat Helton, his voice just as booming, his anger showing, "based on the word of a Pastfinder rat like Jason and a complete stranger? I do not speak the words of fear, I speak the words of *sanity*. The words of our leader, Echo the Endless!"

"Echo never spoke a word of sanity in her life!" I blurted out.

At this, the tower went silent again, but not in a good way. I realized, as soon as I had spoken, what a mistake I had made. Echo the Endless was still a hero to all of them, to criticize her was to alienate the Hollow.

Helton drank this in, an evil flicker in his eyes.

"You dare to fault Echo the Endless, the leader who sacrificed herself for us all?" he said. He squared up to me. "In fact, we say that she sacrificed herself. But indeed, no one saw where she went. All that we know is that you went to confront her, and no one saw her ever again."

He turned back to his mob, who jeered and grunted at his words. "This liar, the boy who fled before he could be questioned, is the person we should trust with our lives? I say we slay this Darkshader and his godless companion before they can corrupt us any further! What say you?"

I did not know how the tower felt, but the mob gathered around Helton certainly were convinced. They bayed in obeisance.

Helton held up his hand, and in his fingers there brandished an almighty shadow-sword, conjured from the gloom about us.

It was an act of war.

But Aelia immediately seized her moment. Within heartbeats, the shadows surrounding us lent their blackness to her hand, forming a dark shield. She leapt forward, and as Helton struck with his blade she hit the sword to the side with her buffer. Then, in the blink of an eye, the shield morphed, forming a string of chains, as Aelia leapt about Helton's back, wrapping them around his neck.

Helton's eyes bulged. Aelia put her foot into the back of his knee, and he collapsed on the floor, his sword form scattered into shade once more as he felt the pain on his throat.

It was faster Weaving than anyone in the Hollow had ever seen. No one had ever witnessed someone using the Mind's Eye to flit from one form to other like that.

The mob, suitably cowed, took a step back, in awe at Aelia.

Aelia announced to the whole tower. "I am going to settle this once and for all. I will show this man the enemy with his own eyes. And he will say sorry for doubting you." Aelia tugged at Helton's neck, and he made a strangled noise. "You're coming upstairs with me, little man," she told him. "I'm going to blow your world wide open."

Chapter Fifty-Three

Aelia began to drag Helton up and push him up the stairs. Everyone was so astonished, including Helton himself, that nobody stopped her. The people gathered on the steps above us, parted, allowing a pathway for Aelia to shove the commander up.

I looked at Helton get manhandled, profoundly satisfied at how much Aelia had been able to undermine him.

"Coming?" Corinthia asked me, as she headed the way of the stairs as well.

"I need to see my family first."

Corinthia nodded. "Of course. Catch up with us afterwards."

Emilian stepped forward. "No way am I putting myself through all of those steps," he said. "I'll take you to them, Jason."

Yen and Corinthia followed Aelia, my friend shooting me a look of encouragement as I left. I appreciated it, but it also increased my sense of anxiety.

Everyone knew what I wanted to do, check on my family. And yet, everyone was acting as if my father were in a bad way. It was not a good sign.

"Go on," I said to Emilian. "Show me where they are."

"Of course."

There were still a lot of eyes on me, and I bowed my head as we trickled through. I recognized nearly all of the faces, we'd all shared the same caverns, the same jungle, the same cliffs, the whole of our lives. And yet I knew that many of them saw me through a prism of suspicion, and I couldn't deal with that if I was also going to be able to cope with my father.

Emilian led me up a few flights of stairs, filtering through the groups of the Hollow that had gathered there. The more we traveled up into the tower, the more it felt like a home, people were talking, eating under the pockets of light emanating from torches, cycling on the stairways. Across the stairs, people had strung up vines, drying clothes upon them. It was messy, dark, and damp. But it was a home, of sorts. As I passed by chambers, I started to notice that they were being used as accommodation, with slumping bodies resting on the floor.

I inquired into Emilian's family, and he assured me that they were as well as could be expected. "They found it all quite confusing, me being invited to help make decisions and order people around and things," he admitted. "But I think they're proud, underneath the utter bewilderment."

"I'm sure they are."

"They'll be over the moon to know that you're here. They never forgot how you saved me. They're always talking about *Jason* this and *Jason* that."

"Honestly, I haven't had any success in my travels, Emilian. I genuinely think the best thing I've ever done was make sure you, Corinthia and Yen were in charge of the Hollow. All my actions have gone wrong since then."

"I don't know," Emilian said. "Whatever you've achieved or not achieved, you've certainly picked up a thing or two. You seem…different.

"I spent nearly all of my travels cowering under the sky and getting messed around with by those more powerful than me. It's hardly a triumphant return on my part, is it?"

Emilian shrugged. "You walked in here like you were ready

to take the world on, Jason. You have changed, whether you realize it or not."

Emilian stopped at a chamber. "I'll wait for you out here," he said.

I thanked him and pushed the door open.

My heart almost cracked immediately at the sight.

It wasn't just seeing my father, who was as I'd left him, restless on the floor, in a feverous sweat, his mind was clearly elsewhere. He had lost weight since I'd seen him last, and the small candle sitting on the floor beside him cast shadows over a thin, skeletal body, lines of dark in the grooves between his ribs.

But it was also the sight of Rana, my little sister. The moment the door opened, she let out a gasp of disbelief before springing to her feet and slamming into my body with her arms coiling about me in a tight hug.

But it was too late. I'd seen my sister kneeling beside my father, patting his head with a wet cloth, speaking gentle words to him. Being a nurse, holding the responsibility of caring for someone else.

She'd been a child only a few weeks ago. Now she was something else.

"You're *back*," Rana said, her words muffled against my stomach.

"I'm back."

She lifted her head to look at me, and I saw, even in the small candlelight, strain and sleeplessness making the mark on her features. Tears glinted as she reached out to me with her gaze.

"Are you staying?"

I nodded. "I'm not leaving you like that again."

Rana wiped some tears. "Emilian's family help a lot. They cook for us, and make sure we have everything. They try to get me to go out and explore the tower and be with my friends. But, I can't leave him. I can't help but think that if I'm there, he's more likely to find a way back, you know?"

I knelt down in order to be level with her. "You've been

everything to him. I'm sure father has appreciated every moment, even if he can't show it right now."

"Did you…" Rana hesitated to ask, pausing to take a breath. "Did you find something to help him?"

"Not something. But some*one*. There are people, in a land far from here, who can help him. We just need to get him there."

Rana contemplated this, and for a moment the old Rana came through, as she tilted her head slightly and I could see her brain turning. "Well, I'm coming with you this time. You're not *both* going to go without me!"

I almost laughed, so overcome was I with admiration for her strength and courage. "Fair enough. In fact, we're all going to go. Everyone in the Hollow. We just need to make sure that we beat some bad people first."

"Bad people? Where are they?"

"They're going to try and beat us here. But we're not going to let them."

Rana took this in slowly, her head tilting again. "Are they worse than the Void?"

I noticed that she'd used the word. She used to be too scared to say the name out loud, lest the topic should evoke our mother's death. "Nothing is worse than the Void," I said. "We survived them, we'll survive the rest."

Rana nodded. "Jason, father's gotten worse."

I went to my father's side, and we looked over him, a sibling on each side. "Worse how?"

"His mind kept on going backwards, for such a long time, but then it started darting about all over the place. It's in snatches here, snatches there. He used to be retreating in the past, but now I think that it's a nightmare version of the past. Like, just lots of all the bad things he remembered, and none of the good. Lots of Void, lots of Echo, lots of Mum."

I placed a hand on my father's head. The hair was slick with sweat, and I hated it. "How can you tell?"

Rana shifted uncomfortably. "I haven't told the others.

Some people still think he's cursed or something. Emilian's family tell me not to pay attention, but..."

"Rana, what happens?"

"It's like his mind... recreates the past in front of him. Not for long, like a cough, or something. But if he's thinking of a memory of a Void, then suddenly a shadow will form the shape of a Void in front of him."

"Like an imagist," I thought out loud. Seeing Rana's puzzled face, I explained as best I could. "I went to the Citadel, a big, big place far from here. There are people there who create images of anything in their mind. They can't make it come to life, they can't make it harden like I do with my swords. But the image is still there, in the air in front of them."

Rana's eyes widened. "That sounds like a mad place."

"It's mad, all right. But it's also a place where they can treat him."

Rana nodded. "That's good," she said.

"I've got to go help fight the bad men," I said, rising. "I'll be back. I promise."

"Jason..." Rana rose as well. There was something else she wanted to say to me but couldn't find the words. "I've seen Dad create all sorts of things. All sorts of memories."

I smiled, encouragingly. "I know. It must have been scary for you."

"A lot of it was scary," Rana admitted. "But that's all right. It's helped make me braver. And there's been some good stuff there, all amongst the scary things. Jason, I saw *Mother.*"

I couldn't speak. The idea of my father, recreating my mother in shadow in front of my frightened little sister... it was too much to take. Tears made my vision swim.

"I'd forgotten what she looked like," said Rana.

My throat felt like it was clogged up, preventing me from speaking. "How did she look?" I managed to croak.

Rana's lips curled into a warm smile. "Beautiful," she said simply.

Chapter Fifty-Four

I raced up the stairs in order to catch up with Aelia and Yen. I left Emilian behind. As I travelled up, the people of the Hollow dropped off, leaving the tower to the ghosts and cobwebs.

It was understandable, really. As much as our culture was based on the idea that to be closer to the sun was a measure of safety, there was also an in-built fear about climbing too high. After all, they believed the deities in the plains above smote humanity down into the Canyons and would only invite them up once they were worthy. To climb up too high was to be in danger of defying the gods.

The tower also became more and more labyrinthine, the further up I went. After a while there was no set structure of a winding staircase in the middle, surrounded by chambers. Now the stairs seemed to climb this way and that, sometimes ending in dead ends, so that I would have to retreat and take another hall. The corridors narrowed, the orientation more difficult. There was also the sense that this part of the tower had not been abodes, but places where people came and went. There were more doors, which had all been boarded shut, leading outside to bridges, which would then take one to tunnels into the cliff walls around the tower.

I rose to the final drawbridge, out of breath from rushing

up all those steps. It was below a loft underneath the roof of the tower: it pointed up over me as if I were in the middle of a giant's arrow head.

There were Aelia, Yen, and Helton. The latter did not look happy, his bewilderment and shock now turning into a scowl of anger.

"There you are," said Aelia. "Just ready for the big show."

"What are you going to do with me?" grunted Helton.

"I'm going to show you what we're up against, so we can all work together to become a little less dead," Aelia said.

I stepped forward. "What if the scout sees us?"

Aelia shrugged. "They know that your people are holed up here anyways. Shouldn't make a difference."

Corinthia had her arms crossed; her brows furrowed. Despite her short nature, her look had an intensity with we all picked up on. When she thought about strategy and defense, Corinthia had the tendency to frown so hard enough the lines of age on her face were accentuated by a decade or two.

"Got an idea, Commander Corinthia?" I asked.

"If I've understood correctly, this scout is hovering over us as a marker, correct?"

I nodded.

"Well then, let's bring them down. Without the marker, the company might take longer to get here and will buy us time to shore up our defenses. Plus, it will show me how difficult it is to fight these people."

Aelia's lips turned into a smirk. "You want to start the fight already? You won't get any resistance from me. I need to lead the charge, someone needs to hold this ruffian instead of me."

"I don't need to be held. Release me, and I will see what there is to see," Helton.

"Which would be all well and good, if I even had the slightest notion you could be trusted."

Yennenga held out her hand, and in her palm shadows crystallized into a shadow-javelin. I noticed that it was in a Therian shape, shorter than the usual Hollow spears, with diamond-shaped blades at its end. She'd been listening to the ghosts, and training hard.

"I'll make sure my father doesn't step a foot out of line," she said, her features hard as steel.

Helton considered his daughter. "You'd kill me, would you?"

"If it meant saving the rest of us."

Helton grew solemn at this.

Aelia gave out instructions. "Jason and I will try to bring the scout down. Jason, I need you to use your Mind's Eye to pair your shadow-spear with a vine."

"You need to do the *what* with the *what-now*?" Yen asked.

I'd forgotten just how much my abilities had changed since I'd last seen her. But now wasn't the right time to explain. Aelia waved her hand, dismissing the question, and I focused just on her.

"That should be fine," I said. "I've trained making that link a little."

"We'll try and take the scout down with spears, and pull them in. If we're going to be able to pierce the light-wings, we're going to need weapons as strong as possible. Use the shadows stored in your core for this form. We'll need to be quick."

Corinthia interjected. "I can try and help with my shadow-whip."

"Good."

I closed my eyes, and concentrated, going into my Mind's Eye in order to pair up different forms. "I'm ready," I said, as I also let shadows seethe into my palm, taking the shape of a shadow-staff with a spear end.

"Then let's do it," Aelia went to the door. "Corinthia, count us down."

Aelia and I gathered in front of the door, with Corinthia just behind us, and Yen with her father behind her. We crouched, steeling ourselves, while the Commander whispered.

"Three…two…one."

Aelia shoved the bar to the side and gave the door a kick. Without thinking for even a heartbeat, I surged forward, leaping out of the tower.

We were on a stone walkway which led into a tunnel opposite. But the top of the cliff and the plains were not far off, only a tree's length away. The sunlight blanched the surroundings, brightening the bridge underneath our feet, the red cliffs about us, it took us a moment to adjust our vision. The sense of being too far up, of threatening to tread in the realm of gods, took Yen and Corinthia's breath. I heard Helton growl, an involuntary spasm of fear at having the sky so close to him.

Aelia and I had to act quickly. We ran across the walkway. I cast a quick glance down, and saw the tower stretch down into darkness below, the odd bridge barely puncturing what looked like a plunge into the underworld itself.

The only thing which blotched the black were the Void, ink strokes of grey against the gloom. Some perched on the walkways, while others circled the tower, predators waiting for an opportunity to fall upon their prey.

The drop was vast, yet something told me that if I were to fall out of the sunlight, I wouldn't make it to the bottom.

"There!" said Aelia, interrupting my thoughts.

I looked up, where the tower's head finished in the shape of a spear, reaching into the sky.

Above it hovered the scout, their light-wings flapping gently. The scout was a man with light brown hair braided in a top knot. He didn't move for a moment, his eyes wide in surprise.

This was our chance. Aelia had a shadow-spear in her hand which she cast aloft with considerable force. It hummed through the air and implanted itself into the scout's left wing.

The scout cried out in surprise as he dropped down to our level, his stability thrown off by the shadow piercing into his form.

I let fly with my own spear. Linked to it was a a shadow-vine. It pitched into the scout's other wing, and I held on.

"Help me!" I cried. I felt Aelia and Yen grab my vine too,

allowing me not to be swept off my feet as the scout tried to escape in an awkward, torn flightpath. Corinthia's shadow-whip lashed through the air, wrapping around the scout's ankle, another anchor.

Still in shock, and not recovering from our attack, the scout did not manage to regain a sense of control. With the lashings on him, his flight was torn off course, and with a shriek he careened straight into the tower.

There was a hideous *thud* as he collided with the monolith, and suddenly all the light dispersed, rushing up past us to rejoin the sky. His weave collapsed, his wings were no more, and I was hanging onto nothing.

Aelia's instincts were quicker than mine. She let go of my useless form and grabbed Corinthia's whip. Together, they held on to the scout as he dangled below us.

He swayed this way and that for a moment, twisting in the gloom. The hungry abyss beckoned for him below.

When he stopped moving so much, I caught a sight of his bloody face.

"Try and weave another pair of wings and I'll shoot you down, Lightguard," growled Aelia into the darkness below. But she didn't have to, with the blood in his eyes, and the way in which one of his arms hung limp, I didn't think him capable of flying any more.

The man coughed, spluttering a few drip of red into the throat of darkness underneath him.

"You're too late," he coughed, his look of shock turning into a grim satisfaction. "They're *coming…*"

"We'll deal with them the same way we dealt with you," I shouted down at him.

"Not just the warriors. *Them.* You'll never last till dawn. Not even you, *traitor.*" This last sentence was directed at Aelia.

The scout looked down at the immensity of the drop. And with a flurry of motion, light cascaded from above, amalgamating into a knife into his good hand. The scout slashed at the shadow-bonds at his ankle and released himself from Corinthia's cord.

He was gulped down into the gloom. He spiraled for a moment, chased by beams of light as he tried to create light-wings mid-flight.

Aelia started creating a shadow-spear, but I put a hand on her shoulder, seeing something else in the gloom below.

"No need," I said gravely.

The scout's fall was broken by a circling Void. It caught him in its jaws, and his fallen body was ripped apart before it could drop further.

I turned to the others. Corinthia seemed to have her head about her, but Yen was completely overwhelmed. She'd seen a Lightguard weaving light and flying. It was all too much for her to process at once.

Helton's reaction was even more marked. It seemed to shake his foundations, bringing him to his knees in the middle of the walkway, his eyes shimmering with desperation, his face wrought. He'd been wrong.

I spoke to Aelia. "Did the scout mean what I think he meant?" I asked.

"What do you mean? He was just trying to scare us..."

I shook my head. "I don't think so. He said *them*. And he said that *we wouldn't last until dawn.*"

Realization dawned on Aelia's features. "*No...*" she said.

"What are you talking about?" demanded Corinthia.

"We've not stopped being the Lightguards' test subjects," I said grimly. "There's a reason the enemy haven't arrived yet. They can only travel under cover of night." I steeled myself before saying the words, as if just uttering them would make the danger more real. "They've developed a new kind of Void. Bigger. Deadlier.

"That's how they intend to wipe us out, by unleashing the new Void upon us."

Chapter Fifty-Five

We picked our way back down through the gullet of the tower. Despite how much we had to say to each other, how much I still needed to share with my friends, we were silent. For all of us, the sense of dread and responsibility weighed down our footsteps.

We needed to figure out how to survive, and what to tell the rest of the Hollow.

Helton's silence was perhaps the most significant. He walked with his head bowed, his head shaking sometimes, as if in dialogue with himself. Clearly, he was still wrestling with what he'd seen. He did not need to be bound anymore, indeed, he did not seem to be threatening anyone, the wind had completely left his sails.

At one point, he stopped, and his stillness was so marked that everyone stopped with him.

"We need to go, Helton," said Corinthia. "There is much to do."

His voice, ordinarily so commanding, was broken. "I saw her do it."

There was a flash of anger in Yen's eyes as she cleared her throat and voiced. "What are you talking about?"

Regret cracked his voice further. "I saw Echo, use light like that once. Like we used shadows. But I didn't question it.

Didn't question anything. She said that it was a privilege of the prophets, and it seemed so holy. I never thought that she could be part of a people who wanted to annihilate us."

I itched to say something. It was his *unquestioning* nature which had led him to do anything Echo asked of him. Including killing my mother for asking too many questions. He might see the error of his ways now, but he would never get my forgiveness for it.

The memory of my sister, seeing my mother in the shadows, tore through me, a fresh pain.

I kept my mouth shut.

"You believed no one apart from Echo," said Yen. Tears made the torchlight dance in her eyes. "You never believed me, or Jason, or anyone else. I thought that perhaps after the Hollow burned down, and after everything that had happened, you might finally come around. You still chose not to trust me. You poisoned people against my leadership, and now, when the sky is about to descend on us, you're still too cowardly to look me in the eye and say sorry. Sorry for all the blood you've spilled, sorry for the corpses you've created. Sorry for betraying me."

Helton nodded. "I'm only brave in the dark. And so... I wanted to have people there with me. In the darkness." He raised his head. "My daughter..."

Yen seethed. "It's too *late*! You can't call yourself my father now!"

He nodded slowly. Every word was a wound, I could see that. And yet he never flinched. Helton had never flinched in his life. "Then I will do the only thing I can. The only thing I know."

He strode forward, leaving us in his wake as he traveled downwards.

"What on the skies does *that* mean?" I said.

"Who cares? As long as he keeps out of our way..."

Corinthia placed a hand on Yen's shoulder... and then drew her into an embrace. For a split second, the Yen I knew, the fierce warrior, the strongest person I knew, flailed. Her knees buckled, and she leant into Corinthia's arms, finding comfort there.

Why hadn't I done that? I thought. *Why hadn't I realized what Yen needed at that moment, and given it to her?*

"Sorry," Yen said, wiping a quick hand across her face. She glanced with embarrassment at Aelia for her tears. "I'm fine. Don't know what happened to me there."

"No shame in tears," offered Aelia.

We walked on. I felt a longing to walk with Yen, and to console her, but something held me back.

She'd given herself that one moment of sadness, in Corinthia's arms. I didn't think she'd allow herself another.

And, unsure of what to do, I held back. I did, however, mutter under my breath to Aelia. "Since when are you so nice and understanding, all of a sudden? Where's my heartless would-be executioner gone?"

"If Yen grew up with that man as a father," replied Aelia, "then she's had enough heartlessness for a lifetime. Trust me, I know." She turned to me. "I'm seeing now how much your people have been pushed to the brink. More than any Shade users in the Citadel. Maybe if we can get out of here, and if the people could hear the story of places like the Hollow, then we'd have a real revolution in our hands."

"*If.*"

"Yes. But apart from the considerable threat of death, I'm starting to think that I made the right decision to come here."

"Forever on the side of the downtrodden, aren't you?"

"Always. And there's few cases as dire as the Hollow."

"That, and the fact that you take my training *very* seriously."

"Speaking of that," Aelia changed the subject a little. "Did you have the same thought as I did? On that bridge?"

I wracked my thoughts. "No…" I admitted.

"Well, I've never been standing on the surface of so much darkness before. All those acres of shadows, pooling beneath us. We should be able to harness it in some way, no?"

Corinthia stopped us. "Soon we will be getting to the

Hollow. We need to stop and strategize. We need to give our people a plan, along with the bad news. Is Helton...?" She looked, but Helton had strode ahead and not heard us.

"Leave him," said Yen, a trace of bitterness in her voice. "He won't factor in our plans."

"I just hate to think about what he will tell the Hollow in our absence..."

"If he needs to be dealt with again, he will be dealt with again," said Aelia.

We stood there a moment, the four of us, wondering who would speak first.

"I suppose the best way to start is to fully consider the danger, then consider how to stop it," proposed Corinthia. She was the expert at defense, she'd been famous for it in the Hollow. I could see that expertise now.

"As I understand it," I said. "This next batch of the Void are about three times as big as the ones we know. They can also withstand fire, they call them the Void Enflamed. So I imagine that we need to consider that monsters that size could break the walls and tear this building down bit by bit. I would also consider the fact that the Lightguard could set the tower on fire, in an attempt to flush us out. It would make sense since it wouldn't affect the Void anyway."

Corinthia nodded. To Aelia, she asked "What threat does the Lightguard pose? What will be their strategy?"

Aelia considered this for a moment. "My best guess is they will bring the new Void in chains overnight and launch the attack in the morning by unleashing them into the shaft. That way, the Lightguard have all the light they need, monitoring from the plains above. They can let the Void do the dirty work below, without any of the monsters traveling back in the light and retaliating against them."

Yen made a groan of despair. "So we'll have the Lightguard at the top, the Void below, and a healthy mixture of souped-up-Void and fire in between? Can I get someone to confirm that that's our predicament before I go and stab myself to death?"

"Well if you put it like *that,*" I started to say.

Corinthia interjected, "I definitely wouldn't..."

"Then it sounds like a death trap. Like we should get out of here."

"We can't move everyone out. You've drawn hordes of Void to our door, they'll tear us apart."

"What about all the bridges, coming out of the sides of the tower?" Aelia asked. "Can't we take one of those?"

Yen shook her head. "We explored all of them. All the tunnels they lead to are dead ends, with the ceiling collapsed. It seems like when the Lightguard slaughtered the Therians here, they blocked off as many routes as possible. They knew how potent this tower was for training up new Shade Users."

Corinthia spoke with certainty. "We are in the best place we can be. We make sure everyone is in the training room, with anyone not on duty cycling. And then we post warriors on every floor. We attract the Void to go for the top floors, away from the citizens. And then we go lower and lower."

"That buys us time," commented Aelia. "But it doesn't give us a way to get out of here alive."

"Buying time is all we ever do," said Corinthia. "Drawing out the battle, and controlling the fight *is* our best chance of survival."

"Even if we draw it out long enough to kill all of the Void Enflamed, the Lightguard will be right there above us, waiting to finish the job."

"Right. But they'll have to come down into the world of shadow to do it. They'll have to contend with the Void here, just like we do. And they'll have to fight us in the dark, which is our territory. If they come down, we kill off all the torches, and use our Senses. We'll be able to see five times as well as they can, hopefully it will be the edge we need."

I sighed. "I get the distinct feeling that this tower is going to be torn apart, stone by stone."

Corinthia nodded. "Maybe. We just need to make sure we take down the enemy with it."

Chapter Fifty-Six

We gathered the people of the Hollow in the training chamber and announced our plans. Everyone, it seemed, apart from the infirm like my father, was there, crammed in among the shrines and the ghosts.

Yen outlined the basic premise of what danger was befalling us, then Corinthia came in and explained the details of how we were going to try and survive it. It was an effective double-act. You could see that everyone hung onto Yen's every word, that she was seen as someone who truly embodied the promise and hope that everyone needed. Even though the Yen I knew had the capacity to be cynical and sarcastic, she had the same effect on me, her presence was one that reminded me to strive to be my best self.

Corinthia, too, made for an interesting contrast. For as inspiring as Yen was, I could also tell that the people of the Hollow appreciated having someone come and outline details with the gravitas afforded by experience.

They both emphasized how much Aelia and I were to be trusted, and how much we had risked to help them. I appreciated this, but then held back as much as possible, trying to blend in with the background. Still, I could tell that people were making up their minds about me. Last time they'd seen me, I was a lowly Pastfinder who they'd barely paid any notice to. Now I was this warrior in strange clothing, a stranger who had brought in an exotic companion.

There was nothing I could do to chase away their doubts, I knew, apart from fighting by their side and proving myself. The suspicion sewn by people like Commander Helton had done its damage, and the result was confusion and insecurity, no matter what Yen and Corinthia told them.

"Emilian will be in the lower floors, managing the warriors there," explained Corinthia finally. "Anyone here who can fight must do so, on four-hour shifts, anyone not fighting should remain in this room, either cycling or resting. We must be ready to leave the tower and evacuate at a moment's notice."

"Evacuate, you mean getting through the Void? They are all right outside the door!" someone shouted.

"We will avoid this at all costs," admitted Corinthia. "However, if that is the only route open to us, we must take it."

Someone started wailing with fear in the crowd, beset with fear and grief. Others muttered notes of fear and dissent amongst themselves.

"We *must* be strong, for everyone in the Hollow, for our future, and for the ones we have lost," spoke Yen, sensing the worry of her people.

"How can the deities test us so?!" someone shouted.

"I do not know," said Yen, avoiding the question of faith altogether. "All I know is that I intend to survive this siege. And any other siege or battle that comes our way. We have been battle-hardened all our lives, whether we were in the Shadowfront or not. I refuse to believe we all endured so much just to die off now."

"But who *are* these people from the skies?" another person shouted out angrily. "How can they be so evil if they come from the Paradise Plains?"

Aelia leant over to me and whispered in my ear. "There is no time for religious debate," she said.

"They are scared," I shrugged. "We are used to being beset

by monsters. But the fact that their faith is being challenged, that scares them on another level."

"We will get answers," said Yen. "But first we have to survive!"

This did not get the reaction required. Ripples of anger and fear and confusion spread amongst the crowd, and the volume of their chatter rose with their indignation. Yen and Corinthia looked at each other, a little uneasy.

If they lost the good will of the people, then everything would be lost.

"Silence!" a voice came, booming from the other side of the room. The crowd parted, bunching together as best they could to let the figure through.

It was Helton, in a line with a few men and women, the same who had supported him when he'd challenged us early.

A cold thought passed through me, like a cool blade stroking down the back of my spine. Had Helton regressed once more, and decided to take power?

He marched through the crowds, and all went silent in his presence.

Yen shot me a look of anxiety. Sensing our tension, Aelia prepared for the worst, uncrossing her arms, ready to Weave at a moment's notice.

Helton came to the front, and in a dramatic gesture turned on his heel to speak to the people of the Hollow. He was every bit the commander who spoke to the people, the man who had taught his daughter to capture attention.

A hero of the Shadowfront.

He spoke, and the room was so quiet that his words echoed off the stone walls. "I wish to say one thing, and one thing only. I have often doubted my daughter and Corinthia since they took on the leadership of the Hollow. I have questioned their every move. I have convinced people to resist them. I took their recommendation to use these strange new forms as an aberration."

He swallowed and made a face like someone who has tasted something sour.

"But now I have seen that aberrations come not just from the darkness. They come from the light too. They even come from the skies above, in the dwellings of the Gods. I have seen a taste of what lies above us, and it is more terrible than I could have imagined. Even Echo the Endless never prepared us for this. Even she, in all her wisdom, did not have the insight to see what would befall us."

He made a pause, my heart pounded to make up for the silence.

"I was wrong to question our leaders," he said finally. "So utterly, utterly wrong. I will carry that regret for the rest of my days. I have seen that, in the face of such horror, we must do what we can to live. We must band together and fight however we can. If we do that, then the Gods will receive us with open arms in our afterlives. I am sure of it."

Helton turned. "I may have been wrong in so much," he said, directed towards Yen. "But I hope that I still have something to offer. I do not have your clarity of vision, that much is clear. But I can slay Void. I've done it my entire life. Now, I humbly offer my services to you, for me and my best warriors to be in the frontline against the beasts."

Yen stepped towards him, her eyes shone with emotion, even as her face betrayed nothing. "I accept your offer, Commander Helton," she said. "With all the gratitude of the Hollow."

She put out her hand, and her father stepped forward and slapped his hand into hers, and they put their foreheads on the fingers, their faces close. A Hollow handshake.

I felt it in the crowds, a swelling of emotion. And then applause broke out, until it became louder and louder, as the father and daughter faced the crowds.

United.

The energy pulsed through everyone, as revitalizing as Anima.

"He pulled through," whispered Aelia, a little surprised.

"I still wouldn't trust him," I warned. "A spray of rain is not a storm, a ray of light is not a summer."

"Perhaps not. But it's a start."

I was about to answer, but then, out of nowhere, there was a crash. Boulders shattering and the whole tower trembled.

"What's that?" I cried, as the floor settled once more.

Aelia gave a pained look as shadows gathered at her fingers. "Seems like the attack has begun early," she said.

Chapter Fifty-Seven

We were shut in, there was no way to see what was happening outside without unlocking a window and peering out of the shutter outside.

Yen and I did so, opening the door a crack, and reaching out with our Senses, to try and see what had happened.

At first, I could not make out any details. Night had fallen, and the light filtering from above was now receding into darkness. All that I could see was a tumult of grey, of more and more Void tussling in the shadows outside of our walls, as numerous as wasps buzzing out of a disturbed nest.

The screeching of the Void, the amount of grey movement, almost made me close the door again straight away, lest they caught my presence and battered their way in. But then I also Sensed other flashes of movement, of stone dropping like rain, cracking onto the ground below.

I closed the door, and turned to Yen and Aelia, who had followed me to the door. "I think a walkway has crumbled," I said. "That's the cracking we heard."

"How could the stone bridges collapse, all of a sudden?" asked Yen.

"Light-blasts," said Aelia. "The first of the light-warriors have arrived and are now tossing explosions down at us. How many Void?"

"Many," I admitted. "More than I've ever seen since the burning of the Hollow. At least three or four hordes, as far as I can tell."

Aelia nodded. "The bridges are meaningless. They know they don't lead anywhere, just as we do. They're just making as much noise as they can to attract more Void."

"Well, they're doing a good job," admitted Yen. "And it's not just the Void they're riling up. It's also a scare tactic, isn't it? Getting us to shiver through the night before the attacks begin in earnest. So, what is a light-blast?"

We explained it to her, while she tried not to betray any reaction. "If there's a light-blast powerful enough to destroy bridges, it could also punch through the walls of this tower."

Aelia nodded. And since there was nothing else to do with that information, we did our best to ignore the blasts, and get to work with preparations. We ushered all the non-warriors to the training hall, and I escorted my family there with the help of Emilian's parents. It was no easy feat to keep people calm, when at intervals of a few hours at a time there would again be a boom, making a hideous noise which sounded like we were caught in the grinding teeth of giants. It broke people out of their meditative states too, breaking their cycling routines.

It seemed to make my father more agitated than he was normally, and he would shout nonsense out loud, and shadows would sometimes form above him, from some nightmarish memory he was reliving. He was disturbing the already frightened community, but there was nothing to be done; and so I gave Rana the biggest hug I could, and tried not to think too hard about how hard her heart was beating when I started up the stairs.

I headed up to the tallest door, where we had captured the scout earlier. Along the way, I saw that the warriors, newly trained, were posted at every door leading onto a bridge. There were so many that often there were only doors where two people could be posted, and many of them had only barely mastered, or in some cases not mastered at all, how to Weave.

These people gripped what physical weapons they had, their teeth set in a grim manner.

At the top, I found what we had decided was the main group. It constituted Corinthia, Aelia, Yen, and myself, as well as Helton with his band. Doing my best to ignore Helton, who volunteered to take the first post guarding, I took some much-needed rest, finding an empty chamber to sleep and cycle, filling my channels and core with Anima, some of it shadow-infused.

The night passed fitfully. We took turns watching at the door, then resting and cycling. Corinthia rested the least, she took it upon herself to monitor all of the warriors in the tower, ensuring that they knew their roles. She paced around the tower many times, until Yen implored her to stop and rest.

But no one got any good sleep. The tower trembled and shuddered, disturbed a blast was dropped outside. It was like the monument itself was fearful of its future.

Then, finally, dawn came upon us. We'd both feared it and wished for it. But when the light came, framing the door and windows with blades of yellow, I got up with dread drying my mouth.

We nodded to each other and reiterated the plan to step outside on the walkway, then retreat inside the tower. Hopefully, that would attract the Void. When they tried to pursue us inside they would be in a bottleneck, and in close quarters. That's when we would do our best to slaughter as many of them as we could before retreating to a lower floor.

It was a method of the Shadowfront. None of it catered to the dropping light-blasts from above, or the scale of the new beasts that would be attacking us. We already knew nothing we did *could* cater for such beasts.

We gave each other the Hollow Handshake, although I made sure never to offer one to Helton, who respected the distance I gave him.

And with that, we swung the door open once more, and stepped into the light, black blades gripped between our palms.

Ready for war.

The light was still weak outside. The sun could not be seen directly yet.

Above us, surrounding the top of the tower, a circle of light. Dawn's titled rays were just reaching across the opening above, and it was like an opening eye of a deity.

Around that circle, silhouetted against that red light, was the enemy.

They were silent figures dotting the lip of the cliff, so that the circle of light above us was fringed with threatening shadows. The lashes to the god's eye.

They looked down upon us, and we looked up at them.

The air was still. Sickeningly so. Moments passed, and then more moments, where I felt like I could hear only the breath passing through my lungs, and the restlessness of my heart.

Still, the silhouettes above did not move. They surveyed us. And waited.

"What are they waiting for?" Helton hissed.

No one answered, for no one knew.

Until, minutes that felt like hours passed, and we got our answer.

First, there was the thumping of heavy footsteps, the sound of thrashing feet on the plans above.

Then came the screams.

They were not the shrieks or brays of the Void we were used to. They were a hundred times more powerful, as loud as landslides. If the high-pitched whine of the Void normally hurt the ears, this sound's guttural impact went straight to our chests, rattling our bones.

This was the sound of something *colossal.*

More cold sweat gathered about me, in the pits under my arms, crawling down my back. Gooseflesh riddled my arms, and my throat went dry.

The screams got louder and louder.

They were not war cries. It was the peeling sound of agony, of torture.

The animals were being primed for violence, I realized. Tortured by the sun's first rays.

Someone next to me, one of Helton's men, started muttering a prayer under his breath. A stuttering prayer to Echo the Endless and the Gods above. I had no such god to pray to, so I tried to center upon my breath, to calm and focus myself as much as possible. To try, against all odds, to not let fear take me.

Finally, around the eye of light, there appeared something. The silhouettes against the dawn sky moved, making space for the arrival of something.

And then it appeared. A slumbering mass, a black figure as large as a tree, wrestled into view. It screamed down into the abyss, and the air shifted from its power.

A Void, but not like one we had ever seen before. The same shape but distorted into gigantic proportions. It had jaws the size of doorways, wings the size of caverns. It resembled nothing I had ever seen, a more nightmarish creation than even the Kukulkan dragon I had slain.

It was scrabbling away at the earth at the edge, it clawed stones apart, sending them clattering down into the darkness below. It wanted to get down into the hole where we stood, it wanted to get out of the dawn. Even the sun's weak rays were pelting it with pain, making it shriek with anger, its grey, pallid flesh turning red and sore.

Light-chains, however, kept it in the sun. Many, many light-chains, along all of its limbs, restraining it, making it more and more mad.

A Lightguard shot an arrow at the beast's wings. I did not understand at first, why were they attacking it? Were they making it even more angry than it needed to be?

But then I remembered. This new Void wasn't just bigger and stronger. It was also able to withstand flame.

The arrow had tongues of light, which then spread across the monster's back, until it was lined in red wroth. This made the monster even more flustered, if possible, and it redoubled its efforts to break free from its chains, and head down into the hole beneath it.

I started to count in my head, unable to bear the waiting, wanting to think about anything but that mass of oncoming death.

One...two...three...

More scrabbling. More screaming. More roasting flesh.

Four...five...six...

Flames emblazoned the creature, making it seem even bigger than before.

Seven...eight...nine...

Then it happened.

An order was shouted out by someone in the Lightguard. The light-chains dematerialized.

And the creature, desperate to get out of the sun, leapt down into the darkness surrounding the Tower of Babel.

Plummeting toward us.

Chapter Fifty-Eight

The humungous creature crashed onto the bridge in front of us, and the bridge made a hideous cracking sound as if it would be torn asunder.

The monster raised itself to its feet.

It loomed above us, a fiery vision of hell. It stretched out its flame-tongued wings, and opened its jaws to howl at us, and the scream was now a threat, a promise of the damage and pain it could cause us.

We spurred into action, the fear we had felt turning into a furious burst of adrenaline. Shadow-spears were cast into the air, spiking the Void's skin, remaining planted in its grey flesh before crumbling into shadows. The monster did not seem to notice or react.

It stepped forward, and loomed ahead with its jaws, ready to snap at our group. It caused a rush of movement, so much so that one of Helton's men lost his footing trying to move out of the way—and was immediately yanked down into the abyss, tumbling into the nothing.

The Void's jaws, big enough to hold an entire person within them, snapped at nothing, but the proximity of the scorching skin caused a blaze of heat to sweep among us.

I wasted no time. With my half-moon blades ready, I dove beyond the snap of the jaw, waving the weapon aloft, trying to tear a line of blood into the creature's throat. It made contact, gouging at the grey skin, but not enough to be lethal. The creature growled and scrabbled at me with its claws.

I felt a singe of heat as the creature's fingers pinned me down, and the whole world was ablaze for a moment. The Void's head hovered above me for a second, and the jaws opened, revealing those dagger-teeth, glazed in slobber.

The mouth opened, ready to close upon my skull, until Aelia leapt in, digging a spear into the floor of the Void's mouth, and then, with a flick of shadows, turning that spear into a trident, the teeth now at the other end of the staff to attack the monster's roof.

The Void made a hiss of annoyance, the sort of noise normally made under one's breath, but at this size was louder than the crash of storm rain.

The claws released me, swiping at Aelia instead. Retreating, she tripped and fell, landing on her stomach. She was in a vulnerable position, with the jaws of death about to descend upon her, but Corinthia's whip lanced through the air, curling around Aelia's wrist, and the Citadel warrior was pulled back just in time to avoid the snap of the Void's jaws.

"Into the tower!" cried Corinthia, but there was no need. We were all running as fast as we could. Now that we had provoked the creature, we just hoped that we could draw the monster to the doorway and then fight it from there.

We piled through the doorway, almost falling on top of each other. But we did not have time to turn and face the creature before it was already upon us.

It did not stop at the doorway. Plunging its long, eyeless head through the gap, it pursued us with such drive that that stone around the door crumbled, and there was a rain of rock. An almighty crash resounded around us, as the stones exploded across the hall.

"Take cover!" commanded Corinthia. But there was no cover to take. The creature's impact upon the tower wall was making everything shake and rock, like the entire monument was about to collapse.

The roof above us crumbled, sending stone hurtling down.

I heard a warrior make a blood-curdling shriek as a collapsed section of the roof rained down on her, crushing her under its weight. Her voice was cut off in a way that felt immediate and permanent.

A large section of the roof hurtled down upon the Void Enflamed, and it raged as it tried to shrug off larger and larger segments of the structure as it struck it down.

I winced, thinking that we would all share the same fate, and that we would all be coated with stone and crushed to death. But there was a humming noise, there amongst the grinding noise of disintegrating walls and the screams of the Void, and I saw that Corinthia had created a shadow-barrier above her head, a shield to give us shelter.

The roof of black was immediately pelted with landslides of stone above me. I knew that Corinthia's barriers could withstand a lot, but surely not this much.

The moment my fear struck me, Corinthia howled in exertion, as if to confirm it. Her arms shook, as the black stretch above started to tear, letting blocks of stone drop in among us.

Corinthia twisted her outstretched wrists, tilting the disintegrating shelter, and there was a rumble as the stones tumbled off of it. The black ceiling disappeared, and above us there was no barrier between us and the raining stone.

Luckily, the worst of the roof's disintegration had passed, and what was left seemed in stable enough shape. The cloud of dust dissipated, clearing the view. We witness how an entire section of the roof had landed on the Void, crushing its right wing. It screamed in protest as it pulled, trying to extricate itself from the rubble.

"This is our chance," I said. "We've got to kill it!"

"You're right," said Yen, baring a set of shadow-khopeshes. "Jason, let's finish it off!"

Before we could, a familiar sound came. A chorus of screeches, a tumult of grey.

A horde of the original, smaller Void swept in, seizing their opportunity for violence. A cloud of gnashing teeth came our way, pouring through the gaps in the walls and the roof. At least two dozen creatures gushed in, swirling in circles above our heads. They avoided the lumbering figure of the Void Enflamed, as if in awe of it.

The larger creature's presence was not enough to stop them from attacking us. The tornado of grey spiraled down towards our group and unleashed their unmistakable brand of carnage.

All about, swathes of grey flitted and tore, this way and that. One of the warriors was taken immediately, stolen into the air, and picked apart by a frenzy of teeth, misting the air with his blood.

Those of us who were left held our Weaves aloft and did our best to plant our blades into the wash of grey flesh. I rotated my half-moon blades, and the weapon effortlessly sliced through the channel of Void, catching one limb of a creature here, a wing of another. Blood spattered along my forearms as I wheeled the blades this way and that, keeping the staff in constant motion.

Beside me, Yen was just as quick, jabbing this way and that with her pair of khopeshes, the curved blades digging into the monsters, as they flew above her.

I swatted one away, slicing off its lower jaw, and it careened away with a shriek, colliding with another Void, I saw them veer into a clumsy fall into the larger Void's back. Immediately catching fire, they leapt away, and their mad trajectory across the fire was a streak of red against the gray.

Blood mingled with stone, dust, and smoke. We battled as best we could, every warrior engaging in a desperate duel with the charge of monsters nosediving upon us. When we could, we helped one another. In one instance, a Void crashed into one warrior, flinging her off her feet. Just as a swarm was about to pounce upon the warrior in her vulnerable position, Aelia and I leapt in, carving through Void-flesh as the monsters swarmed about us.

But still, the onslaught of Void was unrelenting. We were

not going to be able to kill them all, and then give ourselves the opportunity to attack the larger one.

We needed to get out of there before we were slowly picked off.

A clutch of warriors launched Helton into the air, and he performed his famous maneuver, shards of shade sprayed about him in every direction, emitting a wave of black. The hail of shards pelted the Void, making many shriek with pain and sending them blindly into collision courses with the tower walls.

It gave us the precious moment we needed.

We took it and ran. In the brief moments before the Void fell upon us again, we retreated the way we had come, towards a flight of stairs leading down to the lower floors.

Even as we ran, leaping over stone, avoiding the craters in the floor created by falling debris, we felt a presence building behind us as a cloud of monsters gathered and swooped.

One of us stumbled, and Corinthia caught the warrior, to fall was to die. Another decided to turn, readying a shadow-arrow onto a bow, despite everyone calling out for him to keep running. There was a sickening *crunch* behind us as we heard the warrior's death at the hands of the Void.

This is no trained Shadowfront, I thought to myself. These warriors had not lived the lives of soldiers and the rigid discipline that came with it. Spending a month or so under the tutelage of Corinthia, or Helton, was no replacement for a career spent in the art of warfare.

We were in disarray and dying.

We plunged down the narrow steps, leading down into a narrow hall of stone, a corridor that filled immediately with movement.

"Turn!" ordered Corinthia.

Some of us dropped to our knees, others simply turned to draw their weapons. I fell to the floor, letting my half-moon blades disperse as the staff took up too much space.

The Void were coming after us, but in small spaces their wings were hindrances as much as anything else. They scrambled over each other, some even gouging into each other with their claws in their process. They were like a landslide, a tumble of boulders rolling towards us.

With the enemy in a bottleneck, there was no need for accuracy.

"Fire!" barked Corinthia.

A volley of shadow-spears and arrows spewed out of our company: every single one of them hit their mark, somehow causing the melee of Void to become even more chaotic, a turbulence of claw and bone as they crashed into each other, tearing through each other's bodies to get closer to us.

"Once more!" said Corinthia, and another blast of black punctured the deluge of grey. Blood coated the walls, and more twitching, eyeless bodies carpeted the floor.

"Halt!" I said. I hadn't participated in the volley.

Instead, I had been brewing something to bring the fight to a close.

I rose and stepped forward. I held my palms open in front of me—and created two gouts of black flame which sprayed the bodies in the corridor. They immediately ignited, combusting, and it spread through the bodies as if carried by a gust of wind.

The screeching was deafening as it rang through the corridor. The creatures no longer flew nor crawled towards us, retreating back the way they came instead.

I breathed a sigh of relief.

It was too early to do so.

One Void, clearly too far ahead to return, pounced ahead. Its head was coated in black blood, the kind which would have blinded its vision if the creature had eyes. Flames trailed it.

I was first in line, but I had not been prepared for this. My Anima levels were low, and I did not have time to form a new weapon. Completely taken aback, I turned to run, only resulting in falling upon the floor as I did so.

I turned, my hands over my head as if they would somehow stop the arrival of those deadly jaws.

But then, just as the creature's head loomed over me, it was stopped.

A screen of black washed from one side of the corridor to the other, Corinthia had created another barrier of shadow. This one caught the Void in its neck, stopping it in its tracks as its head was one side of the barricade, and its body in the rest.

It was frozen in place, gnashing at nothing but air, with no way to move.

I got up, my heart pounding, and watched as it whined in protest, saliva dripping down to the floor.

"Finish it, Jason," Yen said, appearing before me. She had a shadow-khopesh in her hand, which she tossed in my direction.

I caught the shadow-form, and a frisson went through me. It was rare to handle someone else's Weave, few formations in the Shadowfront entailed it, as far as I knew. It felt odd to hold someone else's khopesh, perhaps even more so because it had been formed from the Anima inside her core. The essence had been purified inside her chest, decorating the form with steel blue.

It was almost intimate.

I bore Yen's khopesh aloft, and then drove it down. It sliced through the Void's neck, separating its head from its body.

Then, Corinthia dispersed the wall of black, and the body of the creature clattered down.

There were no more Void coming to get us now, those who could had left, and those who couldn't were roasting in a fire of corpses.

Smoke, and a hideous smell, coiled about our nostrils.

"Time to leave," Yen pointed out.

I nodded in agreement. "But can I borrow this a moment longer?" I held her khopesh.

"What for?" she asked, frowning.

I looked down at the headless corpse of the Void. "I want its wings," I answered.

Chapter Fifty-Nine

We regrouped a few flights down.

The mood was somber. On the one hand, we had executed our plan with about as much success as could have been expected, we'd killed a considerable amount of Void.

But it was hard to feel a sense of achievement. The Void Enflamed had been more formidable than we had imagined. It would have extricated itself from the rubble, and we would have achieved little more than annoying it. The fact that it so easily knocked a hole in the tower wall meant that we would never be completely safe in the tower.

There was a pause, now. The Void was resting and licking its wounds. The Lightguard above seemed to be forming a new plan of attack.

Right now, it was quiet.

The Void Enflamed was still there, outside the tower. As for the other Void… well, there were plenty more where *they* came from.

We contemplated all of this as we caught our breath. "We are going to have to remain silent," Yen pointed out. "The Void have incredible hearing senses. If the Void Enflamed hears where everyone is sheltering, it could just punch a hole in wall and attack that floor."

"Agreed," said Corinthia. "We need to reaffirm our message to the others, to keep silent as death to not attract the creatures' attention. We lost three warriors back there and gained very little. We are going to have to do better than that if we are going to survive this siege. Any ideas?"

Corinthia shot an enquiring look at Aelia, who was busy adjusting her armor. "Sorry," she said. "I think the baiting-and-killing is all we've got. We don't have the trained army to do anything more sophisticated than that. Get them in those narrow corridors like we did there and kill them bit by bit."

Helton harrumphed. "This means luring them more and more into our home. Hardly how sieges are supposed to work."

Yen shrugged. "We can hold out for a few days like this. If it means cutting them down one by one, and that's the safest way to do it without sacrificing any more lives, that's the way we do it."

Corinthia crossed our arms. "Which deals with the Void, of course. It's the old tactics of the Shadowfront, Helton and I have been that for all our lives. It doesn't deal with the more pressing threat of the Void Enflamed, or the Lightguard above. Before long, I get the impression that they'll start tearing the whole tower down, and then our strategy means nothing."

I cleared my throat, drawing everyone's attention towards me. "I haven't really figured this out properly yet, but maybe I can help."

"Has this idea of yours got anything to do with *those*, by any chance?" she said, her ironic tone making me feel like we were teasing each other as youths again.

She pointed at the wings I had sheared off the corpse of the Void. They were currently folded and strapped to my back, giving me the strange air of an insect.

"*Maybe*," I returned, with just as much sarcasm. "I've used the wing-forms as Weaves before. Only in desperation, and only to glide. But now I actually have the things to study, maybe I could form them better. Maybe I could use them properly."

"And fly?" grunted Helton.

"Wow, you weren't kidding when you said that you hadn't figured this out," added Yen.

"Hear me out," I said, putting up my hands to placate them. "If the bait-and-kill strategy is what works with the Void, and it seems to work with the Void Enflamed, then that's what we have to do."

"The problem is that attacking the Void Enflamed involves bringing our own tower down on its head," Yen interjected. "Not the safest way to survive a siege."

"But not necessarily. There are other ways to bring infrastructure down. The bridges- if we can bring one of *them* down on the monster, then surely we could kill it?"

They considered my plan.

"Except that being outside and on the bridges is where we are at our most vulnerable," Corinthia said. "You've got both kinds of Void, and the Lightguard above. You won't be able to fly quickly enough to escape all of them, let alone have the power to destroy bridges."

"It has to be possible, *somehow,*" I said.

"It might only be the start of a thought," said Yennenga. "But right now, it's all we've got."

"That's true," said Corinthia, her tone uncertain. "Let's keep it in our thoughts. But in the meantime, we need to regroup. Head downstairs, report back, and cycle."

Aelia interjected. "Is the safest way not to head out through the bottom? Try our luck with the Void? Jason and I survived it."

Corinthia shook her head. "They're attracted to noise. With the ruckus we've caused, the area at the bottom of the tower will be swarming with them. No, I wouldn't try and get children and the sick out that way, not unless there was no other choice."

We did as instructed. We headed back down a flight of stairs and went to the training hall. We had to ensure that we weren't swamped immediately: everyone had heard the commotion from upstairs and were wondering how we had fared. We had to ensure that they remained quiet, and that we would only talk in whispers.

I was able to extricate myself, as most of the attention was not directed at me. I caught Aelia's eye, and we went to find a chamber by ourselves to cycle.

"You've got something in mind," she said, as we immersed ourselves in darkness, taking our fill of Anima.

"The Essence-Gathering," I said. "I need to improve it."

"Improve it?" Aelia gave me a look of apprehension; or rather, in the dark, her tone suggested it so much that I felt like I could see it. "You've only just managed to learn how to use it. That's more than any shade user in centuries, as far as anyone knows."

"But it's not enough. And what's more, you need to know how to use it too."

"Since we've come to your end of the Canyonlands, you've really become a lot more bossy, you're aware of that, right?"

"Just listen. If my plan works, and we can destroy the bridges and make it rain onto the Void Enflamed, there needs to be two of us. I managed to use Essence-Gathering to make myself into that statue, right? Well, that gave me a coating of armor which the Quaester couldn't break through."

Aelia held up a hand. "Wait... are you thinking what I'm thinking? Something self-sacrificial and heroic?"

"Possibly."

Aelia sighed. "Skies above..."

"It makes sense. I can be the bait. With the stone-shadow around me, I could withstand the Void. Maybe even the jaws of the Void Enflamed. I could get it to come to me and survive, while you destroy a bridge directly above it."

"Hence you need me to do Essence-Gathering."

"Exactly. We need the equivalent of a light-blast, but with shadow. Something really destructive, that could break stone."

Aelia contemplated this. "You've got a death-wish," she muttered.

"I *really* don't."

"I'm not saying this because your plan is risky. I'm saying

this because your plan *literally involves you dying*. Essence-Gathering wipes you of all your Anima and energy, you saw that when you fought the Quaester. What happens to you when you're in the jaws of this monster, and I bring down a hundred boulders on you?"

I patted the Void wings, which I'd placed beside me during my meditation. "I was hoping to count on these to escape."

"Ha!" Aelia exclaimed, in a dark laugh. "You've only just managed to Essence Gather, and now you think you can make a statue *and* wings?"

"Why not? If I can pair and link forms using my Mind's Eye, why can't I do the same while Essence-Gathering?"

"Because that is the kind of control which only true masters of Essence gain. The prodigies. I've heard of the Emperor being able to do that, back in the day, and Cizin is said to have been able to do that. But you're talking about surpassing a lifetime of training and doing it in the few days we'd realistically survive in here."

"A man's got to hope," I said.

"That man's going to die, if he's as foolish as you are."

"Foolishness has got me this far. I've survived a lot, most of it due to being a fool, one way or another."

There was silence in the darkness for a moment.

"Well, I've got one piece of good news," said Aelia.

"Good news?" I exclaimed. "I don't even remember what good news sounds like, at this point, what is it?"

"I'll show you."

Aelia got up, and with a rod-straight back, exited the chamber and went upon the stairs. With the tower above and the dark below stretching into forever, we faced the blackness, punctured with the odd pocket of torchlight amber. The tower was deadly silent, save the odd bump and shudder as monsters from outside clawed and battered at the stone.

Aelia closed her eyes and put her palms forward. She breathed in and out, a few times, while I waited with bated breath for what was going to happen.

At first, nothing happened. And then, slowly, the air

seemed to change around me. Something pulling at me, tugging at my insides, like I was in a whirlpool.

But then I realized that it wasn't the air that was rushing, nor my insides. No, it was something about the very dynamics of the tower that were changing.

I used my Anima to reach out with my senses. And amidst the stream of ghosts, all chanting their chants, cascading down the steps, the shadows were bending out of their natural course. Untethered from their natural space, they engorged the air about me.

I glanced at Aelia and saw what she was doing.

She was *Essence-Gathering*.

In the air above her palms, there was a form interlacing into shape, and on it was a blue glyph, the sign of core magic.

The shadows plunged down from above us, and swept up from below, converging, swooping, and banking into a ball at Aelia's hands.

She exhaled, and let it go, and the shadows fled once more, leaping back up to higher floors, or plummeting down below.

"Aelia, you can *Essence-Gather?!*" I gasped. "You told me I was the first since Cizin?!"

Aelia passed a hand across her brow, which had become moist with the effort. "Well, I'm hardly an expert. I don't always have the best control over the forms when I Essence-Gather, so I've never used it in battle. But yes, I have been working on making shadow-blasts for a while now."

For a moment, I had a rush of emotion. "Why are you telling me now? Because the situation is so desperate?"

Another monster hit the wall, somewhere up in the tower, we heard the sound of stone crumbling. The building trembled as a result. Aelia motioned up toward the sound with her thumb. "I think that answers your question."

"Was that form what I thought it was?"

Aelia nodded. "Like the light-blasts they've been dropping on us. So *maybe* I can destroy a bridge like you said. But it would be a one-time thing. We'd have to get it right the first time."

I smiled. "Sounds like you're agreeing to my plan."

"I didn't say that."

I felt a little ember of hope travel through my thoughts. "Aelia, you have to teach me *everything*."

Chapter Sixty

Aelia and I shared our experiences of Essence-Gathering.

As it turned out, the form of the blast was not a difficult form. It had not posed great difficulty for Aelia to place the shape in her Mind's Eye. However, what had taken significantly longer was the difficulty of maintaining enough control and stamina to keep it stable. It was just an intensity of shadow, balled together, condensed into a small object. It took significant effort to keep it intact, so that it could then burst apart when released.

Aelia had trained to do it for months. Partly, it had been out of frustration, rather than to use in any combat. After all, just learning to use it was a protest, a sign that shadows could do whatever light could.

She, too, had used an emotion to pull her through the process, her determination, a sense that her efforts to change an unfair world could not end without result. In this way, we found that we used similar trajectories to gather shadows.

"I imagine that I am calling for a greater morality, a greater sense of equality," I told her.

She nodded in agreement. "It's that desire to become bigger than yourself. For the Lightguard, I imagine it's their sense of entitlement. They believe in their own self-importance, that they are best to lead the world, and that they are the only masters who can take on the Demons of the Underworld. For us, it feels like we're breaking the rules of harmony and balance. It's disruptive, it feels wrong."

"And yet sometimes, the world needs to be broken, if it's going to be fixed properly."

"Exactly."

I motioned towards the wings. "Can you tell me how to gather enough that I can maintain these wings around me? I want them *huge,* like the scouts of the Lightguard."

Aelia shook her head. "I'm not an expert. The shadow-blasts I do, I've never even tried to use in combat or release them. They're rudimentary in shape. Just your statue form, which you used in your duel with the Quaester, that's a hundred times more intricate than what I do. But what we *can* do is be there for each other. If we push ourselves, the other can bring them back. Enable us to go further than we've ever gone."

We decided to find somewhere with more space. We ventured up higher in the tower, discussing how best to train.

I passed by Yen at one point as she was prepping a pair of warriors on the current situation. She shot me a quizzical look as we passed by.

"I'll explain later," I said. "Don't worry, it'll be worth it."

"You're excited. Which, given our current situation, is *deeply* concerning..."

"Oh, you have *no idea.*"

She didn't answer; she turned back to what she was doing. I felt a current of resentment in the way she turned away, but I didn't have time to think about it.

Aelia and I headed up, and when we felt sufficiently removed, practiced our forms once more in preparation. First we cycled as much as we could, then I worked on my Mind's Eye. Aelia helped me develop certain links I could make between the different chambers inside my Mind's Eye, especially during the close combat inside the halls of the tower, and out in the open on the bridges, where the Void would swarm about me from all directions.

But then we got down to the more important task of Essence-Gathering. We tasked each other with practicing gathering shadows and have them do our will.

It was a punishing training regimen, one which threatened to wipe out all of our energy. That by itself was a concern. As much as we wanted to improve our skills, we also had to be prepared to enter combat at a moment's notice. Throughout our practice, there were constant reminders of war. Dust shifted and shadows trembled as the monsters thudded and crawled and scraped at the walls outside as they prowled up and down the tower.

And yet we still managed to make improvements. I went first, circling the Anima so that it ejected blue forms into my shadows, creating the core sign which then bent and distorted all the darkness about me.

The problem was that the charge of shadows rarely felt under my control, it felt like the darkness was washing through me, or *tearing* through me, rather than responding to me. The more I tapped into my emotions, the better I concentrated on the form, and the more the blackness obeyed me.

I managed to recreate the statue form which I had used in the duel with the Quaester. This time it was in a better shape than the one I had used before, it was more stable, with fewer shadows leaking and spilling. Aelia marveled at it, for she had been too busy fighting herself to see how I had fared in the duel. She inspected how the shadows had to keep rushing in with every movement I made, recreating slightly different versions of the statue form with every movement, with layers of black interlocking and releasing and reshaping like a piece of intricate machinery.

I found that, even though Essence-Gathering hurt, it was hard to stop once I'd started. It was like the balance between me and my surroundings was broken, and no matter how painful it was I could not repair it. However, Aelia's presence helped. When I started to buckle, and when it seemed that I could no longer breathe, she spoke words which pierced through my panic, "Restore the balance, Jason, restore the harmony."

It was this sense of calm and order, breaking through the storm, which enabled me to regain control of myself, and lose the shadows so that they could be released back into the ether.

We then agreed that these would be the words to use, to anchor someone back if the darkness overtook them, so that we would never become mad like Cizin.

I then took a break, and instead studied the wings I had carved off the Void. I spent an hour simply studying them, memorizing every inch of their surface, storing the memory of it in the chamber of my Mind's Eye along with other animal forms such as that of the fire and the claws.

I took regular breaks and witnessed Aelia refine her own Essence-Gathering. She focused on practicing her shadow-blasts, creating bigger and bigger forms which would have the most impact, and then dispersing the shadows before they exploded. While the tower shook and rattled like a tree in a storm, attacked by monsters outside, she ignored the distractions to form those balls of shadow.

It was an impressive process to watch. Aelia needed a moment of calm, and intense concentration. The calm would seem to break, and her forehead creased into frowns of anger and furious study. Then she would raise her hands, and they would tremble with exertion.

All my life, I had been told that to be a warrior, one's mind had to be calm, like the surface of still water. But here I saw that when Aelia and I Essence-Gathered, it was something else altogether. It was rage and desire that allowed us to wring essence into form.

There was no wonder it brought about madness, if unchecked.

Aelia was almost frightening as she called for the darkness, and as all the black staring to be ensnared in the orb between her hands. It was like she was elemental, a force of destruction.

Do I look like that when I do it?

Her orbs became bigger and bigger. One time, her shapes were as big as a fist, then as a head, then a shield. I could always tell when she was losing control: it was in the sharpness of her breath, a gasping, and a look of panic taking in her eyebrows.

Then I placed a hand on her shoulder and spoke the words. *Restore the harmony.* Nervous myself, given that if her shadow-blast were to mistakenly go off our bones and flesh would coat the walls, I injected a sense of calm and control into my words. They always had the desired effect, Aelia's breaths regained their regularity, and the shadows peeled off in ribbons from her orb until it was completely unwrapped.

When it was my turn to practice once more, I tried to Essence-Gather, and then shape the shadows into huge wings, as wide as that of the Void.

It was not easy.

Even with the form in front of me to copy, laid at my feet, I found that in the mad rush of feeling, my Weave was too unstable. As soon as I created the shape, it started to immediately dismantle.

I tried again and again.

"It's getting better," remarked Aelia. "Every time, the shape is more stable."

Panting on sweating on the floor after an effort, I shook my head. "The form is so big. So intricate. It's not like I can use my imagination to fill in the gaps, every detail has got to be exactly right, or my flying is going to be off."

"You're trying to replicate the design of a killing-machine," Aelia noted.

"Exactly. Everything in it is honed to perfection. If a single stretch is off… it won't work."

"Listen, even without Essence-Gathering, you've managed to glide before."

"I've managed to *just about* avoid dying when I fell. Hardly the same as flying."

Aelia shrugged. "What you've got for now will have to do.

We need to rest and cycle if we're going to be any good for the next attack."

Reluctantly, I had to agree. My body felt like it had taken a beating, but from the inside, it was as if I had a layer of bruises on the wrong side of my skin. I needed to stop.

But when I'd cycled, and then rested, I decided to rest upon the wings, with them stretching out about my shoulders.

I took their shape with me into my dreams.

Chapter Sixty-One

I did not sleep long at all. A few hours, if not less.

I woke to what felt like the inside of a storm.

The battering of the tower was now unavoidable. I peeked out of a window, reaching out with my Senses, and saw what was happening.

There was not one, but two Void-Enflamed that were now encircling the tower. One was the one we had encountered earlier, its flight was a little uneven, and one of its hands seemed a little limp from the roof we had brought down upon it. The flames had died out, and now we could see its skin. It was gnarled from exposure to the sun, blotched with wounds.

The other, however, was a similar shape. It was just as huge, and just as terrifying. At the moment, it was not on fire. Instead, it lumbered about, tearing at the walls on occasion, sometimes perching on one of the stone walkways and braying.

Why, I wondered, hadn't it been ignited like the other?

With this question in my heart, Aelia and I gathered our forces, and went downstairs to regroup with the others. Taking some food from the rations and hastily stuffing it down our throats, we found Corinthia and Yen in the training hall with the rest of the community.

The people were shaken by the battering of the tower: it

was plain to see on all their faces. Every sound of stone collapsing and tottering, half of the people jumped a little, their nerves well and truly frayed.

"You've seen the new beast?" I asked Aelia.

She nodded.

"Why isn't it in flames?"

"We think that the Lightguard might be waiting to light them. That's when they're at their most enraged. So they're letting them rest for now, so that they can strike properly later. Remember, the Void attack in short, sharp moments. They cannot do sustained combat for long. So after the failure of the last attack, I imagine the Lightguard are probably thinking of the best moment to start again, and get better results."

I pointed above, as dust spattered down on us from the ceiling and an almighty groan came from above as something huge knocked into the tower. "You call this *resting*?"

"I do. I'll admit, it's starting to feel like we're waiting down here to die. Is it time for another attack?"

Corinthia nodded. "We have to rest. We cannot let them wear us down like this. We do as we did before, we lure the Void in and slay them. That will at least keep spirits up. Unless your training has given you the key to attacking the Void Enflamed?"

Aelia and I looked at each other. "Not yet," I said. "Aelia can make a blast which could be strong enough to take out a bridge, or a Void Enflamed."

At this, Yen shot Aelia an impressed look.

"But we only have one shot. We'll need the beast to stay in one place. So we'll need to lure it somewhere that Aelia can throw the blast. I thought that I could be the bait, and then fly away when the blast was going to hit. But right now..."

Aelia interrupted. "Right now Jason is at the stage where he could be the bait, but not escape the situation alive."

"Then it's not an option yet," said Yen.

The walls rattled once more, as another bombardment of monsters hit into the tower above us.

"You know," I swallowed, as I realized what I was about to

say. "Maybe it should be. Maybe that's a good trade-off. Me for one of those big beasts."

"No. We need you," said Yen. "And that's not how we do things. Our lives are not to be gambled with."

Yen turned to the others to gain support. But then, in a moment of dread and understanding, I realized that she would not get it. Corinthia did not answer; her face was as still and as unemotional as rock. "That is what we did in the Shadowfront," she answered quietly. "Give our lives for the collective. It was an act of honor."

"Well, the Shadowfront didn't work," spat Yen. Suddenly, anger was taking hold of her, her face was setting into a scowl. "We didn't take leadership of the Hollow to make the same mistakes as our predecessors."

"I watched Jason's mother die," Corinthia said, the pain just underneath the surface of her words, a slight tremble.

I knew that Corinthia and my mother had been in the same Shadowfront company. I had not known that she had been there to witness my mother's death. An emotion made my insides lurch, like a fist closing over my insides.

"There is nothing in the world I would want to see less than to see her son die too," Corinthia continued. "But in battle, there is no want. Desire and wishes mean nothing. Purpose, and survival, that is all there is."

Yen turned to Aelia, hoping to gain support from her.

But Aelia did not give it. She shrugged. "I always thought that I would die fighting for my cause. My ambition was never to win, that seemed too lofty. Only to die well, in the name of rebellion. If that's the path Jason chooses, I respect it."

"You're all mad," said Yen. "If we cannot win with those we love by our side, then winning means nothing. It's just burning the world down and claiming the ashes."

Another emotion pulled me. First, the fact that Corinthia had mentioned the passing of my mother, and then Yen, saying those words.

Those we love.

The words echoed around me as if whispered into my ear by ghosts.

Our thoughts were interrupted before the conversation could continue.

A sound of rocks breaking and crumbling, along with a rhythmic tattoo.

It did not come from above. It did not even come from the beasts outside. No, that sound could not be mistaken. I had heard it from all my youth excavating. It was the regular sound of a pick and axe burrowing through rock and tunnel.

It was coming, faintly, from one of the cliff walls around the tower.

"What is *that?*" I cried, louder than I should have.

No one bothered to answer. Something, or someone, was tunneling their way to us.

That's all we needed to know. The Vanguard, as the group of the leaders had come to be called (along with Helton and his band of priest-warriors), ran upstairs, shadows leaping to our hands as weapons.

The knocking continued to sound about us, getting louder and louder, its regularity cutting through the chaos of all the other noises.

A chaos that was growing in volume. The monsters outside were battering the structure with force, making sections of the stairs and walls rain down, filling the air with dust.

The structure was starting to feel unstable, the further we travelled upwards. It gave a true sense of impending destruction, of a monolith about to crumble upon itself from the top down.

Finally, we arrived at the level where there was a door leading onto a walkway. The other side was a tunnel which had collapsed like all the others, but it sounded like the sound was coming from the other side of the collapsed boulders.

"Here," said Corinthia. She cracked open a slit of the boards stripping the window to see outside. We all gathered around the slit, trying to make out what was happening.

Even from the small strip of vision I had, I could see trouble.

The sound from the other side of the rubble, getting louder and louder, was attracting attention. The air outside the wall was half-choked with Void, the gloom studded with volatile grey. The monsters were amassing on the bridge, lining the stone passage, scrambling over each other.

The larger Void did not seem to be around. But it made no difference. Whoever was in the passage, breaking their way in, they were going to meet nothing but slaughter when they arrived.

"What do we do?" asked Yen, breathlessly.

"We watch," said her father.

Corinthia snapped her head to face Helton with a scowl, clearly irked by the fact that he was volunteering his opinion, but regained composure. "Much as I hate to agree with your father, he's right. We have no idea who is coming, we cannot risk our lives trying to save them."

"But if they've come here, it means that they've tunneled a way out for us. They must be friends, rather than foes, surely?" demanded Yen.

"We don't know that," came Corinthia's response. "What allies could we possibly have? We've only ever had each other. Who would come to help us?"

Yen jerked a finger in the direction of myself and Aelia. "They did," she said.

A thought then occurred to me. A hint of a hope, taking root in my thoughts, as the sound of burrowing got louder and louder.

Could it possibly be…

But my thoughts were interrupted.

The strangers were here. A chink in the rock wall appeared, a space between the rubble.

Quick as thunder coming on the heels of lightning, a javelin emerged from the space in the wall opposite, launched with strength and precision. It sliced through the jaw of a Void, splattering the air with black blood, and continued its trajectory into another's forehead. The latter Void was killed instantly, and in the mad scramble of beasts it was tossed aside, falling lifeless into the cavern.

But I still managed to get a quick glimpse of the javelin protruding out of the monster's forehead as it fell.

It was made of ice.

"It's Tende!" I cried. I leapt down from the window, and flung open the door to the walkway, baring my half-moon blades as I charged into the contortions of grey monster. "Come and help, it's a friend!"

Chapter Sixty-Two

I tore with complete abandonment into the Void. My half-moon blades twirled in perpetual motion, a blur of circular movement, and into the melee it created spurts of black blood which rained upon my armor and feet.

The others did not hesitate, and behind me the vanguard leapt to my aid. Shadow charged into the brittle skin of the Void without mercy.

There was a frenzy of teeth and claws as the Void turned about, as they all had been facing the tunnel. I ran ahead, tearing and slicing through legs and necks.

Aelia leapt to my side, and with her swords she drove forward too, every swing meeting its mark, her black swords blackening further with the blood of the enemy. There was barely any need to aim, every swing of our blade caught something of a Void, and in screeches of pain their mad scramble would do the rest, pushing each other into the precipice, even scratching and bloodying each other in the process as they tried to escape our onrush.

The air about us teemed with blood and gray, filling the air above, below and to the sides, but I ignored it all. I was carving my way to Tende, that was my only goal. I did not even care for slaying; all that mattered was that I made a path to him. Claws raked at my clothing and arms, and scarred my armor, but still it didn't stop me as I ventured forth, sweeping my staff like I was a farmer scything through grass.

Finally, with my perseverance, and with the hum of ten blades behind me making their mark too, the cloud of Void scattered. They leapt off the sides of the walkway, taking off into the air, reconvening for another attack later.

Leaving my sight clear to the debris ahead.

The boulders shifted and broke, a hole in the collapsed tunnel appearing like the opening jaws of a dragon.

Behind that new hole was Tende.

He stepped through the hole, as tranquil as he ever was, his movements as graceful as they ever had been. To see him emerge with a pick made of ice made my heart leap, and he also gave me a quick smile.

He was not alone.

Zyanya and Buress, Shadowfront warriors who had been wounded and left behind to be healed by the Riverkind, were there. Old comrades from the old Hollow. We could not tell whose faces were more relieved to be met once again, them or us.

They were not the only ones who were there. A whole group of Riverkind, with their kaftans, bearing ice-forms, were there.

Tende had convinced a group of Riverkind, a group of pacifists, to change their ways. To intervene and help us.

It was nothing short of a miracle.

"Am I glad to see you," I said.

Tende held up a hand. "No time to speak. Get your people up here, this is a way out!"

Corinthia, who was clearly completely overcome with surprise, immediately regained composure enough to turn to everyone. "Evacuations, every warrior's role is to accompany the citizens of the Hollow up here and through the tunnel! Yen, you lead the escape. I will defend here as best I can. Jason, Aelia, Helton, help me!"

Tende looked up. "I will ascend the tower to its roof. There is still sunlight up there, the Riverkind with me will use ice shields to reflect the sun's rays. It will hurt the Void. Hopefully we can use this to protect the evacuees as they cross the bridge."

He did not stop to give any more explanation, he, and a group of Riverkind pulsed forward in a diamond formation, with no need for further instruction.

Yen sped off, grabbing a few warriors with her as she left in order to start the evacuation. Corinthia organized those who were left, posting them on different ends of the bridge, giving instructions to use spears and arrows to stave off whatever Void arrived next.

My mind, and heart, were racing. This was it. The moment which spelled life or death for the Hollow.

Any escape was a blessing, and yet the bridge we were on, and that we would have to defend, couldn't be more exposed. We might have dispersed a turbulence of Void, but they would come back in their hordes. And the Void Enflamed could not be far off either.

If we were going to get our people across, we were going to have to give our all to defend this bridge. Possibly even our lives.

I was prepared for that. The only thing which gave me pause was my family, who still needed me—and Yen. I still felt like I had so much to say to her about everything I'd seen in the world beyond our valley, and everything I felt.

But that didn't matter, not in the face of life and death.

"Eyes above!" barked Corinthia.

I looked up, tensing immediately, and saw what she was referring to. A Lightguard scout, on wings of light, circled around the tower.

They would not want to stay down here for long. Not here in the shadows, where the Void teemed.

Which begged the question, what were they doing here at all?

"Bring them down!" I shouted.

Some of the more experienced warriors, of which there were few, created shadow-bolts, to be fired from bows. They loosed shafts of black into the air, trying to hit the prowling scout, but to no avail. Buress and Zyanya's spears and arrows came the closest, but still not close enough to draw blood.

The scout's swoop was uninterrupted as it swirled down in gyres, and it flew down past our bridge and further down into the throat of the earth. As it swept past, I saw what it held in its hand, a flaming torch.

Dread filled me as I sensed what the scout's mission might be.

I went to the edge of the walkway and looked down into the abyss. Far below, the tower stretched into darkness, the bottom lost in the black. A few bridges below, the Void Enflamed were hanging upside down, their heads coiled into their wings like bats.

It was what we had said. The monsters were still designed for short, sharp attacks, with rests in between to conserve energy.

I had a feeling that they were going to be awakened, in the cruelest possible manner.

The scout streamed across the hanging figures. In passing, they drove their torch onto the beasts' skin.

It lit up almost immediately, creating a pocket of yellow below us. The Void Enflamed awoke, stretching their wings, and the flames feathered their bodies from head to toe, creating a red glow on the rock around them.

It was like we were looking down into a dragon's throat.

The two Void Enflamed opened their gullets, and let out a hideous, ear-shattering cry upwards, outraged at the flames spanning their bodies.

They started to crawl. Their claws dug into rock, and walls crumbled down in their wake.

They were heading straight up towards us, and their wings, festooned in flame, started to flap as they made to launch into the air and attack.

"Aelia..." I said.

She was beside me. She let out a short exhalation and gritted her teeth. "I hear you."

"I haven't said anything yet."

"Yet I hear you, nonetheless. Time to put our training to the test."

I nodded. We had never had the time to fully form a plan. But an ill-formed plan would have to do.

Even if it was going to take my life.

I looked over at Corinthia. "We're taking the fight down to them. Try and keep them occupied."

Corinthia nodded. "In such cases, we'd normally say something. *For the Endless,* or something like that. We haven't had time to come up with new words."

"*For the Hollow,*" I replied

Corinthia raised her hand. "For the Hollow!" she shouted.

And all the others echoed her words back to us.

I wove a shadow-vine and let it down from the precipice. Aelia grabbed it, as did I, then we flung ourselves down into the black.

Into the dragon's throat.

Chapter Sixty-Three

We dropped down, slithering on the vine as quickly as possible. We didn't want to lose time, especially in mid-air, when any passing creature could take us out. It was rough when we landed on a bridge below, slamming onto the walkway. We rolled, allowing our armor to take the brunt of the fall, but our shoulders still took a beating. I looked up, the bridge where Corinthia and Helton waited was above us, a black silhouetted line against the sphere of sunlight.

I went to the edge of our bridge, and looked down, hoping to be able to swing down to yet another bridge lower.

But there wasn't enough time, the Void Enflamed were just below us, crawling up with their claws digging into the cliffs.

We were going to have to face them here, or lower down. As far away from the escape route as possible.

That meant getting their attention. And, from my knowledge of the Void, there was only one way to get their attention, and that was to make them very, very angry.

Using a link I'd trained in my Mind's Eye during my rest with Aelia, I paired a shadow-vine with a half-moon blade. It created a lasso with a razor-sharp circle of shadow-steel at its end.

I started to throw the blade in a circular motion, swing it around and around, giving it more and more slack, letting it whistle above my head in wider and wider circles. Around me, I felt the air distort, the pull of shadows beckoning, the buzz of Shade. Aelia was Essence-Gathering for her shadow-blast.

She didn't have enough time to create much of one, it took her minutes to form one in training.

So it was down to me to give her time.

I gazed down at the humungous beasts, they were close enough now for me to feel the heat emanating from their burning skin. The mass of flesh and flames was directly below, their normally pallid skin now golden with fire.

One was climbing up the cliffs, the other was climbing up the wall.

I breathed.

This was it.

As a Void Enflamed launched up, leaping into the air, its wings of fire spreading, it was as if time slowed. I let fly my blade, letting it swing down into the chasm below.

It sliced all the way along a Void Enflamed's front, drawing a line of blood. The beast howled in anger, and broke its flight, choosing not to continue upwards, but instead to perch on the walkway on which I was standing.

It loomed high above me, making me feel as small as an insect, as the fiery nightmare squared up to me, screaming with abandon at me, making my hair billow.

But it was not the only monster I had to contend with. To my side, a flaming set of claws dug into the bridge; the other Void Enflamed was clambering up to attack me too.

"How's that blast coming along, Aelia?" I called.

"I need more time!"

I looked over. It was true, her orb was still small, not big enough to cause significant damage.

"Skies above, you need to hurry up!" I shouted. With another loop of my lasso, I swiped at the Void Enflamed on the bridge, making the half-moon blade swing towards the level of the beast's face. It was enough to stop it advancing, making it keep back for a second. I then changed the arc of the swing,

making my blade swoop downwards, underneath the bridge where I was standing.

I didn't have time to aim properly but the Void Enflamed was too big to miss. The swing found its target, and my weapon sliced across some part of the creature hanging under the bridge, I could not pause to see what.

Smoke wafted about us; the walkway we were on cracked and groaned. It was not going to hold both us and the Void Enflamed for long.

"Any time now would be good!" I shouted at Aelia, more out of desperation than anything else. But, I could see she needed more time.

There was nothing else for it.

I swung my lasso one more time, now at the Void Enflamed on the bridge. It swung about its neck a few times, whipping around it twice before the side of the blade at its end dug into the Void's throat.

As it did so, the other beast rose into view, its flaming, nightmarish head rising above the parapet of the bridge, ready to join the fight.

Gripping my end of the vine tightly, I ran. I did not think, to think even for a second was to succumb to doubt.

There was no time for that.

I dropped into the black, launching myself over the edge, holding onto my vine. The shadow-cord tightened, and I dragged the Void Enflamed down with me, yanking onto its neck with my fall.

I collided with a mass of flaming flesh and gnashing teeth, bouncing off the furnaced skin of the beast hanging off the bridge.

I kept on falling.

My mad plan had worked. My weight might not have been much, compared to the form of the Void. But it was enough to drag its head down—and make it topple over the edge with me. Enough for the two beasts to collide, and in a scramble of fire, lose their footing.

Chaos erupted above me as the two beasts collided. I had

some sense of them scrabbling at each other, both trying to use the other to remain stable.

It didn't work, they both spiraled downward, extending their wings in order to stop their flight. I was tossed this way and that as we all fell down deeper into the black, swinging across the emptiness.

I had enough presence of mind to outstretch one hand, trying to grab at some shadows.

I let the vine disperse, untangling into formlessness, and let myself go, leaping at the wall of the tower, shadow-claws at the ready. Digging my claws into the wall, I raked down the wall of stone until I stopped.

I looked around, the next bridge down was not directly underneath, but to the side. Sprouting claws on my other hand, I scuttled around the wall of the tower, and leapt down to it.

I looked up. Both Void Enflamed were now baring down upon me. I had gotten their attention and they were plummeting down, leaving a column of smoke in their wake.

I held my arms out, and held onto my emotions, letting it charge me. All around me, below and above, to each side, was darkness.

That would have to be my savior.

Shadows poured out of my chest, gilded with the blue of Anima. The lines of blue twisted, knotting in the shape of core magic—and then I Essence-gathered.

The black in the air was now being beckoned in two directions, Aelia above, making her shadow-blast, and me here. But it did not matter. Here, there were multitudes of midnight, chasms of dark.

My body burned with the pressure, yet the darkness yielded, flooding toward me like water to a sinkhole. It enshrouded me, embossing my arms, enveloping my chest, cocooning me into shadow-statue.

It was my best chance of surviving. To encase myself in stone, and hope that the layers survived the flames and teeth of the Void Enflamed.

Black upon black, layer upon layer. I made myself the center of a squall of darkness that enveloped me, thickening every part of my body until I was twice my normal size.

And then, it happened.

With the flurries of black churning about me, I had not been able to anticipate the approach of the monster. Through the tempest, fire emerged, and teeth coating with vile slobber.

The jaws closed in upon me.

And the world turned into the stuff of nightmares.

Chapter Sixty-Four

The teeth drove deep into the outer layer of my shadow-stone skin, biting inside, lodging into my head, arms, and torso. Although I felt the pressure, the teeth did not pierce through into flesh.

The world ceased to make sense as the two monsters thrashed at me, tossed me, and tried to rip me apart. I did not know where up or down was, I did not know anything apart from teeth gnashing at me, puncturing my shell, jabbing at every part of my body. I caught moments where I realized that I was in the Void's mouth, where they attempted to chew me, and others where one creature held me in its claws while another bit at my legs.

I was their plaything, their doll, powerless to stop anything.

Yet I was also enraging them, their bites became more and more vicious, and I had the impression that my shadow encasement was getting pummeled with more and more ferocity.

All I could do was focus on the Essence-Gathering. To replace every toothmark, every dent, with more shadow. Dark drew toward me, finding me even though I was thrown this way and that.

But I could not keep going forever. My chest felt like it was about to burst, the shadows felt like they were swamping me, like I was going to drown in them.

Is this what happened to Cizin?

"Aelia!" I bellowed, unsure whether any of my words would emerge from the madness about me. "*Fire*!"

Sure enough, the blast came. For a moment, time seemed to slow down. I peeked through the smoke and the raging fire and shadow and saw the orb dropping down from the heavens.

It plummeted down, bringing with it trails of shadows. It would have been beautiful if it didn't also mean death.

When the orb fell upon the bridge, the result was instantaneous.

A blast of black tore through the air in an eruption of midnight. It made the sound of a hundred landslides. It was a flash of black, as deafening and as powerful as a fist of a hundred shadow-giants.

It dismantled the world around me.

One Void Enflamed was torn in two by the explosion, and a spray of its black blood accompanied the blast. Parts of the creature spattered the tower in sickly crunches. The stone bridge under which we had stood disintegrated, becoming a cloud of dust.

And the creature who held me in its mouth was flung to the side, hitting the stone.

I felt the huge creature collide with the tower, the crash reverberated through my body.

Then came the descent.

The monster was falling and taking me with it.

There was nothing I could do, the creature, either by instinct or design, was clenching its teeth, and there was no way for me to get out. I was there for its fall, I was forced to share its fate.

All I could do was continue gathering shadows and plastering them over my body to keep my armor of stone, and hope it made a difference.

We fell, fire and shadow, down the gullet of the cave, straight down. A monster and I, or whatever was left of it, falling down to the ground below, a cloud of shadows leaping in and out of its mouth as if it were a dragon billowing smoke out of its throat.

The creature tussled. I heard the noise of the irregular flapping of its wings, of the creature trying to stop its fall, and recapture flight.

It didn't work.

There was a mighty crash, and the sound of stone structures breaking. For a moment, in my blinded vision of a world turning and falling, and of shadows streaming, I thought we might have hit the ground. But we kept falling.

We had just smashed through a bridge.

There was more twisting and turning. The Void was still feebly trying to slow down its fatal descent. I heard claws, raking down the cliff walls. I heard more wings trying to find purchase in the air.

We slowed down, a little.

But instinct told me that the ground would still be coming fast.

I braced myself, curling into a ball as best I could with the creature's teeth still implanted in my exterior of stone.

Then we hit it and the world reeled as I was expelled from the creature's mouth, spat out in the collision. I was flung across the air, and thrown through fires and ashes and piles of burning corpses. My body sent flames and embers and parts of Voidflesh scattering, and still I tumbled and rolled, until I finally hit the ground on my side, skidding through more pieces of smoldering Void.

For a moment, I did not feel anything. Shock numbed me to the pain of the collision. It was long enough for me to think that perhaps the Void Enflamed had managed to slow its fall more than I had thought. It was long enough for me to think that being inside the creature's mouth, and then inside my shadow-armor, had cushioned the impact so much that I wouldn't feel any pain at all.

The next moment annihilated that thought completely.

I cried out as pain flooded through my body, and immediately I let go of the shadows gathered about me, knowing I would not be able to control it a second longer.

My armor vanished, shadows racing each other home.

And I was just myself again. Vulnerable, depleted, and coated in bruises rather than shadow.

I tried to pick myself up, but my body protested from the pain. My vision swam, and my legs buckled, and all I did was topple back to the ground.

Propping myself up against the cliff wall, I let myself gather my thoughts.

My vision stabilized, so I cast my eyes about. Along the ground were the strewn parts of a Void Enflamed, the one which had been torn apart completely by the blast. Its long, pointed head, barely connected to anything but the remains of a spine, lay smoldering on the floor.

So one creature had been slain, at least.

But what about the other? The one who had carried me in its mouth, all the way down to the bottom?

I cast my gaze about, through the smoke and fire, and saw movement. It was slow. Like me, the beast was recovering from the fall.

Slowly, it began to move, a silhouette amidst the smoke.

The creature limped across the ground, one wing was torn, a corner hanging at a grotesque angle. And it had to drag one leg. It whined with pain and fury.

But the creature did not stop. It put one claw above another and started to drag itself up the cliff wall.

I groaned. It had been hurt, it needed to recuperate, as I did.

But it had not been killed.

I winced and got up, my legs obeyed my will this time. I looked above me, at the tower spearing up, all the way to the sky overhead. Amidst the network of bridges, I could see clusters of Void, clamoring and screeching, circling the tower.

My people were still in danger.

What I needed to do was fly, to gather shadows once more, and shape them into wings at my shoulders, and rise all the way back to the top so I could help defend the evacuees as they traveled across the bridge to safety.

But I could not. I stretched my hand out and tried to Essence-Gather again, but my body rejected my efforts instantaneously. The shadow-stone armor had taken everything from me.

There was only one other way up, through the tower.

I picked my way across the flames, and smoke, finding some source of energy inside me. I found the door to the tower and saw that it had been burnt half-off. I steeled myself, and ran through the flames, bursting through the crumpling door, to the foot of the tower.

Stairs rose above me. I looked up and saw that it was funneling smoke all the way to the top.

I hoped my father and Rana were all right. I hoped that they were on their way right now, climbing to the bridge, soon to run across it to the tunnel of safety.

And then, as I breathed, preparing myself for the climb, I heard something hideous.

A grinding, a rattling. Cascades of rock tumbled down stairs, crashing through the building and rained down around me.

A hard realization hit me.

This tower is going to collapse.

Chapter Sixty-Five

The tower had taken too much punishment. With the fights, the blasts, the fires, the fallen roof, it was now completely unstable.

It had stood for thousands of years.

Now it was going to crumble.

I started to limp up the stairs, as fast as my legs would take me. The walls were shaking so much that it felt like being in a tree hut during a storm. Streams of dust poured down the walls, and everything shook.

My chest felt completely empty, and coupled with the fact that one leg was not working properly, I had to take the odd moment to breathe. I used the moment to snatch at some Anima. But I did not tarry as there were a lot of stairs to climb, and the tower did not feel like it would last long.

I hobbled along, gradually wearing off the pain of my fall, until I could jog. I wound my way up and up, glad that I was not encountering any Hollow residents. This meant that they'd already headed up, shepherded up by the likes of Yen. Which, theoretically at least, meant that my family might be safe.

I prayed that was still the case, even for a moment regretting not having Gods to pray to anymore.

I passed by walls which had crumbled completely, they

looked like they had been bitten off by monsters with ragged teeth. I passed by those sections with a renewed wariness, knowing that Void could be flying nearby.

And still I kept on climbing, ignoring the pain in my limbs, ignoring the protest of my lungs. Sometimes I even closed my eyes, letting my legs carry me along, and listened to the history of ghosts, the endless streams of history, whispering. They chanted about the Swallow, about warriors, about scuttlers. After all of the madness I'd encountered in the past few weeks, to hear their mutterings was felt normal.

Then, among the whispers, I heard voices.

Up above, only a few flights of stairs up. The Hollow was there, waiting to pass along the bridge and get to safety.

A fresh bout of energy spurred me on, making me run faster, making me leap up those steps.

Making me lose focus.

I didn't even see the hole, the gap in the wall among the smoke in the excitement. But the moment I passed by it, a Void tore in.

It whacked into me. My back hit the banister, and my armor, already dented out of recognition, took another blow for me.

With its claws in my chest plate, the Void loomed over me, ready to bite at my neck.

For close quarters like this, a form I had been practicing immediately came to me. In a flash, a combination between the half-moon blades and the shadow-claws materialized across my fists. The slicing blade stretched across my knuckles in this form, so that my fists were lined with the sharpest steel shadow could mimic.

I drove my elongated fist into the Void's mouth, and sliced its lower jaw clean off. Amidst the gush of dark blood, I kept going, sinking my fists into its pallid flesh until it scrambled away, clumsily darting off and shrieking as best it could with the rest of its mouth.

The shriek was clearly loud enough to call its fellow creatures, though. And through the hole in the wall a batch of Void poured forth, sweeping in and up.

They were going up through the stairwell, to get at the Hollow from the inside.

I shouted out a warning and did my best to stop the Void from entering. I let the half-moon blades grow, until they were at the end of a staff. I stood at the entrance, flinging my weapon this way and that, scraping and carving at the tide of flesh charging through the hole.

It seemed endless, like all the Void in the surroundings were filtering in. I had to stop and fling myself to the side to get out of the way. The Void almost did not notice me after, they all seemed so eager to be streaming in.

Why?

I peeked outside through a chink in the wall, and saw beams of light strafing, directing the Void in.

Of course. The Riverkind were reflecting the sunlight from above, directing the Void.

It was safer, at this point, to have the Void *inside the tower* than attacking the evacuees on the bridge.

Safer for them, obviously.

Less so, for me.

The tower around me was becoming choked with the creatures, they coated the walls. If I was going to make my way up through that, it was going to take a miracle. If I had the strength and anima in order to coat myself in shadow-stone, then maybe I would have a chance.

Just when I was wondering how on earth I was going to get through, things got worse.

The lumbering sound, the rhythmic knock. The surviving Void Enflamed, was making its way up the tower. It crawled awkwardly, like one shoulder and leg were tender, but it crawled its way up, nonetheless.

Its head loomed inside, trying to get away from the strafing light-beams.

Presumably, it took was having light reflected on it, chasing it into the tower. In its weakened and injured state, the beams were probably having an effect on it that they never would have had otherwise.

The Riverkind did not know that I would be in there too. For all they knew, I was dead. So they were stuffing the tower full of the creatures, in order to contain them, not knowing that they were sending all the dangers my way.

The hole enlarged, yawning open, as the Void Enflamed's body pushed through, shattering stone as it tore its way inside.

The jaws yawned open toward me, causing me to panic.

I turned and ran. I went the same way as the other Void. Up the stairs.

Behind me, underneath me, the great creature lumbered, with it came a crash of crumbling stone as it squeezed its way up the column.

Above me, a cloud of Void rushed upward, wafting up the trails of smoke, and it seemed like we were all scrambling away, as fast as we could. All of us tried escaping the larger evil climbing up from below.

The only problem was that I was a lot slower than them. I could only put one foot in front of the other, going round and round in circles, on disintegrating stones.

I ran, and kept on running, sprinting over gaps in the rock, over piles of rubble collecting, while around me the world was a shaking, crumbling prison.

And then, just as I thought that it couldn't get any more unstable, I felt everything change.

At first, I thought it was just my stomach lurching, my balance was thrown off by the rattle of what I had been through. It didn't take long to realize something *far worse* was happening.

This section of the tower was falling apart, pitching to one side.

The world reeled, and the walls around me spun. I was thrown forward, my balance completely lost. Swarms of Void shrieked in confusion as the tower left its foundation. Parts of the building snapped off, and sounds reverberated up and down the spine of the Babel.

But then, as the tower leant forward, it did not fall. With an explosion of noise from above, the tower came to a halt, leaning on its side.

It must be tilting onto a cliff wall, I thought. A whole section of the tower was on an incline, barely connected to its bottom half, linked in the same way a snapped branch could still dangle loosely from a tree.

Thoughts rushed through me. This was not stable, it could not last.

The tower was going to crumble, and fall. It was a matter of moments now.

I got to my feet and found that my balance did not match my vision. The world lurched to one side, and I had to put my foot against a wall as much as the step to remain upright. I ignored the screams in my brain that everything looked fundamentally *wrong* and kept going, first crawling, then running again.

Behind me, the Void Enflamed did the same. The smoke coiled around me, reminding me of its chasing presence.

Around me, there started to be spirals of Void. They were in a panic, crawling over each other, as desperate to get away from the larger beast below and out of the crumbling tower as I was. They did not attack me, but still, the lashings of tooth and claw around me scraped and scratched at my flesh, and fresh lines of blood streaked my arms and legs.

They were slowing me down, and that was the last thing I needed.

"Jason!" came a cry from above.

A voice, a hope.

Someone was in this crumbling tunnel with me, the ghosts, and the monsters.

I looked up. Aelia and Yen stood a few rings of steps above me. They were looking down while the world around them disintegrated, every stone shaken into deluges of stone.

"Get up here!" Yen barked.

"Aelia..!" I shouted back. "Make another shadow-blast!"

"What? Are you *mad?*" Yen cried back down to me.

"Just do it!" I yelled.

All of the creatures were in here. The Void Enflamed was in this tube. All the tower needed was one last push, and it would crumble into oblivion, taking all the creatures down with it.

Shadows around me flowed upward, like reversed rainfall. As I indiscriminately slashed at the grey surrounding me and ran along a wall to get over a chasm where steps had once been, I snatched a glance upwards.

Aelia was already at work creating another shadow-blast. Shadows were draining from around her, condensing into a ball in her hand. It was weak, a leaking form. She too was low on Anima.

It didn't matter. It wouldn't take much to bring the Babel down now.

I kept on running, a familiar hand caught my own. I was pulled up onto a ledge, the remnants of what had once been steps.

"There!" said Yen, pointing to our side.

Beside us, outside a now-disintegrated part of a tower wall, the cliff outside was close enough to reach.

I nodded, and we both turned to Aelia. "Do it!" we shouted at the same time.

The Citadel warrior took the orb in her hands, that ball of condensed shadow, and flung down the throat of the tower.

Straight down where the Void Enflamed was climbing.

We did not wait to see the impact. We flung ourselves through the air, through the broken section of the tower, and outside onto the cliff wall. Yen made shadow-claws, but Aelia and I were too Anima-deficient for that. We grabbed whatever foothold we could, landing on a small ledge just large enough for our feet to make purchase.

Just as we leapt, there was a crack, like the Earth was splitting open. The blast blew a hole in the spine of the tower behind us, and stone vomited into the air, accompanied by the death-knell shriek of the Void Enflamed.

All we could do was hold on for dear life as debris and rock pummeled our back and the wall around us. We closed our eyes, and clung on, while behind us the tower disintegrated, finally crumbling upon itself. It took the countless swarm of Void down with it.

The crash was so loud it was like the earth itself was breaking.

The tower had trained generations. It had been the home to thousands of ghosts. We had sacrificed it to save ourselves, taking the enemy down with it.

Clouds of dust billowed around us, rising from the devastation beneath, and I could see no more.

Chapter Sixty-Six

We took all of ten seconds' rest, before Yen urged us to climb.

There could still be Void around, who had not been claimed by the falling tower, and we did not know what the Lightguard, gazing down from above, would make of all of this.

We had to use the cover of the dust and smoke to get out of here.

As we pulled ourselves upward, my head started to feel dizzy. I had pushed myself to the last and could barely hold on anymore.

Before long, however, hands pulled me up. Tende had emerged, and we pulled ourselves onto the tunnel where the Hollow had evacuated.

A fleet of hands caught me as I almost collapsed onto the floor, and carried me inside. passing me through the hole which Tende's company had created to find us. "Rana... my father..." I managed to splutter.

"They got through. They're safe," someone replied. I thought it sounded like Corinthia, but I was not sure.

All I knew was that a lot of people were huddled in this tunnel, and that meant survivors. That meant the Hollow had been evacuated, and were here, with me.

That meant some kind of success.

I was placed on the floor, and a gourd of water was placed to my lips. The liquid felt foreign to me at first, and I thought about how long it had been since I'd had something to eat or drink. It washed away some of the dirt and blood in my mouth, and after my initial splutters and coughs I greedily slurped from the gourd, taking as much as I could.

After this, my head stopped spinning a little, and the tunnel around me came into focus. Just off to the side, the mist of dust was still greying the air of the chamber of the tower, and it crept in among us, meandering among all of us. Although people were still scared, huddled together and crying, there was also a sense of relief.

We'd made it out of the tower.

Corinthia stood, her back to the shrouds of dust. "Gather your breath, Hollow. The enemy above will have seen everything and will be following us," She gestured towards Tende, and other Riverkind. Some of them had their eyes closed, and I realized what they were doing, they were maintaining columns of ice, propping up the tunnel around us. "I know that it is strange to meet strangers from outside the valley, but we owe these warriors our lives. They will let the tunnel collapse again behind us and slow the enemy's pursuit. But first, we must leave this place."

"Not so fast."

The voice was a strange one. A calm one, one of ease, when all conversations between us had been ones of tension and discomfort.

A hush of fear spread between us, and then the speaker revealed himself, walking in from the clouds of mist.

It was a Lightguard, someone resplendent in perfect armor, strolling in like he was walking into a tavern. His insouciance, his ease, was at odds with our own.

The tunnel filled then, as everyone leaped to their feet. I did too, although I was in no means to fight, and could barely see between the bodies.

Corinthia barred the route, a shadow-trident forming in

her hands. "You will step no further," she said through gritted teeth.

"So be it," the Lightguard grinned, coming to a halt in front of her and brushing the dust off his immaculate robes. His gaze fell upon Corinthia's trident with a trace of amusement. "You can put your weapons down. I am simply here to deliver a message. Or perhaps less of a message, and more...*terms*."

"We have no use for them," Corinthia answered.

The Lightguard made a show of looking at our dismal, dusty surroundings, and our huddled figures. "I think you do, actually," he said. "You are homeless, and vulnerable. And will soon be the enemy of an empire so powerful that your minds have not fully developed enough to understand it."

I let out a hiss of hatred.

"So allow me to explain. We were rather impressed by your demonstration back there, in the tower. We think that you may be even more useful to us than the Void are, in the wars against Cizin. The Emperor will take some convincing, of course, but it might just be that you could have a place in the Empire. If you come with me, we could see what you could do to grant earn entrance to the city. Or you can spend the rest of your short lives as refugees, scampering around in the dirt until we kill you. What will it be?"

There was silence there. I looked around and saw blank confusion in the people's faces around me. They'd had no idea what he was saying. They had no context for his words.

A figure, tall and powerful, pushed past the crowded cave. I didn't even recognize them until it strode to the figure and squared up against it.

It was Helton.

His form, disheveled and dirty, made a contrast to the pristine Lightguard. Helton was doing what he did best, towering over adversaries and hiding every trace of fear in his face.

"You dare to enslave our people, to drop death from above, and then invite us to your city?" snarled Helton.

The Lightguard did not seem at all disturbed by Helton's

presence; a smile played at the edge of his lips. "I give you a choice, when you would otherwise have none," he said, as calm as a man offering a drink at dinner. "Given your circumstances, I'd take it as a blessing."

"We've had lifetimes of your blessings, and each one of them meant death and suffering. You deceived us, made our own minds turn against us. Turned monsters against us. Turned us into monsters. We will never trust you, never obey you, ever."

I could barely take in the words Helton was saying. Was that regret? An apology, of sorts, for what he'd done to me? To my mother?

The Lightguard looked past Helton, dismissing him with his gaze. "Is there anyone with more sense than this man ready to speak? A leader, perhaps?"

Helton stepped to the side, blocking the Lightguard's way forward. "You take one more step, and I'll show you the meaning of fury."

Helton... don't... my mind said. I was too exhausted to do anything. But I knew what the Lightguard were capable of, and now that Helton had finally expressed some kind of regret, I somehow felt a strain of pity for him.

The Lightguard smiled. "We *did* train you well. I can see that. You are most impressive, for people brought up in in dirt and jungles, oblivious to the world. But never forget, we remain the masters. Let me show you."

Helton didn't even have time to move.

There was a snatch of light, bolting in from the cave opening. That light emerged from Helton's back as a sword. The Lightguard had driven his weapon through Helton's chest, all the way through until it gleamed in front of us, barely dimmed with the blood running off of it.

There was a wave of gasps across the cave. Yen screamed, and ran forward, finding her father just in time to catch him as he slumped to the rocky floor.

"Let this be a message," said the Lightguard, letting the

light filter back behind him. "A reminder that you should *really* have accepted our kindness."

Then he left, gathered by two scouts who picked him up and whisked him out.

"Close the cavern," ordered Corinthia, her voice thin with shock.

Tende nodded and cast an eye towards a Riverkind. They released a few ice-pillars, and the tunnel partially closed, blocking off the chasm where the Tower of Babel had once stood.

Yen wailed, tears flooding down her face, dropping onto her father's unmoving shape. No one cried like this in the Hollow, no one showed such raw pain.

But when Yen cried, everyone followed suit, and in the darkness, everyone's eyes gleamed with tears.

"He died for nothing," I muttered, incredulous. "It's a waste."

Corinthia was walking by me, and leant in. "It wasn't a waste. Helton did what he did for a reason. He knew the risk."

"For what possible reason would that be?"

"To unite us."

I turned around, and saw everyone grieving, from Yen, to the warrior-priests who had been Helton's followers, and everyone else besides. It was true. Back in the tower, we had been divided, serving different masters. Now, there were no such divisions.

We were one people again.

We all knew who our enemy was.

Chapter Sixty-Seven

What followed Helton's death, and the battle of the Tower of Babel, was a blur.

We found each other and made counts of the deaths. I found Rana and my father, and embraced them, others were not so lucky, not finding their loved ones and joining Yen in grief.

Although no one believed anymore, we spoke prayers out of habit. We put stones over Helton's body, even though we knew that collapsing the tunnel would bury him anyway. It seemed too cruel to do away with him without any ceremony at all.

And then there was nothing to do but move and put distance between us and our enemy. My father was put upon a stretcher, and I carried him through the tunnels with Emilian. We were a long trail of sadness, everyone shuffled mournfully through the gloom. Everyone in the Hollow had now lost more than one home, and as a result people seemed to plod forward more out of habit than with any purpose.

Our exodus brought us through the Canyonlands.

While I walked, I tried to reassure Rana, I even offered to take her on my back. But she shook her head, telling me to save my strength for carrying our father.

I also tried to speak to Yen, to console her. I felt like I

should be there with her, and asked others to take over carrying my father's stretcher so I could give her company. But she was quiet, and sullen, and brushed off my attempts, so I let her be.

The only ray of light, in this blackness, was to reunite with Tende, and hear what had happened to him.

"The river has always run one way," said Tende. "And the current was always toward peace, towards never harming my fellow man. But after that fight on the bridge, when you'd done so much to save me, and I saw the Lightguard torture you with that charged light-form, I could not see the world in the same way anymore. I knew, then, that the way of the world was imbalanced, and that we should fight to restore the balance. Then, and only then, will the rivers run right again, and we can abstain from conflict once more."

"How is your arm?" I asked. "Last I saw you, you were in a bad way."

"You forget just how talented we Riverkind healers are," he said. "I returned to my valley and was treated by my people. It was then that I managed to convince a few to join me in the fight. My elder was not happy with us, it took some convincing. But I had Buress and Zyanya with me to tell of the sufferings of the Hollow, and that helped." He gave a pained smile. "So now I have my very own company, just like I was in the Shadowfront."

"Well, I am grateful for it."

He nodded. "There are old waterways in the rock, it helped us get to you in ways unseen. We knew that we had to face the imbalance together."

"As always," I said. "You end up being my guide."

Tende shook his head. "Warfare is foreign to me. These are depths where I cannot guide you anymore."

"Well, warfare is in *our* bloodstream," I said bitterly. "We have enough experience for a hundred lifetimes. That's the imbalance, the *injustice* the people of the Hollow have had to suffer."

"Perhaps imbalance and injustice mean the same thing, here. Different sides of the same river."

"Maybe so. In any case, I'm happy that we're speaking the same language."

I had an idea, but I didn't dare voice it out loud yet. Not until I'd spoken to Corinthia and Yen.

We didn't stop walking until we gathered in a small tumble of light from a split in the plains above. Water trickled down along with the sunlight above, and we took it in turns to fill our gourds and wash some of the dirt and blood off our skin. The mood was one of funerial silence. People watched the Riverkind with a mixture of gratitude and apprehension.

I noticed people looking at me, too. It wasn't with the same fear and suspicion as before, instead, they looked at me with curiosity.

I couldn't quite make it out, I didn't know what they were looking for with their gaze. I asked Corinthia, who said the following.

"It's obvious, isn't it?" she said. "They think you have the answer."

I blinked. "The answer to what?"

Corinthia shrugged. I'd rarely seen her do so, her stance was always so poised, so measured. "Well, they're picking up on the fact that I don't have one, at least. No use asking me anymore. I'm part of the old guard. These are new threats." She smiled, and the wrinkles on her face doubled. "You're not a stranger, like the Riverkind or Aelia. But you've seen the world beyond our valley. If anyone knows what we should do next, it's you." She pointed a finger at my chest. "It's up to you now. Give them something. What they've just seen, they don't understand it yet."

"I can't give them much hope."

"Well, you're going to have to."

"That would be cruel."

"*That* would be leadership."

Corinthia stepped aside in order to put her head underneath the water falling from above, running her hands through her hair. "It's been a long time since we had running water at our disposal. It feels good, Jason. It feels good. Your mother always used to say that if a stream was running by your side, then things could never be *that* bad."

I smarted at this. "A river carried her off when she died," I pointed out.

"Some might call it ironic, or cruel. But I'd venture to say that she'd call it fitting."

"She was always seeing the light instead of the shadows," I admitted. "I remember that. The family missed that, after she was gone."

Corinthia pulled her head out of the water, and her hair was flattened and dripping. "Sometimes, a smiling face is a brave one. *Talk to them.*"

She was right. If I kept my people in the dark, I was following the same foul path as Echo the Endless.

The time for censorship was over. Now was a time for difficult truths.

I stepped into the middle of a pool, water tumbled into it from the stream above, coming down in broken curtains. I raised my hand and looked at what was left of our community. Huddled as we were together, for comfort and for water, we seemed pitifully few; just a fraction of what we had once been just a few weeks ago.

"People of the Hollow!" I said, getting everyone's attention. But it was clear that I didn't need to, everyone's gaze was drawn to me anyway.

I cleared my throat, suddenly regretting not giving myself more time to think of what words to use.

"I have something to say," I started uncertainly. It felt odd to hesitate, given that I had to talk loudly enough to have my voice heard over the water. "I have met the Lightguard, the people who killed Commander Helton. They have kept us trapped in the valley of the Hollow. They created the Void. They pitted our people against their creatures in order to test them for a coming war. They are the source of all the pain we've been subjected to for our entire lives. They are powerful, and they are cruel. Echo the Endless was one of them, all that she said was a ploy to keep us obedient, and to keep us in the valley so more Void could be pitted against us."

I looked around to gauge their reaction. I had thought that there would be shock, maybe anger.

It was silent.

Perhaps too much had happened now, perhaps they were ready to believe anything, after what they'd lived through.

In any case, they were no longer the same people who had exiled me and distrusted me for being different. Their minds had broadened, just as mine had when I'd first encountered ghosts.

"These same people would track us down and kill us," I said. "We are without a home, they have made us fugitives. There are many among us who are sick and wounded. I don't know where our lives lead now. But I have a proposal."

A few heads which had been bowed rose at this. Corinthia was right, I realized. Hope and promise. That is what the people needed, it would fuel them.

"I suggest going straight to the enemy. Not all of us. Anyone who doesn't wish to fight can go to Tende's tribe, they looked after Zyanya and Buress, and they would look after you. But those of us who do want to fight, over there, in that jungle, in that city, we can be part of the struggle against the people who enslaved us. Right now, the city is struggling to overthrow the evil Emperor who imprisoned us. With your help, we just might be able to tear him from his throne. We could make them pay for every death, every drop of blood spilled in the Hollow, and free the others who have been imprisoned like us."

I looked about me. "What do you say?" I asked. "Would you run, or would you join the Uprising, a movement that would restore balance and fairness and justice to the Canyonlands?"

There was silence then, a long, terrifying silence.

Then a figure emerged, pushing through the curtain of water.

It was Yen. Water dripped off her, streaking down her body. Hours of tears had made their mark upon her face, and her face was a mask of cold misery.

"I will not hide," she said. "If there's a place where those cowards live, I want to burn it to the ground. Show us where they sleep, and we'll flood it with shadows."

I'd never seen my friend like this, her face clenched with anger, emotions so large that she was unable to contain them.

She raised her hand, and shadows coalesced about her fingers until they became a spear.

"Who's with me?" she said, turning to everyone, holding up her spear in a rally for support.

The Hollow answered her. "I am," said one. "I am," said another. The words were repeated, scattered throughout the remnants of our people.

It was Corinthia who settled it. She stepped into the pool too and fixed me with a gaze of.. was it pride? Fear?

"We all are," she said quietly. "You just need to show us the way."

Chapter Sixty-Eight

"I'm not leaving him."

Rana stood with her arms crossed, her eyes unwavering. There was almost something comical about it, the fact that she was so much smaller than me, and yet completely confident that she would get what she wanted.

We were going to get to a crossroads soon. We'd made our way through the earthwork, through labyrinths of stone and earth, using a combination of both the map that Aelia had taken from the Citadel and secret riverways which Tende knew.

The crossroads was where our people would divide. Those unable to fight, those who were injured, would be escorted back to Tende's tribe people by a member of the Riverkind. Rana had been due to go, along with Emilian's family. I never assumed that my sister would come with me to the foot of the Citadel, that seemed far too dangerous. My father would be left in my charge.

"You said that we wouldn't be separated again," said Rana. "No one knows how to look after father like I do. I can calm him down!"

I sighed. "It's just too dangerous," I said.

Rana shook her head. "You asked me to look over father, while you went off on your... adventure. That's what I did.

That was our deal. Well, I'm looking after him. You can't stop me."

"Let her come," said a voice behind me.

It was Aelia, she strolled in with the suggestion of a smile on her lips. "I learned to fight when I was her age, in the streets of the Citadel."

Irritation made me contort my lips. "Oh, and that was safe, was it?"

Aelia shook her head. "Oh, skies no. But I helped, in my own small way. And that felt like everything."

Rana's eyes were wide with shock. The impressive stature of Aelia in her armor, which, despite everything we had been through was still more resplendent than anything Rana had ever seen in the Hollow, was too much for Rana, and she went shy, bowing her head and fidgeting.

Despite myself, it edged off my irritation. It was rare to see Rana behave so timidly.

"In our home, young girls don't get a chance to talk to commanders," I explained to Aelia. "To say nothing of rebel leaders from faraway lands."

"Well, once we're done with the fight, we'll all be equal. Everyone living in the ground below and the skies above," said Aelia. She knelt, lowering herself to Rana's level. "Sound good?"

Rana nodded enthusiastically, still unable to speak.

"Would you like to help us with that fight, then?"

Rana nodded again.

"Aelia," I said. "I think that this is a decision for family to make…"

Aelia rose again. "And I think that this family is a fighting one. They belong in the center of things. It will do your father good to have Rana there, she can stay with him as he is treated by the Earthkind."

I frowned at this. "If you think that you'll do the whole tough-love-trainer routine with my sister…"

Aelia dismissed this immediately. "I'm not." She looked around as all the refugees from the Hollow filed past us in the cavern. "The thing is, I left my family pretty young. To keep families together? That's always been one of the reasons why I've fought in the first place."

Aelia didn't stop to hear my response, instead, she walked off, leaving me with her words.

Rana found the ability to speak again. "See, *she* says I can come!"

I knew then that I had lost the argument completely.

It was therefore decided that Rana would stay with me, while so many families and the injured left for Tende's tribe. What was left constituted about fifty warriors, some in better shape than others, most of whom barely knew more than the basics of Weaving. But there was determination in their eyes and purpose in their step as we followed Aelia and left for the city, and I was proud of them.

There was no one with more determination in their step than Yen. Indeed, she seemed impatient to get there, like all she wanted was to walk straight into battle. I was worried. She had a pale look, her eyes had a darkness in them I couldn't recognize. Unlike everyone else, she'd barely washed in the waterfall, and she was still grimy from the struggle at Babel. Even her wounds and cuts did not seem like they'd been tended to. Gone, too, were her leadership skills, her instinct to think of others first, and herself after. She, along with Corinthia, had been in charge of the Hollow since I'd left.

She'd abandoned all sense of command. She was walking at the front, but not because she was guiding the others. It was because she was rushing forwards, thirsty for blood.

I could tell that our people were unnerved by it, and I shared their feelings. It was difficult for me to register what Yen was without the fierce commitment to justice, without the sarcastic quips at my expense. This person, buried in her own thoughts, walking their own sullen walk was not the friend I knew.

Asking someone to take my father's stretcher off my hands for a moment, I went forward and walked beside her.

I did not start a conversation, like I had done on my

previous attempts to speak to her. I did not want to be dismissed again.

"I don't need to talk, Jason," said Yen, weariness in her voice.

"I know," I said. "You won't hear me talking. I'm just walking beside you."

"Why?"

"In case words come out in spite of yourself. And if not, well, maybe it's a good thing to just have someone walk beside you."

She seemed to appreciate this, and we strode along together for a while.

After a few long minutes, she said, "I just don't know what to make of it."

I nodded, not wanting to interject. She still wasn't looking at me, so I wanted to give her as much space as possible.

"I was alone. Being in charge means being alone. Even with Corinthia by my side, it's a lonely world when everyone looks up to you. My father endured it his whole life. So despite everything he did, despite all the trouble he caused in the tower, I think I understood him best the moment I lost him."

She turned to me.

"I don't expect you to grieve or understand. To you, he could only ever be the man who murdered your mother. But to me, he was still my father. I can't get away from that. As much as I'd like to."

"He did many things wrong," I said. I chose my words carefully, like treading on steppingstones.

It was true, what Yen said. I couldn't feel sad for Commander Helton. But I *did* feel sad for her. And that sadness felt threatening. Like it could become a fissure between us. I wanted to bridge the divide, to dismiss the tragedies of our parents and put my arms around her and comfort her. But that felt wrong, presumptuous.

All I had were my words, and how carefully I chose them.

"But he did the right thing in the end," I continued. "He

stood up to the Lightguard and forced their hand. He made sure we knew who they are and what they're capable of."

Yen nodded, her head low. "But even the mistakes he made, all the wrongs he did, perpetuating lies and executing Echo's will, I can't hate him for it like I did before. I know that for you, that will never make sense. Maybe you'll even hate me for it."

A fury, deep inside me, one that was still untreated and raw, threatened to make me protest at her words, even though I knew it wasn't the time. "What do you mean?" I said, in a strangled voice.

"Even the awful things he did, like what he did to your family, it was all because he was in charge. He had the burden of being Echo's mouthpiece, of being the commander's commander. If anything will drive you to lose sight of right and wrong, it's that weight, the *pressure*."

I shook my head. I'd wanted to comfort Yen, to be a good friend as she had been to me. But I couldn't agree with her, I couldn't defend Helton's actions.

"You never lost sight of what's right and wrong," I said. "You and Corinthia, you kept the spirit of the Hollow alive as well as its people. There's a difference between the likes of your father and us. We don't lie and punish and execute."

"Don't we? We didn't tell the Hollow the truth for so long. We lied to them because it was easier. Now they know, and that's got nothing to do with me." Yen stopped walking, and faced me fully, and I saw that her eyes were still wracked with grief. "You've never lied, maybe, but only because you left me to do it. Because you wouldn't be a leader yourself."

I swallowed, giving myself time to take all this in. "I couldn't do what you do. They don't look up to me. I'm not a leader like you are."

She pointed back the way we came. "What about that speech you made? I think you're beginning to make a start. When all is said and done, we're going to need you to be front and center. And then you're going to find that you'll have to put on a front and make difficult decisions like I have. To lead people is to wear a mask."

I paused at this. "You sound like Aelia now. I had to wear a mask, back in the city. Deal in lies and deceit. It wasn't for me."

She scowled, and her words suddenly had an edge. "I imagine it suited you as well as it did Helton, or Aelia, or me. We just accepted it nonetheless because it was our job, because it was for the best."

She was just lashing out now, her sadness turning into anger. I stopped talking and let her say whatever she needed to say.

But she stopped too.

We stood facing each other for a moment, while people streamed past.

Instinct told me to open my arms, to offer an embrace. I did so, tentatively. For a moment, Yen did not respond. And then she gratefully accepted, wrapping her arms about me, putting her forehead upon my shoulder, masking her face from the passers-by. I felt her head shudder with sobs. Her mass of hair poked at my face, but I ignored it, and closed my eyes, processing the moment.

"This feels good. You were gone for so long, so far away," Yen said, talking lowly, her breath on my neck. "Even when you came back. You were so far away."

I frowned. "What, because of Aelia?"

Yen took a step back, and through her mask of sadness there was a hint of my teasing old friend. "Oh, *please*. Did you really think that because another woman was on the scene that I would be jealous? Even though I was busy struggling to keep us alive?"

I shrugged. "Honestly, I didn't think about it."

A smile cracked her lips, even as she sniffed. "Well, at least *that's* the old Jason I know. I never got jealous, *obviously*. But it did feel strange, you coming in with those clothes with stories of that strange city. We used to spend every day together in the same jungles, the same caves, you know? Now you're someone different. I'm still coming to grips with it."

"Well, am I better or worse?" I tried my hand at a joke.

She smiled appreciatively. "Hard to be *worse*. Honestly, though, I'd say you're getting there."

"That's patronizing."

"*That*, my friend, is the best you're going to get."

"Yen," I said, looking straight in her eyes, a moment of seriousness again. "About what you said earlier. I'm never going to hate you. I won't let your father do that to us. And it doesn't matter how I feel about him, and what he did, you're still allowed to mourn him. I just wanted to make sure you knew that."

Yen seemed taken aback. She tilted her head pensively, sadness looming once more. "You *are* getting there," she said lowly, almost as if to herself. Finding herself once more, she patted me on the shoulder, the way a friend would. "Now come on, we're lagging behind," she said.

Yen walked ahead. To me, it felt like there was less dread in her step, that she was less trapped in her own thoughts.

I fell in beside her once more. "All right for me to walk beside you a little longer? I won't make you talk, I promise."

"Sure thing," she said, and her weak smile told me that she was grateful for my presence.

I stayed there for as long as I could before going back to the stretcher.

Chapter Sixty-Nine

We traveled to the Canopy. It took many days, but we avoided going up to the plains at all, knowing how much it would disturb the members of the Hollow, and that we would be detected by scouts.

So instead it became a long trek through caverns and valleys, with Aelia consulting her map, and the Riverkind freezing over rivers to let us cross and find old dried-up waterways to use. We were slow, slower than I would have liked. But then, I could not fault the path we took, which kept us hidden from the enemy at all times.

I tried to do my best to enjoy it. Here was a chance to spend time with everyone in the world I cared about. After spending so many days in the city, fending for myself, it was good to be with people I knew. I enjoyed talking with Emilian, and how sheepishly he spoke about his prowess for using Therian Shade forms, like he could not believe his luck. I got the impression that when he made shadow-claws, or shadow-vines, he took far less satisfaction in using them than realizing that he had recreated history, his favorite subject.

It felt good to hear him gush about all he knew, and everything he'd figured out about the past of Therians, and I sometimes laughed when he'd speak for whole minutes straight about the subject, not realizing that I'd lost the thread.

Another pleasure was to see a team of warriors come together. Aelia, the Riverkind, the old ways of the Hollow and the ways of the Therians were endlessly discussed and compared, and I had a vision of the future I wanted for the Canyonlands, of different traditions and minds meeting in amity and with commonality of purpose. I could see my people's minds open before me as they heard Tende describe what he could Sense in the water, and what Aelia told them the Lightguard were capable of.

I could see friendships bloom as a result. It gave me courage.

I trained, too. Every time we rested, I spent time with Aelia, and we pushed each other to perfect our forms. We tried to do Essence-Gathering in a way which was more stable, I'd ingrained enough memory of the Void's wings to get better and better at forming its intricacies. After the battle at the tower, we were conscious of the fact that Aelia's shadow-blasts were of good use, and she worked on perfecting that.

Gradually, we got more and more control of the shadows as we wrestled our way through the Canyonlands. Still though, a frustration lingered. I wished to be able to take many forms, to pair them, even when I was Essence-Gathering. What good was that statue form if I could not also create a blade with it? How good would flying be if I could not also drop a vine to those below?

I felt like there was some barrier I had to break, I just wasn't sure how to break it yet.

Whenever I could, I spent time with Rana and my father. It was no easy thing, my father was often in distress, his mind elsewhere, and nothing I could say ever got through to him. I could see in his eyes that he was in another time, and that he was becoming less and less responsive to what was happening to him in the present.

Being his caretaker was repetitive and draining. I got a sense of what Rana had been through since I'd been gone, the rigorous, emotionally punishing role of looking after my father, and I understood better than ever how much life had forced Rana to mature.

It was not all sadness, though. One night, when I was sitting with my father and Rana, we saw him smile, and we felt like he could feel my presence, somewhere distant, deep inside his heart. I never failed to laugh at how much Rana enjoyed bossing me around when I took care of our father. She'd finally found something in which she had more experience than me, and she relished showing me how to make father comfortable.

After days and days of travel, over an overcast night, we had finally snuck into the Canopy at the foot of the Citadel.

We walked along the roots of the trees, that long tunnel of gnarled wood, and in the gloom the mushrooms and fungi glowed, and my people were in awe.

We set up camp, there among the roots, and there was a nervousness among everyone as the realization dawned that we were so close to the city. During the journey, the place had gained an almost mythical status.

"I'm going to go into the city to get in touch with Cleander," said Aelia. "I'll go now, while it's still dark, if anyone sees me I'll be thrown directly into the Demon's Lock for sure."

Rana appeared by our side, coming out of nowhere. She looked up at us with her big, dark eyes, saying everything that needed to be said in complete silence.

"But, naturally," Aelia said, putting her hand on Rana's head, "we've got something more important to do first, get your father some help."

Nothing had surprised me more, in these last few days, than Aelia and Rana's growing bond. My little sister had the capacity to completely dismantle Aelia's habitually gruff exterior. As for Rana, Aelia was perhaps the most dazzling and exotic person she'd ever met, and she loved her for it.

It made life easier for me. Where I had to push or goad, Aelia could get Rana to do whatever she wanted.

Aelia and I took my father on a stretcher, and Rana did as

she was told, keeping silent and close as we headed out through the root tunnel and through the jungle.

The jungle glowed with life at night, with plants of such vibrant colors that even on the overcast evening the flowers and plants and fungi were marvels, gleaming like stars.

Aelia brought us to a collection of trees where the growth was particularly dense, explaining that here was where Kauri and the Earthkind sympathetic to the Uprising were. The ceiling of trees was low, and the branches were of a wood streaked with red, so much it almost felt as if sunrise had come early over our brows. Curtains of willowy branches dropped around us, draped from the low trunks, veiling our surroundings.

We found the base of one tree where many sprouts shooting in different directions. On the nub, sitting cross-legged, was Kauri.

He noticed us the moment we walked in, and yet it was difficult to make out, given the strange, gaunt, earthy features of his face. He rose, and there was a rustle as he moved, the greenery around him whispering with his movements.

He took one look at us, and without a word he told us to place my father at the center of the nub of trees, with his head resting against a branch. My father moaned softly, and shook his head, sweat beading on his forehead. His mind elsewhere, as usual.

"I beg your leave," said Aelia. "I must go to the city."

Kauri bowed. "Be careful. The wrath of the Emperor awaits you in the Citadel."

Aelia nodded and left.

"So," said Kauri, turning to his patient. "Let me sit awhile with him, see what ails him." He went to my father's side, and placed a hand on his wrist, chest, then forehead. He would whisper to himself in a way which neither Rana nor I could decipher, it almost sounded like the rustling of his foliage again.

Minutes drew on. Rana and I, unsure of what to do, stood awkwardly, waiting for Kauri to deliver a verdict. My heart pounded. I could not bear the tension. I did not know what I would do if there were to be bad news.

I tried to be strong, for the sake of my sister. But she knew me too well, she took my hand and we breathed together, calming ourselves like we did in meditation.

Finally, my father cried something out, and suddenly a gust of shadows emerged from within him and twisted into shapes, showing figures fighting for their lives against creatures with jaws not unlike the Void.

My father yelped, and convulsed, and then the shadows left, and he collapsed and went silent once more.

Kauri stood straight and faced us. "I have thoughts to share."

"Good ones, I hope?" I asked.

"It is good news, to my ears. But I think it will sound like bad news to yours."

I didn't like the sound of that. "What do you mean?" I asked.

"There is no treatment for your father. Nothing can make him go back to the way he was."

The words speared into me, gutting my insides. I almost let go of Rana so I could drop to the ground and despair-- but her presence made me keep my cool.

"How could that be good news?" I said.

Kauri looked at me, measuring how to say his words. I saw that there was kindness in his eyes, even if it was the patronizing kind.

"Your father is full of history. Full of the past. He is reaching into the earth of yesteryear, the roots of our growing world. It may seem like madness and fever to you, but such knowledge is making him wiser. Think of the richness of his mind."

"But, look at him!" I cried. "He's *suffering*. His mind isn't rich, it's lost!"

Kauri nodded with patience. "Because he is fighting with it. Wrestling with it. Instead, he could accept it. Tap into it. The world would benefit from someone with his knowledge, were he able to process it all. He would match the Stonekind in his knowledge of the past."

I struggled with this. "I just want my father back. I don't care about how wise he is. We just need our father."

"Your father has changed. There is no going back. But change does not mean loss. Your father is *growing,* not wilting."

"We've brought him across the entire Canyonlands, carried him with my bare hands. All I ask is for you to *get rid* of whatever's inside of him!"

"Jason," came a whisper from beside me. Rana. She was looking at me, tugging at my hand.

"I'm doing my best, Rana!" I snapped, frustration getting the best of me.

"You misunderstand her," commented Kauri.

I was about to counter this. I know my family better than you, I was about to say. But a doubt took me, and I looked down at her again.

She bade me come close. I knelt, and she went close to my ear, the way she used to when she wanted to tell me secrets.

"I think he's right," she said.

"What do you mean?"

"He's been like this a while now. I figured out that he wasn't going to be quite our dad anymore."

"How could you have known that?"

"Aelia told me. She said, everything else had changed for me, and so why would Dad be any different?"

Tears threatened to spill. "We don't want to lose him, though, do we? Not after Mum."

"But that's it. We're not losing him. He's still there. We don't need to get rid of anything. We just need to calm him down, so that he knows we're there."

I blinked, drinking this in for a moment.

"All right," I said. I hugged my sister and stood up to speak to Kauri. "My sister agrees with you. Trusts you. I don't know how my sister got so wise."

Kauri gave an understanding smile to Rana. "Probably

because you needed her to be. Now, if Rana will stay with me, we can give your father some potions to calm his mind, and together we can help stop his confusion, so he can be present with us once more. The past will still be rushing through him, but then, the ghosts can be a gift, as I think you know." Kauri held out a hand. "Will you help me, little one?" he asked Rana.

She nodded, a little shy. But she stepped forward and took his hand.

She turned to me and said, "You get rid of the Emperor, and we'll get Papa back. All right?"

I smiled, proud of her.

I replied with the words she always used to say. "It's a deal."

Chapter Seventy

For the next hour, I did not want to return to the others. I just wanted to get one last bit of training in before tomorrow. I'd hoped that it would clear my mind; that the cycling and meditation could help process what had happened.

Truly, I just needed time to myself.

I roamed along the jungle, picking my way through its myriad colors, through trees patched with lichen and moss, underneath branches strewn with warts and fungi. I found a place to myself in a mossy patch by the side of a pond.

I sat down and breathed. I took in the Anima of the pre-dawn air, filling my channels, and then my core.

Then I welcomed my thoughts. So much had happened, and I hadn't given myself time to let it all sink in. What had happened with Rana had demonstrated that clearly. She'd been able to get to grips with what was happening to our father in a way that I hadn't.

There was something I was lacking. Something that was holding me back from being the best warrior I could be. In the past weeks, I had gathered knowledge at a dizzying rate, and had come out of it able to pair forms, and flit from one to another. I had learned new shapes. I learned to Essence-Gather, a process which allowed me to continuously grasp at shadows, making forms bigger and stronger than I ever had before.

It wasn't enough. If I had been better, I could have saved more back at the Tower of Babel. I would have been able to fly people to safety. I would have been able to wield a sword while encased in my shadow-stone armor.

So what could I do?

Rana's words came back to me, echoing inside my soul. *Everything else had changed for me, and so why would Dad be any different?*

Perhaps it was this. In order to Essence-Gather, I'd had to embrace something larger than myself, I'd had to embrace the desire to make a mark upon history. To care not just for the injustices against me and mine, but injustice across the Canyonlands.

Could it be that I hadn't embraced it enough? Was I still holding on to the life I knew, like a man trying not to be taken in the current of a river? Was I not ready to let things go and abandon myself to the wider cause?

Rana had taught me that I wasn't. That no matter how strong a warrior I had become, I was still the boy who could not accept the death of his mother, a boy who'd roamed around the valley looking for her ghost.

A boy who couldn't accept change.

That was why it had been so hard to accept that there was no cure for my father. I needed some things to remain as they were, or nothing could be stable anymore, and the world may as well open in cracks and swallow me into the Underworld.

I'd wanted the world to change, but I'd not been prepared for my life to change with it.

The moment that thought came to me, I could not dismiss it. It took root in me and bloomed. It led me to think about the Therians, who had built the Tower, a place of training for generations beyond the original creators. I thought about my conversations with Yen, and how she'd told me that I was going to have to adapt, because the Hollow needed me to lead them.

I thought about being the Blade of Rebels.

I hadn't thought about the title, that grandiose, theatrical role. Not since I'd left the city. I'd been only too glad to abandon it. The suit, the grandstanding, had not been me. I had taken it on because I'd had to, because it was the best way for me to protect my people.

But the real Blade of Rebels did not work for himself. He gave everything to the cause, to overthrowing the Empire and restoring of justice. To the dismantling of the Experiments.

Could I be *that* Blade of Rebels?

The very moment I asked myself the question, the answer came. A gut feeling, from the pit of my stomach.

I have to be.

I shook myself, as if physically letting go of something, and stood. A desire to be that person, to be the one who gives up everything in the name of right and wrong, the person willing to embody the cause they fight for. Anima spun with ferocity in my core.

I stretched my arms out, ready to embrace the dark.

Shadows danced out, embossed with Anima blue. The blue took the shape of Core Magic.

I beckoned to the black, and the black answered. It streamed toward me, like I was at the bottom of the Earth and they were falling. My outstretched arms were interlaced, then coated, then thickened, painted over with shadow. My reach doubled, as my arms were extended with wings of black.

This was not like all the other times I had done this. No, this was controlled. This was with purpose. Before, Essence-Gathering had always come with a sensation of panic, of the world pulling at my chest. But now I knew what the world wanted while I hungrily drained it of its shadows. It wanted my absolute commitment.

For the first time, it had it.

The wings on my shoulders did not leak shadows. There were no trails, no mists of escaping black. They were perfect sculptures, an exact mimicry.

I had the wings of the Void.

I swayed from side to side, and the greenery around me swayed with the displaced air. I flapped the wings downward and felt a lift in my heels.

This was it. I could feel it. Now that the shape was there, and stable, the rest was natural.

I ran, charging through the jungle.

I leapt into the air, my arms outstretched.

This time, my feet did not return to the ground.

Chapter Seventy-One

"Jason, where have you been?"

I smiled at Yen. "Cycling," I said, in a way which suggested much more.

"I don't know if I should be scared or excited by how happy you look," said Yen, eyeing me with suspicion.

I centered myself, shaking off the giddy memories of the past hour. "Sorry. I got a little carried away."

"Look, if you got good news about your father, I'm happy. But I could do with your concentration for a bit."

I nodded.

Aelia had managed to get in touch with Cleander, who had immediately called an emergency Uprising meeting. She had collected Corinthia and Yen and was bringing them to the meeting.

I was only just catching up with Yen as she was about to head into the secret compartment of the Uprising, and she seemed none too pleased. "What on earth is this place?" she asked.

"It's where people plan to overthrow the Emperor," I said.

Yen took this in. "That sounds all right."

"Things are never that simple in the city," I warned her. "People can be duplicitous here. They can say one thing and mean another."

Yen frowned. "Even the good guys?"

"Everyone."

"Yeesh."

"Indeed."

Aelia pushed the door open, and we were welcomed into the chamber. Seats formed at our arrival, stone twisting into shape, and Yen jumped at the sight.

"Ah..." said a familiar, smooth voice. "These must be the chieftains of the Hollow."

It was Cleander, standing to greet us in his fine robes, smiling at us in his slightly patronizing way. I felt Yen take an immediately defensive stance, bristling at his presence, and I felt a surge of affection as I realized how similarly we felt.

Cleander introduced the other members of the Uprising: Fealta of the Riverkind, and the others. Kauri was there too but was quick to explain to me that his treatment of my father had been placed in other, just as capable hands.

They all bowed to Corinthia and Yen, who did the same in an uncertain manner, and we all took a seat in the circular formation on the newly shaped rocks.

Aelia began the meeting, updating the others on what had happened back at the Tower of Babel. "Right now, hidden underneath the Canopy, we have fifty warriors of the Shade. They are not refined, many of them are not properly trained. But they have lived through a lot and have been hardened by a lifetime spent in the Experiments. Like Jason, they wield great promise and heart."

I could hardly believe it. Did Aelia just *compliment* me? Publicly?

Aelia's face almost turned to self-disgust as she realized how kind she was being, and she pushed forward. "Their greatest asset is that they have strange weaves, based on the old techniques of the Therians, modeled on nature and wildlife. That, and the fact that the Lightguard have no idea that this band is in the vicinity of the city. More importantly, they have attuned their Senses to explore caverns and tunnels in a way the Shadekind of the city never have. They could find an old way into the palace and help infiltrate it."

"A tribe of Shadowkind. How...novel," said Cleander. "It's not enough to take on the might of the Lightguard, but it is an intriguing addition. After all, a Shadowkind which is trained in any way, shape or form is a more powerful proposition than the rabble of the Lower Levels."

I noted, once more, that for all Cleander's progressive ideals, he certainly spoke with condescension about those beneath him.

Skies, I hate being back in the Citadel already.

"This may be perfect," he said. "If the Hollow itself, the people of the Experiments, infiltrate the palace and put me on the throne. It will give me even more legitimacy. I will be the symbol of the new, fairer Canyonlands."

Yen shot me a look. *Who is this guy?* Her eyes asked.

To which I could only answer with a shrug.

Who, in fact, was Cleander? I'd trusted him because I'd had to. But he was still too slippery a character for me to truly embrace, and the idea of risking death to appoint him as the new leader was a little difficult to stomach.

I leaned forward. "Forgive me," I said. "But the Shadowkind are no match for the Lightguard. It would be a bloodbath up there. When I left this city, the Uprising had failed. The coup was dead. Now I return to find you all smiles. What am I missing?"

Cleander gave a little chuckle. "You are absolutely right. This must feel all a little disorienting for you. But we Moonguard are known for our stealth. We adapt."

Cleander rose to his feet and started pacing about the room. "There were two simple reasons why we failed the last time. One was that it was too soon and too quick, it was not planned carefully enough. The people of the Canopy did not have time to join in, and they are crucial, as Kauri will be able to tell you in a moment. But also, what I should have realized is that revolutions must come in *two* phases, not one. The riots in the city can therefore be seen not as a failure of a coup, but as a success in *setting the stage* of a coup."

Cleander looked me in the eye, a little twinkle of self-satisfaction in his gaze. "You see, the first movement of a revolution is to show the people *and the elite* that change is inevitable. That the Emperor is weaker, and more vulnerable, than they thought. Then, it is not just the people that riot. It is the Senate who shift too, wondering whether someone else would be better placed to take the throne. Only then can the second phase succeed, the real transition of power."

I frowned. "You've been making deals with Senators."

"Indeed. My battlefield is dinner tables and drinks, Jason. I have considerable support now, after those riots. Lucian looks weak now. Most of the Senate are ready to replace him. They do not wish to be kidnapped and taken for ransom. They do not want to deal with a leader who cannot handle a band of rebels, what chance does such a leader have against Cizin and the Demon Hordes? They want a more stable, trustworthy hand wielding the sword of the Empire."

I stood up too. "But surely we don't want the Senate, in its current form, to persist? The Senators are awful, parasites of the emperor. I saw them slosh their wine and deal out death and suffering like it was nothing at all. If our rebellion is to mean anything, then it means that the Senate needs to be completely dismantled. A clean slate. Your deals and handshakes cannot be part of this."

Cleander's eyebrow arched. "It may not be the revolution you wanted, Jason. But it is the revolution that is presenting itself to us. We saw that during the riots, we cannot govern by the whims of the populace. All they know is destruction and riots. We need people in power with experience. I have spoken to all the Senators we kidnapped, and they saw reason. They pledged themselves to me. They have reached out to convince the others."

The vision of that Senate room, where they drank and ate themselves merry while applauding cruelty and executions, came back to me. I could not stop myself. "These Senators promised to support the person who kidnapped them? What value does that promise have? And what did you do to elicit it?" My nostrils flared in anger. "If the world you promise is ruled by *those* people, the people I saw clapping at the creation of a new form of Void, then I want no part in it. My people died between the jaws of that new Void just days ago."

Cleander's silky voice still showed no sign of irritation. "Anyone who believes that utopias are achieved instantaneously is doomed to never see their utopia at all. The question, then, is this. Would you rather keep Emperor Lucian in power? Do you want to risk keeping him at the helm of the ship when the storm of Cizin's hordes hits our bow?" Cleander took a step towards me. "Or do you wish to take the first step with me, and see if we can take a second, and third, until the Canyonlands become a better place?"

"You see steps taken towards a better world," I said. "I just see a dance. A merry dance of people outmaneuvering and double-crossing each other while the world below them suffers the same shades of injustice."

"You don't believe that," Cleander said sweetly. "Perhaps when you first arrived here in the Citadel, but not anymore. You know better now, that rulers make a difference. Speak to the leaders of your community. Corinthia, Yennenga. I'll wager they had to compromise, and I'll wager more that their compromises saved as many lives as their shadow-blades."

I glanced over at Yen. She did not know how to react, the whole situation was overwhelming to her. But I could see her getting won over by Cleander's words.

I was losing this argument.

Yen cleared her throat. "I barely understand the things you speak of. I have never seen the city, and I have never met the Senate. But if the choice is between trying for something better, or not trying at all for fear of failing, then there is no choice at all." She looked directly at me in the eye. "We cannot walk away from this, and you know it."

Cleander's eyes were kind, but I still saw a note of triumph in his lips. "And you, Corinthia?"

Corinthia nodded, slowly.

"Then I can count on the support of the Hollow, yes, Jason?" Cleander said, turning back to me.

"On one condition," I answered.

Cleander did not expect this, beneath a calm exterior there was a note of surprise that caused a twitch in his nose. "I am impressed. Despite all you say to the contrary, you play the game too, and you play it well. What was it you called it? A *merry dance?*" He let his words sting for a moment. "Well then, name your terms. Let this be in the spirit of a new era of collaboration. What do you want?"

"A promise. You say that your word means something. Here, in front of the whole of the Uprising, is your chance to prove it. The moment you take power, you must liberate all the people suffering in the valleys of the Experiments. Free all of the people who suffer and die like the Hollow did."

It took a moment before Cleander responded. "You have my word," he said. He offered a hand.

I took it. "In which case, you have my sword."

"Good." Cleander's eyes lit up in excitement. "Now let's plan a revolution."

Chapter Seventy-Two

The next phase of the meeting was all about logistics.

Kauri took over the proceedings, explaining his role. "One of the key reasons that the riots failed is that we in the Canopy were not involved," he explained. "After all, we are the roots of the revolution. We are out of the gaze of the Lightguard. They believe that the only things worth looking at are in the city. We have been able to operate without being detected. Recently we have increased the smuggling of Elixir-infused plants. We have also, with the help of the Riverkind, siphoned off the Elixir into blocks of ice, and distributed them around the networks of the city."

I took a moment to take this in. "What is he talking about?" Yen whispered to me.

"It's like the whole forest is made up of Jade Roots," I said. "Every single plant there gives you the same boost."

Yen's eyes widened in the same way mine had.

"We Earthkind have been drinking the Elixir under the noses of the Empire for many years. As such, we have grown far stronger than they imagine," said Kauri. "We suggest that if such a diversion is needed to bring the Lightguard away from the palace, then let it come from below. We Earthkind can storm the Lower Levels of the city, and in the roads leading into the city. We can block roads, creating a little trouble. When all the Lightguard come down to do battle with us in the Lower Levels, we take over the gates and close it behind them. The Stonekind among us will create stone barriers to ensure that the gates remain closed, preventing the guards from coming back up Into the Upper Levels."

"Such a diversion would create great risk for your warriors, and those in the Lower Levels," noted Corinthia, ever the tactical thinker. "You would effectively be caged in with the enemy."

Cleander nodded. "Indeed," he said with solemn gravity, which I did not buy for a second. I doubted he cared a jot as to how many lowly Shadekind and Earthkind died.

Kauri continued. "We are a diversion, not an open battle. We will lure them to the streets of the Lower Levels, and the forests beyond the city walls, worlds we know infinitely better than them. It should be feasible to keep them occupied without too much loss of life. After all, we will all be fighting against the demons of Cizin before too long, every man will count."

Cleander took over the planning. "While they are distracted, the Shadowkind of the Hollow will try to infiltrate the palace. If I remember correctly, there is, indeed, an old tunnel leading to the palace. It was last used many, many years ago and will not be easy to follow. But that, I can leave to your cavern experience. From memory, the tunnel leads to the palace gardens. It is now covered in stone and has a statue resting on top of it. I will be inside the palace, there are a few palace guards who are part of the Uprising. At midday, you must find your way to the opening. Members of the Uprising will use a light-blast to reopen the entrance to the tunnel, and you will emerge.

"If the diversion in the Lower Levels works, there will only be a small group of guards in the palace. Still, they will be fierce warriors, and they will be more powerful than your Shadowkind, so we need to prepare for a fight. I will meet you there with my own warriors, including Aelia, and we will do as best we can. We must keep the enemy at bay long enough to get to the Prism and broadcast our message into the sky. At that point, the fight will be over. At that point, the Emperor will have no choice but to stand down."

"You mean to let him live?" I asked.

"We will see," Cleander answered evasively. "He is a cowardly man, not the Emperor of years past. He may flee at the first sign of trouble. But it is no matter. Once we get to the Sundial, we will reveal to the world the identity of the Blade of Rebels. There, you will endorse me in front of everyone as the new leader… and the battle will be over."

"Hang on," I said. "The identity of the Blade of Rebels is not known? But the Quaester saw me!"

"It is known among the Senate and the Lightguard, but everyone was instructed not to tell the people at large. The Emperor knew how bad that would look. The people of the city still need to be told. Imagine, there, on the eve of a new era, they will look up to the sky, and see an image of their hero, returned to the battle after many weeks. And that hero will be unmasked, revealed to be none other than yourself. They will hang on to your every word. And if you proclaim me to be the next Emperor, right there in the sky for everyone to see, there will be no going back. I will be at the head of the Empire. And I will proclaim right there and then for the fighting to cease in the Lower Levels, and for the Experiments to be stopped immediately. How does that sound?"

"Too good to be true," I admitted.

"Start believing, and start preparing," Cleander said. "At dawn, the world changes for the better."

With that, the meeting adjourned. Dawn light was starting to spill its sepia tones into the jungle, making the vegetation dazzle with even more vibrant colors than before, and we hurried to ensure that we were back inside the Root Tunnel before we were seen by anyone.

There, we relayed the plan to the Hollow. Here I let Corinthia and Yen do most of the talking, as they were used to organizing the warriors, but Aelia and I intervened with descriptions of the layout of the city. While Aelia gave broad descriptions, I went into more detail. I knew that the Citadel was an overwhelming place, and I wanted to mentally prepare them for the fight ahead.

We then hashed out more details of who would have what role, and how we would lead the attack.

Finally, we ordered everyone to rest, and to cycle, stating that we would move upon the city at dawn. My final words were that of invitation, I had filled an amphora of Elixir, and urged everyone to drink from it as the day wore on, so that they could benefit when they cycled. If they ran out, I instructed them to gnaw on the roots, as they contained the same magical abilities as the Jade Roots from the Hollow.

The Hollow were apprehensive, and frightened. This new world was not their own, and they were incredulous that they were to play such a crucial part in this coup when they knew the land so little. But the liquid helped, and soon they were settled, cycling, and resting, readying themselves.

Emilian was particularly nervous.

"Jason, can I be frank?" he asked, approaching me. His round, expressive face was creased with worry.

"Everything all right?"

I felt him nod. "It's just that, well I'm afraid."

"Emilian the Warrior? The man who trains other warriors, no less? Scared?"

My bright tone did not have its intended effect. His face remained as grave as ever. "As horrible as the Void are, I *know how horrible they are*. I have no idea what's happening, up there in the Citadel. I've been trying to imagine it, but nothing comes to mind."

"Then think about it like this," I said. "Think of the fact that, no matter what happens, you'll have walked in the oldest city in the Canyonlands. You'll have walked where our ancestors, and their ancestors, walked. This is the center of all history, Emilian. You want to see that, don't you?"

A look of wonder stole across his face. "I really do."

"Well then, today is your lucky day."

After consulting with Yen, Corinthia, and Aelia about the

last details, I took a corner to myself and started to loosen my thoughts in preparation for mediation.

I felt a presence take a spot next to me.

Yen.

"Do you think this will work?" she asked in a quiet voice.

"I don't know," I said honestly. "Cleander seems confident. But I don't know whether that's good news or bad."

"I don't know what to make of him," admitted Yen. "But I feel like *something's* going to happen. And that means getting a chance to strike back at those who've caused us all of this misery. That's all right with me. I'm still carrying that anger, since my father died, it's fighting to be let out."

I nodded. "Yen, what if we succeed? What if the Emperor is deposed, and Cleander is in charge? What then?"

"I don't think anyone is letting themselves think that far ahead."

"Cleander is," I pointed out. "I bet he has plans. And I bet I'm in them, as a mascot, probably. The Blade of Rebels is what will keep him popular. Otherwise, he'll be a bitter pill to swallow. After all, he's been part of the ruling class for hundreds of years, people will have a hard time forgiving him for that."

"Well, then. It sounds like you'll be busy."

"But, what about you?"

"I don't know. We're homeless. This jungle is incredible, people might want to stay here. Or perhaps, if the Experiments don't exist any longer, they might want to go home. To the Hollow."

I shifted. "And what will you want?"

Yen eyed me suspiciously. "I feel like you're asking me a different question than the one you're actually asking."

I shrugged. "Maybe. I think that someone needs to be here, make sure Cleander is true to his word, and that the Experiments truly end. And I can't help but feel that that person might have to be me. But frankly, this city scares me. I don't want to be swallowed by it."

"You don't want to do it alone?"

I shook my head. "I'm stronger with you by my side."

A silence, one far too long for my liking, settled between us.

And then she placed her hand on mine. "You've got to do what you can for the Canyonlands. I've got to do what I can for the Hollow. Even if I wanted to stay here with you, I'm not sure I could."

"Can we not make any choices for ourselves anymore?" I lamented, even as I knew she was right.

Yen breathed in a deep sigh. "Do you remember how much we wanted to be *important* when we were young? How much we wished we were in charge, and making the decisions? It's strange to think of that now. We've gotten everything we dreamed of, but nothing that we want."

I held a cup of Elixir, and Yen clicked hers against mine. "For the Hollow, then," I said. "And for the Canyonlands. And for us, somewhere further down the line."

We exchanged sad smiles, took our drinks, and closed our eyes to welcome the darkness into our channels.

Chapter Seventy-Three

The rest of the day was spent recuperating, and cycling, and eating, then doing it all over. We limbered up and stretched and took our fill of Elixir while the day etched away, and the sun started to clamber out of the valley. We slept as best we could and took in our fill of Anima.

Aelia gave orders for us to leave just as the sun was starting to rise and the first stars were beginning to fade away in the light of the new day.

Aelia and I gave each other the Hollow Handshake.

"I'll see you in the palace," said Aelia.

"Make sure you do," I said. "Last time I went there, I almost died. I want to avoid repeating that experience, if possible."

"I'll see what I can do. Just find your way through the tunnels. Cleander and I will be there on the other side."

With that, we set off. I led with Yen, while Corinthia and Tende brought up the rear. We filtered through the trees, and then we went into the tunnel where the Elixir flowed, and made our way through the gloom, climbing the stairs while the gleaming liquid gushed down beside us.

There was palpable excitement in the air around us. A feeling that everyone wanted to speak, to give voice to all the doubts and fears and excitement, but no one would. The energy was charged, and everyone's mind was focused on one thing: the battle ahead.

The further we travelled up the more the sounds of the city above came alive, filtering down from the surface.

"The diversion," I murmured, and Yen nodded.

As we spoke, the Earthkind were starting to cause mischief down in the Lower Levels, near the Demon's Lock. We heard thuds, and shouts, all hushed by the layers of rock and stone, and then the thunder of movement as troops came down from above, ordering barking, fighting.

We came to the top of the tunnel, where the Elixir was gushing in from aqueducts in the city above.

I then turned to figure out the next step. Around me, there were a few different choices as to where to go.

I pointed at a slim opening to the side, barely wide enough for my frame to fit through.

"Is that the direction of the palace?" asked Yen.

"More or less."

I reached out into the darkness with my Senses, seeing that the tunnel stretched into the distance, winding, and curving.

"Good enough for me," I said, stepping inside and threading through the path, walking on my side as it was not large enough to walk normally. Behind me, Yen followed, and then came the footsteps of the rest of our company.

"Feels familiar?" grunted Yen, squeezing through a tight passage.

"Exploring caves with the Hollow? It's Pastfinding all over again—the only thing I was ever any good at, if you believe all of our teachers."

"Seems like a lifetime ago."

The tunnel forked and we had to stop.

"I don't know about that," I said. "I've never stopped Pastfinding, one way or another..."

With those words, I reached a little deeper with my Senses, peering into the history of the tunnel. First came the whispers, the voices. And then came the ghosts, the forms of the past.

The Shadowkind from another era, making their way across the halls.

I lifted my hands and felt the history flow past my fingertips in a current, seeing where they led.

There was one path which was more frequented than the rest, a path busy with spirits.

"It's this way," I said, following the Shadowkind ancestors up towards the palace. Together, the Hollow retraced the footsteps of our people from another era.

It was no easy path. Partly, this was because it had been abandoned for so long, and parts had collapsed. For certain sections, we had to climb upwards, using shadow-claws and vines to scramble up facades. But the ghosts were always there to guide me, showing me passages and handholds to grasp which I would have missed.

We climbed upwards for hours.

Finally, I Sensed the ghosts disappear into a rock, a dead end.

Here, then, if we had not taken a wrong turn, was the entrance to the palace gardens, sealed off with a wall of rock.

This was to be our entrance into the battle.

"How long do you think until midday?" I asked Yen.

"An hour, perhaps."

I tried to get everyone to rest and cycle, awaiting the hour when we would emerge into the palace above our heads and play our part in the coup. But it was no easy feat, dread sat in the pits of our stomachs, and the wait was excruciating.

I forced myself to go through all my preparations; I cycled, and stored shadows inside my core. I focused on my Mind's Eye, going through all my forms, ensuring they were all clear in my mind.

I tried to imagine a moment, in a few hours, when the world would be different, when the Experiments were finished, and all Shadowkind were liberated from the cruelties of the Emperor. The images wouldn't come, however.

Perhaps my imagination wasn't as developed as I thought.

"Jason," the voice of Yen.

"Yes?"

There was a pause. My throat went dry when I realized why she'd caught my attention.

There was sound, coming from above us. Commotion, the footsteps of many men.

It was time.

I clenched my jaw and pulled from inside my core, in my hands the darkness took the shape of a staff with half-moon blades at each end.

A moment passed. Then another.

I could hardly breathe. All the warriors of the Hollow were hushed in anticipation.

Silence fell heavy as a hammer. My heart pounded and sweat coursed down my features.

Then it came. A cry from above. The humming sound of a Weave.

I ensured everyone kept their distance, holding up a hand.

There was a cracking sound echoing through the rock. The roof blew inward through as a light-blast exploded on the surface.

The plan had worked, Aelia and Cleander were letting us in.

Dust billowed through the tunnel, and blinding sunlight streamed through the passage where darkness had reigned for so long. Even though rocks were rolling at my feet, I charged ahead, flinging myself into the cloud of dust, reaching for the sunlight. I ran with my half-moon blades brandished, ready to wage war.

But what I found, emerging through the fog of dust into the gardens, was something altogether different.

I stopped in shock.

There was no commotion. No war. Only a ring of Lightguard, at least twenty of them, pointing their weapons at me. Behind that row was a line of senators, they were sitting in the garden on stools, slurping from goblets of wine, and standing among them was Cleander.

An order was given which I didn't comprehend.

I whipped back, but it was too late. The order had been for a Stonekind, standing by the entrance I had just emerged out of, he held out his hand, and rocks moved at this command. A nearby statue disintegrated, its fragments rushing in to fill the hole I had just run through.

All I saw was Yen shriek and call out my name, before a layer of rock groaned into place, and we were separated. The Hollow were still in the tunnel, but I was alone up here with the Lightguard.

"You made it," said Cleander, walking through the guards towards me, a satisfied smile stretching his thin lips. "You are so very...*dependable.*" He took a drink from his goblet and smiled a simile of cruelty. "Welcome to my revolution, Jason."

The guard made way for him, and he loomed close. It was at that precise moment that I realized in my gut that something was truly, deeply wrong.

Cleander was wearing the costume of the Blade of Rebels.

Chapter Seventy-Four

"Cleander, what's going on?" I blurted out.

Cleander continued to speak in his cheery, self-satisfied manner. "We just did so well, Jason. Even easier than expected. Make the right deals, and the right threats, with the right Senators, and just the promise of you arriving here was enough for the Senate to turn against Lucian. He's fled up into the plains above, with his band of faithful warriors. Leaving me in charge."

"So, we've won. The coup has succeeded. You're the new Emperor. Why have you barred my people from coming up? Why are you wearing the costume of the Blade?

Cleander paced around me, like a someone admiring their artwork, pleased with their output. "You represent the people so well, you know. And you were right. The people want a true revolution. A clean slate. But that's simply not possible, Jason. Take it from me, the city cannot be run by the likes of upstarts like you. Not when we are preparing for war. We need steady hands. *Old* hands. And we certainly can't let go of the Experiments. They have been, and will continue to be, invaluable. Lucian didn't see that, he just saw them as tools of oppression. But then, there's much Lucian didn't see anymore..."

"You made a deal—" I started to say.

"I lied. Welcome to the Citadel, Jason. You still don't quite have the hang of things around here, do you?"

Cleander put a hand across my shoulders, as if he were speaking to a friend. "You see, Jason, the Senate are happy for me to assume the complete mantle of Emperor. No counterpart, no one to keep me in check. So long as I have the goodwill of the people."

I threw his hand off my shoulder.

"You won't have it," I snarled. My surprise was just beginning to wear off, replaced with fury. "You're part of an old system. A system which has persecuted the people of the Canyonlands for years. They won't accept you as a new dawn, and you won't unite the people. Not without my endorsement, and there's no way you're going to get it."

Cleander seemed delighted to be asked. "That is why you're so perfect. A boy, plucked from the mysterious experiments. Everyone looks to you. You are the key to all of this. The people look to you to speak the truth. Lucian never quite understood your importance like I did. So when you, a martyr, tell the people that I have mastered the arts of the Shade, and that I was the Blade of Rebels all along, they will no longer see me as part of the old system. I will be heralded as the dawn of a new age."

My blood ran cold. "Did you say *martyr?*"

"Oh yes. So much more effective if you tell the people this in your last dying moments, having battled Lucian, don't you think? Won't that be so effective, painted across the sky for all to see?"

My lip curled. "Is this what you have to do so that your *Senate* will accept you? Lie to the people? Pretend to be someone you're not? Take the credit from others, and then kill them off?"

"That's politics, my boy."

Hatred burned through my body. "Well, you're not going to get your spectacle. I'll never proclaim you as the Blade, or the rightful Emperor. You can do what you want to me, I'd rather die."

Cleander shook his head, and said in his patronizing, smooth voice, “Everyone has a breaking point, Jason. Yours is all too obvious.”

He snapped his fingers in the air.

As a result, there was movement. Someone was being escorted here, dragged this way by guards.

A terror seized me, it grabbed my throat so that I could not breathe.

It was my worst nightmare, materialized. Rana and my father, manhandled by guards, were being led over. A way to make me behave, a way to make me obedient.

My father was in a world of his own, squirming with distress as he was dragged into my sight. Rana was thrashing against her captor, doing all she could to wrench herself out of his grasp; but then she caught sight of me, and her eyes widened with comprehension.

I could barely look at her.

“You see, now,” said Cleander. “I think three steps ahead. That’s why I’ll make such a good Emperor.”

I looked about in panic, gazing for some kind of answer; some reprieve from the nightmare I was living. But there was none. Only the row of guards, and the line of senators beyond. They were laughing amongst themselves, barely even paying attention to what was being said.

My eyes landed on Aelia.

I’d forgotten, she was part of Cleander’s group in the palace. She was standing there, among the other guards under the new Emperor’s order.

My eyes met hers. But I could not read them.

Surely, I thought, she would not let this happen? Surely she would not let Cleander take power in these circumstances?

The cruel answer came to me. Of course she would. She’d said it, from the time I realized she was a revolutionary. She would do *anything* for the Uprising, and for Cleander. She’d spent her life waiting for this moment.

And she’d been ready to kill me to see it happen.

Aelia looked down, avoiding my gaze.

My last hope evaporated.

"So, will you help me, Jason? Will you help me restore peace and defenses to the Canyonlands?" Cleander's words were rhetorical, and barely even sounded like questions.

He'd won, and he knew it.

"Come to the Crystal, Jason," he said. "We will send your message of peace and strength to the world. I promise you, you will get a funeral worthy of a hero. Your body will parade the streets."

I tried to move, to do as he said, but my steps were heavy. I remained frozen. I couldn't even speak.

"Come now," said Cleander. "Or would you rather receive your mortal wound, then be carried over? You might want to get this over with, your sister is looking *ever* so upset..."

A single word boomed across the air. It was a voice so different to Cleander's smooth, calm tones.

A voice of strength.

"No," it said.

I turned. It was Aelia's voice.

She was stepping forward, through the guards. Her face was a scowl of fury. And in her hands, shadows were gathering in an orb, amassing from all corners. She was Essence-Gathering.

The guards around her shifted, turning to each other in shock.

"Aelia, I order you to—" Cleander started.

"You don't order me. Not anymore...*Emperor*."

There was a blur of movement.

"Get her!" Cleander shrieked.

A light-blade materialized in the hand of the guard behind her, it was promptly planted in Aelia's back.

But it was already too late. With a scream of pain, Aelia threw her shadow-blast, her orb of shadows.

It soared through the air and landed on the entrance to the tunnel, the opening which had been blocked again by the Stonekind.

An explosion ripped through the air, just behind me, as stone was once again torn from the mouth of the tunnel, and dust plumed around us once more.

This time, the Shadowkind of the Hollow didn't hesitate. Before the exploded stones even hit the ground, there was the trampling of feet.

The Shadowkind ran into the palace gardens, ready for war.

Chapter Seventy-Five

The world was pandemonium as Yen and the others tore into the courtyard, the hum of shadow-weapons buzzing through the air, accompanying their battle cries. Cleander, still cowering from the blast, plunged into the safety of the line of guards.

I bent down to pick up Aelia, but she howled with pain as she stood, brushing my hand away. "I'll protect your family," she said, before diving to shield my father and sister amidst the confusion of guards.

Before I knew it, the Shadowkind had thrown themselves into the line of attack, rushing into the barrier of Lightguard, some were immediately impaled, falling onto the paved slabs.

Around me, the fight had begun. The remaining warriors of the Hollow fought against what remained of the palace guard now that Lucian had taken his faithful with him. We outnumbered them, but they had skills that we could only dream of.

The first cries of blood and death sounded. An ugly melee started in front of me.

The gardens, with their lush greenery, pleasant fountains, and marble floors, formerly a sanctuary, were now a place of violence, a place where blood would splatter onto immaculate flowers and bone-white walls.

The Lightguard pushed the first attack back, shaking the Shadowkind off like they were flies. Now over their initial surprise, the Lightguard assumed their positions, some advancing with swords, others throwing light-spears and nets towards the crowd of Shadowkind now gathered around me.

Luckily, Corinthia was there. She put her hands out, and a band of shadows appeared in front of the Hollow, creating a black barrier. The light-bolts pelted the wall of gloom and went nowhere, fizzing out against the hum of the shield.

In response, the Lightguard created their own barriers. After a few streaks of light charging through the air, a line of light-shields glowed on each warrior's hand, each one spiked with blades coating the front. With this in hand, they shouted a war cry and fired a barrage against Corinthia's shadow, pushing against it.

The spikes on the enemy's shields punctured Corinthia's barrier immediately. We didn't have long before they would push through and start the slaughter.

"Shadowfront!" barked Corinthia in a strangled voice. "To me!"

Her barrier was disintegrating, torn to shreds by a line of spikes stabbing into it.

It was enough of an opening for the first of the Lightguard to leap over the barrier, launching off of each other's shoulders and starting another melee. I saw Yen leap into the fight, khopeshes in hand, while Zyanya burnished her weapon of choice, a shadow-trident.

The first clatter of light and shadow sounded, over the dins of shouting and cries.

I gripped my staff of half-moon blades. Tende appeared beside me. He brandished ice-hooks, which made their cracking sound as they froze into shape.

We dove into the melee and launched an attack on those who had leapt over the barrier. Around us there was already a sense of chaos, even with the few Lightguard who had jumped in. Adding to the confusion was the fact that their weapons were constantly morphing, flashing from sword to shield to spear to net in a dance of light. Next to such dexterity, the Hollow were slow and ineffective.

I ran up to a Lightguard who was using moonlight to form a morning star, a club with three spiked balls dangling off the shaft. With a shield in one hand, and her morning star in the other, the warrior battered through a member of the Hollow, bringing down her weapon onto her opponent's shoulder.

Tende and I took opposite sides. He caught her arm with his ice-hook, while I whipped my staff in circular motion, battering her shield away with one blade and slashing down her side with the other.

She collapsed to the floor, but there was no time to rest. I looked up, thinking that more would leap over the barrier.

When none came, I looked around, my mind racing as to *why*.

And I got my horrible, horrible answer.

Corinthia's shadow-barrier was broken. A Lightguard had pierced through and driven their spiked shield straight into Corinthia.

The Shadowfront commander shuddered with pain as the spikes rammed into her, piercing her armor. Her arms dropped low, and with them the barrier dropped too, retreating back into shadows.

There was a scream of grief, it sounded like it was from Yen.

Corinthia slumped to the ground, her eyes open and empty. Lifeless.

The moment she fell to the ground, there was a charge from the Lightguard, all of them racing towards us, thirsty for blood.

The Quaester, whom I hadn't noticed before, was at their head.

War came upon us in a dizzying explosion of noise, a storm of darkness and light. Gold and black stretched and morphed and danced like firelight, darting to one warrior's hand and back, and then snatched by another.

It was a chaotic clash, one of nightmarish proportions.

I lost all sense of what the others were doing, the bursts of light and shadow, the eruptions of gold and black, the gush of blood, all of it was background noise, like the rush of a waterfall behind me.

All I could focus on was one enemy at a time.

The Quaester was the first to attack me. He was a little tender, I could tell that his movements were obstructed by the pain I'd inflicted upon him in our last duel. But I could also see his determination and anger, obliterating any restraint or caution he might have felt.

He wanted blood. I could see it in madness in his eyes, the flecks of saliva in his mustache. He wouldn't stop until he'd wreaked his vengeance on me.

In his hand he formed an almighty light-hammer, as big as three axes. It crackled with energy, the kind that would send charges of pain through me the moment it touched my skin. In his other hand he maintained his spiked light-shield, brandishing it in front of me.

I changed my staff into a vine and began twirling my half-moon blades like a lasso above me before letting them loose at the approaching brute.

One of them entangled itself in the spikes of the blades, but the other wound itself around the hilt of the hammer. The blade sliced at his forearm as it spun around the hammer, but it did not stop him moving forward.

I paired one more form, changing the half-moon blade dangling from his hammer into a plume of fire. Black flames rippled along his sleeve, setting his tunic aflame.

But still, he kept running.

Then he was upon me, thrusting his shield at me. I leapt to the side, only to be hit by a blow of his hammer to my chest plate. A bolt of pain rippled through my body, and I was flung back.

He shouted with triumph, and approached once more, completely disregarding the flames embroidering his arm. Madness and adrenaline seemed to have rendered him oblivious.

He threw his hammer this way and that, every movement was magnified with the accompaniment of flame. I backed away, shifting my forms.

I shaped my half-moon blades along the edge of my knuckles, so that my fists were edged with sharp shadow-steel.

My reach would not be far, but I was nimble and quick while the Quaester was slow and powerful.

I dodged to the right, then to the left.

Then I dove forward, just grazing past the spiked shield and slicing along the forearm holding it.

Grunting with pain, the Quaester dropped the shield, and it clattered to the ground with the spikes facing upwards. It immediately started to disintegrate into moonlight, I had to act fast.

Ducking under a swing of the hammer, I fell low, swiping my knuckle-blades at his heels.

Having touched blood at his calves, he howled once more. As he dropped to his knees in pain, I kicked him in the back.

He was flung forward, onto the spikes of his own shield. They were dispersing, but just present enough to momentarily impale him before they returned to the light in the air.

The shield underneath him vanished, but he remained flat on his stomach, his hammer disappearing, his arm slowly getting consumed by the flames.

I had a moment to look around me. Everything was pandemonium, warriors parried and pushed and stabbed, light and dark taking myriad forms. I saw the Hollow's warriors were falling around me, the Lightguard getting the better of them. The Shade users were fighting with passion, but they didn't have the precision or the training of the Lightguard.

They were killing us.

A few light-blasts were tossed overhead, destined to arrive in the midst of the Hollow and rip some of us apart. I shot a plume of shadow-flames at them, and they exploded overhead, cracking an explosion in our heads before they could land among us.

None of that prepared me for a blow which cracked against

my shoulder, sending me staggering back and numbing my arm.

Looking back, I saw who had hit me. Out of the skirmish arrived a form I had never seen before.

A moving statue of marble, a figure of the Emperor in moving stone. Behind it stood a Stonekind, manipulating it like a puppet.

How could I break stone?

I didn't have time to think about it. The statue, with the sound of bones cracking, moved toward me in a plodding fashion. Its hard, lifeless features somehow made it more monstrous than an opponent of flesh.

It immediately gathered me in its arms, pulling me into a cruel embrace. Still reeling from the pain in my shoulder, I couldn't move fast enough before it pinned me to its chest and started to crush me in its cold marble arms.

The air escaped from my lungs as I felt everything tighten and squeeze. I had never encountered such force in an opponent. I tried to push back, to flex my arms and pull them free, but it was as fruitless as punching a cliffside.

My armor cracked, buckling and fraying, crushed out of shape.

My ribs would be next.

My vision started to blur, and panic rose in me. I could not budge. My body felt *wrong*, like the pressure was putting it into an untenable position.

My mind raced. I had taken on rock before and broken it. Marble was just a kind of rock.

I ignored all the pain, and focused, recapturing my imperfect memory of the form of an ahuizotl tail which I'd used to batter rock before. My form was made in a haze. Pinned against the statue's chest, I could not see what I was doing.

Shadows formed around me nonetheless, drawing from the surroundings into a cloud above me, and Weaving into the shape of the monster's tail.

I let the statue have it, whatever leaking, imperfect form I'd made hurtled straight into the statue's side.

There was an explosion. The white marble fractured into shards, and I was dropped to the ground.

I took a second, placing a hand on my chest, almost as if to ascertain that my body was still there as I remembered. That done, I made a shadow-khopesh in my hand. I had to kill the Stonekind before he—

Too late. He was twisting his fingers, his eyes full of intent. And the marble shards were slotting back into place, reforming. Rebuilding the opponent who had almost killed me.

I took a stride forward, but then tripped. The reforming statue was not yet intact, in the air, white pieces were coming together like pieces of a puzzle. On the ground was what was left of a chest, and arm, and half of a face. It was this arm that grabbed my ankle, stopping me in my tracks.

Other opponents noticed me with a marble arm at my ankle and saw their opportunity. A Lightguard next to me created a light-net and flung it over my shoulders.

I was unable to shake it off in time to block the charge of pain that burned through me, sending me into convulsions. By the time I'd ripped the net off, the Lightguard had re-sculpted it into an axe. It was an axe made of moon and starlight, gleaming in the air.

Those marble arms, now attached to a fully rebuilt body, took hold of me once more, grabbing my shoulders with its implacable grip.

Only this time my face wasn't facing inwards into stone, but outwards. I could see the Lightguard approach with his axe, ready to swing it at my neck, using the moving statue behind me as an executioner's block.

I desperately tried to reform the ahuizotl tail but found my mind slow. My vision was still reeling from the pain of the net. Shadows came, but did not form anything material, limply forming a mist before leaking back to where they had come.

The guard held up the axe, a sense of glee in his face.

The axe caught the dusk light, a foreshadowing of the color it would turn after passing through my neck.

I closed my eyes.

And then, nothing.

"No!" someone shrieked. "I need him!"

Chapter Seventy-Six

It was Cleander's voice.

I barely had time to breathe before a light-net fell upon me, and I immediately fell to the ground with the pain of its bolts lashing into me. I howled as my flesh writhed in protest, and the world went a sickening color of blood.

The charge went on for what felt like forever. Even as the net dissipated, and a hand dragged me to my feet, all I could feel was the burning sensation, an agony as overwhelming as a hundred Void screaming in my ears.

The world turned and lurched, this way and that. Around us, the surroundings were painted in smears of darkness and light, and the occasional mist of blood. The thick of battle.

In a haze, I was pulled out of it. My vision settled before I realized, in a stagger of footsteps, where I was.

Cleander had brought me to the crystal. Beside us, ten steps away, the battle raged on, everyone too preoccupied in their brawl to take notice of us. There was only an imagist, waiting to project my image into the sky.

"You will say that I am the Blade, or you and your tribe and your family will be massacred," he hissed into my ear. "They don't stand a chance against my guards, they're dying as we speak."

I managed to turn and catch sight of the melee behind me.

I looked for a moment, before I saw what I needed to see, Aelia fighting off a guard valiantly, even as blood was coursing down her clothes, not letting anyone get close to Rana and my family.

There was hope. There was always hope. I'm not sure why I could still believe this, but I did.

"No," I breathed.

Cleander scowled. In his hands, another light-net materialized, and he made to throw it upon me, inflicting more pain.

Only this time, I was ready.

Pain is nothing, I told myself. *Growing up in the Hollow is to be raised by pain.*

The light-net landed on me, and my limbs were once again scored with those charges. But I launched myself at Cleander and embraced him.

We clattered to the ground, the light-net in contact with us both now. Cleander howled in pain, shrieking in my ear.

He hadn't been brought up in pain. He wasn't even a warrior anymore, not in a true sense. As he'd said, his battlefields were in Senates and meetings, at tables of food and in goblets of wine. His weapons were whispers and shaking hands.

His perfect clothes and immaculate hair had not felt the touch of a weapon in years.

Cleander's light-net dispersed, but he was still writhing on the floor.

Now was my chance.

I took my pain and made it my focus. I let it channel my sense of outrage, the injustice of it all.

Reaching out with my arms, I issued forth shadows and Anima.

I formed a shape, decorated with the glyph of core magic, and all the shadows in the air started to rush towards me, shrouding my body, leaping onto my back, stretching my arms. Giving me Void-wings in the space of a few breaths.

I felt the power surge through me, pass through me, a storm of black becoming my own, personal weapon.

Then I used it.

Cleander was getting to his feet, beams of light formed a dagger in his hands.

I picked him up in my arms and brought him into the sky.

He shouted out in sheer panic as we left the ground, his eyes wide as the world retreated below, and we soared into the dusk.

"No!" he screamed, his ordinarily silky-smooth voice turning into an ugly bark. His face turned dark as he hacked at me with the blade.

At first, his scrambling hit, making shallow cuts around my shoulder. Pain screamed through me.

But here, in the air, with the wind whistling around me and nothing but sky between me and the setting sun, I didn't care. Power, adrenaline, and sheer Essence coursed through me, so much that his flailing stabs did nothing.

I closed my eyes, still bringing us upwards, and took some more shadows, grabbing them from the world below, making it leap up into the air to join me, and it layered over my shoulders and chest with shadow-stone.

When I opened my eyes, it was with a smile of triumph. I had Essence-Gathered *and* paired two forms, making both the statue armor and the wings. I had complete, utter control of the shadows, so that they were still amassing about me even as I flew into the sky.

Cleander could not pull out his knife anymore: it was encased in shadow-stone.

His eyes went wide.

"Where did you learn to do this?" he whimpered.

"In the valley, *and* in the city," I answered. "I am both wing and statue. Creature and stone."

Cleander looked down. We were high now, hovering, the gardens were the height of a building away.

"If you drop me in the Demon's Lock..." Cleander rasped.

But I didn't want to hear another threat. I dropped him.

Cleander shrieked once more as he tumbled down, plummeting back the way he had come. His body turned as it fell, a complete lack of control, his immaculate clothes buffeting, his calm poise turned into a tangle of flapping limbs.

He landed on the point of the sundial, his body impaled on the spike.

His scream was cut short.

I stared at him there for a moment, with grim curiosity, then looked around me, taking everything in. I did not have the Anima to stay like this for long, but I wanted to stay this way for a few heartbeats, nonetheless.

The sky, which had overpowered me before, was everywhere. I was high up, higher even than the plains, and the whole Canopy stretched into the reaches of sight, everything a burning crimson.

Such a short time ago, that sky had overwhelmed me. It had made me cower.

This was my sky, now, as well as everyone's else's. It did not make me afraid. It did not make me feel little.

Not anymore.

I let my wings unspool, little by little, and it lowered me slowly, in a controlled manner, back to the gardens. I passed Cleander's body, spiked there on the Sundial, and did not look at it.

And then my feet found stone, and I was in the garden once more. I'd landed near the Senators, who'd been looking at the fighting like it was a sport.

It was a sport no more. The Senators around looked dumbstruck; the sight of Cleander bleeding there on the monument above them, an emblem of their failure.

I faced them directly, ignoring my wounds and the blood seeping out of my limbs.

"Senators!" I shouted. "You have lost! Order the warriors to stop!"

The Senators looked at each other in fear.

"I will not say it again!" I boomed.

The Senators all called for the Lightguard to cease the fighting.

The melee slowed, and then stopped altogether, although confusion was written across everyone's features.

There were bodies. Too many were the bodies of my people. Anger made my wounds hurt anew.

"Some of you," I continued, "have done things which are unforgivable. You have enslaved people and made them into experiments. I can promise you only mercy, and to treat you better than you deserve." I glowered at them. "There may be a few of you that can be part of a new, larger Senate, where everyone is represented. All of the different people of the Canyonlands. People who can help us protect the Canyonlands. But before that, you have crimes to answer for."

The Senators did not know what to say. They looked at each other, weak and shaking. They had not seen fights, or violence, like the one I had just shown them, in many years. They had gotten too comfortable and spent too much time eating and drinking.

I turned back to my people and walked towards them.

First I found Rana and my father. They weren't hurt.

The reason was clear. Aelia, on her knees between them, a sword still in hand. She was still ready to fight, even though she was barely able to stand upright, and the blood pooled around her like a dozen spilled goblets of wine.

"You can rest now, Aelia," I said. "It's over. Have you ever rested before, Aelia?"

She gave a crooked, lopsided smile. Her teeth were red. "Not since the day I was born. Now come on. Help me up."

I propped her back against a pillar. She growled as I moved her, but didn't complain, and when she was in position, a kind of pride and glow came into her eyes.

She looked across at the frightened Senators. Even with her back bent, and her shoulders slumped, and so much blood streaming down from her head I could barely see her tattoos, there was an animated look in her gaze. "This is what a real revolution looks like," she wheezed. "Been dreaming of this for as long as I can remember." She groaned, and more blood split from her lips. "You want to know what my Mind's Eye looks like, Jason? A city. A free city. Connected with streets, and people."

"Of course."

"Whatever happens now... we brought down the Emperor. I can die knowing that."

I frowned. "But, you're not going to. Die, I mean." My words were hesitant.

"Now?" She shook her head. "Nah. Things are just getting started..." She gave me a last, bedraggled, wheezing look. "Now get out of here. Can't stand you being here, looking all sorry for me."

I got up and looked over the corpses strewn about the garden. Tende was there, and Emilian. Both alive.

Standing up from the side of Corinthia's body, was Yen. She walked, unsteadily, to me, and put her arms around me.

We silently held each other for a moment before we stepped apart again.

I turned to the dial. The blood from Cleander's body was dripping down it, streaking the structure in red. Next to it was the Signet Crystal, the prism onto which messages could be written onto the sky.

"That thing only works with the blood of Cleander or the Emperor," I told Yen. "We have just this one time to send a message to the people."

"Well then," said Yen. "We'd better make this count."

I nodded. "Let's tell them our story," I said.

I made to step forward but felt a tug on my hand. Rana.

"Let him say it too," she said.

At first, I didn't know what she meant. But then I realized that she was speaking of our father.

I looked at him, and he was muttering, as lost in a dream as he had been. And yet I also thought I could see something in his eyes, a determination, a pleading.

Something which told me that there was some part of my father who knew where he was.

"Of course," I said. I told the Imagist to put my words into the sky and put his images there with them.

The Imagist listened.

As soon as this was decided, my father's disturbed mind began to make a series of images, threading shadows together. Pictures of the Senate, pictures of war, pictures of people running from the snapping jaws of Void.

The Imagist threw them into the sky, through the projection ring until it was displayed up there in the clouds in silver.

"But I don't just want the city to see it. I want the *world* to see it," I said.

"Then the angle of the dial must be changed," Yen said.

Tende intervened. "We will do that," he said.

The Hollow and Riverkind worked together, heaving until the ring of projection was angled not just straight above, but towards the horizon.

And with that, we began to send a message to the entirety of the Canyonlands. To those in the city, and those in the Experiments.

My father's images of exploitation, of centuries of subjugation, decorated the sky, rendering the entire skyscape a series of pictures of the evils of the Empire.

"People of the Canyonlands," I said, and the imagist turned my words into writing, scribbling across the sky for all to see for leagues of every direction.

"This is the story of the Hollow," I said. "This is the story of the Experiments. This might be confusing to many of you. Because for many of you out there, our story is yours too. A familiar tale of being trapped in valleys, beset by monsters, led by prophets. But let me tell you, this story is coming to an end. A new tale is starting. One of a new era, where you are free to rise up into the Plains and come to safety here in the Citadel. An era where the Void can chase you no more. One of *freedom*."

I looked about me. All of the Hollow stood solemn, many had tears in their eyes. I almost choked on my own when trying to say more. It was suddenly overwhelming to me.

But then I looked up at the history being painted in the

clouds above, at all the injustices that had been wrought by Lucian and the Empire, and I gathered myself.

That history, being embossed in silver unto the sky, would enter everyone's hearts. There would be people like me, who'd grown up only knowing a life of death and misery, looking up and recognizing their lives in the ones being depicted in the heavens.

The doubt would be sown into their hearts, and their minds expanded.

And that would be the start of the end of the Experiments.

I gazed into that new future, into the story being spun into the stars, and began speaking again.

Telling not just the story of the past, but a new story.

One for the future.

Epilogue

A week passed.

A week when everything changed. Where a new Senate was put in place, and representatives from all of the different communities of Essence Users had spokespeople. They ruled instead of an emperor.

Their priority was the protection of the Canyonlands. Of training everyone, and distributing Elixir equally, and planning to man the Demon's Lock with every warrior available. Immediately, we started drills and discussed strategies, and made plans for evacuation, consulting the maps of the surrounding areas.

Most importantly, we arranged for excursions to be sent out to the valleys of the Experiments, freeing the people there and urging them to come to the Citadel and join the fight against Cizin.

A week where suddenly, even though I wanted the Senate to make all the new decisions, many looked to me, and my choices had more sway than I wanted. At those times, I would consult with Aelia, who was part of the Senate with me, and we would come to decisions together. I began to trust my instincts more and more.

It was also a time of healing. My wounds gave me agony for days, even with the best treatment the Citadel could afford.

Aelia, it seemed, would never quite be the same again. Despite all the best efforts of the Riverkind and the Earthkind, she found her right arm unusable.

After a life of fighting in the streets of the city, she now presided over it, a fighter no more. She roamed the city and reported on what needed to be done, and no word carried more weight than hers.

She seemed content. Her life of fighting was over, she agreed. I still caught her training with her left arm, when she thought no one was looking.

Tende and the Riverkind saw to it that the Elixir was distributed to everyone in the city, from the Lower to the Higher Levels. They worked with the Stonekind to construct new aqueducts to bring the liquid everywhere, and new barriers to place upon Demon's Lock.

The city itself expanded. The Senate agreed that the Canopy, the forest where the Earthkind dwelled, should be officially recognized as a neighborhood of the Citadel. They would be involved in all decisions made for the city and would be protected as if they were within its walls.

This last detail especially made me happy. Rana and my father were back in the forest, spending all their time there, getting treated.

The only thing which didn't slot into place was Yen. She seemed restless, and uncharacteristically reserved. I showed her the city, but it did not fire any interest in her. Rather, she mistrusted the place, and spent as little time as possible there, preferring to spend her time with the rest of the Hollow in the Canopy.

It was on the seventh day of the new era that she came to find me, and we strolled along what had been the palace gardens. It was now used for gatherings, and city talks and speeches, and was open to the public. But still, out of habit, citizens did not tend to come here. Yen and I had a place for ourselves.

I did not know why she had sought me out, and I dreaded

what she was going to say. I knew that I wasn't going to like whatever she had in mind. I'd been so busy that I hadn't spent nearly as much time with her as I wanted. But even when I had been with her, she'd been distant, in her own thoughts. With the coup over, it seemed like she now had the time and space to process the death of the father, and she chose to do so alone.

Somehow, despite everything, I had hoped that we would spend more time together. Every day, it was my wish, and every day I failed. I was pulled in so many different directions, and she did not pull me in at all, indeed it was almost like she was avoiding me completely.

We walked in silence to the end of the palace and looked at the afternoon light slanting down into the valley. It sprayed the city with yellow hues and rendered the lake below a dazzling gold.

We contemplated the valley for a moment, seeing the cogs of life in the city turn. A market was forming on the main square below, and people were shuffling in to buy and sell their goods.

"Jason," Yen finally said, breaking the silence.

I looked at her, a queasy feeling in my stomach. "Yeah?"

"I think it's time."

"Time for what?"

"Time for me to find something else. I'm not sure I know where to fit in here. So... I've thought about where I *do* belong."

It was exactly the words I didn't want to hear, but I'd known were coming. "You could belong here," I said weakly.

Yen scratched the side of her neck, letting my words dwindle to nothing. "I think we're going to need everyone we can against Cizin."

She was building up to something. "What are you saying, Yen?"

"I think I'm saying that that's the best thing I can offer this world. A way to get people out of those Experiment valleys and bring them here."

Her words finally hit home. “You want to be part of the companies headed to the Experiments?”

She nodded. “That message in the sky was the first step. I bet they’re all very scared and nervous right now and asking all the right questions. But they still need someone like me, someone who’s lived through what they’ve lived through, to persuade them to get out of there. I can be that person. I can free them and bring them to the Citadel. That way, we can fight the demons all united.”

I didn’t know what to say. It was exactly right. Yen would be the best person to do that. And yet, a selfish part of me wanted her to stay. And it didn’t feel right not to say so.

I just didn’t know how to put the words together.

I took a deep breath, and made to say something, but not a sound was able to pass my lips.

I was interrupted.

First, it was just a trembling sensation, something that I thought might just be my emotions getting the better of me.

But then it grew and grew. A shaking feeling, like the whole canyonlands was shuddering in fear.

I grabbed Yen, and we looked down, fearing the worst. The shaking became more and more intense, and buildings below us started to crumble, creating plumes of dust in the middle of the city. The people in the market shouted and cried, rushing one way and then another, unsure what would be safer.

Even the woods below seemed to be shivering, with all the trees shaking off their leaves as if in the midst of the storm. Out at the lake, ripples and waves danced along the surface.

It went on for a minute, a minute where no one was able to do anything but hang on to whatever was there and pray that the ground didn’t open up below our feet.

And then, finally, the shaking lessened, then stopped altogether.

There was a cowed silence, as if the whole world had just been told off.

"What was that?" Yen whispered.

My heart pounded. Fear sent a sliver of ice down my spine.

"I think..." I swallowed. "I think that's Cizin, getting ready to invade the surface."

I groaned, doubled over, and took a moment to calm myself. I breathed methodically, my hand on my chest, until I was able to stand once more.

"You know what this means?" I said to Yen.

She bit her lip. Now it was her turn to be afraid of what had to be said. "Maybe."

"The expedition that Emperor Lucian was forcing me to do. The infiltration into the Underworld. I'm going to have to actually go and do it. I'm going to have to go down into the Demon's Lock and see what I can find out."

Yen contemplated this for a moment. She shot a glance up at the cliff, and the plains beyond. That was where she'd told me that she would go. Into the plains, and the valleys to save more people from the Experiments.

But then, with a little shake of her head, she turned away from the view, and slipped her hand in mine.

"You're right," she said with a look as unshakeable as shadow-stone. "But I'm coming with you."

Portal Books - Newsletter and Group

Portal Books is a digital publishing house that specializes in LitRPG, Dungeon Core, Cultivation and Progression Fantasy. Our mission is to bring you the best possible novels, with professional editing, copywriting and cover design.

We only work with authors who have a real passion for the genres and we think this shows in the novels we publish. We know that the heart of LitRPG is solid games mechanics and ensure every story is based on the kind of game system we ourselves would love to play.

If you'd like to try out stories from the other fantastic Portal Books authors, you can sign up to our mailing list for 80,000 words of FREE LitRPG stories. Whenever we add more, you'll get the update, absolutely free.

https://portal-books.com/sign-up

You can also find us on Facebook. Join our group to stay up to date on all our upcoming books, cover reveals, author interviews, giveaways, promotions and more!

https://www.facebook.com/groups/LitRPGPortal/

We also have a Discord server where you'll have a chance to chat with some our authors, members of the Portal Books team, or our community of readers as a whole!

https://discord.gg/GXBNDGYQqT

To find out more about the cultivation and western cultivation genres, you might find these groups to be of interest:

https://www.facebook.com/groups/WesternWuxia

https://www.facebook.com/groups/cultivationnovels

For more general discussions about the genre, these groups may be useful to you:

www.facebook.com/groups/LitRPGsociety

www.facebook.com/groups/LitRPG.books

www.facebook.com/groups/LitRPGGroup

Best wishes,

The Portal Books Team

www.portal-books.com

Join the Group

To learn more about LitRPG, talk to authors, and just have an awesome time, please join the LitRPG Group.

Published by Portal Books, 2023

www.portal-books.com

Printed in Great Britain
by Amazon

42856454R00260